# KILL PILL

**DAVID BARBAREE**

ZAFFRE

First published in the UK in 2025 by
ZAFFRE
An imprint of Bonnier Books UK
5th Floor, HYLO, 103–105 Bunhill Row,
London, EC1Y 8LZ
Owned by Bonnier Books
Sveavägen 56, Stockholm, Sweden

Copyright © David Barbaree, 2025
Internal illustrations by Kristin Inglese

All rights reserved.
No part of this publication may be reproduced,
stored or transmitted in any form by any means, electronic,
mechanical, photocopying or otherwise, without the
prior written permission of the publisher.

The right of David Barbaree to be identified as Author of this
work has been asserted by him in accordance with the
Copyright, Designs and Patents Act, 1988.

This is a work of fiction. References to real people, events,
establishments, organisations, or locales are intended only to
provide a sense of authenticity and are used fictitiously. All other
characters, and all incidents and dialogue, are drawn from the
author's imagination and are not to be construed as real.

A CIP catalogue record for this book is
available from the British Library.

ISBN: 9-781-78576-339-7

*Also available as an ebook and an audiobook*

1 3 5 7 9 10 8 6 4 2

Typeset by IDSUK (Data Connection) Ltd
Printed and bound in Great Britain by Clays Ltd, Elcograf S.p.A.

MIX
Paper | Supporting
responsible forestry
FSC® C018072

www.bonnierbooks.co.uk

*For my mother and father.*

# Day 0

A Ziploc bag of blue powder: chemical perfection.

*Deep breath, Jessica. Deeeeeeep breath.*

She opens the bag, pulling apart the plastic seal. Pink lines turn blue as tiny invisible teeth disengage. It leaves her breathless. Anticipation x 1000.

She turns the bag upside down and taps the bottom and blue powder collects onto her copy of *Samuel Taylor Coleridge: The Major Works*.

*Xanadu, here I come.*

She pauses a moment to consider whether she's more nervous than usual.

*Fuck yes!*

Earlier that morning, Jess met with her dealer, Brad. A short, affable kid from the suburbs of Philadelphia who, rather than wait tables or deliver pizzas, earns extra cash at school by dealing illicit drugs between classes. Brad has been a reliable proprietor of OxyPro for months, but today he was sold out. 'Don't worry,' he said. 'I've got something cheaper. And better.'

'What?'

'Fentanyl.'

'Are you serious? No way. Can't I die just from touching it?'

'If we were talking about the Chinese shit brewed in some cave – then, yeah, it's dangerous. But the product I'm offering you is American-made. I buy the pills and grind them up. All you have to do is snort it. You've done blow, right? It's no different.' He held up a Ziploc bag the size of a matchbook.

'This will make Oxy feel like a daily vitamin. How can you say no to that?'

Brad's sales pitch didn't sell the product so much as the fact Jess didn't have a Plan B. She has been using Oxy on a semi-daily basis for weeks. And if her choice is getting high on fentanyl or not getting high at all – well, that's not really a choice. She's getting high, one way or another.

But she's nervous. With Oxy, she knows what to expect. With fentanyl, there's bound to be a learning curve. It's inevitable.

She stares at the tiny hill of blue powder, listening to the sounds of a mild September morning roll past. Hidden sparrows chirp; a sedan with a squeaky axle crawls down the street.

*Now or never!*

She starts to manoeuvre herself into a good snorting position, but as her left foot slides out, she knocks over a beer bottle filled with cigarette butts. Black water glugs out onto the dusty porch. Her top lip curls in disgust. *Eww. Gross.*

The bottle is an artefact from Josh and his scabby friends. They were on the front porch last night, drinking, smoking weed, calling out to girls as they walked home from campus. *It's the only time they have the courage to talk to girls, in a group, yelling from a hundred yards away.*

Jess considers cleaning up the bottle and puddle of black water. Susan is always harping on about how the porch is a communal area and how everyone is supposed to clean up after themselves. If Susan finds the empty bottle, she'll blame Jess, even if she knows it belongs to Josh. She'll start an argument. 'Come on! You couldn't pick up one measly bottle?' Or she'll do something passive-aggressive, like leave the bottle outside Jess's bedroom door, so Jess either has to trip over it or throw it out.

Jess knows the path of least resistance is throwing out the bottle, but doing so would only reward Susan's bitchy behaviour. In fact, if Jess wants to make a point – if she wants to be Pavlov, not the salivating dog – she should be messier. *That would teach Susan not to be such a bitch.*

On the sidewalk, on the other side of the white picket fence, a mom and a toddler walk past. Jess gives them a big, friendly smile, but the mom sneers and speeds up.

*No way she saw the fentanyl, not from that distance. Could she?*

Jess briefly considers moving inside. She's exposed out here, on the front porch. And if Susan comes home early . . .

Jess isn't embarrassed about getting high. It's just that Susan will ruin it, like she ruins everything. She's too passive-aggressive for outright confrontation. But her sourpuss expression says a thousand words. *You're getting high? Before noon?*

But Jess likes being outside. She likes the front porch. She likes the fresh air, the morning sun, the ancient couch that's somehow still comfortable.

*All right*, Jess thinks, *let's do this.*

Her Visa card does its best Zamboni impression, separating the fentanyl into two orderly lines. Then she rolls a dollar bill into a little tube, lines it up with a blue line, presses a thumb into her left nostril, quickly snorts through her right, and then . . .

Numbness.

Relief.

Joy.

The world recedes. Sunlight melts the earth.

She leans back into the waiting embrace of couch cushions.

*I could get used to this.*

Her eyes . . .

                . . . slowly

                                . . . close

A locked door. No window. No handle.
*Wake up.*
Someone is on the other side.
*Wake up!*
Their voice – who is that?
*WAKE UP!*

White light crushes Jess's eyeballs in a vice.
'Jesus Christ.'
Her brain sizzles; her lungs are packed with cement.
'Sit up. SIT UP!'
Squinting, Jess sees a black shadow. Susan hovering. Susan screaming.
'PLEASE SIT UP!'
She has Jess by the collar. Shaking her.
'Jesus Christ! You're blue. Your skin is BLUE!'
A slap on the cheek.
*Fuck off, Susan. You're such a . . .*
Jess opens her mouth to tell Susan what she thinks, but no words come. Only . . .
Vomit. Warm, wet, burning the back of her throat.
Jess feels tired.
'Don't!'
*I need to . . .*
'Don't close your eyes. DON'T!'
*. . . sleep.*
'Josh! Call 911.'

# PART ONE

# AMERICA'S OLDEST PASTIME

# 1

Eleanor wants to strangle someone. In terms of a victim, she isn't fussed. Any warm body will do. But as she stands on the front steps of her Connecticut home, bone-tired, desperate for a strong drink, searching for house keys in her two-thousand-dollar Celine handbag, she's suddenly struck by an overwhelming desire to cause harm to another person. It's been that kind of day.

Her flight from Heathrow was delayed four hours; she spilled coffee on her favourite blouse, leaving a mud-coloured Rorschach on the white silk; and there was an issue with the Wi-Fi on the flight, which meant she was unreachable for nearly nine hours. When she finally landed at JFK, just after midnight, she was flooded with calls from the Family. Three and counting, all while navigating customs, baggage and the drive home.

First, it was Wells. He needed cash. Again. Ten million. 'That's it, Lenny. Twenty if you can make it work. Can't you wave that magic wand of yours?'

Wells forever straddles the line between billionaire and bankrupt. It would be fascinating if it didn't consume so much of Lenny's precious time.

Next, it was Cindy. She was in tears over the *Times*'s coverage of New York Fashion Week. 'Did they *have* to refer to OxyPro in an article about my new line? It's not like one has anything to do with the other.'

*Well*, Lenny thought, *I'm not sure you could have paid for the latter without the former.* (The market for tie-dye shirts with 'inspirational' words stitched across the front – DIVA, FEARLESS, BOSS-BITCH – isn't as robust as Cindy imagines.) But Cindy has never been one for honest self-reflection, so Lenny merely asked for the name of the reporter and said, 'I'll see what I can do.'

Mitch called after Cindy. That's who Lenny's talking to now, on the phone, outside her front door. Unlike the rest of his family, Mitch doesn't come to Lenny with problems for her to solve. He comes with solutions she has to talk him out of.

'No, Mitch,' Lenny says, 'I don't think it's a good idea to buy the *Daily Beast* and fire everyone who works there.'

'Did you read the article? They're quoting my emails. My *personal* emails. To show I'm some sort of hypocrite or something. First: who isn't? Second: it's not like the company lied.'

Lenny thinks of the sweetheart deal with the Justice Department, the ink still wet. *Apollo Pharma Corp. knowingly misled . . .*

'But Mitch, why do we care about an article in the *Daily Beast*?'

Mitch erupts. 'Where did they get these emails, Lenny? Why haven't we found the leak yet? This has been going on for years.'

This is the moment Lenny feels like throttling someone, after the day she's had and with Mitch ranting in her ear. As a result, she's distracted. She misses the scratches the screwdriver made to the brass lock. She notices the door is two inches ajar – it would be hard to miss that – but she chalks this up to a negligent housekeeper.

*Goddammit, Lucia. If anything's stolen . . .*

She pushes the door open and drags her suitcase inside. The foyer is dark and empty. Her red-bottomed Louboutins echo on the hardwood. She drops her keys on the bureau, kicks off her heels, and heads for the vodka.

The kitchen is lit by moonlight. She has neither the time nor the patience to bother with the lights. She opens the cupboard and finds a dusty crystal tumbler. The bottle of Grey Goose is where she left it, on the counter, beside the knife rack.

'OK,' Lenny says, cutting Mitch off mid-rant, 'I get why you're upset. But what do you want me to do about it?'

'How about your job, Lenny? You're my lawyer. You're supposed to mitigate risk. So fucking mitigate.'

She pours two ounces of vodka into the tumbler and drinks all of it in one smooth gulp.

'I'm the company's lawyer, Mitch. Not yours, not the family's.'

Lenny knows this is a pointless distinction. Apollo Pharma is owned entirely by one family – *The* Family, as Lenny calls them. Still, she finds it useful to redraw the boundaries on the boundless expectations of the Buchanans.

Lenny gathers up the bottle of vodka and heads upstairs.

After a conciliatory pause, Mitch resumes listing his grievances. He's moved on to his upcoming speech at Everly College. The press has been relentless. Lenny can't tell whether Mitch likes the coverage or resents it. She suspects a bit of both.

'Well, Mitch,' Lenny says, 'you could cancel the speech.'

She steps into her bedroom, flips the light switch and . . .

'Not a chance! I'm not going to give *them* the satisfaction.'

. . . nothing. No lights, just darkness and strips of moonlight leaking through the California shutters.

'What the hell,' Lenny mutters, flicking the switch up and down.

'What is it?'

'I don't know. I think my power is—'

Before Lenny can finish her thought a hand covers her mouth. She tastes latex and corn starch powder. She feels the weight of another person along her spine.

Terror surges through her like venom.

She drops the phone and reaches for the hand covering her mouth.

She feels a pinch on her neck, then a euphoric rush.

For a brief moment, she grasps the irony of what's happening...

But then she starts to relax.

Her breathing slows.

She collapses.

A tide of poisonous bliss drags her away.

# 2

'But why are they so angry?'

Harper Scott watches the crowd through the passenger-side window. Kids, mainly. Waving home-made signs, chanting, drenched in the downpour.

Marble-sized raindrops detonate on the windshield. Wipers work furiously to clear the deluge.

Charles Foster shrugs without taking his hands off the steering wheel. 'Everyone's mad these days.'

The protesters have spilled off the sidewalk and onto the road. They can't see past the tinted windows, but the black Cadillac Escalade is the sort of vehicle the focus of their hate would arrive in, so they swarm, like zombies chasing a pulse, forcing the SUV to crawl through campus.

Harper reads the signs. SAY NO TO BLOOD MONEY. BIG PHARMA = MASS MURDER. MITCH BUCHANAN IS AN ASSHOLE.

'All the money these kids pay to go to this fancy school and not one of them can come up with something clever?'

'I don't know,' Foster says, nodding out the driver-side window, 'that one's not bad.'

'Mitch-the-bitch,' Harper says, reading the sign aloud. 'At least it rhymes.'

A hand smacks the hood of the car and Harper's heart rate skyrockets. She reaches for her vape. Not to use it – not yet, anyway. Foster wouldn't approve. But it's comforting knowing it's there. *Half an hour until I can use it*, she thinks. *An hour tops.*

'It's Friday afternoon,' Harper says. 'Don't they have somewhere better to be?'

Foster is too distracted to answer. He's leaning forwards, watching the crowd, trying to anticipate the path of the road he can't see. He's wearing a slate-grey suit and white button-up shirt. The suit's tailored, but with Foster's build – with his broad shoulders and granite arms – it looks painted on.

The SUV labours forwards. The mob starts to chant, inaudible in the downpour.

*Breathe.*

Harper slowly sucks air into her lungs. She exhales.

'Are they right?' Harper asks.

'Who's they? Right about what?'

'The crowd. About Buchanan. Is he an asshole?'

'Who? Mitch?' Foster briefly takes his eyes of the road. He turns to Harper and smiles. 'No way. His brother Skip is the asshole. *Was*, I mean. But it doesn't matter. Mitch is our employer. He pays. We do our job.'

'I thought you were my employer?'

'That's true. But there's still a chain of command.'

'Oh yeah?' Harper can't help sounding sceptical.

'Don't worry,' Foster says. 'Our job is easy. Mitch Buchanan wants to stay alive. That's it. Think you can handle that?'

# 3

Harper was in Croatia when Foster offered her the job, her hiding spot after everything went to shit with Dark Star. She'd island-hopped for a few weeks before settling on Lastovo, a small, remote-ish island a hundred and twenty kilometres west of Dubrovnik. She'd checked her email for the first time in a week and saw a message from Foster. We need to talk. Where are you? How do I reach you? Harper hadn't had a phone since quitting Dark Star, so she gave Foster the number of her favourite hole in the wall by the shore. The next day Foster called and asked to speak to a woman in the bar. 'Black hair,' he said, 'green eyes, tall, maybe nursing a bourbon.' When the bartender demurred, Foster said, 'She's pretty and mean.' The bartender handed Harper the phone.

'Yeah?'

'I heard you were looking for work?'

It'd been years since they'd last spoken, but they'd always had a comfortable friendship, one that didn't require catching up or even hellos.

'Maybe.'

'You're not with Dark Star anymore?'

'Nope.'

'I heard you were fired.'

'Lies. I quit.'

'Not what I heard.'

'You heard wrong.'

'Don't you want to know what I heard?'

'No. Not really. I'm trying to enjoy my time off.'

'What are you doing in Croatia anyway? Vacation?'

'Sabbatical.'

'What's the difference?'

'You take a vacation to relax. A sabbatical is about growing your mind.'

'Oh yeah? How's that going?'

'It's hard work. I could use a vacation.'

Foster laughed. 'I've got a better idea. How about you come work for me?'

'Private security?' Harper had heard Foster had started his own security firm, Spartan Security Inc., but she didn't know much more than that. 'Not really a field you see a lot of women in.'

'Hasn't stopped you before.'

'Charles, are you seriously offering me a job? You need brute strength to do that sort of work. That's not really my bag.'

'What I need is a massive prick and you're the biggest I know.'

Harper bit her lip, considering the proposal. She knew Foster. He wouldn't offer her the job if he didn't think she could do it. *How hard could it be?*

'For who?'

'You ever heard of Apollo Pharma Corporation?'

'No.'

'What about the Buchanans?'

'Nope.'

'Come on. You've heard of Skip Buchanan. The Karma Killer?'

Harper was out of touch when it came to current events and pop culture, but even *she* had heard of the Karma Killer. 'Oh yeah. Sure. Bit late for Skip, though, isn't it?'

'Not Skip. We're working for his brother, Mitch. He's giving a speech this Saturday at Everly College.'

'A security detail at some fancy school in Connecticut? Sounds like overkill.'

'I don't want to get into it over the phone,' Foster said. 'I can tell you more in person.'

'I haven't said yes yet.'

'Scott, it's Monday afternoon and I had to call you at some dive bar. And you're what? Thirty-four? Unemployed, somewhere between a nomad and homeless. You'd be insane to turn this down.'

Harper didn't correct him. It was all true. But all she said was, 'Maybe.'

'Maybe? You stubborn . . .' Foster paused to collect himself. 'Lucky for you I need someone A-SAP. Someone I can trust.'

Harper didn't say anything.

'Well?'

'I'm thinking.'

'That was always your problem, Scott. You think too much. If you're in, I need you here by Friday.'

After she finished her bourbon, Harper headed to the shore to smoke her vape. As she watched the sun set over the Aegean, as blinding pink melted into indigo blue, she weighed the pros and cons of Foster's offer. Harper had cash in the bank – enough to live on for the foreseeable future, but not forever. She'd left the army years ago and had no intention of going back. And while her years with Dark Star paid well, after what happened in Greece . . . that ship had sailed. In truth, Foster's offer was a godsend.

At around 9 p.m. local time, she sent Foster an email.

I'm in.

# 4

Harper landed at JFK in the afternoon. Foster was there to meet her. They drove straight to Everly College, crossing from New York state into Connecticut. Over the two-hour drive – after they caught up, sharing anecdotes of friends they used to serve with – Foster explained the ins and outs of private security. It wasn't until they'd reached campus that Harper started asking questions about Foster's newest client, Mitch Buchanan.

'But I don't understand what they're protesting,' Harper says as the SUV labours through campus. 'They don't even know what Buchanan is going to say.'

Foster, the Picasso of shrugs, offers another masterpiece: shoulders up, head slightly inclined to the left. 'It's not *what* he's going to say. It's *who's* saying it.'

Harper read up as much as she could about the Buchanans before flying home, piecing the story together from whatever she could find online. Today's protest could be traced back nine years, when the school's board of governors voted to retrofit the oldest building on campus, a four-storey library built in the neo-Georgian style. The classic redbrick facade would stay, and a young, modern interior would replace the over-the-hill innards. A facelift in reverse.

But the school needed cash. (An endowment can't grow if it's being spent, after all. That's what wealthy alumni are for.) On the list of potential donors, the Buchanans were at the top of the list.

Across the globe, from Boston to Beijing, museums and universities bore the Buchanan name. The Tate Modern in

London, MOMA in New York, Beijing University. For decades, the family was known primarily for being extremely wealthy and philanthropic. There was only a vague sense of where their money came from. Pharmaceuticals, painkillers, Oxy-something-or-other. Certainly no reason to say 'no' to a sizeable donation.

A deal was struck. In exchange for twenty million dollars, the library would be named after the Buchanan family. They'd get a fancy plaque commemorating their generosity, speeches, a ribbon cutting, and so on. For the Buchanans, it was a steep price to pay for prestige. But if you can afford it, why not? And for the school, it was a no-brainer: an entire library for a plaque and a speech.

Or so they thought. Because nine years later, as the library neared completion, the Buchanan name had become synonymous with the opioid crisis that had killed a million people and counting. Not the sort of association one would like when unveiling a new, twenty-million-dollar library.

And the fact the family was sending Mitch Buchanan to speak only made matters worse. Not only was he a Buchanan and forever tied to the opioid crisis, he was also a prominent conservative donor, which made him possibly the last person on earth an eastcoast liberal university would willingly invite to speak.

But a deal was a deal. The school certainly wasn't going to return the money.

Hoping no one would notice, the school posted news of the ribbon-cutting on its website during the doldrums of July. But a few diligent students noticed and posted about it online. Word spread like a virus. The event had to be cancelled, Mitch Buchanan had to be cancelled, and certainly, under no circumstances, could he be allowed to speak. His very words would cause harm to the student body.

The 24-hour news networks that live for controversy covered the online response. Gasoline on a tyre fire. The death threats came next. A repulsive development given what happened to Mitch's brother Skip. But these days, as with any online controversy, it was probably inevitable.

As Harper read all of this on her flight back to the US, she became convinced the school would cancel the speech and Foster's job offer would disappear. Now she says as much while the SUV crawls through campus.

'If you're asking me if I'm surprised the school didn't cave,' Foster says, 'the answer is yes.'

'What's in it for the school?'

Foster shrugs. 'Twenty million dollars and a new library.'

'You really think Mitch would have demanded the money back over a speech and a plaque?'

'I wouldn't put it past him.'

'I thought you said he wasn't an asshole?'

Foster shrugs. 'He likes the attention. Eats it up with a spoon.'

'Even if it's negative?'

'Especially if it's negative.'

Harper watches as two protesters climb onto the hood of a parked car. The grey sedan undulates under their weight, like a ship in a storm.

'Couldn't they have sent someone other than Mitch?' Harper asks. 'It's a big family, right?'

'It's complicated,' Foster says. 'It was Skip Buchanan who made the donation. And it was Skip who was supposed to give the speech and cut the ribbon. But after what happened ... Obviously, he's not around to give the speech.'

'Right.'

'Mitch is the executor of Skip's estate. So it's Mitch's call. And he chose himself.'

'And the speech is tomorrow?'

Foster nods. 'It's in the afternoon. Outside – which isn't ideal. A lot of variables. I told Mitch the speech should be moved indoors, but he refused. He thinks it would look weak, like he's reacting to the reaction. Tonight will be easier. People from the school are taking Mitch and his nephew out to dinner and then to a play. Shakespeare. Titus something-or-other. It's all indoors. Invite only.'

Harper points out the window at the screaming kids. 'You really think there's a real threat out there? Looks to me like a bunch of kids with too much free time.'

Foster grimaces. 'We've a lot to go over, Scott.'

# 5

Special Agent Louis Diaz watches the screen of his phone light up. Spelled out in capital letters: the dreaded 'UNKNOWN CALLER'.

He kicks his office door shut and answers the phone. 'Hello?'

'Lou? Hi. It's Vincent Borelli.'

'Hi Vinnie. I didn't recognise the number.'

'Well, I'm a private citizen now. New life, new phone number.'

'Right.' Lou feels compelled to make small talk. 'And how's that going?'

'Good. Really good. The network just offered me a permanent role. And I'll be on tonight promoting my book. Actually, that's why I'm calling. I've been getting asked about the story in the *Times*. It's sure to come up tonight.'

'Which story?'

'Come on, Lou. You know the one I'm talking about. Eleanor McMurtry is in the hospital.'

'I can't comment, Vinnie. You know that.'

'Seriously, Lou? I was a federal prosecutor for twenty-three years.'

'Yes, that's true. And you're missed. Believe me. Your replacement is a prick. But now you're – what? A talking head on television?'

'Chief legal analyst, actually. And a bestselling author.'

'Sorry, I missed the memo. Congratulations.'

Borelli doesn't pick up on Lou's sarcasm. Or he ignores it because he needs something. 'Thanks, Lou. Anyway, I'm bound to be asked about McMurtry. I'm just looking for background. I need to look informed. I'm the guy who put the Karma Killer in jail, for crying out loud.'

*We*, Lou thinks. *We put Knox in jail.*

'I can't help you, Vinnie.'

'She's in the hospital, right? The official press release said it was for routine surgery, but I hear she was attacked.'

'Vinnie, my lips are sealed.'

'Listen, Lou, this is what I'd like to do.' Borelli's voice adopts the pitch Lou watched him use on countless suspects, the don't-you-see-I'm-doing-you-a-favour tone. 'I'd like to say that my sources in the FBI assure me this is nothing to worry about. Otherwise, you know what the press is like. They'll blow this out of proportion. The Karma Killer sells. They'll try to tie whatever happened to McMurtry back to Skip Buchanan. They'll say there's a copycat out there, picking up where Knox left off. Put me to work. I can help. I can temper these wild stories in the media.'

Lou wants to say: *Vinnie, you are the media!*

'Sorry, Vinnie. I wish you the best. I do. But this is wasting both our time.'

Lou forces himself to make small talk – How's the wife? And the kids? – and then hangs up. He feels drained afterwards. It's depressing watching someone he once admired transform like this, from a man of substance into a flake.

A knuckle raps on the door.

'Yeah?'

The door opens and Frank Dreser slides his short, burly frame into the gap. 'Who was that?'

'Borelli. He was looking for information about McMurtry.'

'Did you give him anything?'

'Don't insult me, Frank.'

'Good. Guy's a fucking traitor.'

'I bet he's making a *lot* of money.'

'Yeah? How much do you think?'

'Did you know his book is a *New York Times* bestseller?'

'You don't say.'

'Yeah. And he's not shy bringing it up either.'

'Prick,' Frank says, summarising his feelings on Vincent Borelli.

Frank scratches his five o'clock shadow. As usual, he looks dishevelled, as though he slept in his suit and rolled out of bed hours earlier. Frank has always stood in stark contrast to Lou, a trim marathon runner and sharp dresser, who religiously visits his barber every three weeks.

Lou turns to his computer and starts typing.

Frank checks his watch. 'It's after five and you know what they say? There's no problem a drink won't solve.'

'No one says that, Frank.' Lou types for a moment and then stops. 'On second thoughts, maybe you've got a point. I'll meet you downstairs in ten.'

# 6

Charles Foster pulls the SUV into an underground parking garage. The din of the protest fades as they descend the ramp. He parks on P2 and shuts off the car.

Foster turns to look at Harper. His eyes narrow. Harper senses a switch, from an old friend to her new boss, the owner of Spartan Security. 'How are you feeling?'

'Fine.'

'Thirty hours in transit. Maybe you need a nap?'

'I'm good. I got a few hours on the plane.'

'And you're sure you don't have any problem working for the Buchanans.'

'You didn't want to ask me this before my ten-hour flight?'

'Come on, Harper. The incident with your brother . . . I have to ask.'

'Trust me, Charles. As long as I'm getting paid, I'm good.'

Foster nods, apparently satisfied with Harper's response. 'Buchanan is upstairs. I'll take you to your room first. We're staying in a different building, nearby. You'll have time to shower and change.' He points at a garment bag hanging up in the back seat. 'And I've got a suit for you.'

Harper eyes Foster's slate-grey suit. She tries to pinch the fabric along his bicep, but it's too taut. 'Please tell me it's not this tight.'

'I don't care how tight it is, you're wearing it.' Foster is staring at Harper's blue jeans and black leather jacket. 'Mitch would have a heart attack if you showed up looking like that.'

'Fair enough.'

'There's three of us on the team. You, me and Jay. Jay's upstairs with Mitch. You'll like him. He's ex-navy, but we won't hold that against him. Our main responsibility is Mitch. But while we're here, on campus, we're also responsible for his nephew.'

Foster hands Harper a phone. 'This is how we communicate with each other. I've added my number and Jay's into the contacts.' He checks the time on his wristwatch before pulling a tablet off the back seat. He unlocks it, plugging in a nine-digit passcode and hands it to Harper. The screen radiates phosphorescent white, the only light in the car. 'Here. Read. It's good background. We've got time.'

Harper's eyes slowly focus on an email.

To: M.Buchanan@ApolloPharma.com
From: Stuart.Chaney@hotmail.com
Subject: Karma's a BITCH

Your brother got it easy. You know that, right? Not like what I'm going to do to you. I'm going to rape your wife before I slit your throat. Wealthy men like you who made a fortune on the pain and suffering of others – your time has come. I'm Knox's protégé. There's thousands of us.

'What is this? Harper asks.

'An email to your new boss. He gets dozens of these a day.'

'And who is Stuart Chaney?'

Foster shrugs. 'I don't know. Probably some dope living in his parents' basement. We don't have time to follow up on every threat. There's too many. We catalogue them as best we can, and keep an eye out for repeat offenders.'

'Does Mitch have a wife we need to worry about as well?'

'They separated a few months back. And she's in Europe, so she's outside our jurisdiction.' Foster swipes his index finger in the air, like a conductor. 'Keep going.'

Harper swipes through threat after threat aimed at Mitch Buchanan. Emails, DMs on Facebook, replies on Twitter, conversations on Reddit, some private, some public, for all the world to see.

On Twitter, someone with the handle @wordofgod22 wrote: This Apollo Pharma sh!t is 2 much. How many people have to die so the Buchanans get rich? F-That. Karma is coming for these assholes. Let's finish what Knox started. Who's with me? #KarmaKiller.

Harper points at the number beside the symbol of a heart. 'Does that mean that more than ten thousand people liked this tweet?'

Foster nods.

'Jesus.'

On Reddit, there's an entire page – a subreddit called *Bad Pharma* – dedicated to discussing the Buchanans. Foster taps the screen. 'This is the page Knox was posting on before he was arrested. It started as a site people used to complain about the Buchanans and the opioid crisis. But it grew into something darker. The page was taken down after Skip was killed, but now it's back up and the posts are worse than ever.'

Harper scrolls through dozens of screenshots from *Bad Pharma*. In one, a user called @karma733 wrote: Here's Mitch Buchanan's address. Click the link. Die motherfucker.

Harper looks up from the screen. 'This was posted yesterday. Is this actually Mitch's address?'

'That's his house in Manhattan. It's called doxing, posting someone's address online.'

'Can you get it taken down?'

'We did. That's not a live website. You're looking at a screenshot. But it was up for hours before it was taken down. I told Mitch it's not safe to live there anymore, but he's stubborn. He recognises the risk enough to hire security, but not enough to listen to me.'

Harper swipes left. Next up is an article from the Associated Press.

**KARMA KILLER SENTENCED FOR MURDER OF SKIP BUCHANAN**

HARTFORD, Conn. (AP) – former history professor William Thomas Knox was sentenced Friday to 120 years in prison for the murder of Skip Buchanan and four others on Christmas Day last year.

After hearing his fate, Knox showed little emotion, his eyes downcast, as they were for much of the trial.

Outside the courtroom, Knox's supporters expressed disappointment with the verdict. 'He's a grieving father,' said Fay Smithman. 'I don't blame him. I'd have done the same thing.'

After Knox's daughter died from a fentanyl overdose at the age of nineteen, friends said Knox took a dark turn, obsessing over her addiction, which he blamed on her being prescribed OxyPro after knee surgery.

Throughout the trial, supporters of Knox gathered outside the courtroom. Some claimed that Knox's act of injecting Skip Buchanan with OxyPro was meant to be a form of political protest, and that Buchanan's death was an accident. Others believed that Knox was somehow the manifestation of the eastern concept of karma, earning him the moniker, 'The Karma Killer' and 'The Killer of Killers'.

'Somebody had to hold these people to account,' said Alvin Johnson, a retired truck driver, who was outside the courtroom to show support for Knox. 'Lord knows no one else did.'

The Buchanan family owns Apollo Pharma Corp., which manufactures the prescription painkiller OxyPro. The drug is derived from its main ingredient, the powerful synthetic opioid oxycodone (hence 'Oxy'), and the pill's prolonged twelve-hour release system, (hence 'Pro').

After the opioid was developed in the mid-1990s, Apollo Pharma pursued a relentless campaign to influence doctors across the country, marketing the drug as appropriate for any type or degree of pain management, from headaches to serious chronic pain. Sales representatives were coached to assert that OxyPro had a less than one per cent chance of addiction – a claim with no evidentiary support.

Two years ago, internal documents were leaked to the press which demonstrated that the company knew the addictive and possibly fatal effects of OxyPro since the 1990s.

For years, the Buchanan family claimed to have little involvement in the company's day-to-day operations. However, the leaked documents showed the family – particularly Skip and his brother Mitch – were the masterminds behind the company's efforts to market and sell OxyPro.

Apollo Pharma changed its labelling of OxyPro, adding a disclaimer about its side effects and addictive qualities, but not before public sentiment had swung against the Buchanans, and litigation commenced across the country.

Federal prosecutors recently entered a plea arrangement with Apollo Pharma and the Buchanans. Under the terms of that deal, the Buchanans were to pay nearly $4.2 billion from their personal fortune, but with no jail time or criminal conviction. While a significant sum, critics claimed the Buchanans would escape real punishment given the family is worth an estimated $15 billion.

When asked about the prospect of an appeal, John Rekowski, a lawyer with the public defender's office and Knox's lawyer, said only that, 'Time will tell.'

The article is accompanied by two photos. The first is of Knox in the courtroom, his spindly frame hunched over the defence table, with his long unkept hair covering most of his face. The second is of Skip Buchanan, lying dead in the snow, a syringe protruding from his forearm.

Foster takes the tablet back and says, 'So now you've got a better idea of why Mitch hired us?'

'Sure.'

'But you're not worried?'

'Well, these posts, threatening to kill someone, it's horrible. Obviously. But it's all online, right? What people say on the internet – it's just noise.'

'It wasn't with Knox, though, was it?'

Foster looks on the verge of saying more, but instead he reaches into the back seat and grabs a paper bag. 'All right. As for equipment' – he drops the bag onto Harper's lap – 'here.'

Harper un-crumples the bag. Inside there's an extendable baton and belt holster. 'This is it? Are you serious? I need a firearm.'

'Sorry, Scott. Spartan Securities is a New Jersey company. And operating across state lines, with Connecticut's rules about private security – you wouldn't believe the red tape. I know this isn't ideal. But we're working on it.'

'I'm going to feel naked out there.'

'It shouldn't take more than a couple days for the licence to come through. Once we have it, I promise you'll have the biggest gun you want. But if you're *that* worried...'

Harper thinks: *classic male response.* Foster is nearly twice her weight, four inches taller, and while he's on campus he'll have a Sig 9 strapped under his arm. *But he gets to act like I'm the one that's scared to work unarmed?*

Although Foster's response is bullshit, after growing up with three older brothers and serving in the army for six years, Harper can't bring herself to admit weakness. *Why give him the satisfaction?*

'I'll be fine,' she says, 'don't worry about it.'

She starts to reach for the door but Foster grabs her arm. 'One last thing, Scott. How much weed are you smoking these days?'

Harper settles back into her seat. She meets Foster's gaze. She'd expected this. 'Not much.'

'How much is not much? Quantify it.'

'Why?'

'The Harper I knew in Afghanistan smoked a lot of weed.'

'Fuck off.'

Foster's stare hardens.

Harper's tone grows defensive. 'Relax, Charles. I smoke a bit of pot on the weekends. Just to unwind. That's it.'

Foster nods. 'Listen, Harper, what you do on your own time – I couldn't give two-shits. But I need you sharp and sober when you're on the clock. OK? If you're working, you're clean. If anything happens, I need the brave motherfucker I went to war with. OK?'

'OK.'

'And one last thing.'

'How many last things can there be?'

'This is it, I promise. These intellectual types – they like to pick and choose which military campaigns were *just*.' Foster uses air quotes for emphasis. 'Mitch is cool, but I'm not sure about anyone else you'll meet this weekend.'

'I get it,' Harper says. 'No war stories. My lips are sealed.'

'Good. And for the love of God, don't mention Dark Star. I'm not sure they'd grasp the world of corporate espionage. If they ask, you were in the army before moving to the private sector. That's it. It's fine to keep the details fuzzy. They didn't hire you for your mental recall.'

'I'm a moron in a nice suit. Got it.'

Foster smiles. 'You're a good soldier, Scott.'

# 7

They take the elevator up to the ground floor and exit the building. The rain has stopped, replaced by the last gasps of summer's heat. The sky is the colour of a polished stone.

Foster nods at the four-storey building on the other side of a soggy field. 'We're staying there, in Appleton Hall, an old dormitory. It's empty and scheduled to be torn down next spring. Buchanan asked for rooms for us and this is the best the school could do.'

'Isn't he a billionaire? He couldn't spring for a couple of hotel rooms?'

'There's only one hotel in town and it isn't an option. It's fifteen minutes away and we need to be close.'

They follow a winding stone path, across the field, a cluster of maple trees to their right. Outside the residence, Foster unlocks a rusted steel door with a key card. On the second floor, outside of Room 212, Foster says, 'This is you. I'm next door.'

Inside, the room is dated, like it was built in the Seventies and left to rot. The colour of the carpet reminds Harper of a two-day-old banana peel. Twin beds line the walls, perpendicular to the door. A window looks down onto the field they crossed moments before.

Harper drops everything she'd been carrying onto one of the twin beds. There are no sheets, just a bare mattress, stained and with the faint outline of springs trying to escape through the threadbare fabric.

'You've got an hour,' Foster says. 'Then come back the way we came, to Cielo House. Redbrick, six storeys. You can't miss it. Text me when you're headed over.'

Foster starts to leave, but Harper grabs his arm. 'Charles, thank you. I mean it. For everything.'

Foster smiles. 'Glad to have you, Scott.'

Once she's alone, Harper decides to get high. She promised Foster she wouldn't smoke weed on the job, but *technically* she's not on the clock yet. And besides, Harper needs this. After the flight, the airport, the drive through campus – the release valve needs to be opened.

This is how Harper conceives of her internal psychology. Stress, anxiety, her heart beats per minute. Pressure builds and builds until she opens the valve and the pressure eases. Some veterans have PTSD or anxiety. Harper has a release valve that she needs to open from time to time.

Four drags. That's the right dosage for tonight. Four drags and Harper can relax, but still remain sharp for the night ahead.

She hauls one of the desk chairs to the window, takes out her vape, turns it on, and waits twenty seconds for the miniature convection oven to warm the cannabis flower.

Drag Number One: the valve turns a quarter inch and the intensity gripping her insides slackens. The improvement is incremental, but it feels, as it usually does, like a miracle.

Harper examines the redbrick building across the field. She tries to spot her new employer through the sixth-floor windows but doesn't have any luck.

*Hopefully, I like him*, she thinks. But Harper knows that's unlikely. The Buchanans are pretty easy to despise. William Thomas Knox murdered Skip Buchanan in cold blood and not an insignificant portion of the country thinks he's a hero. That's how hateable the Buchanans are.

Drag Number Two: the valve turns another quarter inch. Her heart rate slows, her shoulders relax.

Harper wonders what her grandfather would think of all this. Not that he would have told her. Jack Scott wasn't much of a talker. He'd never have said, 'Harper, you're working for the Buchanans? How could you? What about Derrick?' If he were disappointed, he'd have conveyed it through his unique brand of telepathic stubbornness, radiating it like toxic waste in a cartoon, bright green and pulsing. If her grandfather were still around, maybe Harper wouldn't have taken the job. But he's not, so she said yes.

Drag Number Three: the valve turns half an inch.

Harper thinks about her talk with Foster, how he made her read screenshots of online posts, like someone posting on Reddit was anything more than some dweeb with a keyboard. He seemed – not on edge; this is Charles Foster after all, a walking slab of granite. But he wasn't himself. *Stressed* might be the right word. Harper can't remember Foster ever acting like that during their tour together, so it can't be the job itself. Protecting some rich billionaire is child's play compared to the Korengal Valley. *It could be the pressure of running his own business*, she thinks. *Maybe I'm not helping, getting high before my first shift . . .*

Drag Number Four: the valve turns another half inch. Harper holds the vapour in her lungs. One. Two. Three. She exhales.

*. . . but it's better this way. Foster doesn't want both of us stressed out.*

Harper showers using the washroom at the end of the hall and changes into her new suit. It fits perfectly. Foster thought of everything, dress socks, belt, leather shoes with a subtle yet functional heel. She fastens the extendable baton to her belt and stands in front of the mirror, admiring the fit. Red lines in the whites of her eyes draw her closer to the mirror. She mutters, 'Yikes,' and then fishes eyedrops out of her bag, tips her head back, and, with expert ease, soaks each eye in Visine.

Harper admires herself in the mirror one last time, slides her vape into the breast pocket of her new suit, and heads out the door.

# 8

Foster is waiting for Harper on the sixth floor of Cielo House. The hallway reminds Harper of a five-star hotel, with its plush carpeting and framed paintings every twenty feet.

'Do students live here?'

'No. The building is mainly for events. This floor has a suite for visiting A-listers.'

'Too bad we're not A-listers.'

'We're the help, Scott. We're not even on the list.'

Foster leads Harper to a door at the end of the hall. An engraved gold plate on the wall says, PRESIDENTIAL SUITE. He knocks on the door, looks up at a small camera mounted above the frame and nods. The door opens. The man on the other side has a shaved head, red beard, and slate-grey suit, just like Foster's. There's a fragment of a black ink tattoo – the tail of a snake, maybe – on his neck, just above the collar of his shirt.

'Harper, Jay Hollinger. Jay, Harper Scott,' Foster says as they step inside.

Jay nods and dissolves back into the room.

Harper studies the suite. The warm, inviting ambience from the hallway is doubled here. Soft lighting, brass lamps, a bookshelf filled with hardbacks.

When Foster speaks again his voice is at a noticeably higher pitch. 'Harper, let me introduce you to Mitchell Buchanan.'

Harper's new employer is short and paunchy, with thinning auburn hair flecked with grey. Harper is struck by how average

Mitch Buchanan would look – like a middle-aged accountant – if not for his smile, which radiates unyielding confidence.

'Nice to meet you, Ms Scott,' Mitch says. 'Charles here has told me quite a lot about you. What did they call you? The Hero of Kabul? You'll have to tell me that story sometime.'

Harper looks questioningly at Foster. His reaction is subtle: the hint of a smile, the tiniest shake of his head. Harper wonders if Spartan Securities has been doing the same kind of marketing that got Apollo Pharma into trouble. *I'd be happy to tell the story*, Harper thinks, *just as long as Foster tells it to me first.*

'I must confess,' Mitch says, 'I was hesitant to take a woman on as part of my security team. I'm as forward-thinking as the next man but, well, usually . . . women and men have different strengths, obviously. But Charles insisted. What was it you said, Charles? You had such a colourful description. Ah yes. You said: "She's a bulldozer, Mitch. She can flatten anyone or anything." Is that what you did in the army, Ms Scott? Flatten your enemies?'

Because Mitch Buchanan doesn't seem the type of man who appreciates modesty, Harper says, 'That's me all right. A bulldozer.'

Mitch's smile grows wider. 'That's what I like to hear.' He looks across the room. Harper follows his gaze and notices for the first time a man sitting on the sofa watching the news. 'Tommy! Come meet Ms Scott.'

'Sure thing, Uncle Mitch.'

The man stands and walks to his uncle's side. He has dark eyes and is wearing a houndstooth blazer. Harper figures he's a few years younger than she is, his late twenties maybe.

'This is my nephew, Tom,' Mitch says, throwing his arm around his nephew's shoulders. 'He's a PhD candidate right here at Everly College, in cognitive psychology. Tom, meet the newest member of Charles's team, Harper Scott.'

Tom's dark eyes seize onto Harper. His large grin is incongruent with the moment. At first, Harper can't quite place why.

'*You* are a security guard?' Tom asks. 'But you're so . . . pretty.'

There is an awkward moment of silence, as the room absorbs the stupidity of Tom's comment.

*Great*, Harper thinks. *This is the last thing I need, an employer with a crush.*

Mitch Buchanan slaps his nephew on the back. 'Oh Christ, Tommy, we don't want an HR complaint five minutes into Ms Scott's tenure. Make yourself useful and mix me a Scotch and soda. I'm going to freshen up.'

Tom snaps out of his trance. He blushes. 'It's nice to meet you, Ms Scott,' he says, before retreating to the bar.

With the introductions over, Foster stations Harper by the couch and Jay by the door. Harper keeps her eyes trained on a painting across the room, a bowl of fruit, heavy on the oranges. Perhaps the dullest painting Harper has ever seen, but still better than making eye contact with Tom following his self-immolation.

When Tom is using the washroom, Foster sidles up to Harper. He can't hide his smile. 'I think you've got a fan.'

'Fuck off,' Harper whispers.

'Want me to do anything?'

'Like what?'

Foster shrugs. 'Castration?'

'I'm not his type. He'll move on soon enough.'

'Maybe. Maybe not. Say the word and I'll get my shears.'

# 9

Half an hour later, Mitch Buchanan emerges from his bedroom wearing a navy suit and red power tie. He makes a Scotch and soda and joins Tom on the couch. On PBS, there's a story on a potential second impeachment inquiry into the president. The 2020 election is more than a year away, but there is no shortage of Democratic candidates weighing in.

Buchanan sighs. 'Come on, Tommy. There has to be something better on than these self-satisfied pricks.'

Tom changes the channel. CNN is airing interviews of the protesters at Everly College, from earlier in the day, before the rain started. They're sweating in the lingering summer heat, shirts clinging to their chests. '*Mitch Buchanan is a mass murderer*,' a young woman shouts at the camera. '*His mere presence on campus is violence. He must be stopped!*'

Tom watches his uncle sympathetically. 'I can turn it off, Uncle Mitch.'

Buchanan cocks an eyebrow. 'Do you think I'm offended? Please. If a crazy person hates me, it means I'm doing something right.'

Next, the reporter asks a couple what they think of the death threats aimed at Mitch Buchanan. The couple hesitates. They look at each other, then back at the reporter. '*What's happening online*,' the man says, '*it's just the powerless expressing themselves. It's got nothing to do with what happened to Skip Buchanan. And it's not like Skip was an angel.*'

Buchanan shakes his head. 'My God! Can you believe that question? It invited the answer.'

'OK,' Tom says, aiming the remote at the television, 'I'm changing the channel.'

On MSNBC an anchor is interviewing a man in his early fifties.

'*I'm joined now by Mr Vincent Borelli,*' the host says, '*former federal prosecutor and the man responsible for putting the Karma Killer behind bars.*'

Mitch makes a sound in the back of his throat signalling disgust.

'Want me to change the channel again?' Tom asks.

'No, no. Let's see if he's found a new way to profit from our family's misfortune.'

'*First,*' the host says, '*congratulations are in order, Vincent. Your book,* The Killer of Killers, *debuted on the* New York Times *bestseller list. And I hear a Netflix series by the same name is in the works?*'

'*Thank you, Stacey,*' Borelli says. '*It's an exciting time.*'

'Jesus,' Buchanan says, 'the ego on that man.'

Tom looks over at his uncle. 'Maybe I should turn this off?'

'No, no. I need to hear this. Keep your enemies close.'

'*While we have you here,*' the host asks, '*do you have any comment on the story in the* Times *about Eleanor McMurtry, Apollo Pharma's general counsel? The company's official press release said she's in hospital for routine surgery. However, the* Times *says she was attacked.*'

Harper twigs when she hears this. She tries to make eye contact with Foster but he's fiddling with his tablet.

'*Well, I'm retired from the prosecutor's office,*' Borelli says. '*I know as much as you do, Stacey.*'

'Could someone please mention the fact that I called 911 and saved Eleanor's life?' Mitch shouts at the television. 'God forbid anyone gives *me* credit.'

'*The article implies the assault was inspired by Knox, a copycat of sorts, because of its similarities to the murder of Skip Buchanan. Both were doxed, and then, within twenty-four hours, they were attacked or killed.*'

'I don't think the article uses the word "copycat". That's your word, Stacey.'

'*But according to the* Times, *Ms McMurtry was injected with some kind of opioid. Just like Skip Buchanan. The similarities are striking.*'

Borelli waves his hand, cutting the host off. '*Like I said, Stacey, I know as much as you do.*'

The host changes tact. '*You'd agree that Knox has a large online following?*'

'Yes. I believe some call themselves Karma Disciples. Or the Knox Hive.'

'*Yes, that's right. And these Karma Disciples – they admire Knox and what he did?*'

'Yes, but I'm not sure that's anything new. Charles Manson, Ted Bundy, they had admirers as well. I'd say the difference now is that we are more aware of Knox's fans because of how organised they are online. In my book, I compare Knox's impact to terrorist organisations, the way the marginalised find and radicalise each other, by immersing themselves into an ideology. Before Knox, I prosecuted Islamic extremists and I see a lot of parallels.'

'*Some have claimed you helped glorify Knox by writing your book.*'

Buchanan nods vigorously. 'Thank you!'

'I'm changing the channel,' Tom says.

'Don't you dare.'

'*Listen, Stacey,*' Borelli says, '*the murder of Skip Buchanan struck a chord with the American public. The hashtags started well before I published my book. One of the reasons I decided to write my book was to diffuse the mystique that had built up around Knox. He wasn't a mastermind as the press liked to insinuate. He was mentally ill and, quite frankly, lucky to have gotten as far as he did.'*

'Then why did you name the book, *The Killer of Killers*?' Mitch screams at the television. He's on the edge of his seat now. 'Ask him *that* for Christ's sake.'

*'And do you think your book did that? Diffuse Knox's mystique?'*

'Oh, for fuck's sake!' Mitch puts his head in his hands. 'How is that her follow-up question?'

'That's it,' Tom says. 'I'm turning it off.'

Ten minutes later, as Mitch is mixing himself another Scotch and soda, Harper finds Foster in the corner of the room, fiddling with his tablet. On the screen is a black and white image of the hallway.

'That's the camera outside the door?' she asks.

Foster nods, then flicks the screen with his thumb and it divides into six frames. 'I've got cameras set up in the hallway, the foyer downstairs, two in Appleton Hall, and one on Tom's front door. The feeds connect to this tablet and another back in Appleton Hall.'

Foster resumes whatever he'd been doing on the tablet. Harper hovers.

'What is it?' Foster asks, without looking up.

Harper flicks her chin in the direction of the television. 'How much of that is true?'

'How much of what?'

'What they were saying on the news. That the company's lawyer, Eleanor What's-Her-Name, that she was doxed and attacked.'

Foster meets Harper's eyes and smiles. 'Well, Scott, I coaxed a highly trained veteran to fly halfway around the world to – in your words – a sleepy college. What do you think?'

# Day 1

'Can you hear me?'

A heart monitor, steady and precise.

*Beep. Beep. Beep.*

'You, little lady,' – a man cast in shadow looms overhead – 'are lucky to be alive.'

Fluorescent lights hum a nauseating tune. A teal curtain divides the room in two.

The man leans closer. He has a white moustache and gentle brown eyes.

'Do you know where you are?'

Jess tries to answer, but her tongue has doubled in size.

'That's all right. You relax, we're not in a rush. You need your rest.'

Or so he says. But then the doctor forces Jess's right eye open and shines a flashlight into it.

'Mmhhmm.'

He does the same to the left.

'Mmhhmm.'

'Fucking hell.'

'She speaks! Excellent.'

The doctor turns to inspect the heart monitor.

Jess doesn't have the energy to ask what happened. Anyway, she knows. When the realisation hits her something breaks in her chest. She moans, something weak but terrible, like an animal dying. She fights back tears.

The doctor turns away from the monitor and pats her shoulder. 'There, there,' he says. 'Everything will be OK.'

Jess finds this small act insanely comforting. Now she's certain tears will come.

But it turns out she's too exhausted to cry. She closes her eyes and drifts off to the sound of the doctor's voice.

'There, there.'

# 10

'There's not much to tell.' Foster hasn't moved from the corner of the room. His initial response to Harper's questions was a series of indifferent shrugs, but Harper kept pressing and now Foster is ready to talk. 'Eleanor McMurtry – everyone calls her Lenny – she's Apollo Pharma's top lawyer. She was in London on business. Sunday night, she landed at JFK and a company car took her home. She was on the phone with Mitch as she pulls up to her house. Mitch said it was a pleasant conversation, but – well, you've met Mitch. He has a way of demanding one's attention.'

In unison, their eyes drift to Buchanan. He's on the phone, pacing in the opposite corner of the room, red-cheeked, gesticulating. 'I can see that,' Harper says.

'So probably Lenny's attention was focused on the call, as she said goodbye to her driver and walked into her home. The door was ajar but she blamed the housekeeper. And she didn't notice the power's been cut and the entire security system is down.'

'How'd she miss that?'

'She was in a rush to have a drink, I guess. She didn't even bother to turn the lights on. Just grabbed a bottle of liquor and headed up stairs.'

'She drinks in bed?'

'If you worked for this family for twenty years, I bet you would too.'

Harper smiles. 'Maybe.'

'Lenny got to her room and finally tried to turn on the lights. But the power didn't work. Mitch could tell she's distracted. He asked her what's wrong. She told him the powers out and then – poof – she stopped talking. Mitch thought he heard the sound of a scuffle, then someone struggling to breathe. After what happened to his brother, he thinks the worst. He grabbed his other phone – he has three, don't ask – and called 911. The police arrive six minutes later and find Lenny on her bedroom floor with a needle sticking out of her neck.'

'No shit. Just like Skip?'

'Yes. Just like Skip. Except it didn't kill her. She lived.'

'How?'

'She'd built up a tolerance.'

'What do you mean? She's . . . an addict?'

Foster nods. 'She had surgery years ago, and was prescribed OxyPro for the pain. She's been using ever since. And opioid users – you probably know this with Derrick – they develop a tolerance for it. A dose that would kill an average person won't kill an addict.'

'So, being addicted to opiates saved her life?'

'Apparently. But since the company has always said OxyPro isn't addictive – Lenny included, in sworn testimony no less – they've tried to keep a lid on the story.'

'What did Lenny say? Did she get a look at the guy?'

'No. One minute, she's standing there in the dark, fiddling with a light switch. The next, a needle's in her neck. She passed out, and woke up in the hospital hours later.'

Harper goes quiet for a moment, as Foster's story sinks in. 'What do the cops make of all this?'

Foster shrugs. 'I used to serve with someone in the FBI who's working the case. They're involved because of the similarities to what happened to Skip Buchanan. From what I can tell, they have no clue what to make of the attack on Lenny.'

'Similarities? Like using an opioid as a weapon?'

'That's the obvious one, yeah. But also how the doxing went down. You remember that site I showed you on Reddit, Bad Pharma? Two days before Skip Buchanan was killed, someone doxed Skip Buchanan by posting the address to his home in Connecticut.'

'Was it Knox?'

Foster shrugs. 'I'm not sure anyone knows. The username was @Karma and then a number. 9-5-6, I think. It had never posted before and it never posted again. A different username posted Lenny's address a day before she was attacked, @Karma again, but with a different number. This time it was 1-3-1-6.'

'And the screenshot you showed me earlier today, of Mitch getting doxed. Wasn't it a similar address?'

'Yup. But the number was new again: 3-7-3-3.'

'If Mitched was doxed yesterday, you're expecting him to be attacked soon?'

'If the pattern holds, yeah. But the good news is Mitch won't be home. And I'm not sure many people know where he's staying in Petersburg.' Foster smiles and slaps Harper on the shoulder. 'I told you this would be fun.' He nods at Buchanan, whose call is wrapping up. 'Come on. Mitch isn't paying us to chit-chat. Back to work.'

# 11

Twenty minutes later there's a knock at the door. Foster checks the video feed of the hall on his tablet before giving Jay a thumbs up. Jay opens the door and two new faces shuffle into the room, a man and a woman. They look uneasy, like they're the French elite rubbing elbows with the Nazi occupiers.

'Uncle Mitch,' Tom says, 'I'd like you to meet Olivia Perkins, the vice-dean of Everly College, and Professor Stuart Collins. Mr Collins is a bestselling author and a bit of a celebrity around here. He's published – how many books now?'

Collins is the stereotype of an East-Coast professor come to life – white hair, tweed jacket. He smiles, feigning embarrassment. 'Oh, eighteen or so.' His accent, which may have been German to start, has diluted over the years into an American hybrid.

'Of course,' Mitch says. 'You wrote *From Gutenberg to Facebook: The Way Technology Shapes How We Think*. I couldn't put it down.'

'You read my book?' Hearing the name of his book has a medicinal effect on Professor Collins: his shoulders relax; he smiles. 'Wonderful.'

The vice-dean is grimacing. She's a severe-looking woman – tall, thin, angular. She's wearing glasses and her blonde hair has been marshalled up into a tight bun.

Collins turns to the vice-dean. 'Olivia, Mr Buchanan has read my book. Isn't that wonderful?'

The vice-dean can't bring herself to agree. The best she can do is force her grimace into a pained smile. Her disdain is palpable. Mitch, however, doesn't notice or care.

'Please call me Mitch.'

The four sit and talk. Harper stands beside the window and stares into space. Normally, she'd abhor eavesdropping, but she can't help it: they talk as if she weren't there.

'We're still a go for tomorrow?' Mitch asks. 'The ribbon-cutting. My speech.'

'Yes, of course,' Collins says.

'Fantastic.' Buchanan accepts a Scotch and soda from his nephew. 'To be honest, I'm surprised. I thought the school would capitulate to the crazies. These days, it's the path of least resistance.'

Harper didn't think it possible, but the vice-dean's pained smile tightens. She looks like she's having a toe removed. 'Well,' she says, 'the library is stunning.'

Buchanan nods. 'So I hear. When can I expect to see it?'

'We are hoping to take you through tomorrow morning. If the weather will cooperate.'

'It's inside. Who needs the weather?'

'Yes, well . . . We'll try.'

'Try? What's stopping us?'

Buchanan stares at the vice-dean, with the impatience and entitlement one would expect of a billionaire. Her only response is her toothless, pained smile.

Professor Collins politely interjects. 'I'm sure tomorrow morning won't be a problem. The weather is supposed to be lovely. Sunny and this heat is finally, fingers crossed, supposed to break. And don't discount tonight. We'll have a grand time. The play is *Titus Andronicus*, Shakespeare's meditation on revenge. It's quite violent, but revenge is a dirty business, after all.' He laughs. 'And the students can't very well do *Hamlet* every year. Or *A Midsummer's Night Dream*. Or *Lear*. Or . . .' Collins takes a deep breath and changes course. 'Tell me, Mitch, were you able to make it through campus unmolested?'

'Oh yes,' Buchanan says. 'I've capable hands looking after me.' He nods at Foster. 'On the advice of Charles here, I came in early this morning, while most of the student body was still nursing a hangover.'

Collins chuckles. 'Brilliant in its simplicity. What about you, Mr Buchanan?' Collins says to Tom. 'Have you escaped the animus that's plagued campus as of late?'

'It's Mr Park, actually,' Tom says. 'My mother didn't take my father's name, but I did. And I'm *actually* a PhD student here.'

'Ah,' Collins says, his cheeks reddening. 'I'm sorry. I believe I already knew that.'

The vice-dean checks her watch. 'We'll have to leave now if we want to make dinner.'

She wants to walk, but Foster says it's out of the question. 'It's too exposed. We'll drive you.'

Perkins sighs. 'It's only a few blocks.'

'Drive or stay here,' Foster says, 'those are your options.'

The vice-dean does something Harper suspects she has little experience in: she relents.

# 12

Dinner is held in a French bistro a few blocks from campus, in a private room between the kitchen and dining room. Wine racks built with dark, oiled wood loom over the table. Foster has the team rotate positions every twenty minutes. Harper and Jay start in the hall, on either side of the door to the dining room.

'Charles says you were working for Dark Star before this.'

'Yup.'

'I hear the pay's good in corporate espionage.'

'Dark Star is a private intelligence agency,' Harper says, as though she's reading the webpage. 'We didn't do corporate espionage.'

Jay winks. 'Sure. I understand. What was it like, working in' – he uses air quotes – 'private intelligence.'

'Fine.'

'Why'd you leave that for this? I bet it's more exciting.'

'I didn't see eye-to-eye with management.'

Harper doesn't elaborate; and Jay, distrustful of authority in general, doesn't ask for more of an explanation. He nods and says, 'At least you won't have that problem with Foster. He's cool.'

'He's all right.'

'I think the nephew is sweet on you. Can't say that's happened to me before, a client wanting to fuck me. Usually it's the other way around.'

Harper cocks an eyebrow. 'Well, I'm a catch, Jay. You're not.'

Jay smiles. 'Foster said you were mean. Now I see what he was talking about.'

When it's Harper's turn inside the private dining room, the president of the school, Winston Flowers, arrives. He's a short, bald man who sighs constantly.

'You look stressed, Winston,' Buchanan says, as Flowers takes a seat. 'I don't know what you could be stressed about?'

Flowers chortles. 'I wonder how you do it. The press, I mean. Dealing with them as often as you do, the coverage with this level of intensity. It's exhausting.'

Buchanan is watching the waiter fill his wine glass with a twenty-year-old Côtes du Rhône. 'I think of the press as a class of toddlers. There's no point in losing your temper. Patiently answer their inane questions, and then hope their parents pick them up on time.'

Vice-Dean Perkins and Professor Collins are noticeably silent. The vice-dean is staring at her plate with extreme intensity, as though she's trying to will it into a wormhole that will transport her to another dimension.

Buchanan says, 'I'm indebted to you, Winston. I know you've taken flack for not cancelling the events this weekend. It would have been an embarrassment for me. I won't soon forget this.'

'No need to thank me. We're not going to let the students decide who can and cannot speak at this school. It's an illness that's sweeping academia across the country, but not here, not at my school.'

Buchanan turns to the table and says, 'Now that right there – *that* is real courage.'

The vice-dean looks on the verge of throwing up.

# 13

By the time a second bottle of wine is opened, the atmosphere has shifted. The group is less stiff, their voices an octave or two higher.

'You know I have sympathy for you, Mitch,' Professor Collins says as he's buttering a roll of bread. 'Being on the wrong side of the internet mob. It's a terrible place to be. The glee that people exhibit – the *schadenfreude* – revelling in your misery. It really is quite disgusting.'

'You're not one of those people who think our family deserves this?'

'No, no. Of course not. Although . . .' Collins stops to sip his wine mid-sentence. 'I have *some* sympathy for the mob as well.'

'How so?'

'It's the technology. You've read my book, haven't you? The internet – social media, especially – has run roughshod over our mental faculties. Swift technological advances inevitably breed unrest – civil, political, religious. The printing press was invented and a century of religious war followed.'

Buchanan scoffs. 'Technology brings about tremendous change. I agree with you there. But you'd absolve someone of their sins because of technology?'

'Not absolve. Understand. Sympathise. Pity.'

'Pity?' Buchanan wags his finger. 'Let's take your example, the turmoil that followed the invention of the printing press. You'd pity a member of the Spanish Inquisition, someone responsible for torturing and burning heretics. Surely such a man is a sadist?

The circumstances just gave him an opportunity to be cruel. He doesn't deserve your pity because of *new technology*.'

Collins tips his head to the side thoughtfully. 'Doesn't he? He was a product of his time, a prisoner of the period's ignorance. As are we.'

Vice-Dean Perkins interjects. 'But Stuart, no one hates Mitch and his family because of *new technology*.' She uses air quotes to show her unwillingness to engage with the term. 'Our students are angry about a crisis that has killed more than a million people in this country.'

'Oh please,' Buchanan says. 'Apollo Pharma sold an FDA-approved drug. What people did with those drugs was beyond anyone's control, including mine. I don't see anyone blaming the executives over at Rolling Rock for the alcoholics in this country?'

Perkins turns her attention to her Caesar salad. In a soft voice she says, 'Rolling Rock never misled doctors, though, did they?'

President Flowers was not prepared for his vice-dean to openly challenge the school's guest of honour; his eyes bulge in horror. But rather than take offence, Buchanan appears to be enjoying himself. He leans forwards, angling his body towards Perkins. He bares his teeth, flashing his billionaire smirk. 'Actually, I'd say the good people at Rolling Rock misled everyone. Pretty packaging, advertising that sold a lifestyle as much as a drink. And does a bottle of Rolling Rock list the number of alcoholics in this country? No, of course not. The difference between Rolling Rock and Apollo Pharma is the standards you hold them to.'

'The point *I* am trying to make is that we need empathy for our fellow man.' Collins smiles and looks at the vice-dean. 'Or woman. It's the only way forwards, towards the light.'

Buchanan is sawing into his steak. He stops and points his serrated knife at Collins. 'An attitude like that, Stuart, will get you eaten alive. If the mob comes for you, you can't have any room for pity. Believe me. I've survived all these years through one trick of the mind.'

'Oh? What's that?'

'They may hate me, but I hate them more.'

# 14

Harper can't remember the year: 2008, 2009 maybe. The day is out of focus, the details fuzzy. It's the kind of memory you keep bottled up for so long that when you search for specifics, you can't find them. Harper's tour in Afghanistan had ended. Back then, she'd usually spend a night or two drinking with the boys near Fort Bragg before heading home. Not this time. She hadn't seen Derrick since the injury, so she came home to Ohio as soon as she could.

Harper found her eighty-two-year-old grandfather on the front porch, a bottle of Budweiser in his hand. This was new. Drinking before five.

'Where is he?' she asked.

'Where else? His room.'

Harper detected sarcasm in her grandfather's voice, but Derrick was in fact in his room, sitting on the floor in the dark, playing Xbox, his crutches strewn on the floor. Harper hit the lights and Derrick recoiled like a vampire. 'Shit! Come on, Harps. Turn that off.'

'You're alive?'

'Course.'

Harper scanned the room. It was filthy. Open drawers, empty beer bottles, bed unmade – a scene once unthinkable under their grandfather's roof.

'How's the leg?'

Derrick paused his game and looked at the brace strapped to his calf. 'Out of the cast. It hurts like hell but they gave me some pills that help.'

Harper saw prescription bottles on the dresser. One was empty and lidless, lying on its side. The other looked half-full. She picked up the empty bottle and examined the script. 'OxyPro. 80 milligrams.' Harper couldn't remember what they'd given her after she was injured in Kabul. Morphine, then something else. 'What's in these?'

Derrick shrugged. 'I don't know. They're pretty amazing, though. And popular. Grandpa and I were leaving the pharmacy and kids were offering cash in the parking lot. Eighty dollars for one pill. Did you have eighty dollars when you were sixteen?'

Harper laughed. Later she'd think it cruel, but back then it just sounded like kids being kids. Getting drunk, getting high – it was all the same, wasn't it? Anything to dull the tedium of small-town Ohio. 'Well, if you need extra cash, I guess you could swing by Central.'

Derrick restarted his video game and a close approximation of artillery crackled on the television's speakers. 'Central's gone. It merged with Centennial after the McClusky factory moved to Mexico. And a lot of families left. Less kids, I guess.'

Harper nodded. The description fitted with what she saw on her drive through town. Closed store-fronts, abandoned buildings, the once vibrant city dying a quiet, slow death.

'Well, that's depressing.'

She flopped down onto the carpet beside Derrick. He handed her a beer. They clinked their bottles together before taking a sip.

'Are they tearing the school down?'

Derrick hammered away on his controller. 'I don't know. It's still there, empty and unused. It's like a graveyard.'

'When did the McClusky factory close?'

'No idea.'

Harper sipped her beer. 'Well, this is turning into a hell of a trip home.'

'On the plus side, you get to see my beautiful face.'

'Beautiful? How many of those pills have you had today?'

'Fuck off, Harps. That's no way to talk to your older brother.'

Harper pinched Derrick's cheek. 'Older only in years. I practically raised you.'

When Derrick took his hand off the controller to swat away Harper's hand, his avatar died a bloody death.

'Damn it. Look what you did.'

Harper's eyes drifted up to the dresser. 'Just be careful with those pills. OK?'

Derrick shrugged. 'They have to be safe, right? FDA-approved. VA's handing them out like candy.'

'Right. Sounds safe enough.'

# 15

'Oh, come now, Olivia. It's all performative.'

'I'm not sure I agree,' the vice-dean says. 'Our students are passionate in a cause.'

Buchanan scoffs. 'You mean my death?'

'Let's not confuse online death threats – which I won't defend – and today's peaceful protests, which concern your family's role in . . .'

President Flowers waves the wine list like a white flag of surrender, trying to bring the debate to a close. 'Perhaps we should order another bottle of red? Mitch, would you do the honours?'

Buchanan doesn't take his eyes off the vice-dean. 'You can say it, Olivia. Opioids. My company sold opioids. The *best* opioids, actually.' He thumps his hand against his chest. 'The most effective.'

'I think we can both agree the opioid crisis is serious,' the vice-dean says. 'How many people have died? Hundreds of thousands? A million? To be angry about that is perfectly reasonable, isn't it? More reasonable, I'd say, than the apathy shown by the rest of the country. These students, the mob as you like to call them – they have a conscience. And they are exercising their constitutional right to protest, to express how they feel.'

'If their protest was about me, I'd agree with you.' Buchanan is leaning back in his chair, swirling his wine, entirely at ease. 'But it's not about me. Or my family's company. Or the opioid crisis. It's about themselves. About showing the girl in your sociology class what a great guy you are. Getting angry is the new foreplay. In my day, you wore a leather jacket and drove a nice car. Now, to get laid, one needs to publicly flog themselves. It's all a performance. What did Updike call it? The ecstasy of sanctimony, America's oldest pastime.'

'Actually,' Professor Collins says, 'I believe it was Philip Roth who wrote that – *The Human Stain*.'

Buchanan waves away the comment like an annoying fly, his eyes never leaving the vice-dean. 'This week it's me and the so-called opioid crisis. Next week it will be some other cause. They yell and scream and then they move on, without actually having done anything. And it's all so hypocritical,' he says, 'justifying their shitty behaviour – or even a murderer like Knox – because they think our family did something wrong.'

'In a way,' Collins says, 'it's deontology versus utilitarianism. A philosophical debate for the ages. I'm a Kantian myself.'

'And the way these people interact online,' Buchanan says, ignoring Collins' remark, 'the us-versus-them mentality, the closed system of logic – it's a cult.'

Perkins says, 'They're in a cult because they agree with each other?'

Professor Collins nods his head at Tom. 'Well, we have a bona fide cognitive psychologist in our midst. Should we ask him?'

Tom looks at his uncle and smiles, sympathetically. 'Sorry, Uncle Mitch. Isn't that a bit of a cliché, to compare people you disagree with to being in a cult?'

Buchanan waves his hand, dismissing the comment, and turns back to Perkins. 'Our family has done more for this country – for this planet – through our philanthropic efforts than any of those spineless nodes you call your students.'

'You pay to put your name on buildings,' Perkins says, her voice rising slightly for the first time. 'That makes you vain, not charitable.'

President Flowers' eyes bulge in horror. 'Thank you, Olivia. Thank you for . . . expressing your thoughts so freely,' he says, clearly meaning the opposite. 'We do love a spirited debate here at Everly College.'

Buchanan's eyes are fixed on Perkins. His smile is gleeful. *He's a pig knee-deep in shit*, Harper thinks.

'Mark my words,' Buchanan says. 'All these people who admire Knox, a convicted murderer – that's the ultimate performative display.'

The vice-dean dabs her mouth with her napkin and then smiles her cold, toothless smile. 'Have you ever considered, Mitch, that through your obsession with performance, perhaps you are merely describing yourself?'

'What do you mean?'

'Isn't your speech right now, isn't it performative, a well-practised distraction?'

Buchanan winks and holds his wine up to toast the vice-dean's insight. 'The world's a stage, my dear.'

As they're eating dessert, Foster informs the group that because of the crowd outside the theatre, he's arranged for them to enter through the back.

'Not a chance,' Buchanan says. 'I'm not scurrying in the back like a coward.'

'I can't guarantee your safety if we go in the front.'

'You may be worried about a few angry kids, Charles, but I'm not. I go in the front.'

# 16

Foster and Jay drive Mitch and Tom Buchanan and President Flowers in one of the two Escalades. Harper drives Professor Collins and Vice-Dean Perkins in the other. As they did at dinner, Harper's passengers talk as if she weren't there.

'Well, he certainly wasn't the monster the media makes him out to be,' Collins says. 'I found him quite charming.'

'You can't be serious? You argued with him the whole time.'

'We disagreed with each other, but we hardly argued. There's nothing wrong with a spirited debate. I enjoyed it.'

'God, the pain that man has caused! He's basically a Mexican drug lord. The El Chapo of Connecticut.'

'That's hyperbole, isn't it, Olivia? What his company did – no doubt, it was deplorable. And everyone involved should answer for that. But we don't know what Mitch's role was.'

'It's Mitch now, is it?'

'Can't we be civil, even if we disagree with him?'

'Can and should are two different questions.'

'I think, despite your best efforts, he actually liked you. If I didn't know any better, I'd say he was flirting with you.'

'That's disgusting, Stuart.' She sighs and looks out the window. 'If there were justice in this world, Mitchell Buchanan would be in jail. Or worse. But no, our school has invited him to speak.'

'Or worse? And by that you mean – what? – dead in a ditch somewhere? Are you the next Karma Killer?'

'I didn't volunteer to do it myself.'

'You must admit, it's brave of him to come.'

'I'm not so sure. Did you see him at dinner? The smile on his face? He loves the attention, the controversy.'

'Most families in the Buchanans' position would have taken their donation back. After all, the man that killed their sibling was a professor here.'

'Only briefly, thank God,' Perkins says. 'So brief most people have forgotten all about it. And speaking of brave, I see you didn't mention to *Mitch* that you were friends with the man who killed his brother.'

Harper had been doing her best not to listen and to keep her eyes on the road, but now she can't help herself. She'd read countless articles that described Knox as a former professor, but the specific school was never mentioned.

Harper's eyes drift to the rear-view mirror. She watches as Collins stares out the window, lost in thought. 'Friends is an exaggeration,' he says. 'We were both in the history department, but he didn't last two semesters. I barely knew Knox. I recall you being closer to him than I was.'

'Well, we can both agree that Winston has put us in an awkward position, forcing us to have dinner with Mitch Buchanan.'

'I'm surprised to hear you say this, Olivia. Winston said you advised him not to cancel the speech.'

'What? Oh God, that is false. Believe me. If Winston hadn't told me to attend this dinner and tonight's show, I'd be out there, with our students, demanding that Mitch Buchanan not be allowed to—'

She stops mid-sentence as the Escalade turns the corner, when she sees what's waiting for them outside the theatre.

# 17

The protesters, who had spent the afternoon spread out across campus, have now converged on the theatre, along a single block, crammed between steel barricades, churning in the lingering summer heat.

'Good God,' Professor Collins says. 'Look how many there are.'

Harper's stomach turns. She instinctively reaches for her vape in the breast pocket of her suit. *Not yet*, she thinks. *Not while you're on duty.*

A narrow lane along the road has been cordoned off, as well as a carpet-lined walkway from the road to the theatre. Harper parks. The distance from the Escalade to the theatre is about fifty yards or so.

*Distance is relative*, Harper thinks, *and that's a long fifty yards.*

She steps out of the SUV and onto the street. The crowd is chanting: CANCEL BUCHAN-AN, CANCEL BUCHAN-AN.

Harper walks around to the other side of the SUV and opens the door. As Collins and Perkins step out, they're met with a chorus of boos. Collins gives Perkins his arm, but it's Perkins who pulls Collins forwards, towards the theatre. Harper walks behind them. When they're close, campus security open the doors to the theatre. Collins sighs loudly once they're inside. Perkins mutters a curse.

'Wait here,' she says. 'I'm going to help with Mitch and Tom.'

Outside, Harper sees the second Escalade parked behind the first, and Foster and Jay standing beside the back door. The crowd can sense Buchanan. Their chanting builds to a feverish pitch. Spittle and hot breath fill the air.

When Harper reaches the SUV, Foster puts his lips to Harper's ear. He has to yell to be heard. 'You take Tom and Flowers inside first. We'll follow with Mitch.'

Jay reaches for the door handle. The crowd quiets with anticipation.

*The eye of the storm.*

The door opens. Tom steps out, then Flowers. The crowd recognises the school president. They call to him, mockingly, "President Liar, President Fascist."

The colour has drained from Tom's face. Harper grips his arm above the elbow. 'We have to keep moving.'

Tom nods, and then, with Flowers at his side, starts walking towards the theatre. Harper follows at their heels. When they're halfway, the crowd erupts with pure venom. Harper looks back and sees Mitch Buchanan stepping out of the car. He shrinks from the seething crowd, cowering like he's exiting a helicopter and fearful of the spinning blades above.

Harper feels a drop or two of rain on the back of her neck. She has Tom and President Flowers ten yards away from the theatre doors when there's a loud bang behind them. She turns back and sees a section of the barricade has gone down. Half a dozen protesters wearing all black and balaclavas stream onto the red carpet.

Foster and Jay spin Buchanan around and barrel him back towards the SUV. Harper pushes Tom and Flowers towards the doors to the theatre. Flowers doesn't need any encouragement. He runs forwards and through the doors. Tom, however, turns back and shouts, 'Uncle Mitch!'

Harper grabs Tom's wrist and screams, 'It's not safe.'

A second barricade goes down and more protesters stream onto the red carpet, cutting Harper and Tom off from the theatre.

Something is fluttering around them. Paper, like oversized pieces of confetti. It's only when one sticks to Harper's arm that she sees it's fake money stained with red spray paint.

Blood money.

With their route to the theatre blocked, Harper hollers, 'Back to the car,' and pulls Tom back the way they'd come. She uses her free arm as a fender, knocking protesters back. Their progress is slow.

The rain picks up, heavy sheets begin to drench the melee.

Some kid in a Yankees baseball cap steps forwards and screams into Harper's face. No words, just pure rage, fuelled by the crowd around him.

In Harper's experience, angry mobs are, for the most part, comprised of cowards. They need to see someone else land a kick or a punch without consequence before they work up the guts to do it themselves. And the so-called 'leaders' – the ones who will throw the first punch – they aren't that much braver. They usually wait for a moment of weakness to do what the dark part of their soul has been asking them to do. Harper knows ferocity is their best shot at making it to the SUV in one piece. Show weakness, flinch even once, and the crowd will have the opening they need.

So, with a screaming twenty-something blocking their path and on the verge of something much worse, Harper's response is, by design, swift and terrifying. She swings her elbow, in a controlled motion, every ounce of energy perfectly accounted for, and connects with the kid's orbital bone. He falls backward, unconscious before he hits the ground.

Harper grabs Tom's arm and pulls him forwards. Once they reach the Escalade, she opens the door. But before she can push Tom inside, a shoulder slams into her ribs. She stumbles and a horde of men wearing black balaclavas surround Tom. They're shaking something in their hands. Harper hears the hiss of an aerosol can and thinks the worst, bear mace or acid.

Tom throws a feeble punch at the nearest attacker. Harper removes the baton from the holster on her hip and lengthens it with a flick of her wrist. She steps forwards and snaps the ballpoint end into the knee of the nearest man in a balaclava. He falls to the ground, screaming in pain.

Rather than work together to disarm Harper – there's three of them and they could easily overwhelm Harper if they tried – the other men in the balaclavas stare in shock as their comrade writhes in pain on the ground.

Harper snaps the baton into the elbow of the next closest man. He hollers and back-pedals. She kicks him in the stomach, sending him tumbling into his friends.

Tom is covered in red and for a brief moment Harper thinks it's blood. But clarity comes in a matter of seconds and she realises he's covered in spray paint, not blood. She opens the door to the SUV and pushes Tom into the back seat. She jumps on top of him and then pulls the door shut. She locks the doors and tells him to stay down. She hops over the arm rest and into the driver's seat.

Foster's SUV has already pulled ahead of them. It's surrounded by protesters. Foster is lurching it forwards, trying to escape without killing anyone. When any space opens up, he picks up speed, which in turn gives him more space. The staccato acceleration lasts for fifty yards until the SUV is finally free of the crowd.

Harper puts the car into drive, hammers the horn, and starts inching her way forwards.

# 18

Once they're clear of the crowd, Harper looks at Tom in the rear-view mirror. He's panting, trying to catch his breath. He drags himself off the floor and onto the seat.

'Well, that was *in*sane.'

'Are you hurt?'

'Only my pride.' He looks down at the streaks of red across his shirt and seersucker blazer. 'And my wardrobe.'

As they drive, Harper presses two fingers into her neck and checks her pulse. She forces herself to take two long deep breaths, then reaches into her pocket and starts heating up her vape. She watches Tom in the rear-view mirror. When she's certain he's focused on his phone, she takes a drag. The valve turns a quarter inch and another miracle works its way through her bloodstream.

Harper drives another four blocks away from the theatre before pulling over and calling Foster.

'How's the nephew?'

'Shaken up, but OK. How's Buchanan?'

'The same. It gave him a scare, but he'll live.'

'I just got a text from Professor Collins,' Tom says. 'The play has been postponed. Flowers made the call, but it sounds like the police didn't give him much of a choice.'

Harper relays the news to Foster.

'Good,' Foster says. 'I couldn't convince Mitch to cancel. That was a disaster. And the only thing to do with a disaster is to walk away.'

'What's the plan?' Harper asks.

'You take the nephew home. After that, go back to your room. Get some sleep. Come relieve me and Jay at 5 a.m.'

'I don't need to sleep, Charles. Give me the night shift.'

'I'm giving you the worst shift, believe me. No way any of us are sleeping after that. I want two of us on tonight. Tomorrow morning, after things have calmed down, you can hold down the fort while Jay and I catch a few hours.'

Harper hangs up and twists in her seat to face Tom. 'I'm supposed to take you home.'

'I'd like to see my uncle first.'

'Don't worry, he's in good hands. The best thing you can do for him is to give him time to' – she thinks of the right word – 'decompress.'

For a moment, Tom looks on the verge of arguing. But he eventually nods and Harper starts the car. Tom directs her to a residential street lined with white clapboard homes and rain-soaked lawns. It's a nice street, but not what Harper would have expected from an uber-rich Buchanan.

Harper parks and turns in her seat to look at Tom. His breathing has slowed, but he still looks shaken.

'It will pass,' she says.

'What will?'

'That out-of-body experience you're having, like your brain went for a walk and left your body behind.'

'It's awful. Any way to speed it up? Getting through it, I mean.'

Harper bites her lip, thoughtfully. 'In my experience, weed and alcohol help. But I'm probably more fucked up than I realise. I wouldn't follow my example.'

Tom mulls this over. 'I think . . . long-term, those sound . . . But right now I'm focused on the short-term. So . . . I'd like to try your method. If you're offering.'

'You think I just have something on offer?'

Tom smiles. 'That's exactly what I think.'

Harper's first thought is of Foster. He'd be furious if she smoked weed with a client.

*But*, she thinks, *how can I say no after that debacle? We both need medical intervention. One or two puffs – that's totally reasonable in the circumstances. And Foster doesn't have to know.*

'Fine,' she says to Tom. 'But let's take it inside.'

# 19

Tom Park's home is so clean and meticulously ordered Harper's first thought is: *he's a psychopath*. White walls, white furniture, not a dirty sock in sight. Harper fights the urge to kick over a chair.

'Nice place.'

Tom detects something in Harper's voice. 'You're surprised a Buchanan owns something this modest?'

Harper shrugs.

'I'm just a grad student here, remember? It's better to fit in than stand out.'

'Right.'

Tom points at Harper's lower back. 'Uh-oh.'

Harper has to contort her body, twisting her spine, in order to see the red spray paint Tom discovered. It's on her blazer and white button-up shirt.

'We're matching,' he says, holding up his ruined blazer. 'Don't worry, I've got something for you.'

Five minutes later, Harper and Tom are wearing matching grey hoodies with EVERLY COLLEGE inscribed across the chest. They sit on the couch in the living room. Harper pulls out her vape and, once it's ready, takes a drag. Tom watches intently. The glowing tip is a bright blue circle, like the exhaust pipe of the Millennium Falcon. Harper inhales twice more and hands the vape to Tom. He turns it upside down, examining it. 'How does it work?'

'A little oven inside cooks the weed. Suck that end.'

Tom slowly takes a drag. It's obvious he appreciates the distraction, even before the numbing high sets in.

'Do you do this often?' he asks.

'Only when I need to.'

'When's that?'

Harper shrugs.

Tom takes another drag. 'When did you start?'

'Afghanistan. When I served.'

Harper feels the cannabis gradually enter her bloodstream, slowing it to a nice meander. Her shoulders relax. She can feel her breathing slow. She watches Tom take another drag. His cologne has a medicinal flair. It reminds her of her grandfather's aftershave.

'First time?' she asks.

'Smoking weed?' Tom laughs. 'I haven't done it in years. But, believe it or not, I partied pretty hard in high school.'

'Oh yeah? I can't picture it.'

'It's true. I actually had a short career as a drug dealer.' He smiles and shakes his head. The stress of the theatre is miles away now. 'I only sold to rich kids who went to my private school in Manhattan, so the stakes were low. I thought it was cool and dangerous. I didn't realise I was being such a conformist.' He sees Harper's questioning look and adds, 'Selling drugs is the family business.'

'I pictured you more as an overachiever in school,' she says, 'not a delinquent.'

'I was both. Great grades, but bad decisions otherwise. A mess, to be honest. My dad died when I was fourteen. We were close and I didn't take it well.'

'I'm sorry. About your dad, I mean. Was he Mitch's brother?'

'My dad? Oh God, no. My mom, Bonnie – she's Mitch's sister. Actually, my dad – Herald Park – had nothing to do with the Buchanans.'

'Oh yeah?'

'My mom met my dad at school. They fell in love and got married. But my grandfather disapproved.'

'Why?'

'Well, Dad was Korean. Actually, he was born and raised in Queens, New York. But to my racist grandfather, Dad was Korean, full stop. By any reasonable measure, Dad was a catch. He had his MBA, and eventually worked on Wall Street. He was honest, hard-working, handsome. But none of that mattered to old Maurice. Dad was Korean and that was all that mattered. End of discussion. And so my mom was kicked out of the family business and written out of the family trust. She and my grandfather only reconciled after Dad died from a heart attack. He was fifty-one.'

'You must have hated your grandfather?'

Tom nods. 'Sure. I hated the whole family for a long time.'

He tries to hand the vape back to Harper, but she waves it off. Tom takes another drag.

'What about you?' he asks. 'If you didn't smoke weed until you served, does that mean you were a good kid?'

Harper smiles. 'Oh yeah. I was a bit of a dweeb. Church, school and basketball. That's all I cared about. I don't think I touched a drop of alcohol until college.'

'Which school did you go to?'

'North-Western.'

'Really?'

Tom's surprise rankles Harper, though the weed dulls the sting. *He probably thinks everyone living west of the Appalachians are lucky to make it through high school.*

'Why'd you quit?'

Harper shrugs. 'I was a teenager when 9/11 happened. I was pissed, but I was too young to do anything about it. Then the

Iraq War started, when I was in school. There was an insurgency killing Americans. And my grandfather had served. It was in my blood.'

'That's admirable.'

'I was young and naive.'

Tom shakes his head. Harper can tell he's high now, by the way he moves, his languid pace. 'No, no, no. You had a sense of duty.'

Harper shrugs. 'Maybe.'

'You don't have that now?' Tom asks. 'A sense of duty?'

Harper laughs. 'Fuck no.'

'What happened?'

Harper doesn't answer. She takes another drag. Holds it, feels it burn in her lungs, then exhales.

'What did you do after you served?' Tom asks.

'I worked for a company called Dark Star, a private intelligence agency.'

'What kind of work is that?'

Harper lacks the energy to give Tom the practised answer she gave Jay hours earlier. 'Surveillance, hacking, blackmail, witness intimidation. I stole some patents.'

'How was that?'

'Soul crushing.'

'I can imagine.'

'But the people we targeted – they were shitty people. Believe me. Liars, thieves, criminals, tech-bros. They deserved whatever we did. My boss, Mordecai – I always thought of him as Robin Hood.'

Tom smiles. 'And you were part of his merry band of thieves?'

Harper laughs. 'Sort of. But I lived in Marriotts across the world, not some forest.'

'I'm sorry.'

'Sorry about what?'

'You probably thought this job would be – I don't know – less stressful. But you left one bad situation for another.'

Tom places his arm on the back of the couch, a few inches from Harper's shoulders.

Harper's initial impression of Tom was that a bit of good looks and a lot of money had made him pompous and insufferable. But he scored points when he'd called his uncle a cliché. *Maybe he's charming*, she thinks, *in a nerdish sort of way.*

She tries to remember the last time she was with someone. There was the New Zealander in Croatia a few weeks back. He'd quit his job to *something* around the world. Surf? Kiteboard?

Tom drops his arm until it makes contact with Harper's shoulders.

*Is he charming?* Harper thinks. *Or is it the weed?*

She suddenly thinks of Foster and the limb he crawled out on when he hired her. She hops out of her seat. 'I better get going.'

The weed dampens Tom's disappointment. Harper guesses there will be more to come when he's sober. He walks her to the front door.

'Can I return the hoodie tomorrow?'

'Of course.'

The drive back to Appleton Hall is lit by moonlight. Harper passes pockets of kids dressed in black, with signs under their arm. They're chatting casually, as though the day-long protest and melee outside the theatre never happened.

Back in Room 212, Harper sits by the window and fiddles with her vape, staring up at the half-moon. She considers smoking more – she's technically off-duty after all. But she feels guilty, smoking with Tom, against Foster's explicit direction, so she settles for staring at the wall. Her mind drifts. She thinks of Mitch

Buchanan, how proud he was of the pills his company marketed and sold; and then she thinks of Derrick, the pain in his leg, the pain he could suppress but never escape.

Harper knows Derrick wouldn't care how she made a living. *Would he?*

Just then something above the door to the hall catches her eye. She drags the desk chair closer, hops up, and examines a symbol etched into the wooden frame.

It's small, no bigger than Harper's thumb. She runs her fingers over the pattern. She thinks she may have seen it before, but can't quite place it.

But she soon loses interest and goes to bed. She strips down to her underwear and listens to the fluorescent lights in the hallway, humming like cars on the freeway.

# 20

Special Agent Louis Diaz watches his phone buzz to life on his kitchen table. He mutes the television and answers the phone. Frank doesn't bother to say hello. 'You saw what happened?'

Lou's eyes briefly drift up to the television and the melee outside the theatre at Everly College, which CNN has been playing on a constant loop.

'I'm asleep, Frank.'

'Fuck you, you're asleep. Did you see it?'

Lou tosses a green M&M into his mouth and cracks the candy coating between his molars, applying the perfect amount of pressure.

'Sure. I saw.'

'What a mess.'

'It's late, Frank. Tell me you didn't call me this late to discuss the obvious?'

'What do you care? You're still working.'

Lou shuts his laptop. 'I'm in bed.'

Frank laughs. 'Fuck you, you're in bed.'

'Fine. I'm up. But couldn't we talk about this tomorrow?'

'That's not why I'm calling.'

'No?'

'There's been another post on Bad Pharma.'

'And?'

'Someone's posted an address at Everly College.'

'Where?'

'Cielo House, sixth floor.'

'Shit. Does it say anything else?'

'It says, "This is where Mitchell Buchanan is staying at Everly College. Karma do your work."'

Lou crushes a peanut M&M between his molars. 'What's the username?'

'It's new but like the others, @Karma and then some numbers. It could be related to the other posts. Or maybe some kid followed Buchanan home from the theatre and posted the address for a cheap thrill.'

'Maybe.'

Frank asks, 'What's the quality of the protection Buchanan's hired?'

'They're ex-military. Capable, for sure. But I'll reach out, give them a heads-up.'

'You want me to head over there and check in?'

Lou checks his watch. 'The drive from New York to Everly College is over an hour. You wouldn't get there until the middle of the night. Why don't you call the local sheriff's department, get them to drive by? You can head over in the morning.'

'Done.'

Lou searches the yellow bag for another M&M.

'You going to pay him a visit?' Frank asks.

'Who? You mean Knox? No. The last thing Knox needs is more attention. He's locked up, with limited internet access. Whoever made those posts, it wasn't Knox.'

'Then who was it?'

'I don't know. Probably one of his loyal fans.' Lou shakes his head, still unable to comprehend Knox's online following.

'You think it's the same person who attacked McMurtry?'

'All I know is that we closed this case a year ago and I hate the fucking internet.'

# Day 2

Someone is watching.

Jess is half-asleep, with her eyes closed, but that feeling – the silent presence of another person – is inescapable.

She opens her eyes and sits up with a jolt. Blood rushes to her head and she winces. Once she's recovered, she opens her eyes again and sees a woman sitting on a chair beside her hospital bed.

'Addict?' the woman asks, 'Or did you try to kill yourself?' She looks like the star of a romcom, with lustrous blonde hair and big blue eyes, except for the cuts on her face and the cast on her arm. Crutches are propped up against the chair. 'You were crying in your sleep, saying you were sorry. So I figured it was' – she leans in, lowers her voice to a whisper – 'attempted suicide. Are you going to try again? They don't have you on suicide watch or anything. Should they?'

Jess looks around the room to get her bearings. 'I didn't try to kill myself.'

'Then you're an addict?'

'I'm not an addict.'

The blonde cocks an eyebrow in disbelief. She radiates confidence. Her certainty is overwhelming, so much so that Jess wonders: *maybe I am an addict?*

'I just wanted to get high,' Jess says, already giving away more information than she'd intended. It's like the blonde's self-confidence is sucking information out of her.

'Why?'

Jess keeps looking around the room for answers that aren't there. Her brain is stuck in mud. 'Why what?'

'Why did you want to get high?'

'Why does anyone want to get high? It feels good.'

'Puny.'

'What?'

'Puny.'

'What does that mean?'

'Small.'

'I know it means small,' Jess says, exacerbated. 'I said getting high feels amazing and you said "puny". Why? What does that mean?'

The woman tilts her head, considering Jess. 'My name's Alex. My mom is coming in an hour. She's swinging by Juga Juice first. Do you want a shake? Before you answer, let me assure you, the food here is a catastrophe.'

'I'm OK.' Jess lies back, settling into her hospital bed. Her head is pounding and the movement makes it worse.

Alex is wearing a bathrobe over the top of her hospital gown, a monogram sown onto the left breast. It looks expensive. She exudes trust-fund entitled-ness. Usually, this would make Jess gag, but Alex has a way of pulling it off without pretension.

'I'm getting the Guava Sunrise,' Alex says as she's typing out a text on her phone. 'I'll tell my mom to get two. You'll thank me when you see dinner.'

Jess nods at Alex's crutches. 'What happened to you?'

Alex briefly looks up from her phone. 'Car accident. Some kid was racing his friends. Ploughed into my Beamer. Totalled it. Tragic, really. But I'm happy to be alive.' She leans forwards and lowers her voice. 'Do you know the feeling? Or is this all an annoying epilogue?'

'I didn't try to kill myself.'

'Are you sure?'

Jess is spared the effort of coming up with a decent reply when the doctor knocks on the door. 'You're up? The nurses were supposed to tell me.'

'Hey, doc,' Alex says, looking over her shoulder. 'Should she be on suicide watch?'

Jess is mortified at the question. The doctor stares at Alex. 'You should be resting, Alexandra, and certainly you shouldn't be bothering our new arrival.'

Alex staggers back to her bed on the other side of the room, a crutch under her right arm. She moves gingerly, without putting any weight on her left foot. Only now can Jess see there is a cast wrapped around Alex's left leg, from her toes to her knee.

The doctor shines a light in Jess's left eye, then her right. He holds up a finger and tells her to follow it. He folds over the sheets at the bottom of Jess's bed and pokes her feet with a pen. Jess winces with each jab. When he's finished, the doctor asks, 'How are you feeling?'

'Horrible.'

'Well, you should consider yourself very lucky. Opioid overdoses' – he shakes his head – 'they can be horrible. The media only covers the deaths. But even when people live there can be severe brain damage. Those cases don't make the news or the grim figures in the paper, but they're just as tragic.' He sighs and pats her shoulder. 'A neurologist is on her way. She'll examine you, but the fact that you're alert and talking, that you have feeling in your legs . . . it's nothing short of miraculous.'

# 21

A maze of alleyways, dark and narrow. Harper is running, unarmed and helpless. She's already out of breath. Her shirt is glued to her back with sweat. The sound of gunfire is distant but growing louder. She hears footsteps, heavy boots racing after her.

She runs faster, her legs near the point of failure. She turns corner after corner. If she slows down – if she stops running for even a moment – she's dead. She knows this, feels the certainty of her own demise nipping at her heels.

And then an alarm drags her back to the waking world.

Harper sits up in bed, gasping for air, like she'd stopped breathing in her sleep. She sees the time: 4:51 a.m. *Better hurry*, she thinks. *Foster and Jay must be exhausted.*

She dresses quickly, donning a fresh button-up shirt and her suit pants, which miraculously survived the melee outside the theatre. She re-examines the blazer in the light of day, but it's stained with spray paint and probably ruined. She figures Foster would prefer her slightly underdressed than wearing jeans and a leather jacket, so she leaves the blazer on the bed.

The walk to Cielo House seems shorter the second time, one hundred yards or so. She follows a winding path through the field, maple trees to her left, and redbrick buildings to her right. It's quiet at this hour, not a soul in sight.

Harper enters Cielo House using the key card Foster gave her, then crosses the lobby to the elevator and impatiently taps the up button. The door opens. She steps inside and taps the button for the sixth floor. The door closes. The elevator starts with a lurch.

On the sixth floor, the door slowly slides open. Harper starts to enter the hallway but stops abruptly when she nearly steps on something. She looks down and sees a body lying face down. The green carpet is stained with a pool of blood.

Harper freezes for half a second before back-pedalling into the elevator. She crouches to the ground. Her heart rate quickens.

*Breathe.*

She sucks air into her lungs.

The elevator door starts to close. Harper waves her hand to set off the sensor and the door reverses course. She uses her hand to keep it open. From her knees, she examines the corpse. There's a hole the size of a fist in the back of the head, and a tattoo along the neck, what looks like the tail of a snake.

Jay's tattoo.

She pokes her head into the hallway. Once she's satisfied no one is there, she steps out and kneels beside Jay's body. She doesn't check Jay's pulse. There's no point. Instead, she skates her hands under Jay's jacket and feels the leather underarm holster and the dense composite metal of a firearm. She wrenches free a Sig 9, checks the chamber and the clip, unlocks the safety, stands, raises the gun, and slowly walks down the hallway, towards Buchanan's room, the presidential suite.

The door is ajar. Harper quickly peers inside, scanning the room, gathers herself, and then advances forwards, her gun leading the way.

The glass coffee table in the living room is shattered. Shards of glass crunch under her shoes. She hears a groan from behind an overturned couch. Foster is lying on the other side, bleeding from his shoulder and abdomen.

Harper kneels. 'Hey, old man. Can you talk?'

Foster moans. He's alive, but not fully conscious.

Harper dials 911.

'Hold on, Charles. Hold on.'

'911. What's the exact location of the emergency?'

'Cielo House at Everly College. Sixth floor. A man has been shot. Twice. In the abdomen and shoulder.'

The operator starts to ask Harper questions, but she ignores him. She puts the call on speaker, places the phone on the floor, and then quickly and methodically checks the rest of the suite. The bathroom and first bedroom are clear, but in the second there's a body lying on the carpet, at the foot of the bed, arms outstretched, like Jesus on the cross. Harper recognises the face, though the confident smirk is gone, replaced by a pallid finish and gaping purse. Harper kneels and is about to check Mitch Buchanan's pulse at the carotid artery, but stops when she sees a syringe sticking out of his neck.

Once she's certain the suite is clear of any threat, Harper rushes back to Foster and starts ripping a bolt of curtain off the window and tearing it into strips.

'Hello?' The 911 operator is still on the line. 'Are you still there?'

Harper folds the bolt of curtain and presses it onto the wound on Foster's thigh, then uses thinner strips to hold it in place.

'I'm here.'

The operator tries again to ask Harper questions, but Harper knows he's only trying to distract her, to keep her calm.

Harper wipes sweat from Foster's forehead. 'You're going to be OK, Charles. You're going to be OK.'

*What am I missing?* she thinks. Jay is dead. Mitch Buchanan is dead. Foster is shot.

And then Harper remembers Tom.

'Listen to me,' Harper says, interrupting the operator. 'You need to send police to' – Harper combs her memory for Tom's address – 'One hundred and thirty-two Melcher Way. There's a man there. Tom Park. He's in danger.'

'Ma'am, I need you to calm down. I've already told you an ambulance is on the way.'

Harper tries to argue but he won't listen. *He thinks I'm losing it.*

Moments later Harper hears a buzzing siren. The ambulance took five minutes. An eternity and faster than she expected; a miracle but maybe not fast enough.

It's another forty-five seconds before Harper hears the ding of the elevator doors. Because there's a dead body in the hallway and she doesn't want them to get confused, Harper hollers, 'In here!'

Paramedics burst into the room. Harper steps back as they converge on Foster. She picks up Jay's Sig 9 off the floor and rushes out the door.

Outside, the Escalade is where she left it, parked on the street. She jumps in and races to Tom's. She parks on the kerb and jumps out of the car with the engine still running and races up the walk. She hammers on the door and is about to kick it down. She steps back, readies herself – and then the door opens. Just a crack.

'Harper?' Once Tom sees Harper, he opens the door all the way. 'What the hell is going on?'

Tom is in his boxer shorts. He's alive. Relief washes over Harper.

'What is it?' Tom asks. 'Is my uncle OK?'

# PART TWO

## REVENGE IS SOUR

# Day 3

'This is Stevie. Isn't he the cutest?'

A black and white picture of a Chihuahua fills the screen of Alex's phone.

'Adorable.'

Jess wraps her lips around a straw, inhales her cinnamon oat milk Frappuccino, then licks her lips.

Half an hour ago, Alex's mom arrived with three Frappuccinos and stayed just long enough to complain about the line at Starbucks before disappearing. Once they were alone, Alex hobbled over to Jess's bed and signalled for her to slide over. Now they're sitting side-by-side on the narrow mattress, scrolling through Alex's Instagram feed.

Jess is grateful for the distraction. Their shared hospital room is devoid of diversion. No TV, no magazines, just a dreary view of the parking lot. Plus, Jess hasn't had any visitors. She's done the math and she's fairly certain it was Susan who called the ambulance. So Susan knows Jess nearly died.

*It's a little fucked up she hasn't visited*, Jess thinks. *But would I want her to? God no. Could you imagine? The sanctimony?*

Jess thought about calling her dad for about half a minute, but she's pretty sure he's in Singapore. Or maybe Hong Kong. Sure, she nearly died. But would that be enough to make him drop everything and fly home? Probably not. Anyway, the idea of Mr Straight and Narrow, coming here, seeing her like this, after OD'ing – the look of disappointment would be worse than overdosing. 'Your brothers never did this to me, Jessica,' he'd say.

Alex continues to flick her index finger and pictures scroll past.

She stops on a picture of a young man sitting cross-legged on the floor.

'Who's that?'

'My boyfriend, Brent.'

'He's handsome. Is he a yogi?'

'What? Oh, you mean because of how he's sitting? No, that's actually our meditation group. Here, I'll show you.' Alex opens her cloud-based photo album and scrolls through hundreds of photos. She stops at a picture of a large, open room, with exposed brick walls. Dozens of men and women are evenly spread out, sitting on the floor, cross-legged, their eyes closed. Everyone is dressed head-to-toe in athletic gear, all in the colours of a Buddhist monk, maroon or saffron orange.

'I've never heard of a meditation group.'

'But you know what meditation is?'

'Yeah. Of course.'

'All right, well, we do that – meditate – but we do it together. You should come check it out. The group changed my life. Honestly. I mean, I look at you, and I see myself four years ago.'

'What does that mean?'

'Believe it or not, I used to use as well. I was lonely, depressed, filled with anxiety. My heart used to beat so fast I thought it was going to jump out of my chest. I hated myself. No, I *loathed* myself. My dad left' – Alex counts on her fingers – 'eight years ago, something like that. Turns out, he'd had a second family in California. Two kids, a wife. I guess he got sick of living two lives. Because one day, he picked the other family. He moved out west, and I've barely seen him since. I didn't dive off the deep end. It was more a slow walk from the shallow side of the pool. Mom was beside herself, trying to help me. She was worried

I was going to kill myself. Maybe I was ... I don't know. Honestly, I look back on who I was then ...' She shakes her head. 'Mom tried everything. Therapy, pharmaceuticals. She brought me to the meditation group as a last resort. And it saved me. I know it sounds flaky, like something out of GOOP or *The Power of Now*, but it did.' She sips her drink and then suddenly seizes Jess's arm. 'Hey! I've got an idea. Why don't you come and see what it's all about? I swear it will change your life.'

'Yeah?'

'Come to just one session, Jess. I promise you won't be disappointed.'

'Maybe.'

'I'm serious, Jess. I'm not going to take no for an answer.'

# 22

New York City, the Upper East Side. The Uber rolls to a stop. Harper Scott starts to open the car door, but stops when a bike messenger barks profanities as he zips past.

'Christ,' she mutters.

A chorus of car horns seeps through the crack in the door. Tom – a Manhattan native and therefore immune to near-death experiences – pushes Harper out and onto the sidewalk. The doorman opens the door and smiles. 'Welcome back, Mr Park.'

Inside, two men are standing to the right of the elevator bank. Grey suits, sombre expressions. *More security?* Harper wonders. *Or law enforcement?*

On the elevator, Harper checks her phone and is relieved to see she hasn't missed a call. One of the nurses at the hospital said she'd call if Foster's condition changed. *No news is good news*, she thinks.

Yesterday, after Harper found Tom alive and well, she raced to the hospital. She didn't want to leave Tom alone, so she dragged him with her. Shaken by the news of his uncle's murder, Tom readily agreed. They spent the next eight hours in the waiting room. The sheriff's department came and took statements; then the FBI, an agent named Frank Dreser. He grilled Harper, like she was the FBI's number one suspect. And he was the same with Tom, even though he'd just lost his uncle.

Once Foster was out of surgery, there was good news and bad. Foster had made it through alive – that was good. But he'd slipped into a coma. Agent Dreser was there and swore out loud at the news. He'd lost his chance to interview the only eyewitness to the murders. Before he left, he told Tom that the FBI was convening a meeting with the Buchanan family in New York City the next morning.

'Am I supposed to go as well?' Tom asked.

Agent Dreser shrugged. He didn't seem to care one way or the other. Perhaps because Tom's last name was Park, not Buchanan, and he wasn't interested in expanding his remit. 'That's up to you.'

With Foster's condition stable, Harper drove Tom back to his bungalow. When she started to follow him inside, he told her, 'Don't worry, Harper. You're off the hook. I'll be fine. Why don't you go back to the hospital and be with Foster?'

Harper shook her head. 'Foster paid me for two weeks, so you have me for another twelve days. When my two weeks are up, you can find someone else – if that's what you want. But until then, I'll be glued to your side.'

Tom put up a fight, but his heart wasn't in it. He was only doing what he thought was expected of him, some macho I-can-handle-anything-myself-bullshit. In fact, he was relieved. Harper slept on his couch that night and they drove to New York City in the morning. With her grey suit stained and ruined, they made one stop on the way so Harper could purchase a new suit. She opted for black this time, with a matching black turtleneck for underneath the blazer.

Now the elevator door opens – not to a hallway, as Harper had expected – but to the foyer of a massive penthouse. Glossy marble floors, vaulted ceiling, a wall of windows looking down onto Central Park.

'Tommy, you poor thing. How are you?'

Tom embraces a tiny woman. Her torso is drowning in a merino cardigan.

'Lenny, hi,' Tom says. 'I should be asking you the same thing.'

'Oh, I'm fine. Really I am.'

Or so she says. But Eleanor McMurtry looks frail enough that a strong wind could knock her over. She moves slowly, her complexion a sickly matte grey. Only her dark eyes reveal a certain tenacity. She looks Harper up and down. 'And who is this?'

'My bodyguard.'

'A woman? Really?'

'I know what you're thinking, Lenny. But you should have seen her Friday night. She got me out of a dicey situation.'

Lenny keeps her eyes on Harper. 'Fascinating. You're like Muammar Gaddafi, with his Amazonian bodyguards.'

Tom beams with pride. 'Exactly.'

On the surface, Harper remains stoic throughout this exchange, but inside she's seething. She pictures the younger version of Lenny, rising the corporate ladder, having to navigate an endless river of sexist bullshit. *Is there anything worse than a hypocrite?*

Actually, there is. Tom's behaviour is worse. By treating Harper as some quirky Band-Aid to his security problem, rather than the best man or woman for the job, it undermines Harper's authority. It reduces her to a novelty. She's the lioness at the circus forced to jump through hoops. The audience focuses on the hoops and misses the point: she's a *fucking* lion.

Growing up with three older brothers, Harper is (a) used to this feeling and (b) conditioned to bite back. She doesn't even think about it, only waits for the lion tamer to give her an opening. Which he just did.

'Wasn't Gaddafi murdered by his subjects?' Harper asks, her voice as sweet as honey. 'And his corpse was sodomised, right? With a bayonet?' She slaps Tom on the back. 'Let's hope you fare better than that, *Tommy*.'

Lenny's expression doesn't change, but there's something in her eyes that wasn't there before, a devious twinkle. 'She's feisty, Tommy. I'll give you that.' She takes Tom by the elbow. 'Enough small talk. Follow me, everyone's here.'

## 23

Harper spots a familiar face in the library, Agent Frank Dreser. He's whispering with a man wearing a sharp indigo suit. The Buchanan family is spread across the room, sitting on leather couches, standing by the window. There's an elderly man in a wheelchair, sporting a large gold medal pinned to his navy blazer. A woman half his age is whispering in his ear.

Harper stays on the edge of the room, while Tom dives into the group, saying hello, fielding rapid-fire questions. 'How are you?' 'Did you see his body?' 'Have you spoken to the press?' 'Keep Tom away from me. He's bad luck.'

Tom takes a seat next to a woman Harper recognises from photos as Bonnie Buchanan, Tom's mother.

On the drive to New York, Tom had broken down the two branches of the Buchanan family, established by two brothers, Maurice and Edgar, and an endless list of children and grandchildren. According to Tom, every member of the Buchanan family falls into one of two camps: the Alphas (Maurice's side) or the Betas (Edgar's side).

Maurice has been dead ten years, so Harper figures the old man in the wheelchair must be the patriarch of the Betas, Edgar. If that's Edgar, then the woman standing by his side would be his third wife, Abigail.

Tom described his cousin Wells as a 'perpetual man-child', so Harper assumes the man dressed like a teenage snowboarder – camouflage hoodie and backwards baseball cap – is Edgar's youngest son.

With both Skip and Mitch murdered, the Alphas take up less of the room than they used to. Harper guesses that the couple trying to corral a toddler is Skip's son Terry and his second wife, Cindy. Terry must be in his fifties, while Cindy is in her mid-thirties and attractive. According to Tom, Terry's life is now dedicated to supporting his wife's career, the 'fashion icon wannabe,' he said. 'She sold a few hoodies for half the cost of producing them, and Terry thinks she's a genius.'

Tom and his mother Bonnie round out the rest of the Alphas.

The number of Buchanans in attendance is nowhere close to the names Tom listed on the drive down. Maybe the others couldn't make it. Or maybe the FBI only picked those with the highest profile. Harper isn't sure.

'Harper?' The man in the sharp suit has crossed the room and is holding his hand out for Harper to take. 'I'm Louis Diaz.'

'Have we met?'

'No, but I know Charles. We served together. I'm with the FBI now. I figured he'd mentioned my name, but maybe not.'

Harper takes his hand. 'Nice to meet you.'

'You as well.' Lou's expression softens briefly. 'I'm sure he's going to be fine.'

Harper fights back a lump in her throat. 'Yeah . . . well, if you know Charles, then you know how tough he is. He's in bad shape, but he'll pull through.'

Lou nods. 'There's nobody tougher.'

'Are you going to find the person responsible?'

'Yes.'

Harper likes how he says this, with absolute confidence.

'Your friend over there didn't seem too optimistic.'

'Did Agent Dreser give you a hard time? Don't take it personally. He's a great agent, but he lacks people skills.'

'Like how not to be an asshole?'

'And,' Lou says, diplomatically avoiding the question, 'he doesn't know Charles. Or you.'

'You don't know me. You're nice enough, so far.'

'Actually, Charles told me quite a lot about you. How you saved his life. He even ran the idea of hiring you by me.'

This takes Harper by surprise. Foster wasn't exactly an open book. She can't imagine him talking with anyone about Afghanistan, let alone some agent with the FBI.

Lou changes the subject. 'I was looking over your statement, the one you gave to Agent Dreser. He didn't ask you about Jay Houser's gun.'

'What about it?'

'Well, I understand Jay and Foster carried a firearm. But you didn't.'

'That's right.'

'Because you didn't have a licence.'

'Yeah. So?'

'We managed to locate Foster's weapon at the scene. But not Jay's.'

'OK.'

'Odds are whoever killed Jay took his weapon. But I thought maybe there's a chance you found it on Jay.' Harper starts to respond but Lou talks over her. '*And* if that's what happened, I don't care. You can give us the gun and that's that. We only want to know what happened. And I don't want to waste time looking for a firearm you've got stashed away somewhere.'

Harper's instinct is to lie. Jay's Sig 9 – which is currently strapped under her left arm, in a holster, underneath her suit jacket – won't make or break the FBI's case, and it's far more valuable to her than it is to them. Plus, she doesn't know Lou. He seems OK, but in Harper's experience, there's no bigger scam than when a cop says, 'I only want to know what happened.'

'I didn't take Jay's gun.'

Lou nods. 'Well, I figured it was worth asking.' He flicks his chin at Tom. 'Are you going to keep working for Mr Park?'

'Foster paid me for two weeks, so I'll be with him for that long at least.'

'Well, if you need any help' – Lou hands Harper his card – 'call me. Foster's friend is my friend.'

## 24

Lou joins Agent Dreser at the front of the room and together they try to quiet their audience. The family doesn't notice. They talk over each other until Lenny lets loose a vicious whistle. 'I know we're all upset,' she says, 'but let's please give Special Agent Diaz the floor.'

'Thank you, Eleanor,' Lou says. 'And thank you everyone for coming. I'm sure this is a difficult time, and that you're all devastated about Mitch.'

'Are we?' Wells asks in a whisper loud enough for everyone to hear.

Bonnie glares at him. 'Shut up, Wells.'

Lou ignores all of this and keeps talking. 'The FBI is working with our colleagues in the local sheriff's department to investigate Mitch's murder. Unfortunately, I can't get into specifics. But I can give you enough information here, today, for you to understand why – if you didn't know already – it's vital that you all retain private security for the foreseeable future.'

A murmur ripples across the room.

'Why isn't the FBI providing us with protection?' Wells asks. 'Do you know what we pay in taxes? I pay enough to cover your salary and everyone else in your department.'

Terry shakes his head. 'That's not how it works, Wells.'

Lou ignores the bickering and indirectly answers the question. 'My team is working with local law enforcement and the Federal Marshals Service to determine how best to protect everyone here. But that's going to take time to get in place. Your family has the resources to immediately hire private security.

Professionals who can keep you safe right now. We believe it's imperative that you have twenty-four-hour protection until we've apprehended the person responsible for Mitch's murder.'

'They say we need to hire security,' Abigail shouts into Edgar's ear. He nods, but still looks confused.

'Let's be honest,' Wells says. 'Mitch was a legendary asshole. Just like Skip.' He sees his family recoiling and puts his hands up in the air, defensively. 'Hey, don't get me wrong. I loved them both. But we know that outside of this family, they weren't exactly considered the second coming of Mother Teresa. The rest of us have a lower profile. Aren't we overreacting, thinking what happened to them will happen to us?'

'That would be a dangerous assumption,' Lou says. 'And I'll explain why.'

He nods at Agent Dreser, and Agent Dreser turns on a digital projector connected to a laptop. An image appears on the wall. It's blurry at first, lost in the window's light, until Lou lowers the blinds, using a light switch on the wall. As the room grows darker, the image on the wall crystallises into an email.

'This is an email Skip Buchanan sent to many of you years ago. And to Mitch. It was leaked to the press and published in the *LA Times*, among other places.'

'How could we forget?' Barry says. 'It made the John Oliver show. I *still* have to apologise for this email. And I didn't even send it.'

Harper reads the email.

From: Skip Buchanan
To: Eleanor McMurtry
Cc: Mitch Buchanan, Bonnie Buchanan, Edgar Buchanan, Terry Buchanan,
Wellington Buchanan, Sandy Spitzer, Carl Watson

Eleanor,

I read your email. You made four points. I agree with one of them. The other three are – excuse my French – absolute horseshit. I've copied the other members of the board so we are all on the same page.

Yes, the statistics are big. I'll agree with you there. And the optics aren't great. But I think you are being a tad dramatic to call it a 'nightmare'. If there is – as you put it – 'an opioid epidemic sweeping the country', no one can reasonably blame Apollo Pharma.

This is a messaging issue. We have to hammer the abusers, here. OK? They're criminals, scum of the earth. The pills aren't the problem. The users who can't control themselves – THEY are the problem.

And do we even agree with these statistics? Doesn't the DEA have their own agenda? Fifty thousand people died this year from OxyPro overdoses? Are we sure about that? Maybe the DEA is trying to justify their existence. At the very least, that's a talking point. I pay you to think, Lenny, to come up with solutions. Not to compose elegies.

The DEA is breathing down our necks. Fine. Let them. We know where that will go. A fine – big on paper, nothing to us in the long run – a few Hail Marys, and then it's business as usual.

I hear you on the lawsuits. But this is America. Lawsuits are inevitable. Damages are a part and parcel with making a profit. We'll deal with that as it comes. But we are not scaling back production and sales. If anything, we should ramp up to cover future liabilities. We have an obligation to our shareholders to maximise profit. You're the company lawyer, Lenny, not the company deacon. You're paid to help us generate revenue and reduce risk. Not to cry wolf. Dry your tears, roll up your sleeves, and let's sell some goddamn pills.

Yours,

Skip Buchanan
CEO and Chairman of the Board, Apollo Pharma Corp.

Harper reads the email, but has trouble getting past the bit about hammering the abusers. She thinks of Derrick. *What am I doing here?*

'Not Skip's finest hour,' Wells says. 'We can all agree on that.'

'Jesus, Wells,' Bonnie says. 'Don't speak ill of the dead.'

'Come on, Bon. Don't protect Skip. He fucked us. All of us. Writing emails like this. Remember when this became public and Skip said, "Don't worry. This will blow over. The media will have a new villain soon enough." He was wrong. Dead wrong.'

Cindy says, 'It was more than the email, though, wasn't it?'

'Oh please, Cindy,' Wells barks. 'You're more than happy to live off the money Skip made for this family. Your private flights around the world, that shitty clothing line you started.'

'Fuck off, Wells,' Terry says, defending his wife.

'Am I the only one who read Borelli's book?' Wells says. 'This and all those other documents that were leaked to the press – the story ran weeks after Knox's daughter overdosed and died. This email didn't kill Skip and Mitch,' he says, pointing at the email projected on the wall, 'it was the fact Apollo Pharma's confidential internal communications were sent to reporters. Once we find out who the leak was, we should sue *them*.'

Lou clears his throat. 'If I could—'

'Cindy's right,' Terry says. 'The public is angry because – well, it's more than the one email. Opioids are a real problem.'

'So are car accidents,' Wells says. 'You don't see Henry Ford's great grandkids being murdered in their sleep.'

'What did Maurice used to say?' Bonnie asks. 'Humans have been using opium since Helen of Troy. Anyone who thinks opioids are new hasn't been paying attention.'

'Actually,' Cindy says, to no one in particular, 'my clothing line was recently featured in the *Times* style section.'

'OxyPro was a godsend for people struggling with pain,' Wells says. 'The whole world has conveniently forgotten that it *is* a miracle drug.' He points at the email projected on the wall. 'And Skip was right. Addicts *are* the problem.'

Harper fights the urge to jump across the room and take Wells Buchanan by the neck.

'As I was saying,' Lou says, trying to regain command of the room, 'Knox murdered Skip, the author of this email.'

'Can we skip the part we know?'

If Lou is frustrated, it doesn't show. He smiles calmly, waiting for his chance to continue. *He deserves a medal*, Harper thinks. *I'd have shot three of them in the knee by now.*

'And,' Lou continues, 'Knox – the Karma Killer – he wrote about this email and the Apollo Pharma documents leaked to the press.'

'You mean his manifesto?' Wells asks.

'His what?' Cindy asks.

'Like the Unabomber. Some crazies write down their bullshit to justify why they're so freaking crazy.'

'It's called the Utility of Murder. It's on Reddit,' Wells says. 'I read the whole thing last summer. Fucking trippy.'

Lou holds up his hand. 'I wouldn't go so far as to call it a manifesto. Knox wrote a series of posts, which hardly had any engagement prior to Skip's murder, and following Knox's arrest, we worked with Reddit to have the posts removed, so as not to give life to Knox's ... views.'

'What did he say in his posts?' Tom asks. 'Why show us this email?'

'I'm not sure it's helpful to get into everything that Knox wrote about,' Lou says. 'Essentially, Knox claimed that he was bringing about some sort of moral revolution by punishing wrongdoers. His aim was to start with an example to inspire the world.'

'And are we the example?'

'Yes,' Lou says. 'Knox said he was going to administer karmic justice to everyone on Apollo Pharma's board – specifically, everyone who received this email.'

'Only directors – only *their* lives are in danger?' Wells asks. 'I *knew* I shouldn't have gone to work for this goddamn company.'

'And,' Lou adds, 'their children as well.'

'Because Knox lost his daughter?' Tom asks.

'Yes. Precisely.'

'That's what Knox said before he murdered Skip,' Tom says. 'But how do you know this is related to Mitch's murder?'

'We don't know for certain,' Lou says. 'It's only a theory at this point. But there's online chatter quoting Knox's original posts.'

'How do you know it's not Knox who's posting this?' Bonnie asks.

'I can assure you,' Lou says, 'it's not Knox. He's in a secure facility, under constant supervision, with limited internet access. If he was making these posts, we'd know.'

'Do you know if it was the same person who attacked Lenny and killed Mitch?' Cindy asks.

Wells snorts sarcastically. 'Haven't you been listening, Cindy? They don't know *anything*.'

'There are similarities,' Lou says. 'Patterns that we're analysing.'

'Lenny was injected with fentanyl. Right, Lenny?' Bonnie looks at Lenny but doesn't wait for a reply. 'But wasn't Skip killed with OxyPro? Why the switch?'

Before Lou can respond, Terry interjects: 'Fentanyl is cheaper and deadlier. It's shipped in from China every day, boatloads of it. Easier to buy, easier to kill with.'

Wells waves his finger. 'You aren't online enough. This is all part of Knox's plan, to have the murders escalate from Oxy to fentanyl, just like happened to his daughter before she OD'd.'

Lou raises his arms like he's trying to calm a spooked horse. 'I'd caution against reading too much into what people are saying online. And we're still investigating what substances were used in the attacks.'

'Do you have any suspects?' Tom asks. 'Any at all?'

The Buchanans quieten down, waiting for Lou's response.

'No.'

Wells moans. Terry swears out loud. Cindy starts breathing in an exaggerated way, like she's hyperventilating. 'Oh-my-God.'

'I can understand your concern,' Lou says. 'But we are on top of this. We'll find the person responsible. In the meantime, I am imploring you to hire private security if you don't already have it in place, professionals who can protect you.'

'Mitch had protection,' Wells says. 'And look where it got him?'

The room stares at Lou. A few critical eyes drift to Harper.

'Vigilance,' Lou says.

'Oh Christ,' Wells says. 'That's your advice?'

Terry shakes his head. 'Do you know how many death threats I get a day? I quit Twitter, made my Facebook and Instagram accounts private. And still I'm bombarded with death threats. How are you going to find a killer when half the country is literally threatening to kill me?'

'We're following every lead.'

'Great,' Wells says. 'While you're busy looking under every rock the killer is going to inject fentanyl into my *fucking* veins.'

Cindy puts her hands over her toddler's ears. 'Wells, will you cool it on the language.'

'Language is the least of our problems.'

'Was everyone doxed before they were attacked,' Tom asks, 'Skip, Lenny, Mitch?'

'There is a pattern we've observed, yes.'

'How long after their address was posted were they attacked?' Tom asks.

'It varies,' Lou says. 'But within forty-eight hours of the post.'

'Has anyone been doxed since Mitch was killed?'

Lou's audience collectively holds its breath.

'No.'

A few family members exhale with relief.

'Should we bet on who's next?' Wells asks. 'My money's on Terry.'

'Fuck you, Wells.'

# 25

Tom has had enough. He escapes the library, signalling for Harper to follow. He leads her outside, onto a large stone balcony with a view of Central Park, fifty-one blocks of green surrounded by towers of glass and stone.

'Do you have your vape?'

'I'm working.'

'Save it, Harper. I know a crutch when I see one. I bet you need it to brush your teeth.'

'Fine. Here.' Harper hands Tom her vape. 'But let's keep the personal attacks to a minimum. OK?'

Tom takes a long drag. Harper has the urge to ask who needs the crutch now, but Tom has had a rough forty-eight hours, so she lets it go.

The sliding door opens and Eleanor McMurtry steps onto the balcony. She stands beside Tom and lights a cigarette. 'Can you believe this shit?'

Harper steps back, against the wall, to give them space to talk.

'No,' Tom says, 'I can't.'

Lenny's hand is shaking as she smokes. 'I could have avoided all this, you know.' She'd been looking out at Central Park, but now she turns and looks at Tom. 'Carl – you remember Carl; the company's former general counsel; he was copied on Skip's awful email – Carl told me, he said, "Lenny, leave now if you can."' She ashes her cigarette. Her hand continues to shake. 'Do you remember? When Carl and Sandy fell on their swords, to protect the family?'

Tom squints. 'Sort of. But I was young.'

'It was fifteen years ago. The AG sued Apollo Pharma. They sued Carl and Sandy, the highest-ranking executives without the last name Buchanan. (Back then, your families' political connections could still protect them.) Carl and Sandy pled guilty. They paid a fine and they had to do some community service. It was embarrassing – poor Carl was beside himself. But it was a good result for the company. Carl had to leave. Sandy, too. That was part of the deal. But Skip and Mitch took care of them. Five million each.'

Lenny lights another cigarette. The tremor in her hand has travelled up her arm to her shoulder.

'Did you know Skip and Mitch offered me the same option? A golden parachute. We can clean house, they said. Start over with a new legal team. But they talked big about changing how the company operated. No more outright lies in our marketing material. That was part of the plea deal, after all. So I stayed. But it was all bullshit. Soon, Skip and Mitch were laughing about the plea deal. And why wouldn't they? The penalty was a slap on the wrist. In the end, we didn't change so much as a comma in our marketing material. "Less than a one per cent chance of addiction." Give me a fucking break.' She shakes her head, staring out into Central Park. 'If I'd taken the five million, I'd be . . . I don't know . . . in the Lake District, maybe.' She ashes her cigarette and looks at Tom. 'Sandy ran a charity until he died a few years ago. Homelessness. Or cancer. Something like that. As exciting as watching paint dry. But you can bet no one stabbed him with a needle.'

'I've never seen you like this, Lenny. What happened?'

'You mean when I was attacked? Mitch didn't tell you?'

Tom shrugs. 'You know Uncle Mitch. The story was always about him.'

Lenny puts her cigarette out on the stone railing and quickly lights another one. 'I'd just flown home from London. It was late, I was exhausted, and I was on the phone with Mitch. You know what that's like, his booming voice in your ear. Whoever had broken in had cut the power. But I didn't even realise. I came in, made a drink, and went up to my bedroom. I tried to turn on the light, but, like I said, the power was out. Then someone grabbed me, covered my mouth. He was wearing a glove. I can still taste the latex.' She sticks her tongue out in disgust. 'And then he stuck a needle in my neck.'

'And then what?'

'Well, I got high. I suddenly felt like I was in a warm bath, without a care in the world. But it was short-lived. Soon my lungs felt like they were filled with water. I couldn't catch my breath. Luckily, Mitch called 911.'

'So he *did* save your life? I thought he was exaggerating.'

Lenny nods. 'He did. Absolutely. And also . . .' Lenny ashes her cigarette. 'You probably heard, didn't you? I'd . . . built up a tolerance?'

Tom gently places his hand on Lenny's arm. 'How long?'

'How long have I been using? Let's see. I hurt my back in Aspen,' she counts her fingers, 'ten years ago. The doctor gave me a prescription and that was that. I couldn't stop. The irony, right? All the letters I've written, the emails, my testimony to Congress. All the times I claimed OxyPro wasn't addictive, and I was addicted myself. I'm glad Skip and Mitch never found out. Could you imagine?'

'They loved you, Lenny. They'd have helped, given you whatever support you needed.'

Lenny laughs sarcastically. 'Oh, sure. Skip and Mitch were known for their empathy.'

A pigeon lands on the corner of the stone railing. It coos three times and then flutters away.

'Did you see or hear anything else?' Tom asks.

'When I was attacked? Not really. Once my body relaxed and I stopped fighting – I'm not sure what I was thinking – but I asked a question out loud. I said, "Why?" Strange, right? The "Why" isn't really up for debate. It's the "Who" – that's the real barnburner.'

'And then what?'

Lenny shrugs. 'Fade to black.'

'Was it OxyPro?' Tom asks. 'The FBI seemed reluctant to say.'

'You mean was it Oxy that was dissolved into a liquid and injected into my body against my will?'

Lenny pauses to collect herself. Meanwhile Harper – who had been quietly watching this exchange from the edge of the balcony – blurts out: 'But I thought the pills were reformulated.' Tom and Lenny turn to look at Harper. 'So they couldn't be crushed and snorted,' she adds.

Tom's expression says, *How the hell did you know that?*

'The pills were reformulated,' Lenny says. 'That's true. But they're pretty sure whoever attacked me used fentanyl. The dosage was low enough that I could hold on until the ambulance got there.'

'Fentanyl,' Tom says. 'Jesus! And you survived? I realise you'd built up a tolerance . . . but still.'

'Whoever attacked me missed a vein. So the fentanyl didn't hit my bloodstream right away. If they'd gotten a vein, the doctors said I'd have been dead in a matter of seconds.'

They're quiet for a moment, smoking in silence.

'Do you know why Penelope didn't come?' Tom asks.

Lenny shrugs. 'She hasn't left home in how many months?'

'True.'

'And after what happened to her ... it's understandable.' Lenny sucks on her cigarette, then blows smoke out of her nostrils. 'I wonder if they're going to talk to her.'

'Who?'

'The FBI. You heard them. What happened to me and Mitch – somehow it relates to what happened to Skip. What annoyingly vague language did they use? "Patterns". "Similarities".'

The door to the balcony slides open and Wells plants one foot outside. 'Sorry, Tommy,' he says. 'Looks like you drew the short straw.'

'What are you talking about?'

'You've been doxed, my friend.'

# 26

Tom and Harper find the family where they'd left them, in the library. But now they're on their phones, reading intently. Tom shuffles into the room and their eyes drift to him, their expression a mixture of sympathy and relief – relief that it's someone else's neck on the chopping block. Agents Diaz and Dreser are in the corner of the room, each barking instructions into their phones.

'Is it true?' Tom asks as he enters the room.

Barry throws his arm around Tom's shoulders. 'Sorry, Tommy. It's on Reddit.'

Tom's mother Bonnie is crying. 'My poor, sweet boy.'

'It was me who found it,' Cindy says. 'I just had this feeling, you know, that something was off. The FBI was still doing their presentation and I thought: why don't I have a look?'

Wells rolls his eyes. 'Yeah, quite the achievement, Cindy.'

Tom fumbles in his pocket for his phone.

'Here, Tommy,' Barry says, holding his phone up, 'look at mine.'

'Oh my God! It's my house in Petersburg, near campus.'

Harper pulls up Bad Pharma on her phone. It doesn't take her long to find the post doxing Tom. Someone with the username @Karma992 posted a Google Maps link to Tom's address and a picture of his front door. 'Tommy's next,' the post says, 'Bye-bye.'

'Someone was there,' Tom says, 'outside my home. What am I supposed to do?'

The room turns in unison to stare at Agent Diaz. He's off the phone now, standing with his arms crossed. 'We're looking into it.'

'Looking into it,' Lenny says. 'How wonderfully vague.'

Wells is laughing. 'Once Tommy's dead, they're going to look into that too.'

Lou keeps his focus on Tom. 'We have agents on their way to Everly College as we speak. We're going to find who did this. But in the meantime, do you have anywhere you can go? Another home or apartment?'

'I've got a little place here in the city.'

'I'd suggest you stay there for the time being, until we get movement on the case.'

'So, basically forever,' Wells says and then laughs at his own joke.

'Stop being cruel,' Bonnie says. 'This is my son.'

'Oh please, Bon! We're all in danger here.'

The bickering builds until nearly every Buchanan is shouting. Except for Tom. 'Let's get out of here,' he says to Harper. 'I can't take this anymore.'

As they're leaving, Lou pulls Harper aside. 'Every attack has come at night,' he says. 'Once you're inside, lock the doors and don't come out until morning.'

'All right,' Harper says. 'Tell me again you're going to get this guy.'

'Just do your job and I'll do mine.'

# Day 6

A car horn sends Jess to the window. She spots a white BMW parked on the street, then takes one last look in the mirror. Her outfit – light pink T-shirt, black bike shorts – is not the hues of a Buddhist monk, like Alex had suggested, but it's the best she could do on short notice. It's not like she was going to buy a new outfit for her first – and probably *only* – visit to Alex's meditation group. It's nice Alex extended the invite, but Jess knows meditation won't be her thing. She likes to fret, to ruminate, to seethe. Detachment has never been her strong suit, unless it's via chemical assistance.

But thank God Alex kept in touch. Jess has been out of the hospital for eighteen hours and all she can think about is getting high. Alex's steady stream of text messages and phone calls have been a welcome distraction. And if Jess hadn't planned on spending the day with Alex, she'd probably be off looking for Brad, her dealer.

As Jess steps into the hallway, she hears a door slam shut. Since returning from the hospital, Susan and Josh have avoided Jess like she's radioactive – which is fine, obviously. Jess couldn't stand them before OD'ing. It's not like a few nights in the hospital changed that. *But it shows their lack of character, how shitty they are*, Jess thinks. *Your roommate nearly dies and you can't say, 'How are you feeling?'*

Outside, the BMW is parked on the street. Jess sees the shadow of someone in shotgun, so she slides into the back seat, next to a set of aluminium crutches. Alex is behind the wheel, wearing a saffron orange tank top and matching leggings. She looks different than she did in the hospital: her hair has a new lustre, her eyes a smoky-smouldering look. She was beautiful in the hospital. But here, in the outside world, with access to a shower and makeup, she's gorgeous.

Alex introduces Jess to her boyfriend Brent. He's friendly and handsome. 'It's great to finally meet you,' he says.

Jess feels a pleasant tingle in her chest. She can't imagine the angelic figure behind the wheel talking about her.

'How do I look?' Jess asks.

Alex stares at Jess in the rear-view mirror. 'Contemplative. It's perfect.'

The meditation space is forty minutes outside of town. The building is large, one-storey, and built out of grey cinderblocks. Alex parks. Jess steps out of the car and instantly feels a certain energy, friendly and non-threatening. Alex is swarmed, like a politician entering a pancake social. Smiles, hugs, kisses on the cheek. She looks down at her cast and says, 'Yes, don't worry, I'm fine.' Jess tries to remember names and faces, but it's a merry-go-round of people, dizzying and eclectic.

Once they finally make it inside, the ceremony – the GME, as Alex calls it, for Group Meditation Experience; one of a thousand acronyms she's used this morning – has already started. Jess takes off her shoes and slips them into one of the cubbies lining the wall.

The room is carpeted, with a stage opposite the entrance, empty at this point, except for a large white-leather chair. Participants are spread out across the room. Most are sitting cross-legged. A few of the older, less flexible members are sitting on stools.

# KILL PILL | 127

Everyone is dressed in the hues of a Buddhist monk, saffron orange, maroon red, canary yellow. Alex grabs her by the hand and pulls her to space near the front.

Jess feels a slight strain on her knees as she contorts into the right position. She wonders how long it's been since she sat cross-legged. Now that she's close to the stage, Jess sees there are actually three chairs, with two smaller chairs flanking the leather throne. A woman dressed in black walks onto the stage and sits on one of the smaller chairs. The other remains empty.

Alex leans in and whispers, 'That's Meryl. Mom usually sits in the other chair.'

'She couldn't make it today?'

'Something like that. She'll be back soon.'

A gong chimes and the room grows quiet.

Alex closes her eyes and begins to breathe deeply.

On the drive here, Alex gave Jess a pep-talk on what to expect, on how to get the most out of her first session. 'Focus on your breathing. It's not about clearing your mind. It's about making your thoughts singular, focusing on the present. But remember: it's hard to do, especially the first time. So don't get frustrated or mad at yourself. It's like a muscle. You need to train it. And listen to Lama Aaron. His instruction – it works for any level.'

Jess closes her eyes and tries to focus on her breathing. But her mind immediately drifts. She thinks of how she got here, moving backwards through time: meeting Alex in the hospital, overdosing on her front porch, buying and snorting fentanyl for the first time, her use of Oxy, which started casual and grew into something else, something dark and inescapable. The year from hell that had her chewing Oxy just to escape the shittiness of it all. *This is why meditation won't work for me*, Jess thinks. *My mind is too messy for singular thought. Anyway, Oxy is more reliable. It's a light switch, instant relief. Not a 'process'.*

Just then Jess senses a shift in the room, a wave of excitement, stifled 'ooohhs' and 'aaahhs'. Jess chances opening her eyes and sees a man is making his way through the crowd. Occasionally, he bends down and whispers in a congregant's ear or pats a shoulder. He's short and chubby, with dark, piercing eyes, a tangled mop of hair, and a five o'clock shadow. He is somehow both unassuming and charismatic. His presence is like a magnet, pulling all attention towards him. He's wearing a headset, with an earpiece connected to a microphone, and his jogging pants and T-shirt are saffron orange. The combination is absurd, as if the Dalai Lama took a job as a telemarketer. But somehow he pulls it off.

Alex told Jess about her 'guru' in the hospital. 'His name is Lama Aaron, and he is *a*-mazing.' According to Alex, Aaron trained in Eastern medicine and meditation, first in China, and then India. 'And he's a Rhodes scholar, with a doctorate in philosophy.'

As Lama Aaron makes his way towards the stage, his gentle whispers are transmitted through hidden speakers. 'Good morning, class. Good morning.'

He draws close to Jess.

Her heart flutters nervously.

He places a hand on her shoulder. 'Welcome. We are so very happy you decided to join us.'

He walks to the stage.

Jess turns to Alex. Wide-eyed, Alex mouths the word, *Wow*.

Even though two minutes ago Jess couldn't have spotted Aaron out of a crowd of two, she feels something, a lightness welling up inside her. She tells herself this feeling is separate and unrelated to the envy she senses rippling through the crowd.

On stage, Aaron sits cross-legged on his white leather throne. 'Good morning, class.' He closes his eyes. 'Let us begin.'

# 27

Tom's 'little place in the city' turns out to be an Upper East Side brownstone. As Tom keys in a ten-digit code to disarm the security system, Harper takes in the grandeur of the foyer. Framed paintings, sculptures, hardwood floors, an eye-catching art-deco chandelier. Unlike his clapboard home near Everly campus, this is what she expected from a man of Tom's means. She can't imagine how much it would cost. No number would surprise her. Twenty million? Thirty? She whistles: it seems like the only appropriate response.

'I'm going to order Thai,' Tom says. 'You good with that?'

'I lost my appetite.'

Tom laughs. 'My family has that effect on people. Don't worry, it will pass.'

Harper escapes to the Escalade, which is parked down the block. She told Tom it was to get their bags, but really she wanted to spend some quality time with her vape. It's been a long day and the release valve needs to be opened. She sits behind the wheel, takes a tiny puff, just enough to turn the valve a quarter of an inch, and then eases into the leather seat, closes her eyes, and waits for another miracle.

Once she's relaxed, she removes Jay's Sig 9 from its holster under her arm and examines the firearm. She thinks back to earlier that day, how she lied to Special Agent Diaz about the gun. *Maybe that wasn't the wisest decision, but there's no going back. You can't un-lie to the FBI.* And with a killer on the loose and Tom recently doxed, she isn't about to get rid of her only firearm.

She slides the Sig back into her underarm holster, turns off her vape and pockets it, and then heads back inside.

Plastic takeaway containers sit lidless on the kitchen island. Tamarind perfumes the air.

Tom opens two Rolling Rocks and tries to hand one to Harper. She refuses. 'No, thanks. I'm on duty.'

'Relax. I've got a state-of-the-art security system here. You can have one drink.'

'I'm good.'

Tom looks disappointed. Maybe he doesn't like drinking alone. Or maybe he wants to pick up where they left off in his living room the night of the protest. Harper imagines Foster's I-told-you-so moment. 'That's why you don't get high with a client. If you remove a boundary, you can't redraw it.'

*Point taken*, Harper thinks.

'So, what did you make of my family?' Tom asks.

Harper shakes her head. 'You don't want to know what I think.'

'If you're afraid to tell me they're monsters – don't be.'

'Well, now that you mention it.'

They both smile.

'They're rich, oblivious, and entitled,' Harper says. 'I was expecting that. But what I don't understand is how did *those* people create a multi-billion-dollar company?'

'They didn't. The Buchanans who made Apollo Pharma – they're all gone now. It was my grandfather Maurice and his brother Edgar who formed the company. And when Skip was named CEO in the Nineties – that's when the company really took off. Maurice had always been a Renaissance man. He played the violin and was an avid art collector. Skip was the polar opposite to his father. He was myopic. He only cared about Apollo Pharma. He was a pill-selling robot. That email you saw – there's a million more like it. He worked twenty-four hours a day, haranguing everyone from Lenny to the janitors, trying to increase revenue. OxyPro was his baby. The mother of all painkillers. Oxy took the company's revenues from millions to billions.'

'How'd Mitch and everyone else fit in?'

'The Alphas and the Betas are supposed to have equal representation on the board. The idea was to share power. But everyone pretty much deferred to Skip and Mitch. They knew how smart they were. And the Betas . . . you saw them. If they didn't have Lenny, I think they'd be broke by now.'

Harper shovels a forkful of pad Thai into her mouth.

'Speaking of Lenny,' Tom says, 'what did you think of her story?'

Harper shrugs. 'Pretty messed up.'

'Yeah, but how do you think it fits with what happened to Mitch?'

Harper looks up from her plate, surprised at the nature of the question, though she couldn't exactly say why. 'I have no idea. Why?'

Tom takes a deep breath, like he's readying himself for a fight. 'Do you want to catch the person who did this? The man who killed my uncle and put your friend in a coma?'

'The FBI is on top of it.'

'I'm not convinced they know anything at this point.'

'They're professionals,' Harper says. 'This is what they do.'

'Did you hear them? *We think. Our theory.* Clearly, they don't have anything concrete. It's all theory and supposition.'

Harper drops her fork and stares at Tom. 'Why don't you tell me what you want me to do, so I can say "no", officially?'

'I want to find the person who did this. And I want you to help me.'

Harper laughs, her first time in two days. 'Me? Why would I have any more luck than the FBI?'

'I think it's a mistake to assume the FBI is any good at finding a killer in these circumstances.'

'It's the FBI. They do this for a living. They have unlimited resources.'

Tom gives Harper a condescending smile. It reminds her of Mitch Buchanan's, the billionaire smirk. 'I think, as an institution,' Tom says, 'the FBI has a poor record of handling novel cases. Take the Unabomber. That was a unique case – bombs being sent through the mail – unlike anything the FBI had encountered before. Do you know how long it took the FBI to catch Kaczynski? More than a decade. I don't intend to hide for a decade. I'm sure Agents Diaz and Dreser mean well. But institutions are prone to error. Groupthink, faulty reasoning, post-hoc justification.'

'What the hell are you talking about?'

'Cognitive biases. It's what I study.'

'OK,' Harper says. 'You have concerns about how the FBI is going about the investigation. I get that. But why do you think *I* would be any better at it?'

'You won't be doing it alone. I'll direct you.'

'You?'

'Yes,' Tom says. He sees Harper's fighting a smile and adds, 'I was doxed, Harper. How long did Agent Diaz say from when you're doxed to when you're attacked? Forty-eight hours?'

'Different house, though, right?'

'Is that supposed to give me comfort?' Tom shakes his head. 'I'm not going to sit back and wait for the FBI to screw this up, but I can't do a lot of what needs to be done myself. For one thing, it's not safe. Also, I'm not the most recognisable family member, but I'm still a Buchanan. I won't exactly have the anonymity an investigator needs. I can direct you. We can work together.'

'And how would I even start this . . . investigation?'

'*We*. How would *we* start?' Tom says. 'We talk to my cousin Penelope. She was there, the night my uncle Skip and my aunt Cecilia were murdered.'

*Is Tom in shock?* Harper wonders. Starting some half-cocked investigation two days after your uncle is murdered is not exactly a rational decision. But if he wants to pay Harper to ask a few people some questions, what's the harm?

'How much?'

'The motivation to find the person who shot Foster isn't enough for you?'

'I want to find the man responsible, sure. I just don't think there's a chance in hell we'll be successful. So if I'm going to run around playing detective – I want to get paid.'

Tom's back straightens. He looks offended. 'That's what you think this would be? A hobby?'

'Listen, Tom, I get that you're upset. I get that you don't want to sit on the sidelines. And you seem smart enough. But in terms of conducting a murder investigation, we're so behind in information, resources and experience, we might as well call it a hobby. Because it's no different than collecting stamps or training for a half-marathon. But if you're the brains, and I'm the muscle, who cares what I think?'

Tom nods. 'OK. If we find the person who killed my uncle, I'll pay you a hundred thousand dollars.'

Harper nearly chokes on her vegetable roll.

'Can I get that in writing?'

'Of course.'

Harper reaches her hand out. Tom takes it.

'You've got a deal.'

# 28

'But why Penelope?'

The leftover Thai food is in the fridge and the used utensils tossed in the sink. Tom is on his second beer. Harper is drinking a Diet Coke.

'I think we need to start from scratch,' Tom says. 'Skip's murder is ground zero.'

'There was a trial. Knox was convicted. What else is there to know?'

'I don't think we should take anything for granted.'

'You think the police and Borelli had it all wrong? And the jury?'

'You're thinking about it all wrong. You think the police and Borelli were rational actors, without biases, in complete control of their thought processes.'

'They're not?'

'No, they're not. The human brain is – for lack of a better term – a mess. Not just the police and Borelli. Everyone. We are in a constant state of self-deception. It's unconscious. We not only can't control it, we don't know it's happening. Law enforcement has a history of falling prey to cognitive biases, such as confirmation bias and anchoring. They give the initial evidence too much weight and they think every fact they uncover proves their original theory. All of the wrongful conviction cases you hear about don't happen by chance. How do we know the Knox case didn't have some of the same issues? What do we know about the Karma Killer? A cell tower logged a list of telephone numbers that were within a fifty-kilometre radius the night Skip and Cecilia were killed. This led the police to Knox, a man whose daughter died from an opioid overdose. They found someone with a motive who they could prove was there – or at least nearby. Any information that didn't fit with their theory was ignored or pushed aside.'

Harper is sceptical. 'Didn't Knox admit to killing Skip Buchanan? Aren't we making extra work for ourselves?'

'That's a misconception,' Tom says. He disappears and returns with a copy of Borelli's book. 'Here. If you read this closely, you'll see the holes in the case against Knox. Knox said over and over again that Skip Buchanan deserved to die, but that's not a confession. And at the trial, his lawyers – the only argument they had was Knox didn't confess. Plus, there was evidence that was never explained. The cigarette butt with lipstick on it, for example.'

'But the authorities looked at all this. Didn't they?'

'Have you heard of sunk cost fallacy? Say you're out to dinner and the food is terrible. You know a few bites in that you don't like it. Do you finish the meal or do you stop?'

'If I have to pay for the meal, I finish it.'

Tom flashes his billionaire smirk. 'That's what most people do, but it's false reasoning. You're going to have to pay the money anyway. Eating more of something you don't enjoy is pointless. You're not recovering the money invested.'

'I'm supposed to drop my fork and walk out of the restaurant?'

'Yes,' Tom says. 'That's the logical conclusion. Law enforcement often make the same mistake. The police and Borelli committed too much time and money into Knox's conviction to pause when any evidence they uncovered didn't fit. The wheels of justice only move forwards, never backward.'

'Listen,' Harper says, 'I get this is what you do for a living, and it's backed up by research, but I think you're discounting the experience the police and Borelli bring to their work. I was in the military. Experience is – it's everything.'

'Harper, please. The military? That institution suffers more from groupthink than maybe any other.'

'Group *what*?'

'It's another cognitive bias. Groups of individuals make mistakes in how they think. We learn from each other, but we can learn something that's wrong. And we feel pressure to agree with others. We'll change our views just so we don't rock the boat. Bad ideas spread like a virus, and they mutate, into more polarised versions of the original bad idea.'

'I wasn't some brainwashed soldier, if that's what you're getting at.'

Tom sighs. 'Don't take this personally, Harper. We all suffer from these biases. And overcoming them takes more than just knowing they exist. Let me show you an old trick. OK?' He grabs a yellow legal pad of paper and a black Sharpie from the table. 'Close your eyes.'

Harper obliges. She listens to the squeak of the black Sharpie on paper.

'OK. Open them.'

Harper opens her eyes. Tom hands her the pad of paper. He's drawn two lines.

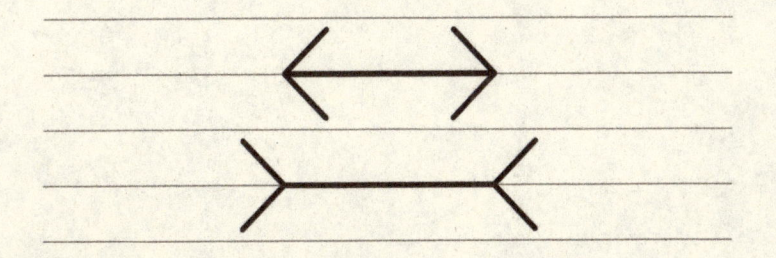

'Which line is longer? A or B?'

'Easy,' Harper says. 'B.'

Tom hands Harper a ruler. 'Measure them.'

Harper measures the lines. They're the same size.

'OK,' she says. 'Neat trick.'

'All right. Now put the ruler away and look at the lines again. Which one is longer?'

Harper looks at the lines again. She wants to say B.

'Tell me what your instinct tells you?' Tom asks.

'Like I said. Neat trick.'

'You want to say B, don't you? This is the Muller-Lyer illusion. Even after you've measured the lines and know they're of equal length, you want to say one is longer. This is how your mind works: biases are hardwired into how you think. Intuition can be useful, and expertise is important. But sometimes you can be blind to the truth and it's anywhere from difficult to impossible to overcome.'

'And how are you going to make sure we don't make the same mistakes?'

'We won't take anything for granted.' Tom holds up the ruler. 'And we measure everything.'

# 29

'Skip was obsessed with opium. The history of it, its chemical makeup, each step in its development that led to OxyPro.'

Tom has run out of beer, so he's pouring himself a generous glass of Pappy Van Winkle.

'At a party,' Tom says, 'or in a speech to shareholders, Skip would lovingly describe opium's chemical makeup, how complex it is. Proteins, latex, sugars, ammonia, alkaloids. He liked to refer to Oxy by opium's ancient epithets. The Ultimate Siesta, the Hand of God. He thought it was clever, tying OxyPro back to its ancient origins.'

The alcohol is finally getting to Tom: his cheeks have a rosy hue, his voice a slight slur.

'No one really knows why poppies produce opiates. Skip's favourite theory was that poppies developed opium simply to make sure that humans would cultivate them, to ensure their own survival. Which means humans and poppies have a symbiotic relationship.' He shakes his head. 'It's strange to say now, given what's happened, but he was proud of OxyPro. He thought it would help a lot of people.'

'But didn't he lie to sell the pills?'

'I'm not saying Skip was an angel. Or Mitch. I just mean . . . It's complicated, you see. Their motivations weren't black and white.'

'The same could be said of Stalin, though. Couldn't it?'

Tom opens his mouth but he can't think of a decent reply. He shrugs and sips his bourbon. He stares at Harper and eventually asks, 'How'd you know about the pills?'

'What do you mean?'

'Today, when I was talking to Lenny, about how Apollo Pharma reformulated the pills as an abuse deterrent, so Oxy couldn't be snorted or injected, how the chemical makeup was changed to harden the pills, so they couldn't be crushed or dissolved, and instead it would just turn into a gummy substance if you tried – you knew about the reformulation. How?'

Harper remembers the look Tom shot her on the balcony. *How long has he been waiting to ask this?*

'Isn't it common knowledge?'

'It's not a state secret or anything, but it's not the sort of detail the average person knows about. If you're going to work for me, we have to be honest with each other. Right?'

Harper stares at the wall.

*Just tell him. Get it over with.*

'My brother Derrick also served in the army, like me. He was on tour in Iraq when an IED fucked up his leg. He didn't lose it or anything, but it was pretty bad. Broken femur, nerve damage. He had surgery and he was in a lot of pain. The VA prescribed OxyPro. His leg got better, but he kept using the pills. He was living with our grandfather in Ohio. The Oxy scene in our hometown was bad. There were pill mills everywhere. Derrick had trouble finding work, and with his leg getting a script was easy. So he'd visit three pill mills a day and sell what he wasn't using.'

Tom had been standing, but now he drags a stool closer to the island and sits.

'Derrick started out chewing pills,' Harper says. 'But he built up a tolerance. Just like Lenny. So he started crushing the pills and snorting them. He never wanted to use needles and held out for as long as he could. But when the pills were reformulated and they couldn't be crushed into a powder . . .'

Harper's voice trails off.

'The reformulation was supposed to stop people from abusing the drug,' Tom says, his tone defensive. 'What happened to Derrick? Did he . . . ?'

'He eventually stopped using Oxy.'

Tom puts his hand to his heart. 'Thank God.'

'Chewing the pills couldn't give him the high he needed so he started using heroin.'

'Oh.'

'He OD'd a few times. Our grandfather found him. The second time was a close call. The ambulance arrived and used one of their kits – Narcan, or whatever the fuck it's called. The nasal spray that saves people OD'ing. It reverses the effects of opioids or something. My grandfather said it was like Lazarus, back from the dead.'

There is a long moment of silence. Tom waits for Harper to continue. When she doesn't, he asks, 'Did he keep using?'

Harper nods. 'The last time he used, he'd bought heroin laced with fentanyl. That's what the police told me.'

'Is he . . . ?'

'Derrick died. Four years ago.'

# Day 6

After the GME, they grab coffee at a Starbucks, fifteen people or so sitting around a long communal table. Jess thought the atmosphere in the parking lot before the meditation session was good, but the feeling afterwards, sipping lattes and raspberry iced tea, is even better. Everyone is lighter on their feet, unburdened. And they're all thrilled Jess has joined them. All anyone can talk about is the hand that Lama Aaron placed on her shoulder.

'He must see potential in you, to single you out like that.'

'Honestly, that *never* happens!'

Going in, Jess had been sceptical of the whole meditation thing, worried it would be weird, and when Alex asked her about it afterwards she'd have to lie. *But it wasn't weird. That's what's weird.* There was something elegant about the process. For half an hour Aaron quietly led the group through guided meditation. His voice and instruction was meant to coax you back to being present, to help push out thoughts and distractions.

It wasn't what Jess imagined meditation to be. It wasn't a process of clearing her mind. It was more like changing gears, from drive to neutral. The engine was still on, but there was no gas or ignition. Then Aaron spoke to the room, drawing on history, philosophy, religion. That part was super cheesy, and Jess had to fight back the thought of her dad, the cynic, putting up his hand, and asking, 'How, pray tell, does this help me pay my mortgage next month?' But practical questions would have missed the sermon's inherent wisdom. Aaron's focus was on truth and how to be a better person. *It doesn't get more useful than that.*

As Jess sips her mocha Frappuccino, she feels content for the first time in a year and a half.

And then someone cuts her down with two words. The woman is around Jess's age, with unusually long brown hair tied in a braid. Her name is Tara. 'Oh my God! I remember where I know you from. You're that girl, from Everly College. What did they call you?'

Jess is suddenly on the verge of throwing up. *Fuck. Kill me now.*

Alex is at the other end of the table. She was mid-conversation, but when she notices Jess is upset, she stops talking and watches Tara closely.

'Yes,' Tara says, clapping her hands together in excitement. 'I remember! Hermione Goebbels. That's it. That's what the school paper called you, didn't they? What was the story again? Some fight with your roommate?'

Jess thought she could escape that name, if just for the afternoon. But no, that name – that *fucking* name – will follow her wherever she goes.

The whole table is watching now. Jess feels dizzy.

Tara turns to Alex and says, 'You've brought a celebrity, Alex. I—'

Alex raises her finger and says, 'Stop, Tara. Don't say another word.'

Tara is mortified. 'I . . .'

Alex's eyes are blue comets sent to destroy Planet Tara.

'You, Tara,' Alex says, 'have *not* reached the right frequency to speak to a guest of mine like that.'

Tara looks at her fellow congregants but they've lowered their eyes, not wanting any part of whatever Tara has got herself into. 'Those rules . . . I am not sure they apply to . . . we're not at the . . .'

Alex tips her head to the side. 'You're going to lecture me on the rules and how they're interpreted?'

Tara shakes her head. 'No. I . . .' She looks at Jess. 'I didn't mean anything by bringing up that story. I'm sorry if I offended you.'

'And,' Alex adds, 'I don't think I have any choice but to raise this incident with my mother and Meryl.'

'Oh, God, Alex. Please don't.'

Alex stands. She looks at Jess and says, 'Shall we?'

Jess stands abruptly. Alex takes her by the arm and they leave together, with Brent trailing at their heels.

They don't talk about the Tara incident in the car ride home. It's torture for Jess, waiting to know what Alex thinks. She's only known Alex six days and already she can't imagine life without her.

They barrel down the interstate, blowing past acres of farm land, tilled rows of black soil, stretching vertically, towards the horizon, like swaths of corduroy.

They pass a sign advertising FRESH CUT FRIES.

'I'm starving,' Alex says, staring into the rear-view mirror. 'Anyone else?'

'Hell yes,' Brent says, holding his belly.

'Sure,' Jess says, despite having zero appetite.

They pull over beside a food truck, order a tray of fries, and share them at a picnic table. It's noon and the sun is blindingly bright. Alex and Brent are wearing large designer sunglasses. Jess is less prepared. She squints and uses her left hand as a visor. Brent dives into the fries, eating three at a time. Jess forces herself to eat, but can only stomach one solitary fry before the agony of not knowing what Alex is thinking is too much to bear. 'I should tell you,' she blurts out. 'I mean . . . what Tara was talking about.'

Alex shakes her head. 'Not interested.'

'What?'

'I'm not interested. What did Tara reference? A school paper? I went to Everly. Remember? I know what it's like. I'll get my news from real sources, not the *Everly College Gazette*, or whatever it's called.'

'It's more than a story in the school paper. I was accused of something horrible.'

'Honestly, Jess, I couldn't care less. There are good people in this world, and there are bad people, and I *know* you're a good person. I'm certain of it.'

'Don't you . . . I should . . .'

Alex raises her hand. 'Stop, Jess. I mean it. Tara is just jealous of the attention you got from Aaron today. She's been with the Movement for six months and he's never so much as looked at her.'

'It's true,' Brent says, his mouth brimming with mulched-up fries. 'We could all see how jealous she was.'

'I . . .' Jess's voice trails off. She feels something, a strange combination of relief and sadness. 'Thank you. No one's ever taken my side like this. Usually people are happy to assume the worst.'

Alex pushes the tray of fries to the side. With a pen, she starts sketching something onto the wooden picnic table. 'Don't thank me,' she says. 'I had a moral obligation to come to your aide.' She taps the pen at her sketch once it's finished.

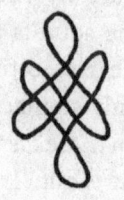

'What's that?'
'You've heard of karma?'

'Yeah. Of course.'

'Karma is the principle that our actions have consequences, good and bad.'

'Cause and effect,' Brent adds. 'What goes around, comes around.'

Jess nods and says, 'Sure.' Her appetite resurrects. She takes two French fries and stabs them into the glob of ketchup.

'This' – Alex taps her drawing on the picnic table – 'is the endless knot. It symbolises how karma works. There is no beginning or end.' Alex traces her pen along the pattern she's sketched. 'Put something out in the universe and it comes back. Do you see?'

Jess nods. 'Right.'

'Lama Aaron, in his teaching, stresses the importance of karma. What we do matters. Put bad energy out into the universe and, eventually, the universe sends it right back. Tara's been with the Movement long enough. She knows this. She let jealousy cloud her judgement. She was rude to you. She tried to humiliate you.'

'So what will happen to her? In the next life, she'll be a mosquito or something?'

'She humiliated you,' Alex says. 'So, what do you think the *just* outcome would be?'

'Humiliation?'

Alex, proud of her disciple, smiles. 'Precisely.'

# 30

Penelope Buchanan is a tiny, wisp of a woman. Her shoulder-length black hair is messy and falling across her eyes. She lives alone on the Upper East Side. The shades are drawn, the room cast in a grey gloom. The home has an Eighties aesthetic, austere and monochromatic, like something out of *American Psycho*.

Penelope is from the Alpha side of the family. Skip was her grandfather; Terry her dad, and Cindy her stepmom. Tom called Penelope his cousin, though Harper lost track of how exactly and what degree.

Tom called ahead before visiting. 'Penelope doesn't deal well with surprises,' he told Harper. 'Or strangers. I'm shocked she's letting you join, even if I'm stretching the truth.'

Tom told Penelope he was bringing his new girlfriend for a visit. He'd warned Harper about this in advance. 'If I say the word "security" she'll never be able to relax.'

They went over all of this in the morning because the night ended awkwardly. After Harper revealed what happened to Derrick, Tom apologised profusely. He blamed himself and his family and even admitted the decision to reformulate the pills wasn't intended to prevent abuse but a ploy to extend the patent. 'The original patent for Oxy was twenty years. With the reformulation, they extended the patent another twenty. It wasn't about deterring abuse. Everything the company did was aimed at profit. Everything.'

Harper told Tom the truth. She never blamed Apollo Pharma or the Buchanans for her brother's death. She blamed the doctor that prescribed Derrick the pills with little warning or direction. She blamed the pill mills in Ohio who made millions selling pills to Derrick and thousands of others. She even blamed Bill Clinton and the North American Free Trade Agreement, which sent manufacturers to Mexico and China, destroying their hometown in the process, and leaving the residents – the ones who stayed – with nothing to do but sell pills and get high.

But Tom was drunk by that point. He kept apologising, telling Harper, 'If you only knew' – whatever that meant. And it was all too much. So Harper fled, escaping to the guest bedroom. She spent a few hours scanning the copy of Borelli's book that Tom had given her before falling asleep.

A man wearing a black turtle neck and black jeans delivers a tray of tea and biscuits. Harper wonders if this is the modern butler attire, Zorro without the mask.

It was Zorro who greeted them at the door, asked them to remove their shoes, and place their mobile phones in a small wicker basket. 'Penelope is afraid to have her picture taken,' Tom said on the walk over. 'She was hounded for months after the murders. Requests for interviews, gangs of cameras camped outside her door. And she gets the same death threats the rest of us do, endless messages saying Knox made a mistake leaving her alive.'

'If she's that spooked, will she even talk to us?'

'She will for me. I'm her favourite cousin.'

They start with small talk. After discussing yesterday's rain and today's humidity, Penelope asks, 'So, how long have you two been dating?'

Harper smiles and looks at Tom. 'Oh, feels like forever.'

'A few months,' Tom adds.

'And what do you do, Harper?'

'I, uh – I was in the army.'

'Really? Tom's type is usually . . .'

'Let me guess,' Harper says. 'Rich and nerdy?'

Penelope smiles. 'That's right. How did you know?'

Harper winks. 'Just a hunch.'

Tom is annoyed. He likes to be the observant one, not the observed. 'Maybe we can skip the part where we discuss my ex-girlfriends?'

'Sorry, Tommy,' Harper says. 'Low-hanging fruit.'

Tom changes the subject. 'Are you still seeing Doctor Asimov?'

She nods.

'Good. Are you—'

'Still taking my medication?' Penelope is miffed at the inquiry. She stares sullenly at her mug of Earl Grey. 'Don't worry. I'm still highly medicated.'

Harper tries to lighten the mood. 'Can we keep discussing Tom's ex-girlfriends?'

Penelope's mood lightens immediately. She leans forwards, towards Harper. 'You have to be the absolute opposite of anyone he's brought home.'

'What's going on, do you think?' Harper asks, smiling. 'Is this some sort of early midlife crisis?'

Penelope laughs, a feat that seemed impossible seconds earlier. 'It must be.'

'All right,' Tom says. 'Can we change the subject?'

Ten minutes later, once Penelope is as relaxed as she can ever be, Tom clears his throat and says, 'We need your help.'

'So this is more than a social call?'

'I'm afraid so. Yesterday we met at Edgar's apartment. With the FBI.'

'I know.'

'They talked to us about hiring security.'

'Don't worry about me. I have Jonathan, an excellent security system. I even have a panic room.'

'The FBI thinks Uncle Mitch's murder is . . . not an isolated incident . . . And . . . well . . . Harper and I . . .'

Tom stares into his mug of tea. It looks like he's fumbling through a difficult topic, but Harper thinks he's putting it on, trying to appear sympathetic before asking for help.

'What is it, Tommy?' Penelope asks.

'I'm not sure what to make of the FBI. Maybe they'll figure it out. Maybe they won't.' He finally looks up from his tea. 'But you know me. I can't sit idle, even for a day, leaving my fate in someone else's hands.'

'So – what? You're trying to figure this out yourself?'

'Sort of. I want to understand what happened to Uncle Mitch to stop it happening again. In order to do that, I need to understand what happened that night . . . at Skip's.'

Penelope recoils at the mere mention of that night. 'I don't know, Tommy.'

'Please, Pen. Harper and I – we just want to hear your story. From you. Some of the details might be important.'

Penelope takes a deep breath. 'OK.'

# 31

Zorro pours Penelope a second cup of Earl Grey. When she starts her story, her eyes are on the steaming mug in her hands. 'Dad had just married Cindy. I hated her, she hated me, and I did my best to make both of their lives miserable. Of course, I wasn't conscious of it at the time. Doctor Asimov has helped me understand what was happening. I had this unconscious desire to hurt them and me. So I acted out. It started to get bad at the end of last year. Late one night, I invited this random guy over. We were snorting coke in the kitchen. Dad caught us. He lost it. The next day he drove me to Skip and Cecilia's before he and Cindy flew to Europe for the holidays.

'It was always a relief going to stay with them. Making Dad and Cindy miserable was a full-time job. So visiting Grandpa's was like a vacation.' She looks at the wall, lost in thought. 'Sometimes I think about what would have happened if I hadn't acted out. If I hadn't driven Dad nuts to the point he had to leave me with Skip and Cecilia. Maybe Skip and Cecilia would have gone on a trip. Or went to a show that night in New York and stayed overnight at their apartment. Maybe if I'd not been such a selfish little bitch, they'd still be alive.'

Tom leans forward and touches Penelope's knee. 'I get the impulse to ask those questions, Pen. But Skip barely left home after he was forced to step down as CEO. And he loved having you visit. If anything, you made his last days more enjoyable.'

Penelope sips her tea. She nods.

'I'd been there almost a week when it happened,' Penelope says. 'It was Christmas Day. I remember there'd been a big snowstorm the day before and then the temperature dropped, so the snow had this hard, shiny crust. Because it was the holidays, Grandpa had given most of the staff the night off. It ended up saving their lives. Except for Miguel and Maria.'

Harper knows these names from Borelli's book. The maid and groundskeeper, a married couple, who lived in the basement of Skip Buchanan's home. They were there that night. So was Cecilia Buchanan's childhood friend, Ester Grange. She was visiting for the holidays. Their deaths are rarely talked about.

'Cecilia had renovated the barn, the one at the bottom of the hill. She'd turned it into a woodworking shop. You know Skip, he wasn't one for hobbies. But Cecilia wanted to keep him busy. So she put him to work on a birdhouse. He worked on it every day I was there.' Penelope shakes her head and smiles. 'His progress was minimal. He called it "that goddamn birdhouse".

'In the evening, a few hours after dinner, Cecilia and her friend Esther were having tea in the kitchen. I brought Grandpa a cup, and just stayed to hang out. I liked the workshop. I loved the smell of sawdust. There was a stool in the corner I'd sit on and use my phone, scrolling Instagram. Grandpa was blasting the Beatles, and he had some machine on that was even louder.

'The bandsaw?' Harper asks.

'Yes. Right. It was loud, but I still heard something. I knew it was gunshots – I just knew it. Skip turned off his machine, and I turned off the music and then we heard three more gunshots.'

Tom interrupts. 'What time?'

'Around nine o'clock. Skip said it was deer season and nothing to worry about. But then he got out his gun. It was stored in a lock box on a shelf in the barn. You know Skip. He was a force of nature, nothing fazed him. But I could tell he was worried. He told me to go up into the loft of the barn, and to stay there until he came back. He made me promise. Once I was there, he took down the ladder and hid it, so it wasn't obvious there was a loft. And then off he went.'

'He saved your life?' Harper asks.

'Yes.' Penelope looks at her lap a moment, to collect herself, to fight back her tears. 'I couldn't see anything in the attic. It was pitch-black. So I just sat there in the dark, listening. And then I heard another gunshot. This time it was louder. Like a crack of thunder. I'd promised not to move, so I stayed put. But every day I think I should have gone to him. There was no ladder, but I could have jumped.'

'You'd have been killed as well,' Tom says. 'You kept your promise.'

'Maybe. But I wouldn't have to live like this. With the pall of being a coward hanging over me.'

'You're not a coward, Pen,' Tom says. 'You're the bravest person I know.'

Penelope ignores the comment. She's well practised at dismissing interpretations of Skip Buchanan's murder that don't align with hers.

'It was so quiet that night, I could hear everything outside. The crunch of the snow as Skip tried to crawl away, his breathing. It sounded like he was hyperventilating, like he couldn't catch his breath. And I could hear Knox's footsteps, I think, trudging along the frozen path.'

'Did you hear Knox say anything?'

'No.'

'Did you hear anything else? Like Knox dressing Skip's gunshot?'

According to Borelli, Knox was so intent on Skip's murder being with an opioid, after shooting Skip in the shoulder, he'd dressed the wound and stopped the bleeding, and only then did he stick the needle filled with boiled down OxyPro into a vein in Skip's forearm.

'No,' Penelope says. 'Once the scuffling stopped it was quiet for a while.'

'And Knox came into the barn afterwards?'

'Yes. I think so. I'm not sure what he was looking for. Me, maybe. I stayed absolutely still. I didn't even look down. I heard him poking around but he left after a few minutes. I'd forgotten to bring my phone to the loft, so I couldn't call 911. I just lay there, in the dark.'

'You spent the whole night in the loft?' Harper asks.

'Yes. The sheriff came into the barn in the morning. I was terrified, they didn't announce themselves or anything. I just heard them poking around. I chanced looking down because – I don't know. Maybe because the sun was up, I was braver. But once I saw it was safe, I called down.'

'And Knox killed everyone in the house before your grandfather?' Harper asks.

'That's what the police think. And the prosecutors.'

'What do you think?' Tom asks.

Penelope hesitates. She looks on the verge of saying more but then shakes her head. 'I think you should go now.'

Tom puts his hands together in prayer. 'Please, Pen. Any little bit of information helps.'

Penelope stands. 'Jonathan, can you see Tom and her friend out?'

Tom begs, 'Please, Pen!' But Penelope is already walking out of the room.

Zorro waves his hand in the direction of the front door. 'This way, please.'

# Day 32

Bodies surround the kitchen island: inert electrons ringing the room's nucleus. A blender pulses. Aaron steps through the sliding glass door holding a tray of vegetarian hamburgers. 'Dinner. Is. Served.'

'About time,' Alex teases.

The guests – ten lucky souls, here at Aaron's invitation – laugh amiably.

Meryl hands Jess a salt-rimmed virgin margarita. She waits for Jess to take a sip.

Jess has been sober for more than thirty days, since she OD'd and nearly died. She'd kill for a real drink right now, and the overly sweet substitute Meryl's handed her certainly isn't scratching that itch. But she doesn't want to hurt Meryl's feelings, so she says, 'Wow. That *is* good.'

Meryl winks. 'See. I knew you'd like it. Who needs tequila?'

Aaron's guests line up, single file, and start to fill their plates with veggie burgers, bean salad, and corn on the cob.

The group is eclectic: one bank executive, a mechanic, an heiress, two professors, a grocery store clerk, and two students. Jess knows most of them by now, and would even say a few are – shocker! – friends. Since her first GME Jess has been inundated with phone calls, texts, Instagram friend requests. At first she thought people only wanted to be her friend because she knew Alex, and Alex was obviously popular in the group. But the more she interacted with her fellow congregants, she realised they didn't have an ulterior motive: they truly wanted to be her friend. It was as simple as that.

The only person Jess wasn't looking forward to seeing tonight was Tara. Hours earlier, Alex had called and invited Jess to dinner at Aaron's, but warned her that Tara would be there as well. 'You don't need to worry about her, though. Trust me. Even if she had the guts to talk to you again, she won't have time.'

And Alex was right – at least so far. Tara is playing the role of caterer tonight, taking drinks orders, preparing dinner. Alex described it as a sort of penance for how she treated Jess, after he raised it with her mom and Meryl. But Jess doubts that's true. *I've only been with the Movement a few weeks. So what if Tara was rude to me?*

Aaron's home is a two-storey clapboard house on a quiet residential street a stone's throw from Everly campus. While the outside is very suburban, inside has a distinctive eastern vibe: sparsely decorated with Japanese calligraphy, Samurai swords, half a dozen chubby gold Buddhas, incense perpetually burning in the corner of every room. Only the kitchen looks like any other suburban kitchen, including an island and Ikea cupboards.

The evening began with the group sitting around Aaron's living room, drinking virgin margaritas (Meryl's secret recipe), while Aaron, with his hands on his large belly, asked the group philosophical questions. Jess appreciated how Aaron was careful not to push his opinion onto the group. He'd offer up a question, let them debate it, and then move on to a new dilemma. At first, the critical part of Jess's brain thought it was all first-year philosophy mixed with a new-age zeal, one part John Stuart Mill, one part healing crystal. But the longer it went on, she saw there was something ingenious in going back to the fundamental questions. Aaron seemed to be operating on a different level than everyone else. Pulling strings, teaching them without lecturing them. He had this happy, benevolent expression the whole time, mirroring the chubby gold Buddha in the corner.

Aaron ended the debate with a ten-minute monologue about the importance of tribalism. 'The media tries to say it's bad, but this is one hundred per cent wrong. Tribalism is good. It's healthy. It's helpful. Since the dawn of time, the human race has travelled in tribes. It's the only way to make sense of the world. And it's what we secretly do anyway. The best way to be moral, in the modern world, is to consciously choose who deserves to be in your tribe, and who doesn't.'

Aaron only stopped the debate when Meryl tugged at his sleeve. 'If you don't fire up that barbeque soon, we'll be eating at midnight.'

They eat outside, on Aaron's back deck, under a web of white lights, balancing plates on their lap, chatting amiably.

Dana, a mother of three, is sitting beside Jess. She leans in and asks in a near whisper: 'No sign of Alex's mom tonight?'

Jess shakes her head. 'No. Actually, I've never seen her at the GMEs. What's going on there?'

'She was Aaron's second-in-command for years, but a few months ago . . . it's only rumour, so I shouldn't say.' Dana stops to sip her drink. Perhaps she meant to leave it at that, but she can't help herself. She looks across the room, to confirm Alex is deep in conversation with someone else. 'I heard there were accounting discrepancies. Money missing from a bank account. Apparently Meryl discovered it and told Aaron.'

'Are you sure?' Jess asks. 'I think Alex would have told me about something like that.'

Dana shrugs. 'This is only what I've heard.'

'Was there a lot of money missing? I can't imagine there's a lot of money in the account. Aren't the meditations free?'

'No way. Each GME costs money. One-on-one sessions with Aaron are super expensive. And there's an initiation fee and a fee every time your vibrations improve and you move to the next level. Alex probably paid for you. She's super generous like that.'

Jess is touched. She looks at Alex on the other side of the room. Their eyes meet and they both smile.

'I wonder how her mom's doing?' Jess says to Dana.

'You want my advice? Don't get caught up in the politics of it all, the fight for Aaron's attention. It's never worth it.'

Near the end of dinner, Aaron stands in front of the sliding glass doors, back lit by the kitchen pot lights. 'All right, everyone, there's something I need to address. Where's Tara?'

Jess feels a flutter of nerves in her chest at the mention of Tara's name.

Tara stands and slowly makes her way to Aaron's side.

Jess looks inquiringly at Alex, but Alex's only response is a knowing wink.

Aaron says, 'Many of you know that, recently, Tara committed an offence against a fellow congregant. Specifically – and it's important to be specific because only then will we know the correct form of punishment – she humiliated said congregant.'

Jess's cheeks suddenly glow with embarrassment. She feels like everyone's focus is on her, but no one is looking at Jess. All eyes are on Aaron and Tara.

'And so,' Aaron says, 'as we all know, karma demands that Tara experience the same humiliation that she visited on this congregant. An eye for an eye.' He looks at Tara and then back at the crowd. He sighs, as though he wished none of this were necessary. 'And, of course, this will help Tara. Better to even the score now. Isn't that right, Tara?'

Tara can't bring herself to look at Aaron. She nods, with her eyes aimed at the deck.

'Excellent.' Aaron smiles amiably, then he opens his arms, like a circus ringleader, before walking away.

For a brief moment, no one moves.

Until Brent whips a half-eaten cob of corn at Tara. It hits her in the breast with a heavy thud.

Brent's act of aggression opens the flood gates, giving others permission to do the same. Alex throws a handful of potato salad; Dana flings a vegetarian patty like a Frisbee; and then everyone but Jess starts throwing their dinner.

Tara is filthy in a matter of seconds. Condiments stick to her like paint. Waste collects at her feet. She looks on the verge of tears. Aaron and Meryl watch, like Greek gods, unable, or unwilling, to intervene.

At first, Jess is horrified. But the pull to follow her new friends is too strong. She throws a half-eaten burger and is surprised to find that she doesn't, as she expected, feel guilty. In fact, she experiences a rush of excitement. It reminds her of the thrill she had shoplifting as a teenager. She keeps throwing food until her plate is empty.

Tara slips and falls ass first to the deck. She starts to sob.

Aaron finally steps forward and puts up his hands. The onslaught stops.

'Oh no! Tara, are you crying?' Aaron is smiling sheepishly. 'Tears of joy, I hope. This was supposed to help you.'

Tara gets to her feet and wraps her arms around Aaron's tubby frame. The group starts to clap.

'Well done, Tara,' Aaron says. 'Well done.'

Tara nuzzles her face into Aaron's chest. 'Thank you,' she says, through her heavy sobbing. 'Thank you.'

# 32

The hospital's underground parking lot is poorly lit, dense black broken only by the odd cone of white light. Harper takes one last sip from her Dunkin' Donuts coffee, then unclicks her seatbelt. Tom does the same. Harper stares at him like he's an extra appendage. 'I think you should stay in the car.'

Tom bristles at the suggestion. 'Why?'

'It's safer.'

'Sitting alone in an abandoned parking lot is hardly safer than going into a well-lit, busy hospital.'

'If anyone wanted to track you down, waiting by the hospital room of the sole survivor from Friday would be a good place to start.'

'Isn't this the same SUV every network in the country filmed me getting in and out of on Friday night? What if someone is looking for it? Maybe someone took a picture of the licence plate. Maybe this Escalade was doxed and we just don't realise it.'

As Harper mulls this over, Tom – knowing he won – flashes his billionaire smirk.

'Fine. But stay close.'

Foster's room in the ICU is empty. Harper immediately thinks the worst. 'What the hell?'

'I'm sure he's OK, Harper. They would have contacted you if something had gone wrong.'

Tom flags down a passing nurse.

'The patient's name?'

'Charles Foster.'

'He's been moved.'

'Moved? Is he out of the coma?'

'No, but his condition has stabilised. He's been moved to the ninth floor. The nurses' desk should be able to direct you.'

'Can he have visitors?'

'Yes. Although you might have to wait until the FBI has finished with him first.'

Harper pictures Agent Dreser hounding an unconscious Foster. Her fear that Foster died alone mutates into wrath. It grows as they make their way upstairs. She's ready to lay into Dreser, to tell him to leave Foster the fuck alone. She pictures shoving Dreser until it escalates into a full-fledged fight. But as she barrels into the room, it isn't Agent Dreser sitting on the edge of Foster's bed. It's Agent Louis Diaz. He's holding Foster's hand, his eyes red and raw. When he sees Harper, Lou quickly stands and straightens the jacket of his indigo blue suit. But he doesn't try to hide his tears. What's the point?

Harper's anger evaporates. *I'm an idiot*, she thinks. *How did I miss this?*

Lou tells Harper the story over coffee in the abandoned hospital cafeteria. Tom – trying his best to both give them space to talk and follow Harper's instructions to stay close – parks himself at the next table and busies himself with his phone.

'Foster was living in New Jersey,' Lou says. 'He operated Spartan Security from there because he wanted easy access to rich clients in New York and Connecticut, but with cheaper rent. I was working out of the FBI's field office in Manhattan.

We'd known each other in Iraq. He says we flirted, but I have zero recollection. I don't think we did.'

Steam spews from Lou's coffee cup. Through the haze, his face is distorted and imprecise, like a desert mirage.

'Anyway,' Lou continues, 'we reconnected through Facebook. He added me as a friend and wrote something like, "Hey, long time. What are you up to these days?" When we realised we were so close, we made plans to go for a drink. I didn't think of it as a date. One, maybe two, drinks to catch up. That was my plan.' Lou smiles as the memory blooms. 'It's strange, isn't it? You can know someone at one stage in your life and there's nothing there. Then, years later ... I felt something the moment I walked into the shitty dive bar he'd picked. Foster felt it, too. We didn't even need to talk about it. It was just there, and we both knew it. We've been together ever since.'

'How long?' Harper asks.

'Six months.'

'And you recommended Spartan Security to Mitch Buchanan?'

Lou blows on his coffee. The steam dissipates briefly, then reforms.

'I knew Mitch from the Knox case. After McMurtry was attacked, he called me up and asked for advice. I gave him three names. He picked Foster. I knew he would. Foster has that everything-will-be-fine presence to him. He made Mitch feel at ease. And I was happy to help Foster out. That's how I thought of it, at least. But maybe I made a mistake. There was a conflict there. I should have disclosed it. And if I had, maybe someone else would be in a coma.'

'Not much of a conflict,' Harper says. 'And like you said, Buchanan would have picked Foster anyway. He'd have been crazy to pick anyone else.'

Lou stares at his coffee. 'Maybe.'

His phone chimes. He checks it and frowns.

'Everything OK?' Harper asks.

Lou nods. 'Yeah. Fine.' He puts the phone away. 'So how much longer are you sticking around? In New York, you told me you were going to finish your two weeks and that was it.'

'I changed my mind.'

Lou nods. 'Good.'

*If you're going to ask for help*, Harper thinks, *now is the time.*

'Actually, Tom hired me – not just for protection – but also . . .' Harper loses her nerve briefly. She made the deal with Tom, but it sounds absurd now that she's saying it aloud: '. . . to help him find the man who murdered his uncle.'

Lou makes a face, like Harper just said two plus two equals forty. 'No offence, Harper, but what do you know about tracking down a murderer?'

Harper knows there's no point being offended. She said the same thing yesterday. Still, she feels compelled to defend herself. 'Before working for Foster, I worked for Dark Star.'

'Corporate espionage?'

'We preferred the term private intelligence.'

'A guy I served with went into *corporate spying* – or whatever it's called.' Lou's tone, bordering on the sarcastic, makes it clear he doesn't think much of the profession. 'Reading between the lines of his bullshit job descriptions, it sounded to me like his main job was stealing corporate information from one company, like the design of a new drug, and selling it to another. He also described what sounded an awful lot like witness intimidation. Some company gets sued and they'd hire him to track down every scrap of information about the other side's witnesses. You think a few years of that qualifies you to find a killer? That you're going to do a better job than the FBI?'

'It's not like that. Tom just wants a pair of fresh eyes looking into this.'

'Fresh eyes?'

'He's worried about cognitive bias. Groupthink. Stuff like that.' Harper shrugs. 'You think this is a dumb idea?'

'I think his family is impervious to irony.'

'Now you've lost me.'

'Listen, Harper, if Tom wants to feel in control, great. Good for him. But why'd you tell me this? Whatever you're angling for, just ask already.'

*Tough and matter of fact*, Harper thinks. *He's definitely Foster's type.*

'What can you tell me about the investigation?'

'You've already heard everything I can say.'

'Can you take me through the crime scene?'

'You've been through it.'

'I was a little distracted the first time, saving Foster's life and all.'

Lou shrugs. 'Too bad.' He straightens his back. Harper can tell he's pissed off now. The feeling of sentimentality they'd shared through their connection to Foster is gone. 'You know, Harper, I've been thinking about Jay Hollinger's Sig. Maybe you can explain something to me?'

'OK.'

'So you step off the elevator, you see Jay. He's been killed, shot in the head. Right?'

'Yeah.'

'And so you're unarmed, you don't know who shot Jay or where they are, and you just walk down the hall and into Mitch Buchanan's room?'

Harper meets Lou's eyes. 'Yup.'

'You know it's a federal offence to lie to the FBI during an investigation.'

'Once I find Mitch's killer, maybe I'll help you find Jay's Sig.'

Lou stands to leave. 'We've got this, Harper. You stick to keeping Tom safe, and we'll find who did this. And if you ever find Jay's gun, let me know.'

# 33

Harper sits with Foster for an hour, her eyes fixed on the endotracheal tube protruding from his mouth, like an alien life form. She can't square the image of the man clinging to life in the ER with Lieutenant Foster, the force of nature from Mustang Company.

In Afghanistan, Foster's battalion was deployed to the Korengal Valley, their camp dug into the steep slopes of a nameless mountain dotted with ancient cedars. Harper's police battalion was asked to send soldiers to tour with Foster's all-male company because they needed women to talk to, and search, the local women. Just like growing up with three older brothers, Harper had to prove herself.

At first, some of the men in Foster's company were pricks to Harper, a weird mix of misogyny and come-ons. She was the only woman on that mountain and it felt like it. But she didn't have any of that from Foster. From the start, he acted like she belonged there, like she was a valued member of the team. And once she started kicking ass, that's when he started comparing her to a bulldozer. 'Careful, son,' he'd tell the kids in the company when they'd cross any line, 'a wuss like you, she'll flatten you.'

She fights back tears and thinks, *I'm going to find whoever did this to you, and when I do . . .*

Tom eventually grows impatient. He starts to pace. He sighs, checks his watch.

'I'm sure you'd be fine in the hall for five minutes,' Harper says.

'Would I?'

Harper can't tell whether Tom's question is serious or sarcastic. And she's not sure of the answer. *Would he?*

'OK,' Harper says, finally. 'Let's go.'

Harper parks the Escalade on an abandoned street outside of Appleton Hall. She reaches for the glovebox and removes a black case the size of her hand.

'What's that?' Tom asks.

Harper shuts the glove box and unclicks her seatbelt. 'Stay here.'

'Haven't we been over this?'

'I'll be five minutes. Tops.' Harper opens the door and places one foot onto the pavement. 'Plus, I'm about to commit a crime. So, probably a good idea for you to sit this one out.'

'You're going to what?'

Harper hears the locks of the SUV click into place as she jogs towards the residence.

First, Harper goes to Room 212, where she slept the night of the murders, and throws her belongings into a green duffle bag. Next, she breaks into Foster's room using her lockpicking kit – the black case she'd removed from the glovebox. Mordecai, the CEO of Dark Star, gave her the kit back when she was his star pupil. She opens it and removes a hook and tension wrench and picks the lock to Room 204. She turns the hook counter clockwise and the deadbolt slowly exits the wall. The dull click she hears as the door unlocks is almost better than sex. *Almost.*

Harper slides into the driver's seat of the Escalade. She's carrying her green duffle bag and Foster's black backpack.

'Whose are those?' Tom asks.

Harper removes a tablet from the backpack before flinging the bags onto the back seat.

'Is that Foster's?' Tom asks. 'Did you just break into Foster's room? I thought the FBI took his tablet.'

'He had two. The FBI took one, this is the other.'

Harper powers on the tablet. Enter Passcode is spelled out in capital letters.

'Do you know the password?'

'Not exactly.'

The tablet needs nine digits to open. Harper inputs combinations of different numbers – Foster's birthday, his old army unit – anything that gets to nine digits.

'Isn't this pointless?' Tom asks. 'It could be entirely random.'

Harper ignores him. After ten attempts, the screen disables for five minutes. Harper curses and whips her head back into the headrest.

Tom smiles. 'See.'

Harper tosses the tablet onto the back seat and starts the engine.

'Where to now?'

'Let's go to my house near campus. All the work we need to do is here.'

Harper shakes her head. 'Not a chance. Your house isn't safe. It was doxed. Why don't we go back to your home in New York?'

'We're not going back to Manhattan, we've got too much work to do here.'

'Fine. Then where to?'

# 34

The Admiralty Inn is a two-and-a-half-star hotel near the highway. Tom rents two rooms on the third floor connected by a door that locks. The decor consists of beige paint and oil paintings of schooners cutting through rough seas. Tom's lip curls slightly when he sees their new abode. 'It's not the Ritz, that's for sure.'

Harper showers for the first time in thirty-six hours and then changes into jeans and a white T-shirt. They reconvene in Tom's room. He raids the minibar and mixes two whisky and Diet Cokes. He tries to hand one to Harper but she says, 'No, thanks.'

'More for me then,' Tom says and downs his first drink.

Harper wonders if Tom always drinks like this or whether this is a reaction to the death of his uncle and the ongoing threat to his life. *Either way*, she thinks, *you're not one to judge*.

As Tom starts on his second drink, Harper takes another stab at Foster's tablet, plugging in different combinations of numbers or letters before the screen disables. This time it's for ten minutes.

'Motherfucker!'

'Can't you call Agent Diaz?' Tom asks. 'They took the other tablet, right? Maybe they've cracked the code?'

'He won't help.'

'How do you know until you ask?'

'Not only is it against the rules, he's insulted.'

'How's that?'

'I told him what we're doing, conducting our own investigation. He's pissed off we didn't think the FBI was up to the job.'

'That's awfully narcissistic,' Tom says. 'It's not about him. Scepticism is healthy, it's valuable.'

'Yeah, well, I think he's having trouble seeing the forest for the trees on that one.'

'That's very short-sighted of him.'

'Listen,' Harper says, 'you tell someone humans are shitty decision-makers, and all they hear is that *they're* shitty decision-makers.'

Tom shrugs. 'All right. Well, you're not getting into the tablet. So what's our next step?'

'I'd like to see the crime scene at Cielo House. I asked Agent Diaz, but he said no.'

'Let me see what I can do. But we can't lose sight of the Knox aspect of this as well.'

'Does that mean you're ready to talk about Penelope now?'

'What does that mean?'

'You insisted on talking with Penelope, but you haven't said a word about it since we left New York.'

Tom sighs, then nods reluctantly. 'It was hard, hearing what happened, seeing the effect it's had on her. We're very close. Or we were.'

'Do you think she was holding back?'

Tom nods. 'I love my cousin. And I trust her. But yes, I don't think she told us everything. Did you see how awkward she got near the end?'

'It was strange. She was too scared to tell us something.'

Tom bites his lip, lost in thought. 'We can go back to Penelope. Eventually. But you saw how delicate she is. Press her too much and she'll break. Let's give her time. Right now, let's focus on Knox. Who he was, what he was like, who his friends were. Did you know he taught at Everly College?'

'Yeah,' Harper says. 'Your friends the vice-dean and Professor Collins both knew him. They were all in the history department together.'

'How do you know that?'

'They talked about it Friday night, when I was driving them to the theatre.'

'Then that's where we start tomorrow morning, with Perkins and Collins.'

'All right. But I think I should go on my own.'

'Not a chance. I'm coming with you.'

'Listen, Tom, if driving those two taught me anything, it's that they think I'm dumb and not worthy of keeping secrets from. And having a Buchanan present might screw that up. I'm sure you can find some theory that explains the effect your presence would have on them – cognitive shyness, something like that.'

Tom ignores Harper's sarcasm. 'Maybe you've got a point.'

As Tom's mixing himself a third whisky and Diet Coke, Harper checks the tablet to see if the screen is disabled.

'What's the point?' Tom asks.

'You don't think I can crack the code?'

'I don't think you have a chance in hell. It could be any combination of letters or numbers.'

Harper shakes her head. 'You don't know Foster. I know he looks big and mean, but he's sentimental. His password isn't going to be random. It's going to be the name of his favourite pet, his best friend growing up, the love of his life.'

Electricity travels down Harper's spine. Her back straightens.

'What is it?' Tom asks.

Harper inputs nine numbers: 5-8-2-4-3-4-2-9.

Or L-O-U-I-S-D-I-A-Z.

The tablet unlocks.

'What was it?' Tom asks, more dumbfounded than impressed.
'I guess Charles was in love.'

Harper scrolls through the tablet, opening files and apps. She finds the research Foster took her through Friday night, some he didn't. She checks Foster's emails, but there's not much there. A few from Lou and Foster's brother. *None of my business*, she thinks, leaving them unread. She opens the security surveillance app and the tablet suddenly has seven camera views. Two from Appleton Hall, one of Tom's front porch, and three from Cielo House.

'The cameras still work?' Tom is looking over Harper's shoulder. 'Is it too much to hope that there's a recording from Friday?'

'Let's see.'

The recordings are stored in folders, broken down into days, and then into hours. There are folders up until Saturday morning. The last folder is labelled 12 a.m.

'It looks like the whole system stopped recording Friday night, just after midnight,' Harper says. 'And it hasn't been recording since.'

'So what happened? Suddenly the whole system just goes down the night my uncle is killed? How does this make sense?'

'It doesn't.'

Just then there's a pop-up notification from the app. Harper taps on it and then the feed from Tom's front porch fills the screen of the tablet.

'What happened?' Tom asks.

'I don't know. The camera must have picked up movement on your front lawn.'

Harper and Tom lean closer towards the screen.

'Is that . . . ?'

They can make out the outline of someone, a man, standing just beyond the reach of the porchlight, near the sidewalk. They watch him move forwards, slowly, towards the door. The hood of his black sweatshirt is up, his face lost in shadow.

'Could be anything. Right?' Tom asks. 'Maybe he's delivering a package or something.'

Harper taps the screen and the camera starts recording.

The man steps onto the front porch and gets so close to the door, they can only see the top of his head. He starts fiddling with the door handle. At first, he tests it gently. Then he shakes it violently.

'Jesus,' Tom says.

The man steps back from the door. His hood has fallen back to his shoulders. He's wearing a balaclava.

'I think I'm going to be sick,' Tom says. 'What do we do?'

## 35

Special Agent Louis Diaz is contemplating the utility of murder.

He's been in the hospital, at Foster's bedside, for more than an hour. His second visit that day. After his coffee with Harper – to give her space and time alone with Foster – he'd visited the medical examiner for an update on Mitch Buchanan's autopsy. After the medical examiner demurred – 'Is there *really* a rush? I think we both know what was in that needle.' – Lou headed back to the hospital. He had an endless and growing list of tasks to complete for the investigation, but he felt compelled to be with Charles.

Lou had known he cared for Charles Foster, but it took a bullet tearing through the lining of Charles's stomach to realise he couldn't live without him.

Lou was never at one with his emotions. Growing up without parents will do that to a person. They died when he was eight. Cancer. Different types, totally unrelated. Both illnesses discovered, fought, and lost in the same year. Just the worst luck ever visited upon an eight-year-old boy. Lou and his sister Steph went to live with their Aunt Jenny in Houston. Their aunt tried her best, but she was a nurse, which meant long hours, so she wasn't around much. Lou and Steph had each other. Still, it was a lonely childhood. To survive, Lou put up emotional walls. Big, Babylon-size walls. Walls no one could scale. The two women and nine men he'd dated (in that order) from age sixteen to thirty-eight never had a chance. Lou never let himself love and be loved by another person. Not until Charles Foster walked into that terrible dive bar six months ago.

But Lou had been oblivious as he'd fallen in love with Foster, as they reached milestones couples reach: exchanging keys to each other's apartment; that line you cross where you talk every day, no matter what. It was only when Frank called Saturday morning and said that Mitch Buchanan and a member of his security detail had been killed, and Lou felt horribly ill and needed every ounce of will power he had not to fall to his knees – only then did Lou realise he was in love.

Lou hasn't decided yet whether their whole relationship was a mistake. He'll wait to see what happens. If Foster lives, it was worth it. If he doesn't, Lou will have exposed himself unnecessarily to pain. He knows this is faulty reasoning, to work backwards from the result. But he doesn't care.

The irony of all this is that now, as he's plagued by rage and helplessness, unable to do anything for Charles other than wait patiently to see if he lives, Lou finally understands the Karma Killer's online following. Lou had always found anonymous threats of violence inexplicable. He could never fathom what would compel a person to do something like that. But now, if he knew who shot Foster, the least he'd do is send a death threat.

This is what Lou is thinking about when his phone rings. He answers. It takes him a moment to place the voice, even though they'd spoken earlier that day.

'Harper? What is it? You've got to slow down . . . Wait, what?'

# 36

In the parking lot of the Admiralty Inn, Lou is standing with his arms crossed, waiting for Frank to finish.

'And ask her what the hell she's doing with that tablet. On Saturday, I asked her about the cameras. I asked her about tablets. I asked her about any *goddamn* passwords. Do you know what she said? She said there was one tablet! One! The one we found at the crime scene. She didn't say shit about a second. And she didn't say shit about any password. "I joined the team yesterday," she said, batting her eyelashes. Clearly a fucking lie. And if she's lying about the tablet, you can bet she's lying about Hollinger's gun. She's wearing a firearm. I could tell at the meeting in New York. I guarantee it's Hollinger's gun. And if she's lying about that . . . Who knows?'

'Take it easy, Frank,' Lou says.

'Take it easy? You must be fucking joking! Take it easy?'

'I hear you on the tablet,' Lou says. 'And maybe the gun. I'll ask her again about the gun. But let's not go accusing her of something bigger than lying, OK?'

Frank's temper heats up quickly, but cools just as fast. He takes a deep breath and is at least twenty per cent calmer when he's done. 'You didn't find anything outside of Tom Park's home?'

'No,' Lou says. 'Nothing.'

'You think she's telling the truth?'

'I don't know.'

When Harper called Lou two hours earlier, she said someone was outside Tom Park's home, poking around, wearing a balaclava. Lou was grateful for any lead and didn't think to ask any questions. He scrambled to Park's house and called the sheriff's department along the way. He also called Frank, but he was in New York and more than an hour away from Everly College in Petersburg, Connecticut. Lou met a deputy outside Park's and together they searched the premises. It wasn't until the excitement had died down that Lou wondered how exactly Harper had access to the camera outside Park's home.

'These two running around campus, playing cops and robbers,' Frank says, 'someone is going to get hurt. She's *supposed* to be protecting him. They were *supposed* to stay in Manhattan. But they've come back to campus where the guy's uncle was murdered? How fucking stupid are they?'

'Take a walk, Frank. I'll go in there and I'll talk to them.'

'Good. You talk to them. Lord knows what I'd say.' As he searches for his keys in his pant pockets, Frank says, 'By the way, how did you get to Park's so quickly?'

'I was in town.'

'Doing what?'

Lou thinks, *Visiting my boyfriend's sickbed*, but instead he says, 'Talking to the medical examiner.'

Lou hasn't told Frank he's gay, let alone that he's in a relationship with one of the victims they're investigating. And given the number of times Frank has tried to discuss the anatomy of women with Lou – 'Look at the tits on her,' etc. – Frank has no idea Lou's gay. Lou wonders how his friend, maybe the least progressive person Lou knows, would react if he found out. *Bewilderment*, Lou thinks. *And anger maybe. A conversation for another day.*

To Frank, Lou says, 'I'm going inside. I'll meet you back here in twenty.'

'Don't let her suck you in with those green eyes of hers.'

'Not to worry, Frank. That won't be a problem.'

# 37

Tom Park is pacing his hotel room. Harper is sitting on the bed, her back against the headboard.

'What did you find?' Tom asks as Lou steps inside the room. 'Did you catch him?'

'I went to your house with a deputy from the sheriff's department,' Lou says. 'We didn't see anyone or anything.'

'But he tried to break in,' Tom says. 'Can't you do something?'

'Well, that depends,' Lou says, as his eyes meet Harper's. 'Did your camera record anything useful?'

Harper shrugs. 'We recorded the last few seconds. But like I said on the phone, he was wearing a balaclava.'

Lou crosses his arms. 'Strange you didn't mention this second tablet before.'

'No one asked.'

Harper is too calm for Lou's liking. She should be begging for forgiveness by this point.

'I'm going to have to take it,' Lou says. 'The second tablet.'

'No.'

'No?'

Harper sips her whisky.

'It's owned by Spartan Security, a company I still work for. We're in the middle of an important job. We need it.'

Lou fights the urge to smile. *I can see why Charles likes her. What did he call her? A bulldozer?*

Lou looks around the room but can't see the tablet. 'Where is it?'

Harper shrugs.

'Harper,' Lou says. 'You want my help, then you have to work with me here. Did you find any recordings from Friday night?'

'Doesn't your partner have the other tablet?'

'We don't have the passcode to get in. You didn't give it to us. Remember? We can't break in without a warrant. Which we're working on but these things take time. And who knows if we can break through Foster's encryption. Just give us the second tablet and the passcode. Don't you want us to catch the man who shot Foster?'

'Take me through Cielo House tomorrow, through the crime scene.'

'We're not negotiating.'

Harper shrugs.

'I'll tell you what,' Lou says, 'give me the tablet, give me the passcode to unlock it, and I'll *think* about bringing you through the crime scene. It would have to be later in the week, but I could probably figure something out.'

Harper shakes her head.

'Or I could get a warrant and seize the second tablet. That wouldn't be hard, seeing as how you lied to the FBI. And if we start searching for the tablet, maybe we find Jay's gun as well.'

Harper doesn't blink. 'You won't find anything.'

'Maybe, maybe not.'

Lou looks at Tom. 'What about you? You don't want to go to jail for lying to the FBI, do you?'

Tom's eyes nervously dart to Harper and then back to Lou. 'There's no recording from Friday night,' he blurts out. 'We checked.'

Harper grimaces as her bargaining chip evaporates.

'Thank you, Tom,' Lou says, politely. 'That's helpful.' He turns to Harper. 'But I still need to check the tablet myself. You understand that, right?'

Harper writes a note on the hotel stationery on the desk. 'For the record. I didn't know the passcode when your partner asked. We cracked it about two hours ago.' She hands Lou the note folded in half. 'Both tablets have access to the cameras and the security app. This password worked on the tablet we have. It will probably work on the one you have as well. I started recording just before the guy in the balaclava left.'

'You don't want to pull yours out now and we can look together?'

'No.'

*She thinks if she shows me the second tablet, I'll rip it out of her hands*, Lou thinks. *Maybe I would.*

'Any chance I can convince you two to go back to New York tonight?'

'Well,' Tom says, 'we're in the midst of . . . when we're ready . . .'

'No,' Harper says, bluntly.

'At least I can say I tried.'

Frank is still pacing in the parking lot. 'Where the fuck is the tablet?'

'I gave it up in the negotiation.'

'Christ! That fucking woman.'

Lou holds up the sheet of paper Harper gave him. 'But I've got the password.'

'That's something, I guess.'

Lou unfolds the paper and is surprised to see his name spelled out in capital letters: LOUIS DIAZ.

He bites his lip, fighting back tears.

Frank can't see what Harper wrote. He only sees his partner's reaction. 'What the hell is wrong with you?'

# 38

The department of history resides in a Seventies-build, a victim of the brutalism style. Grey concrete, small windows, more a prison than academic refuge. The door to Professor Collins' office is open. The professor is sitting at a desk lost under a mess of paper and books, clutching a gnarled pencil in one hand, the spine of a hardback in the other. Harper knocks on the frame of the open door. Collins looks up and squints, labouring under the strain of working out who Harper is.

When he finally remembers, he looks even more confused. He stands. 'Ms . . .'

'Scott.'

'Scott. Yes. Of course . . . Um . . . Are you here to see me?'

'I am, actually.'

Collins doesn't hide his astonishment. 'Whatever for?'

'I was hoping to talk. Can you spare five minutes?'

'I–uh . . .' The answer is clearly yes, but it takes him a moment to admit it aloud. 'I suppose so. But what would you want to talk to me about?'

Harper knows if she says 'the Karma Killer' too early, Collins might clam up. She avoids the question and points at the two chairs facing his desk. 'May I sit?'

Collins is reluctant but his politeness takes over. 'Yes, of course.' He waits for Harper to sit, then sits himself.

'How's Gutenberg?' Harper asks.

'You have a good memory.' The professor's smile is cautious, as he replays everything he said Friday night. 'I was very sorry to hear what happened. A tragedy, of course. I am praying for Mr . . . your colleague.'

'Charles Foster.' Harper nods. 'Thank you.'

'Any news on who is responsible?'

'No,' Harper says. 'Actually, I was hoping you might be able to help with that?'

Collins straightens up in his seat. 'What information could I possibly offer?'

'We want to find the person who killed Mitch Buchanan and shot my friend. And we believe that whatever happened to Mitch is related to his brother's murder.'

'Who is the "we" you're referring to?'

'Tom Park hired me to help him find Mitch's murderer.'

Realisation washes over the professor's face. 'I see. You heard Ms Perkins and I discussing Mr Knox. And you told this to Mr Park, and now . . . you're here.'

'That about sums it up.'

'Well,' Collins says, 'if you were *eavesdropping*, you heard what I said. I barely knew Mr Knox.'

The professor's voice has an edge that wasn't there before. *He won't help, if he's pissed off*, Harper thinks.

'I'm sorry, Professor,' she says, flashing a friendly smile. 'Let me start over. Did I tell you I read your book?'

'You did? Which one?'

Harper looks over Collins' shoulder to a row of books under the window. '*Gutenberg to Facebook*, of course. And *Social Media: Old As Time*.'

The professor relaxes, as if naming one of his books automatically releases dopamine in his system. 'Well, I'm always happy to speak to a reader.'

'I know you're busy. And I certainly don't want to take up too much of your time. I'm just trying to get a bit of information. For

Tom. Mr Park, I mean. During this difficult time, as he grieves the death of his uncle.'

Collins nods. 'Yes, I completely understand. But I honestly didn't know William that well. While our history department is small, he focused on a very niche area, revolutionary Russia.'

'And you're what? Medieval?'

'I am not defined in such a way. I write big sprawling books about whatever I choose. And I have a name – I'm not famous-famous, but I'm academic-famous, if that makes sense. So, the school lets me float in the history department. I rarely teach anymore, to be honest. I mainly write. Books, a bi-weekly column for the *Globe*, the occasional op-ed. And I'm frequently interviewed. Television, podcasts.'

'Podcasts?'

'Oh yes! It's a wonderful format. I'm invited on and I can extemporise on any topic for hours.'

'You don't have to teach? Sounds like a good gig.'

Collins shrugs. 'I'm out of fashion, anyway. I consider history through the prism of personality. I like to write about people who changed the world.'

'Like Gutenberg and Zuckerberg.'

'Precisely. These days, however, the trend is to see the world only in terms of power. Who has it and who doesn't. A useful lens with which to judge society, certainly. But it's terribly dull to write about. It leaves no room for the individual, you see. I sold thousands of copies of my latest book worldwide. And I guarantee you, I wouldn't have sold ten copies if I'd only written about . . . Am I losing you, Ms Scott?'

Harper forces herself to smile. 'Not at all.'

'I've taken us far afield of your line of inquiry, haven't I? Where were we?'

'We were talking about Knox. You said he focused on revolutionary Russia.'

'Yes, indeed. He wrote a book, on Dostoevsky and Czarist Russia, *Raskolnikov and the Russian Revolution*.' Collins stands and peruses his bookshelf. 'Here we are.' He hands Harper a slim book with a blue cover. 'A bit reductive, in my humble opinion.' He flops back down into his seat. 'It certainly didn't sell well. There was no humanity in it, you see. At the time, I thought it was simply a matter of the writing being poor. But after what happened – well, I realised he wasn't capable. The ability to empathise with the past, it was beyond him.'

Harper examines Knox's book. 'I thought everyone said he was a nice guy, until his daughter died?'

'Well, he wasn't violent or anything like that. There was no indication that he would seek . . . revenge . . . in the manner he did . .'

Harper raises an eyebrow. 'Revenge? You make it sound like something other than cold-blooded murder.'

Collins shrugs. 'Maybe if you view revenge as some sort of positive act. But I certainly don't. Do you know what Orwell said about revenge? He called it sour, a childish daydream. An act only the powerless want to commit. The impotent. Something like that.' He scratches his head. 'Shoot. What else did he say? It's a lovely quote. I go back to Orwell often these days. He's good for the soul. He helps clarify the oddities of our age.' He looks at Harper and smiles. 'My outlook is probably too academic for a veteran, too highfalutin. You probably have some mantra you go to in order to lift your spirits. *Hoorah*. Something succinct like that.'

'That's the marines,' Harper says, but then, because it seemed a genuine inquiry, the first she's had in God knows how long, she considers the question. 'I had a captain when

I was in Afghanistan, O'Neil. He had some line whenever anyone complained. He'd say: "It doesn't matter what you bear, but how you bear it." Something like that. I always liked it. It helped somehow, when we had a sixty-pound pack digging into our shoulders in ninety-degree heat.'

'Who said that? Kant?'

'I don't know. Seneca, maybe.'

'Ah, you're a Stoic. That makes sense.' Collins winks at Harper.

'I'm not anything.'

'No?'

'Not if I can help it. Once you start calling yourself something, you're liable to stop thinking for yourself.'

'But you like the quote? You find wisdom in the words?'

'I think it can help you get through the day. And isn't that all we try to do?'

Collins smiles. 'You're sounding an awful lot like a Stoic.'

'Well, I'm not. I'm not anything.'

'So you said.'

Harper tries to steer the conversation back to the matter at hand. 'Were you surprised when you found out what he'd done?'

Collins winces at the abrupt change of direction. 'Who do you mean? William? Yes, of course. It was shocking.'

'There weren't any signs?'

Collins shrugs. 'You're really asking the wrong person. I barely knew him. Olivia would be much more insightful.'

'The vice-dean?'

'Yes. She was head of our history department before she became vice-dean. She denies it now, understandably, but she and Knox were close. Closer than he and I certainly. And she spearheaded the media triage after we learned a former professor had murdered four people in cold blood. She manhandled the other professors in the department, blocking any attempt they made to speak to the press. There was a time when we thought the school might be defined by that one brutal act.'

'All right. I'll speak to Ms Perkins.' Harper holds up Knox's book. 'Can I borrow this?'

'Keep it. And' – Collins looks over his glasses and smirks – 'tell Olivia I sent you, will you?'

# 39

The walk through campus is hot and muggy. Students are everywhere, milling from one class to the next, lounging on grassy fields and park benches. The contrast between Friday and now is striking. The rancour, the violent threats, the seething mob – all of it gone without a trace.

The vice-dean's office is in a redbrick building set back from a large quad. Today there's a line of stalls, each with a different potential employer offering summer internships. Blue-chip corporations, banks, telecommunications, Silicon Valley. Their signs have a whiff of desperation: WORK–LIFE BALANCE ... SAFE SPACES ... FREE LUNCHES ... REMOTE WORK ... PING-PONG TABLES ON-SITE.

On the second floor, there's an assistant outside of Perkins' office. Harper says she'd like to speak with the vice-dean. 'She's not expecting me, but it's a matter of life and death.'

The assistant, perhaps particularly sensitive given what happened Friday night, nods vigorously and hurries into the vice-dean's office.

Harper hears one side of the conversation – 'Who? Outside my office? Why?' – before the assistant comes back and says, 'Please go in.'

The vice-dean's office is not what Harper expected. The furnishings are minimal. Her transparent desk is made of thin strips of black metal and glass. Behind her is a large abstract painting, a swirl of bright pink and indigo blue. To Harper's right is a window that looks onto the busy quad below. The opposite wall is filled with framed photos of the vice-dean meeting and shaking hands with important people.

The vice-dean's blonde hair is once again in a tight bun. She stands, smooths her pencil skirt, before offering her hand. 'Hello, Ms Scott. This is unexpected.'

She stays standing, clearly hoping to end the conversation reasonably quickly. Harper flops into the chair opposite the desk. Outmanoeuvred, the vice-dean sits as well.

'Well?' The vice-dean's pained smile is back. 'What can I help you with?'

'I'd like to talk to you about the Karma Killer.'

Perkins is better at hiding her surprise than Collins. Only her left eyebrow moves, arching like a scared cat. 'And why is that? I don't mean to be rude, but since you were here to protect Mr Buchanan, and he is now no longer with us, I would have thought your time at our school would be over.'

Harper has to hand it to Perkins. She has a way of telling you to go fuck yourself that seems both logical and polite. She suspects most people leave conversations with her thinking: *she's right, I should go fuck myself*.

'I'm going to be here for the foreseeable future, actually.'

'Is that right?'

'Tom Park hired me.'

'Oh? For security?'

'Yes. And to find the man who killed his uncle.'

'I thought the authorities were handling that? The FBI?'

'Two heads are better than one.'

Perkins nods, although it's clear she doesn't agree with the thesis. 'So, you're going to help Tom find the man who killed Mitch Buchanan, yet you started by saying you wanted to know about Knox?'

'Mitch's murder is related to Skip's. We don't know how exactly, but there's a connection.'

'If you say so.'

'So you'll help?'

'In truth, Ms Scott, I doubt you will do anything to advance the investigation. If you have any expertise, it's in security, not murder investigations. And you didn't have much success with the assignment you *did* have.' She lets that one sit a moment, to make sure Harper feels the sting. 'But I think it's fantastic you're helping Tom. Distractions are vital in times of crisis. Please, ask me anything you'd like.'

'You were Knox's colleague?'

'Superior, actually. I ran the history department during his tenure here. He was a visiting scholar, from Austin. He was here for a year and a half before his daughter died. Tragically.' She adds the last word as a matter of course, like she's said that particular statement a thousand times. 'She'd struggled with addiction. William moved here in the hopes that his daughter would have a new start. But, alas, that is easier said than done.'

'And she overdosed?'

Perkins frowns. 'Certainly. It is perhaps the most famous motivation for murder in America since Charles Manson and Helter Skelter. Girl dies of opioid overdose. Father kills the man who made a fortune selling opioids.'

'I'm curious what Knox was like before his daughter died.'

'I'd say we saw two Williams. The first year he was diligent, highly rated by his students, kind to his colleagues. And he was passionate about his area of expertise.'

'The Russian Revolution?'

The vice-dean eyes the book in Harper's hands. 'Yes, that's right. He wrote a book on the topic. It looks like you've already picked up a copy.'

'Courtesy of Professor Collins.'

Perkins flashes her pained smile.

'So,' Harper says, 'the first Knox was a sweetheart. What about the second?'

'There was a great change in William his second year here. He was irritable, withdrawn. He ignored his responsibilities at the school. Now, knowing what we know, it's understandable, considering what he was going through. But at the time, it caused me great consternation. I'm sorry to say it, but I thought he was lazy. Or that he was drinking too much.'

'But his daughter didn't die until the spring, isn't that right?'

'Yes, but she had trouble before she died. She fell in with the wrong crowd. She overdosed and barely survived. She tried rehab. It didn't work. But, as I said, I didn't know this at the time. I only saw the changes in William. And then when the story came out, after the murders, it all made perfect sense.'

The vice-dean's cold demeanour hasn't changed. *She's a walking ice cube*, Harper thinks.

'She died in June,' Perkins says. 'William took a leave of absence. It was – what? – December when he killed Skip Buchanan.'

'And four others,' Harper adds.

'Yes, of course. Terribly tragic, even if you can see poetic justice in Mr Buchanan's end.'

'You think Skip had it coming?'

The vice-dean shakes her head. 'I didn't say that. I merely point out that Skip Buchanan was not entirely innocent when it came to the pain and suffering in this world. One can understand William's anger, and why he directed it where he did.'

'Was Knox close to anyone? Did he have any friends?'

The vice-dean shrugs. 'He was friendly with most of the people in the department.'

'No one he was particularly close to?'

Perkins sighs, signalling her desire to end the conversation. 'No. At the time, we had five professors in the history department.

There was William and Professor Collins, who you've met. Two were fired. They chose, against strict direction from me, to talk to the press after William was arrested. Delacroix and Doherty. I have no idea where they are now, and I don't care. I haven't spoken to either in some time. Selwyn White went on administrative leave eight months ago. It was a media circus here, at the school, and he wasn't up to it. I can give you his contact information.'

'Please.'

Perkins writes an address and phone number on a piece of paper. 'If there is anything else, Ms Scott, you know where to find me.'

# 40

Lou meets Frank at Sunny Side Up, a diner near campus they'd grown fond of last year, while investigating the murder of Skip Buchanan. It was one of the few spots in town that was affordable and relatively fast, but wasn't overrun with Everly students.

Lou slides into the booth opposite Frank. Frank has the hard copy of the *Post* spread out on the table.

'Any luck?'

Lou hands Frank a manila folder. Inside, there's a photo of a man wearing a balaclava standing outside Tom Park's front door. The quality of the image isn't great but it's the closest thing to a lead they've had, so Frank smiles. 'I can't believe it. Green eyes came through?'

'She did.'

'The password she gave you worked?'

'It did.'

'What was it anyway?'

Lou is staring at the menu. He doesn't look up. 'Random numbers as far as I can tell.'

The waitress takes their order. Lou orders tea and an egg white omelette, Frank coffee and the steak and eggs.

Frank holds up the photo. 'So this is our man?'

The question was meant to be rhetorical, but Lou shakes his head. 'We don't know that. Maybe it's the guy who killed Mitch Buchanan. Maybe it's the guy who attacked McMurtry. But for all we know, it could have been some nut job who saw Tom Park's address online.'

'No way. It's him all right.'

'We'll see.'

Frank squints and brings the photo an inch from his face. 'What do you think? Six foot? A hundred and eighty pounds?'

'Give or take.'

Their lunch arrives. Frank starts sawing his rib-eye with a serrated blade. 'What else did you find on the tablet? I figure if there'd been a recording you'd have called me.'

'The cameras were turned off just before midnight.'

'Of course they were. Why would anything about this case be easy?' Frank chews a hunk of steak with his mouth open. 'You served with this guy Foster, right? Does this make sense to you? Would he just stop recording?'

'No,' Lou says, 'it doesn't make sense.'

With his mouth full of steak, Frank mutters, 'This fucking case.'

As their waitress is clearing away their plates, Lou's phone rings. He stares at the screen and sighs.

'What is it?'

'It's someone at the school. The vice-dean. A lot of hand-holding. Since Friday she needs constant updates.'

'So don't pick up.'

Lou shrugs and answers the call. 'Hello.'

Frank rolls his eyes.

Lou says, 'yes', several times, then closes his eyes in mock pain. 'Fine. Tomorrow morning. I'll give them an hour.'

After he hangs up, Frank asks, 'What is it? What did she want?'

'The rich, Frank,' Lou says, as he sips his coffee. 'The leash they get in life, the concessions. I swear to God.'

Frank puts up his hands. 'Stop. Don't tell me. You'll ruin my breakfast.'

# 41

Back at the Admiralty Inn, Harper fills Tom in on what she learned on campus. He flips through Knox's book on Dostoevsky and the Russian Revolution. 'Raskolnikov. He's from *Crime and Punishment*. Right? Maybe we should pick up a copy?'

'Do you have a copy at your house?'

Tom shrugs. 'Honestly, I have no idea.'

Tom opens up his laptop and they Google the names of Knox's old colleagues. They end up on YouTube watching interviews of Delacroix and Doherty, the two professors Perkins fired. They were interviewed again and again and always gave the same tired routine: Knox was nice on the surface, but there were signs of the cold-blooded killer underneath. They told anecdotes about Knox that were meant to allude to the murderer he would become, but that didn't amount to much. While happy to tell their story to any reporter that asked, neither were called as witnesses at Knox's trial. Borelli must have concluded that Delacroix or Doherty were full of it. But the cable news networks couldn't afford to be as discerning. They needed talking heads – anyone with a pulse – who knew Knox before he became a killer.

Harper calls the professor on leave, Selwyn White, but no one answers. Tom Googles his address and discovers he's close, less than a ten-minute drive.

'I'll go,' Harper says.

'I'm coming with you,' Tom says. Harper starts to protest but Tom adds, 'I don't think you realise how scary you are.'

Harper shrugs. 'Maybe you've got a point.'

Selwyn White lives on a residential street a short drive from Tom's. A tiny red hatchback is parked in the driveway.

Harper rings the doorbell and a small dog barks wildly. They can hear claws tap-dancing on a wooden floor and a man trying to soothe the dog, but no one answers the door.

'Hello,' Tom says. 'Mr White, could you open the door?'

'Go away, please.'

'We'd just like to talk with you for a moment.'

White doesn't respond. The only sound is a dog pacing on hardwood.

'We just have a few questions for you,' Tom says. 'It won't take more than ten minutes.'

'I don't talk about him.'

'Him?'

'Knox.'

'We're not with the press, Mr White. And if you're worried about the school, about Vice-Dean Perkins, don't be. It was Ms Perkins who gave us your name.'

The door unlocks and opens just wide enough to see White's face. He's in his seventies, short, with a tiny mouth. He looks like a turtle wearing expensive glasses. 'Olivia sent you?'

'She gave me your name and address,' Harper says. 'I'm ...' Harper struggles to define what she is right now. '*We* are private investigators' – *Close enough*, she thinks – 'hired by the Buchanan family. We're trying to learn what we can about Knox. To help protect them. I'm sure you've heard about what happened to Mitch Buchanan.'

'Did Knox escape?'

'What? No. Why would you think that?'

'He's a genius. It's only a matter of time until he escapes. I heard about what happened ... on Friday... and I just assumed...'

'He didn't escape.'

'How do you know? Have you seen him in jail?'

'No. But it would be all over the news.'

'The media is complicit. They made him into a hero, with the names they gave him. The Karma Killer. The Killer of Killers.'

*All true*, Harper thinks.

'Mr White, it's quite hot out,' Tom says. 'Do you think we could have this conversation inside?'

White purses his little turtle mouth. 'I've told the police everything I know. And how do I know you aren't with the media? They've tried this before. Tricking me, to get inside, to ask me questions.'

'Mr White, please—'

'No, no, no. I've made up my mind. Please don't come back. Bad enough I have to see his old haunt every day. I don't need the media conning their way into my home.'

'Old haunt?' Harper asks. 'You mean the school?'

'No, his home. He lived just down the street.' White points over Harper's left shoulder. 'Thirteen Geraldine Avenue. When he lived there ... Women coming and going in the night. He lived a very promiscuous life, you know. Finding solace in sexual deviancy. They wrote about it in the news. His orgies.'

'Number thirteen?'

'Yes, thirteen. Goodbye.'

White slams the door.

## 42

Harper and Tom stare at the house White had pointed out, a bungalow on a parallel street. Without a word, they start walking towards it. They pause at the foot of the empty driveway. The grass is long, tipped over under its own weight. Half a dozen newspapers are piled up on the front porch.

Harper would never have spotted it on her own, but now that she's here, 13 Geraldine Avenue looks familiar. The clips they watched on YouTube, cable news segments and the home-made conspiracy videos featured countless shots of Knox's former home, but often with menacing scores and dark lighting.

They walk up the driveway. Green weeds are sprouting up through cracks in the asphalt.

Harper rings the doorbell. No one answers. She looks in the window. The living room is empty. The kitchen, too. 'Looks abandoned.'

Tom peers over her shoulder and nods. 'It's been months since Knox was arrested. Would the house have stood empty since then?'

'I wouldn't want to buy the home of a convicted serial killer. Would you?'

Tom squats beside the pile of newspapers. 'The last six days are here,' he says. 'That's it. Which means someone is coming and collecting them.'

Harper stares at the front yard. 'No for sale sign. The grass is a bit long, but it doesn't look months old, does it?'

Tom, who has never mowed a lawn in his life, shrugs.

Harper removes her lockpicking kit from the breast pocket of her leather jacket and kneels beside the front door.

'Jesus, Harper,' Tom says. 'What are you doing?'

'Relax.' Harper inserts the hook and tension wrench into the lock. 'I'll be in and out in five minutes.'

Tom nervously bustles behind Harper as she works. He looks up and down the street, before standing in front of Harper, arms crossed, trying to block her from the eyes of any potential passers-by.

Once the door is unlocked, Harper says, 'Wait here,' and disappears inside.

She starts in the kitchen. It's as empty as it looked through the window, except on the table there's a handful of letters. Most are addressed to Knox or 'Dear Homeowner', but two are addressed to '976451 Delaware Corp.'. Harper organises the letters face up on the table, takes a picture using her phone, and then recreates the pile she'd found them in.

The rest of the house is as empty as the kitchen. Upstairs, the living room, the laundry room.

She reconvenes with Tom on the front porch. A small black cat is rubbing its side against Tom's right shin.

'It's the same story inside. The house is empty,' Harper says. 'But I found letters addressed to Knox and some numbered company.' She shows Tom the picture she took.

'Strange,' Tom says. 'The house is empty. And yet someone's clearly looking after it, picking up the mail and newspapers, and maybe cutting the grass.'

'But it's not sold,' Harper says. 'Not torn down.'

Tom frowns. 'It's stuck in purgatory.'

'I can relate.'

# 43

'Can you ask Agent Diaz?' Tom asks back at the Admiralty Inn. 'He'll have all the ownership information at his fingertips.'

'Are you serious? Did you see our last conversation? He was furious.'

'He didn't seem *that* mad to me. No harm in trying.'

'He'll say no.'

'How do you know until you ask?'

'It won't work. I don't want to jeopardise the relationship any more than I have.'

Tom's irritation is obvious but fleeting. He thinks for a moment and then snaps his fingers. 'I might know someone who can help.' He starts tapping away on his phone. 'When I bought my house in Petersburg, there was a local lawyer I used. I mainly dealt with his clerk, Stacey. We got along and – if I'm being honest – she had a crush.'

Sceptical, Harper arches an eyebrow. 'Is that right?'

Tom holds his phone to his ear. 'Definitely. I'm sure she'd do me a favour.' Then, in a cheerier tone: 'Stacey? Hi. It's Tom Park calling... Oh good, you *do* remember me. It's been ages... How are things?... You did? Good for you. That's amazing... Me? Oh, I'm OK. You know. Working a lot... I know, I know...'

Harper listens to one side of their conversation. It goes on for a few minutes. Finally, Tom says, 'Listen, Stacey, the reason I'm calling, I was hoping you might be able to pull some information for me. About a house. I was thinking of maybe moving closer to campus. There was a house I had my eye on... You would? That would be amazing. You're a saint. The address is Thirteen Geraldine Avenue.' Tom makes eye contact with Harper and flashes a victorious smile. 'Oh wow! Are you serious? . . . I had no idea that was Knox's house. You've caught me completely off guard.'

Harper is impressed. Tom's faux surprise seems genuine. *He's spent so many years pretending he's not a Buchanan, he's a young Anthony Hopkins.*

'Yes, my lips are sealed. Yes, Thursday works.'

Tom grabs a pen and a scrap of paper and starts writing. 'Mmhmm. Mmhmm. Conveyed to who? . . . Oh, I see . . . Thank you so much, Stacey. I owe you one. Yes, I'll see you Thursday. Can't wait.' He hangs up.

'Sounds like that went well,' Harper says.

'Yeah. It only cost me a Thursday night.' He reads the note he made. 'The house was sold three years ago, to Knox, just before he started teaching at Everly College. And then it changed hands again.'

'To whom?'

'The same company that was getting mail there: 976451 Delaware Corp.'

'She said maybe Knox transferred the house to a company he owns. Or he sold it.'

'When did the transfer happen? After he was arrested?'

'No, that's the thing. He did it three months before the murders. Stacey is going to do a corporate search and get more information on the company. She said she'd have it sometime tomorrow.'

'So what do we do now?'

They order Chinese to Tom's room and go over everything they've learned so far. Tom has a notebook he's been filling up with handwritten notes. He flips through it as they talk.

'What did you make of what Selwyn White said about Knox?' Tom asks.

'He seemed . . . what's a nice way to put it? Off his rocker. So, I think we should ignore everything he said.'

Tom shakes his head. 'You're missing the point of everything we're doing here, Harper. Dismissing what someone like White said is exactly what the police or Borelli might have done. We're not doing that.'

'OK. Fine. Do you want me to find out who attended these orgies? Or do you want to handle that?'

'That's not what I mean. Sure, the inferences he's drawing seem out of touch, but that doesn't mean his information isn't valuable.'

Harper takes off her leather jacket and stretches. Out of the corner of her eye, she sees Tom's eyes linger. Harper thought she'd waited out his crush, but maybe not.

'All right,' she says. 'What did White say that was helpful?'

'Everything we've read or heard about Knox – the videos on YouTube, Borelli's book, what Perkins told you – everyone described him as a loner. But White said Knox had people visiting at all hours of the night.'

'For orgies.'

'Again, just because White drew strange conclusions about what happened *inside* Knox's home, doesn't mean Knox didn't have visitors.'

Harper takes a bite from her egg roll. 'Maybe.'

Tom's phone rings. He answers.

'Hi, Cindy. Thanks for calling me back.' He takes down information in his notebook. 'Great.' He looks at Harper and smiles. 'Yes, Cindy. Yes, I understand . . . She'll respect the process. She won't interfere. I promise.' He hangs up. 'Good news. I've got you access to the crime scene.'

'You did? Great.'
'Yes, but there's a catch.'
'A catch?'
'Yes, and I don't know if you're going to like it.'

# 44

Valentina Giaconda prefers to be called a 'medium'. Psychic, as she often says on her television show, makes her abilities sound mystical. When she's simply a conduit between the living and the dead. Hence 'medium'.

And that's the title of her show: *New Jersey Medium*. Technically, it's reality television, but in truth it's better scripted than most studio shows. Each episode follows the same formula. There's one paid gig, where a family hires her to commune with a dead friend or relative. She visits their home, asks a series of vague questions of the family – *horses? Did he like horses? Did anyone in the family like horses? Sam liked horses, didn't he?* – which the family answers, giving Valentina enough information to convey generic statements she insists are communications from beyond the grave.

Once she has them on the hook, she provides platitudes about life and death, about family and moving on, her clients cry, and that's about it. These serious moments are intercut with domestic 'dramas', which are meant to be half-funny, half-embarrassing, but one hundred per cent relatable. Her daughter didn't get invited to a dance. Her son needs to buy his first stick of deodorant.

According to Tom, Cindy Buchanan is a major fan of *New Jersey Medium*. In fact, she's hired Valentina on several occasions, not only to personally communicate with the dead, but also for dinner parties and charity events. And so, while most of the Buchanans, upon learning of Mitch's murder, called their friends in law enforcement or their priests to ask for help or advice, Cindy called her medium. 'She's totally dependent on her medium,' Tom said. 'She thinks the best person to explain what happened to Mitch is Mitch himself.'

And the relationship is lucrative enough that Valentina wants to keep Cindy happy, even if she's out of her comfort zone at a murder scene. 'In gambling parlance,' Tom said, 'Cindy is a whale. And you don't turn away a whale, no matter what.'

Cindy asked the school to allow Valentina to walk through the crime scene. And the school, wanting to maintain its lucrative relationship with the Buchanans, said yes. Because Cindy put in her request before Tom, and given everything had to be coordinated with law enforcement, the school strongly suggested that Tom (or whoever needed access to the crime scene) go with Cindy and her medium.

'Sorry,' Tom told Harper. 'But this is our only option.'

Harper finds the group waiting for her outside Cielo House. Valentina stands out like a sore thumb: she's extremely short – not so much a medium as an extra small – with a large bouffant of black hair and heavy eyeshadow. She's standing with a uniformed deputy from the sheriff's department, Cindy Buchanan, and Special Agent Lou Diaz.

'If it isn't Detective Scott,' Lou says, as Harper nears the group, 'are you here to examine the crime scene?'

Harper shrugs. He's making fun of her, but he's right. That's exactly why she's here.

Cindy introduces Harper to Valentina and the deputy. Valentina speaks in a thick New Jersey accent. 'You're a detective?'

'Something like that.'

Lou rolls his eyes.

'You're too beautiful to be a detective,' Valentina says, smiling. It's the smile of a politician: unnaturally wide and a touch too confident. 'With those green eyes! My cousin, Eddie – oh my God, he would love you.'

'Shall we?' Lou says, waving his hand at Cielo House.

The group walks together to the main entrance. The deputy swipes a key card to unlock the door, then holds it open as the other four saunter inside. Valentina stops in the foyer. 'Oh. My. God.' Her eyes are wide with shock. 'The murderer came through *this* door.'

Cindy clutches her chest. 'Oh my God.'

Harper tries her best not to smile, but she's only human. Lou catches her eye. He's also smiling. Harper leans towards Lou and whispers, 'Game changer?'

Lou grimaces, trying not to laugh.

Valentina bows her head, apparently deep in thought.

Harper turns her attention to the door they entered. She examines the hinges and the lock.

'And,' Valentina adds, 'the killer left this way as well.'

Cindy shakes her head, as though her medium is providing too much information at once.

The group starts towards the elevators. Harper, still examining the hinges, hangs back. 'What is it?' Lou asks.

'The door's intact. No sign of forced entry. Are there other entrances?'

Lou stares at Harper, like she's an annoying fly and he's deciding whether it's worth the effort to squash her. She thinks he's going to ignore the question, but he doesn't. 'There are three ways inside the building, including this one. No signs of forced entry. We don't know which door the killer used.'

'Until a psychic told you.'

Lou smiles. 'That's right. Until now. And she prefers *medium*.'

The elevator doors open at the end of the hall.
'So the killer had a key card?' Harper asks.
'Or he stole one. Or someone let him in.'
The deputy calls from inside the elevator. 'You two coming?'

# 45

Harper's heart rate triples as the elevator comes to a stop. She half expects to see Jay's bloody corpse, still lying on the floor. *I should have gotten high for this.* She reaches for her vape in the back pocket of her jeans, just to make sure it's there.

She can feel Lou watching her. He looks concerned.

The elevator door slowly opens. Jay's body has been removed. The smell of bleach is overwhelming.

Valentina waits for the deputy to signal which direction to go, then she slowly walks down the hallway. Cindy follows, tentatively, like she's stepping on eggshells, so as not to disturb the process.

Harper can't take her eyes off the floor.

Lou is beside her. 'Did you know Jay well?'

'No.'

At the end of the hallway, the deputy unlocks the door to the presidential suite.

'Did it happen in here?' Valentina asks.

The deputy nods. Valentina closes her eyes and drops her chin to her chest.

Harper whispers to Lou, 'Did she fall asleep?'

Lou starts to laugh. Whatever escapes through his hand sounds more like a snort. Cindy whips around and glares at the two stragglers.

Valentina starts to breathe heavily. Cindy bends down, so she's eye-level with the extra-small medium. 'Are you all right?' she says. 'Do you need a minute?'

The medium opens her eyes. She feigns a feeble smile. 'I'm . . . all right. It's just hard because I feel so much pain coming from this room.'

Cindy grimaces, like she can feel it too. 'Wow.'

'What about the hallway?' Harper asks. 'Any pain out here?'

Valentina turns to Harper. 'Yes,' she says, nodding her head. 'The room, the hallway. Not only pain, but also anger.'

Vague and unspecific, reading the clues her audience gives, until she has enough information to bullshit. *A true con artist.* Harper has the urge to give Valentina shit. Her schtick was amusing at first, but as Harper's anxiety grows – as they walk the scene where Foster was shot and two others killed – the medium's routine is mutating into the grotesque. But Harper bites her tongue. There's no point in confronting Valentina. Con artists never admit to the con, and it will only piss Cindy off.

The deputy steps inside the room. Valentina and Cindy follow. Harper lingers in the hallway. She examines the door, which has no damage, and then looks back towards the elevator, where she'd found Jay's body Saturday morning.

Lou is watching her. 'What is it?'

'There's no sign of forced entry. And Jay's in the hall, by the elevator.'

'That's true.'

'It's strange, isn't it? Jay being in the hall, and everyone else in the room. Maybe Jay was on his way to the elevator, doors open, the killer is there, he shoots Jay. But if that happened, Foster would have heard. And if he heard a gunshot, no way he would leave the door open. He'd have been worried about Jay, but his duty was to protect Buchanan. He'd have locked the door and done everything he could to protect his client.'

'If your question is: does it make sense?' Lou says, 'the answer is no, it doesn't.'

'Any theories?'

'None I'm going to discuss with you.'

*Or maybe none of your theories are any good?* Harper thinks.

Inside, the room feels different compared to Friday night, like the ambience died along with its A-list guest. What was once warm and luxurious is now empty and grim. The couch and rug with Foster's blood have been carted off to the lab. The floorboards underneath are stained where Foster's blood seeped through the carpet.

Harper feels a sense of helplessness and regret, something akin to nostalgia, but more powerful. She's been fighting it since the elevator, but now it's verging on overwhelming. She's woozy, her legs weak.

Lou is watching her. Harper wonders what she looks like because Lou looks worried.

'When Charles was shot,' he says, 'we think he was standing about here, in front of the coffee table, and the force knocked him back into the couch, knocking it over.'

Harper knows Lou is only telling her this to distract her, because he feels sorry for her. Still, she's grateful for the diversion.

'Why did the killer leave Foster alive?' she asks.

'We don't know. It didn't make sense to leave a witness. And the killer clearly had no issue with taking lives. Maybe he was too focused on Buchanan to properly deal with Foster.'

Valentina is wandering the apartment, occasionally stopping to close her eyes and commune with the dead. Cindy is on her hip, issuing an 'Oh my God', when appropriate.

Harper asks Lou, 'Mitch was killed with fentanyl, right?'

'That detail isn't public yet.'

Harper keeps pacing the room, aggregating information. 'The killer gets in somehow, he shoots Foster. Buchanan runs to the bedroom. The killer chases him down and then injects him with fentanyl. What's the theory here? That Foster or Buchanan knew the killer?'

Lou looks at the others in the group, to make sure they're not listening. 'That's one theory. Someone who knew Mitch Buchanan, wanted him dead, and is trying to use the internet trolls doxing the Buchanans – all the Karma Killer hashtag bullshit – as cover. Mitch had a lot of enemies.'

'But that doesn't explain how Jay ended up dead in the hall.'

'No, it doesn't.'

'Or the guy in the mask outside of Tom's place.'

'Or that.'

Harper stands where the killer might have stood when he shot Foster. She starts to raise her hand, like she's holding a gun, but sees Lou watching her. Embarrassed, she drops her arm.

'What about the online death threats?'

'What about them?'

'Can you follow up on any that are suspicious?'

'What's the difference between a death threat and a suspicious death threat. If you know, I'm all ears. And we can't chase down every threat online. There wouldn't be time for anything else.'

Valentina is on the threshold to Buchanan's bedroom. 'Oh my God.' She dips her chin to her chest and closes her eyes. 'The pain . . .'

Cindy whimpers.

Harper can't take any more of the New Jersey Con Artist. She tells Lou she'll meet them downstairs.

The group reconvenes in the lobby twenty minutes later. Cindy's eyes are red and raw. She looks exhausted. Valentina is offering her words of comfort as they walk towards the front door. Lou's phone rings as they're exiting Cielo House. He takes the call in the foyer as he walks away from the group. He stops walking and says, 'You're shitting me.'

Cindy and Valentina walk outside. Harper stays back.

'When?' Lou says into the phone. 'You're sure?'

He hangs up.

'What is it?' Harper asks.

'Tom's been doxed.'

'Again?'

Lou nods.

'Where? What address?'

'Where do you think?'

# Day 41

'You've been sober this whole time?'

Milk froths, emitting a supersonic whistle.

Jess nods, proudly. 'Yup.'

Pockets of conversation and easy laughter fill the Starbucks.

'That's extraordinary, Jessica,' Dana says. She wraps her lips around a paper straw and inhales. 'Has it been hard?'

'Oh my God, yes! It's been *so* hard. But Alex,' – she nods at Alex who's in conversation with Abby at the other end of the communal table – 'she's really stuck with me. Whenever I feel myself slipping, she'll drop whatever she's doing and come keep me company. And without Lama Aaron . . . who knows where I'd be.'

Dana leans forwards, her voice quieter than before. 'Speaking of our fair leader, are the rumours true?'

'What rumours?'

'I heard you had a PME?'

Jess is now well acquainted with the Movement's cadre of acronyms. PME – or Personal Meditation Experience – is a one-on-one session with Lama Aaron himself.

'It's true.'

'Oh my God, I am *beyond* jealous. I've been with the Movement more than a year and I still haven't been invited to a PME.'

Jess forces her smile to flatten. *Don't gloat*, she thinks. *Envy turns to hate pretty darn quick.*

Dana briefly aims her chin at the ceiling, summoning the resolve to continue. 'OK. Tell me everything. Was it at Aaron's home?'

'Yes.'

'I figured. Which room?'

'There's a room upstairs. Have you seen it? It's all white – white walls, white carpeting. It's pretty much empty except there's the Buddha in the corner.'

'Oh my God, I've never even been upstairs. You lucky duck.' Dana sighs and again collects herself. 'OK. How did it start?'

'He gave me one of his tonics. The one with turmeric and apple cider vinegar.'

'*That* I've had. It tastes terrible, doesn't it? But it's done wonders for my anxiety and digestion.'

'Yes! I totally agree. Anyway, after I drank the tonic, Aaron dimmed the lights and we both sat cross-legged on the floor, facing each other. I closed my eyes and tried my best to be as present and focused as possible.'

'Of course. That makes sense.'

'Then he led me through a meditation. Which, you know, one-on-one with that voice of his . . .'

'I'm so jealous. I'm *dying*.'

'And then, when I was *super* focused and relaxed, he asked me about the first time I used. I had to describe the day, how I was feeling. And, I mean, I probably shouldn't get into it too much here, but he had me thinking about my drug use in such a different way. I had to approach it rationally, looking at the root causes. He helped me see the connection between when I started smoking weed and my dad cheating on my mom, and their divorce.'

'Wow. That's so . . . deep. Has it helped?'

'Yes. Definitely. Like I said, I haven't used since I overdosed.'

'Oh my God, Jess. That's just so . . . I'm really happy for you. We all are. You must be so committed now.'

'Yeah, of course. I mean . . . I owe Aaron everything. He's a genius.'

'I guess you'll be first in line to move to the ashram when it's finished?'

'Maybe. It would definitely be an improvement on my living situation. I have two roommates who are the *worst*. I'm counting the days until I can move out. What about you?'

'Oh, they can't stop me from moving in. Did you see the plans? It looks incredible. There's going to be tennis courts, a gym, a pool, a steam room.' Dana looks up and down the table and then leans forwards, her tone quieter than a moment before. 'I'm glad to see you're not feeling guilty.'

'Guilty about what?'

'About Tara.'

'What do you mean? What about Tara?'

'Do you not know? I thought you knew.' Dana leans closer to Jess, her voice grows quieter. 'She's gone missing. I heard she might be using again.'

It takes Jess a moment to digest this.

'That's terrible. Are you serious? Is this . . . Is it because of what happened? At Aaron's, I mean.'

Dana shrugs. 'Who knows? If she's relapsed, this wouldn't be the first time. And God knows Aaron can't save everyone. But like I said, you shouldn't feel guilty. She brought this on herself. You heard what Aaron said. You can't stop karma.'

'Is there anything we can do?'

'If there is, I'm sure Aaron will tell us.'

# 46

'I think you're overreacting.'

Tom is pulling T-shirts out of an open drawer and dropping them into his suitcase. Harper signals for him to hurry up, spinning an imaginary wheel. 'Less talk, more packing.'

'I doubt there's any danger, Harper, let alone a sense of urgency. Can't we talk about this?'

'Skip Buchanan was doxed and then killed. Eleanor McMurtry was doxed and then attacked. Mitch Buchanan was doxed and then killed. There's a pretty clear pattern here. This rat trap of an Inn has been doxed, so we can't stay here. It's not safe.'

When Lou told Harper that Tom had been doxed, she'd raced back to the Admiralty Inn. She didn't know how long the post-doxing Tom had been up and thought the worst. But she found Tom in good spirits, reading Borelli's book while having a bubble bath.

'I'm not sure you're thinking about this logically. Correlation doesn't equal causation. Maybe I've been doxed dozens of times and no one's bothered to tell me. If that's the case, then the chance of anything happening this time is incredibly low.'

'It's not safe, Tom. You know I'm right.' Harper is pulling aside the thin curtains and looking out the window.

'I don't even work for the company. How is this fair?'

Harper shrugs. 'Word is out that you're a Buchanan. And, for whatever reason, all the assholes on the internet have turned their sights on you. Groupthink, right? No one thinks for themselves.' Harper smiles as she uses Tom's own words to explain the world to him. 'And for these Everly students at least, you're the closest Buchanan on hand. Low-hanging fruit.'

'Right.' Tom sighs, defeated. 'Someone obviously followed us and posted the address of the Admiralty Inn. How do you know they won't do it again?'

'You're right. I thought once we left New York, after you were first doxed, we'd be OK. But clearly we weren't careful enough, and someone followed us here.'

*Whoever it was*, Harper thinks. *Some kid with a Reddit handle or the killer himself.*

'I'm going to take better precautions this time. We'll disappear before I take you to the next location.'

Tom stops packing and looks at Harper imploringly, 'Can't we go to another hotel at least? A nice one this time? What you're proposing – the amenities are non-existent.'

Harper smiles. 'Trust me, Tom. We're going to the last place on earth anyone would look for a billionaire like you.'

# 47

'Here we are.' On the second floor of Appleton Hall, Harper unlocks the door to Room 212, the room Harper slept in the night of Mitch Buchanan's murder. 'Home sweet home.'

'Jesus,' Tom says as he steps inside. 'This is positively third world.'

'Oh, come on, Tom.' Harper drops her duffle bag on one of the beds. 'You like to show how down to earth you are compared to your family. This' – she holds his arms up, encompassing the room – '*this* is down to earth.'

'This is slumming it, Harper. Unnecessarily.' He sits on the bed and tests the mattress with his hand. 'Oh my God,' he mutters, 'maybe I can get a Casper delivered here.'

'They say a firm mattress is great for your back.'

'What do they say about sharp metal springs stabbing you in the night?'

Harper ignores the question. 'You hungry? I'm starved.'

Tom shrugs without taking his eyes off his new bed. 'Sure.'

Harper orders a pizza. It's a small town, so the man on the phone knows Appleton Hall is abandoned.

'Is this another prank?'

'It's not a prank.'

'No one lives there.'

'I live here.'

'You have to meet us outside.'

'When are you coming?'

'Under forty minutes.'

'You want me to stand outside for forty minutes?'
'Yes.'
'Fine.'
'You'll be outside?'
'Sure.'

Harper hangs up and flops down onto one of the beds.

'You're not going down?' Tom asks.

Harper fishes the tablet out of her duffle bag. 'The cameras Foster set up have sensors. The one downstairs should trigger when the pizza guy gets here.'

Twenty minutes later, the tablet buzzes to life. Harper clicks on the app and sees, via the camera outside, a man in a green windbreaker standing out front, pizza in hand, unimpressed no one is there to meet him. Harper bounds down the stairs and is out front just as he is about to leave.

'I thought you said you'd be outside.'

'I'm here now.'

Back upstairs, Harper and Tom eat pepperoni pizza and continue their research. Tom reads Knox's book, *Raskolnikov and the Russian Revolution*. Harper watches YouTube videos on the tablet. On the right-hand side of the screen, the algorithm cues up the next video, each more extreme than the last. The first few detail how the Buchanans made billions selling opioids. Clips of the family living a lavish lifestyle are cut against images of the opioid epidemic, addicts in the streets, bodies in the morgue. Next, the algorithm takes her to clips of talking heads on cable news debating Mitch Buchanan's murder. Did he have it coming? Is there a Karma Killer copycat on the loose? Before long she's watching home-made videos about the murder of Skip Buchanan. The first few stick to the story Borelli tells in his book, more or less. Then the videos start to embellish, before becoming full-blown conspiracy theories. The Buchanans staged Skip's murder to save the family from going to jail; Knox was a prophet, sent by God, to bring justice to an immoral world.

Harper moans.

'What is it?' Tom asks.

'It's poison.'

'What is?'

'The internet. YouTube. I've been watching conspiracy bullshit for two hours and I'm starting to think it all makes sense. Have you had more luck?'

Tom had been lying down. He sits up, placing two feet on the floor. 'I've been reading Knox's book. Do you know who Raskolnikov is? He's the protagonist from *Crime and Punishment*. Raskolnikov is this poor student living in St Petersburg. He becomes mixed up with revolutionary ideas and convinces himself that great men can change history, that if he kills a greedy pawnbroker, it's morally acceptable. In Knox's book, he engages with Raskolnikov's idea of murder, how the ends can justify the means, and how it fits with the revolutionary fervour taking over Russia. If Knox didn't kill five people, it wouldn't be so obvious, but the seeds of his ideas' – he taps the book – 'it's right here.'

'What are you saying? The murder of Skip Buchanan wasn't about Knox's daughter?'

Tom shrugs. 'Forensic psychology isn't my speciality. But clearly he had ideas about murder long before his daughter died. And you can see his line of thought, how it developed over time, from his views on Revolutionary Russia to his mad ravings online, before he was arrested. The idea that evil acts can justify just outcomes.' Tom rummages in his bag and pulls out Borelli's book, *Killer of Killers*. 'Look. Read this.'

Harper reads the portion underlined in blue pen.

## CHAPTER 18: THE UTILITY OF MURDER

Knox was arrested on March 28, eight weeks after the Buchanan murders. Federal agents surrounded him in the parking lot of a local Walmart. He was forced to his knees, and then onto his chest. He was handcuffed and ushered into a waiting vehicle.

Later that afternoon, Federal agents raided his home. Forensics found little physical evidence tying Knox to the murders. He must have disposed of the clothes and shoes he wore that night. And whatever computer he'd used to draft the various online posts that some collectively refer to as his 'manifesto', *The Utility of Murder*, was also destroyed or disposed of well in advance.

A decision was made jointly, across the various law enforcement agencies involved and with the cooperation of the tech companies who controlled the sites Knox posted on, not to publish Knox's manifesto and to remove whatever remained online. The decision proved a prescient one. At the time, Knox had only a small but passionate cadre of online followers. No one could have predicted that Knox would become a sort of folk hero, for angry, disaffected, and powerless people across the country. It is for this reason alone, I am certain we made the right call not publishing the manifesto.

With that said, I recognise the counterargument. Some say Knox has benefited from his ideas living in the shadows because they have not had to bear the scrutiny of the light of day. By keeping him half-revealed, Knox has generated a mystique. It is for this reason that I have below reproduced portions of Knox's manifesto. My aim is to expose his horrible ideas. Like the Wizard of Oz, we must look behind the curtain and see there is nothing there but smoke and mirrors.

* * *

## THE UTILITY OF MURDER

1. Modernity has been a calamity for 'SOCIETY'. This truth is self-evident and expresses itself through the daily humiliations humanity must endure.

Harper stops reading. 'Sorry, Tom, I can't do it. Knox's manifesto, I mean. I can't read it. My brain will melt.'

Tom takes the book back. 'But it's right here. Listen.' He excitedly traces his finger along the page. 'He talks about the principle of "do no harm", and how it's become misunderstood. Knox wrote, "In the pre-industrial world, humanity was divided into tribes, and what was left unsaid – what was obvious then, and what the world forgets now – is that the principle of do no harm in fact meant do no harm to a member of your own tribe." Then he goes on to say that in order to do no harm to your own tribe, it's not only necessary but good to harm those who threaten your tribe.'

Tom looks at Harper. 'Don't you see – right there – he's justifying hurting others? Then he talks about utility. He wrote, "What matters is not one person's happiness, but the overall happiness of the universe. It is preferable for one person to suffer so a hundred do not." And then he says karma is the natural partner to utility. How people he called "Karmic Soldiers" could protect their tribe and from those who threaten it.'

Tom looks up from the book. 'Well? What do you think?'

'I think Borelli is a flake. It's not safe to publish Knox's thoughts, but here's a few titbits to help sell my book.'

'But what about Knox, his ideas?'

'What do you want me to say? Knox is clearly a loon. If any more insight is required, I think that's your department.'

Tom is disappointed but his phone rings before he can reply. He answers it. 'Hello. Oh! Hi Stacey . . . You did? Amazing.' Tom gives a thumbs up to Harper and starts writing down information. 'Thanks, Stacey. You're a lifesaver. I'll see you Thursday.'

Tom hangs up.

'Anything helpful?'

'It just gets stranger and stranger. According to Stacey, the numbered company that owns Knox's house, it's owned by Nelson Hamilton.'

'Who?'

'The Hamiltons – Nelson and his sister Abigail – they're rich. Old money. Something to do with steel and banks. Stacey gave me Nelson's address. It's about an hour's drive. We can go first thing tomorrow.'

Harper shakes her head. 'I don't know. Maybe you'd be safer here.'

'There is no way I'm staying in *this* abandoned building all day. It gives me the creeps. I'm coming with you. I won't get out of the car, I promise.'

# Day 99

'I'm day two hundred and seventy-six.'

Candles burn before a gold Buddha the size of a large cat. Incense perfumes the air with cinnamon and pine.

Thirteen bodies form a circle. Legs crossed, hands on knees, palms aimed at the ceiling. In unison, they say, 'Welcome day two hundred and seventy-six.'

The man next to Jess says, 'I'm day one hundred and ninety-two.'

'Welcome, day one hundred and ninety-two.'

When it's Jess's turn, she feels a nervous flutter in her chest. She forces her mouth open, hoping the words will come. 'I'm day ninety-nine.'

Lama Aaron's smile is resplendent. After the circle offers its collective welcome, Lama Aaron says, 'Congratulations on attending your first criticism circle before your hundredth day. That's quite the achievement.'

Pride wells up inside of Jess.

Alex is next. She pushes her shoulders back and announces, 'I'm day four thousand, five hundred and three.'

The circle nods enthusiastically. Everyone knows Alex has been with the Movement longer than most, but it's still impressive hearing it said aloud.

'Welcome all,' Aaron says. 'For those who are attending their first criticism circle – Day ninety-nine and Day one ninety-two – congratulations. Tonight will be a major step on your journey to becoming a better person, as we interrogate our past. Because we can only truly improve our karma and achieve the highest vibrations, if we are honest. *Brutally* honest.'

Aaron is wearing his favourite saffron-coloured T-shirt and matching jogging pants, the picture of casual enlightenment. The congregants, meanwhile, are dressed head-to-toe in black.

Aaron narrows his eyes and looks around the circle, making eye contact with as many as he can. 'Our novices are no doubt asking: why do we reject our given names in the criticism circle? Why are we named after the number of days since we were first introduced to the Movement? The answer is simple. We – humanity, that is – are constantly changing, like the water in a river. We are not static. We are a process, moving forwards. Who you are today is not who you were yesterday, or the day before. And so tonight we recognise change and reject stasis.'

As Aaron talks, Jess's eyes drift to Day 192, the other criticism circle rookie. Jess can't help but compare herself to him and feel a certain level of satisfaction that she's been with the Movement nearly half as long. Even Alex admitted she was jealous. 'Most people have to wait at least a hundred and fifty days, sometimes two hundred, before they get an invite.'

Jess is honoured, obviously. But she also deserves this. She's put in the time, she's done the work. She hasn't missed a single GME since meeting Alex; she's undergone two PMEs, fully committing the time and energy required; she's bought, read, and studied all of Aaron's books. (All this she's done at the expense of her Everly classes. She's so behind, she wonders if she'll ever catch up.) And so when Alex called and invited her to 'an exclusive but difficult night' at Aaron's, she was nervous, but she also thought: *I'm ready for this*.

Once Aaron concludes his opening remarks, he closes his eyes and takes a deep breath. When he finally opens his eyes, his face is a touch more serene. 'Let us begin.' He claps three times and then turns his small, dark eyes on Jess. 'Day ninety-nine, tell us what you're most ashamed of.'

The circle turns their collective attention to Jess. Their faces are cold and expressionless.

Jess didn't realise she was smiling until she feels it fizzle, like water hitting a hot stone. She looks to Alex for help. *Why didn't she warn me about this?* But Alex only stares blankly at Jess.

Lama Aaron is impatient. 'Day ninety-nine, do not look outward. Do not look at your friend. Look inward. You cannot purify your soul without being open, honest, and scathing about your past. There is no escaping what you've done. But we are here to help you, to hold you to account. Tell us what you are most ashamed of. Tell us now or leave the Movement forever.'

Every soul in the circle stares at Jess. Her cheeks are on fire. She feels sick. She wants to run away and hide. *But where would I go?*

'Don't you trust me, Jessica?' Aaron asks. 'Don't you trust the Movement?'

'Of course, I do. I just . . .'

'Then answer my question. What are you most ashamed of?'

Jess knows there's no escape. She has to answer the question. Without thinking it through, she says, 'My father never loved me.' Jess has never said these words to herself, let alone to a group of her friends. But it's true. 'He loved my brothers, but not me.'

Aaron frowns, disappointed. 'That is not something you should be ashamed of. That is a pall on your father's account, not yours.'

Warm tears start to slide down Jess's cheeks. 'I'm ashamed that I cared,' Jess says. 'I'm ashamed of the way I acted, to get his attention. I drank. I used drugs. I slept with people. I tried to hurt myself, to hurt him.'

'Good,' Aron says. 'Good.'

The man to Jess's immediate left – Day 525, a man Jess hardly knows – turns to her and says, 'You're pathetic.'

The woman sitting to Day 525's left says, 'You disgust me.'

Everyone in the circle takes a turn.

'You spoiled little bitch.'

'Slut.'

Even Day 192, who looked lost when they started, doesn't hesitate when it's his turn. 'You're a stupid little cunt.'

Jess starts to sob. When it's Alex's turn, Jess holds her breath.

'I don't blame your father,' Alex says. 'How could he love someone so pathetic?'

Jess can feel her world coming apart at the seams. She collapses to the carpet and moans.

Aaron sits beside Jess, opens his arms wide, and she falls into his embrace. She continues to cry. 'Well done, my little acolyte,' he whispers into Jess's ear. 'Well done.'

The circle waits as Jess recovers in Aaron's arms.

He eventually moves back to the middle of the circle and resumes the process. 'Day one ninety-two,' he says, 'tell me, what crimes have you committed?'

Jess can feel the circle's focus shift from her to Day 192. Her relief is immediate.

At first, Day 192 admits to speeding tickets. Aaron shakes his head, points at the door, and tells him to go. 'There is no point being here if you lack the bravery to hold yourself to account.'

Day 192 drops his head and stares at his lap. When he finally lifts his head, his pallor is white as chalk. 'I hit someone with my car. I was seventeen. It was summer. I'd been drinking, with friends.' He swallows, loudly. 'He was crossing the street in the middle of the night.' Day 192 looks around the circle for a sympathetic face, but doesn't find any. 'I kept driving. I don't know whether he lived or died.'

Every congregant in the circle takes their turn insulting him. When it's Jess's turn, she doesn't hesitate.

'Murderer.'

Once the criticism circle is complete, Meryl turns on the lights. The group looks as exhausted as Jess feels. They stand up and slowly start to make easy conversation, like they hadn't flung insults at each other for more than an hour.

Alex finds Jess and gives her a big hug. 'You did amazing.'

When Jess hears her friend's voice return to its usual pitch – to hear the icy, judgemental tone from earlier eradicated – relief washes over her.

'What was that?' Jess asks.

'That,' Alex says, pulling her in for another hug, '*that* was progress, all part of your journey to a newer, better you.'

Afterwards, they relax on Aaron's back porch, under a string of white lights and with Meryl's famous virgin margaritas in hand.

Jess feels as though a massive weight has been removed from her shoulders. She looks across the porch to the other rookie, Day 192. She nods in his direction and asks Alex, 'How do you think the other newbie did tonight?'

'Fine, I guess.' Her gaze narrows. 'You know who that is, right?'

'No, I haven't really seen him before.'

'That's Tara's dad.'

'Seriously?'

Alex must have heard something in Jess's voice, because she places her hand on Jess's shoulder. 'You can't feel guilty, Jess. OK? If she's going to make it, it's on her.'

Jess sighs. 'Maybe you're right.'

'Did you seriously not know Tara's dad?'

'No. Should I?'

Alex shrugs. 'He's a professor at Everly, so I figured you knew him.'

'Honestly, no. I don't think so. What's his name?'

'I always forget his first name. I just know him as Professor Knox.'

# 48

Harper is racing along the quay. Sweat drenches her back and forehead. Humidity fills her lungs. She's running–sprinting for her life. Stop, even for a second, and she's dead.

She looks down at her hands. She's holding a gun. A Glock maybe, though it's hard to tell. It's so heavy she can barely lift it. It hangs at her side like she's running with a twenty-pound dumbbell.

She reaches the end of the quay. Ten-foot waves are smashing against the cement. A man is standing there, with his eyes closed and his arms tied behind his back. He's on his knees.

The gun grows heavier. Then it spasms, trying to escape Harper's grip, like a fish out of water.

Somewhere a child is screaming. The sound starts in the distance, but it slowly builds and mutates into a deafening mechanical screech, drowning out the smashing waves.

The man opens his eyes. Each is a vivid lime green – not just the irises, but the entire eyeball.

'Who's there?'

Harper raises the gun and presses it against the man's left temple.

'Who's there?' the man asks again.

She pulls the trigger.

Harper sits up in bed gasping for air, covered in a cold sweat. She looks around the room to get her bearings. Tom is asleep in the neighbouring bed, lost under a heap of blankets. She goes to the washroom down the hall and splashes cold water on her face. She closes her eyes and takes a series of regimented breaths, counting each inhale and each exhale, until she reaches ten.

Back in the room, knowing she can't go back to sleep – not yet, anyway – she turns on the bedside lamp, warms up her vape, unlocks the tablet, taps the YouTube app, and resumes her descent down the rabbit hole.

She starts with a clip from CNN. A guest informs the very tanned host that Mitch Buchanan, as horrible as his murder was, had it coming. 'It's the settlement the family made with the government. A fine! A fraction of their net worth! Again, no one is condoning murder. But when you're so rich you can negotiate yourself out of any real penalty, if your connections let you escape repercussions . . . well, you can understand why someone felt the need to take justice into their own hands.'

Harper watches whatever the algorithm suggests, video after video. She wonders if this is how it happens, how one becomes indoctrinated or a conspiracy theorist. She'd always thought it happened to a certain type of person, those who lacked the necessary brain cells to think for themselves. But as her mind turns to mush, she wonders if it's simply prolonged exposure. Maybe stupidity is like radiation: it wins out in the end.

Eventually, in the queue, there's an instructional video on administering Narcan – a term Harper's all too familiar with. She wasn't there the first time Derrick overdosed. But her grandfather told her what happened, how the EMTs saved Derrick's life.

Curious, she clicks on the video. It starts with a nurse explaining what an opioid does to the body, how it reduces, on a cellular level, the body's drive to breathe. An animated video shows an opioid invading the bloodstream, cordoning off certain cells, before Narcan, like a peacekeeper, enters the fray and contains the opioid, letting the body breathe again. The animation ends and the nurse demonstrates how to administer Narcan. Her volunteer, pretending to be overdosing, lies on his back. The nurse removes a canister the size of a credit card from its plastic packaging, peeling back a thin layer of foil, inserts the nozzle of the canister into the man's nose, and, with her thumb, pushes the plunger up into the canister.

Harper had always pictured Narcan as a needle, something massive and industrial, like the one Eric Stoltz slammed into Uma Thurman's chest in *Pulp Fiction*. She's surprised how innocuous Narcan is, like something you'd use for a common cold.

The video ends with the nurse imploring anyone and everyone to have Narcan close at hand. 'This tiny little miracle can save a life.'

On a whim, Harper Googles 'Pharmacy near me'. The closest is a seven-minute drive away.

*What's the downside?* she asks herself. *If Tom gets injected with an opioid, it could save his life.*

She dresses and leaves quietly, making sure not to wake Tom, locking the door behind her. At this time of night, there's not a soul out on the road. The drive is less than the predicted seven minutes.

The twenty-four-hour pharmacy's powerful fluorescent lights glow like an alien ship in the night. Inside, the aisles are empty. 'Candle in the Wind' is playing over the speakers. Harper walks to the back counter and finds the pharmacist.

'Can I help you?'

'Do you sell Narcan?'

# 49

In the morning, on the road, Tom runs through what he'd found on the Hamiltons. 'Their great grandfather made his money manufacturing steel. Their grandfather took that money and invested in a little bank in Manhattan, which they eventually renamed Hamilton Bank.'

'Right,' Harper says. 'That's why their name is familiar.'

'From what I can tell,' Tom says, 'Nelson and Abigail don't have much to do with the family business. They're your standard rich, Connecticut socialites. To be honest, I'm surprised I don't know them. Online, there's pictures of them attending the Met Gala and premieres of documentaries they produced. But the last two years or so, they've kept a low profile.'

Tom holds up the tablet and Harper chances a quick look away from the road. On the screen is a picture of red-headed siblings. They're standing arm-in-arm on a red carpet.

'Any connection to Knox?' Harper asks.

'Not that I could find.'

'Why would Knox give his home to a Connecticut socialite like Nelson Hamilton?'

'I don't know. Do you think Nelson will tell us?'

Harper smiles. 'No. But there's no harm in asking.'

The president of 976451 Delaware Corp. lives twenty-one miles northeast of Everly College. The ink-black asphalt driveway snakes its way up a hill, past a barn doubling as a luxury car garage. As they drive past, Harper spots an Aston Martin inside, sunlight glinting off the silver paint. On the crest of the hill, there's a redbrick home in the style of an English manor.

As Harper slows the Escalade to a stop, the double front doors open and a man the size of a house steps outside. He walks onto the driveway and then waits patiently with his hands behind his back.

'If he can see me,' Tom says, 'is there any point in me staying in the car?'

Harper shakes her head. 'No, there's not.'

They step out of the car and walk towards the giant. Movement in the second storey of the house catches Harper's eye. She looks up just in time to see a curtain drawn closed.

'Hello,' Harper says. 'Is Mr or Mrs Hamilton home?'

'Are you expected?'

'We'd just like to ask them a few questions.'

The giant presses a Bluetooth headset with his index finger as he listens to instructions. Then he says: 'Identification?'

Harper already regrets how they did this. *We should have done more recon. We should have known this was going to happen, and been prepared for it.*

Tom, however, doesn't share Harper's concern. He takes his driver's licence out of his wallet and hands it to the giant. Harper reluctantly does the same.

The giant takes photos of both IDs using his phone, texts them to someone, waits, and then says, 'OK. Follow me.'

He walks them around the house. In the back yard, there is a long, rectangular swimming pool and tennis court, hemmed in by a chain-link fence. Two men are on the court, rallying.

As they get closer, Harper recognises Nelson Hamilton as the redheaded man playing tennis. The other looks like a tennis pro, with his tan and crisp tennis whites.

Harper and Tom follow their guide to the chain-link fence. Nelson keeps rallying, without acknowledging their arrival. His aim is good – he can pick the corners with some regularity – but he lacks power. The rally ends when Nelson finally hits the net. The pro lavishes praise on his pupil, but Nelson's attention is now on Harper and Tom. He hands his racket to the pro, 'Thank you, Jonny.'

The pro starts collecting the balls and Nelson walks towards his guests, dabbing his brow with a towel. 'It's not often I receive visitors unannounced.'

There's something about his manner – his ease, his arrogance – that Harper finds grating.

'We're here to ask you about the Karma Killer,' Tom blurts out.

Nelson barely reacts. His smile is subtle, a slight curl on the left side of his mouth. He waves his hand at the table beside the pool. 'Shall we sit?'

# 50

Nelson takes his breakfast by the pool. A poached egg, toast, a carafe of coffee, and the print edition of *The New York Times* – all literally delivered on a silver platter. He offers his guests coffee. They accept.

The giant stands on the back deck, arms behind his back, watching the new arrivals intently.

'Now where were we?' Nelson breaks the yolk of an egg. Yellow liquid leaks like an oil spill across his plate. 'I believe you'd asked me about Professor Knox.'

Harper and Tom nod in unison.

Nelson saws off a square of multigrain bread, dips it in yolk, and brings it to his lips. 'Well, I'm happy to answer your questions, but perhaps you can tell me a bit about yourselves and *why* exactly you want to know about Professor Knox? You don't strike me as reporters. And if you are not reporters, then who are you?'

Tom says, 'My last name is Park, but my mother's maiden name is Buchanan.'

'Ah,' Nelson says, as he saws at his toast. 'My condolences. But surely Professor Knox's actions have been explained – as much as any murder can be explained? Mr Borelli's book was quite thorough. I have a copy myself.'

'All that detail,' Tom says, 'yet he didn't write about you, or about Knox giving you his home.'

'Is it not in the book? Of course, Mr Borelli knew about me. And about the house. I spoke to him on several occasions. And the FBI.'

'If it's public knowledge, then you won't mind explaining it to us?' Tom asks.

'Of course.' Nelson stirs milk into his coffee before taking a sip. 'My sister, Abby, struggles with drug addiction. Opiates. Unless you've had someone in your family suffer from this disease, it's difficult to describe how dark and brutal the addiction is, for the user and their family.' He shakes his head. 'There was a meditation group in town. It offered help to those struggling with addiction, and their families. I brought my sister to the group as a last resort. Professor Knox and his daughter were members of the group as well.'

'What was the name of the group?' Tom asks.

Nelson laughs. 'It didn't lack for names. They were always rebranding. When Abby and I started attending classes, it was called Revive. Later, it was called the Movement. Now? . . . I'm not sure. I haven't been involved for some time.'

'What did the group do?'

'It wasn't very complicated. They offered meditation sessions and, more importantly, a support network.'

'Did it help your sister?' Harper asks.

'With her addiction? Yes. Very much so.'

'How were you introduced to Knox?'

'There were social events. Barbeques, picnics. We had a few here, in fact. I was friendly with Knox. We all were.'

'So friendly he gave you a home?' Harper asks.

'It was not a gift. After his daughter died, he quit his job. He had no income and little savings. He knew of our family's wealth. He asked Abby for a loan. And then another. And then another. Abby is very trusting, you see. She didn't see that Professor Knox was taking advantage of her. By the time I found out about the loans, Will's debt was more than two hundred thousand dollars.'

'What was the money for?' Tom asks.

'Will told me it was for gambling debts, which made sense. He was very self-destructive after his daughter died. Before he focused his rage outwards.'

'Sorry,' Harper says, 'how exactly was the house connected to his gambling debts?'

'Once I found out how much Abby had given to Knox, I was . . . frustrated. I intervened and Knox agreed to sign his home over to me, to satisfy the debt.'

'Is your sister here?' Tom asks. 'Could we speak to her?'

Nelson shakes his head. 'No. She's overseas.'

Harper thinks of the movement she saw in the second-floor window when they arrived.

'Any idea why Borelli didn't mention this meditation group in his book?' Harper asks.

Nelson shrugs. 'You'll have to ask Mr Borelli.' He checks his watch. Diamonds catch the sun. 'Now, if that satisfies your curiosity, I have a morning I would like to resume.'

On the car ride back to town, the odd drop of rain splatters on the windshield.

Tom asks, 'What did you make of Nelson Hamilton?'

'Nothing fazed him,' Harper says. 'You brought up Knox's name out of the blue and he just smiled. And he's shrewd.'

'What does that mean?'

'I don't know. The whole conversation felt . . . calculated.'

'You think he's covering something up?'

Harper shrugs.

Tom stares out the passenger window. 'Did you buy what he said, that the FBI knew about the house? Did Agent Diaz?'

'I don't know,' Harper says. 'Let's ask him.'

# Day 266

'Why are you reluctant?'

A cold February wind whistles through bare branches overhead.

'I'm not.'

'No?'

'No, I just ...' Jess keeps her eyes on the icy road. 'I just think it makes sense to wait until summer. After the semester ends.'

Aaron's parka is bright orange, deer hunter meets Buddhist monk. 'The semester? Hadn't we agreed you should pause your studies for now?'

The wind picks up. Jess retreats into the collar of her parka. 'Right,' she says. 'That's true.'

It's after midnight. The residential street is abandoned. An hour earlier, they set out on one of Aaron's legendary midnight walks, which normally involve Aaron opining on life, philosophy, religion, how to live the good life.

Aaron texted Jess earlier that evening with the invite. They met on Aaron's front porch and Aaron handed Jess a Yeti travel mug filled with hot chocolate. They trudged down his driveway and into the great unknown of his subdivision.

'I wonder, Jessica, what's pulling you back to Everly College?'

'What do you mean?'

'You seem drawn to the place that has only caused you pain. During your PMEs,' Aaron says, referring to a Personal Meditation Experience, a one-on-one guided meditation with

Aaron. 'I've tried to address this trauma. And you've steered away from it.'

'I–I just don't like talking about it.'

Aaron sighs and sips his hot chocolate. 'Do you want to know my theory? You think that if you're still at school, attending classes, then you don't have to treat the trauma. If time doesn't move forwards, you don't have to look backwards. Is that right?'

'I don't know.'

'Jessica, you can't even say it aloud. Can you?'

Jess shakes her head.

'Yes you can, Jessica. I know you can.' Aaron nods at a park bench and they take a seat. 'Close your eyes,' he says.

Jess closes her eyes.

'Take a deep breath. In through your nose, out through your mouth.'

Jess breathes deeply.

'Now tell me what happened.'

'It started with my roommate.'

'Yes. Tell me about that.'

'Her name was Brooklynn. Like the borough, but with an extra "N". I should have known something was off the first day I met her. Mom drove me. (Dad was too busy with work, obviously.) When we came into the room, Brooklynn was already there, at her desk. I was excited. I walked over, put out my hand, introduced myself and she sneered – *literally* sneered – and didn't shake my hand. We hung out with kids on our floor for the first few weeks of school, and she seemed OK. But you can tell a lot about a person when you first meet them. Like you always say, you can sense a person's vibrations, if you focus hard enough.'

Aaron nods, as if Jess received extra points for quoting him.

'There was a boy on the floor named Emilio that I was ... with. And I think that made Brooklynn jealous. If you ask me, that's why she did what she did.'

'And what did she do?'

Jess sighs. 'We had this mandatory sensitivity training on our floor. It was mainly about microaggressions. Do you know that term?'

Aaron gives no indication one way or another.

'The presenters said microaggressions were acts, however small, that "convey hostile or prejudicial intent". Something like that. They said microaggressions could be intentional or unintentional. It didn't matter whether you meant to hurt someone else or not. They asked us to talk about microaggressions we felt that we'd been experiencing. Right away, like she'd been waiting for the opportunity, Brooklynn put up her hand. She said she had a problem with my tattoos. Specifically, the one on my left forearm. You've seen the one, right? The image of a raven. It was my first tattoo. I got it when I was sixteen. The Harry Potter books had meant a lot to me. I could relate, you know, with his adoptive family not wanting him and all.'

Jess pauses a moment, half expecting Aaron to say 'how juvenile', or something like that. But he doesn't. He looks at Jess, waiting for her to continue.

'When I decided to get a tattoo, those books were the first thing I thought of. It's stupid, I know. But, like I said, those books meant a lot to me. I always thought of myself as a member of Ravenclaw. In the books, the wizard school, Hogwarts, was divided into houses. Ravenclaw valued wit and intelligence above all else. I would read the books as a kid and think, "That's where I'd be. Ravenclaw." I printed a picture from a fan site, of a raven, and brought it to the tattoo parlour.

'So, anyway, I'm at Everly College, living in residence. Brooklynn never mentioned the tattoo – not until she put her hand up during the sensitivity training. She told the meeting – a room full of my friends and floormates – that, to her, the tattoo was representative of Nazi imagery. She wasn't Jewish herself, but she said she had a lot of Jewish friends, and she found my tattoo incredibly painful and offensive. She said the tattoo was a violent act, aimed at her, even though I got it years before we met. You should have seen the faces change of everyone who was there. It was like a switch was flicked. One minute they were my friends; the next, they hated me. I tried to explain *why* I had the tattoo, to defend myself, but the presenters said that it didn't matter what the tattoo meant to me. What mattered was how it made Brooklynn feel.'

'What happened after that?' Aaron asks.

'For weeks, I was bullied. I was called a racist and a Neo-Nazi. I had a whiteboard on the door to my room and people would leave mean messages for me. "Why don't you kill yourself?" Stuff like that. The whole floor blocked me from our Facebook group. Brooklynn posted Instagram stories where she'd cry about how painful it was living with an anti-Semite. She loved the attention, the chance to be a victim. She's pretty and her parents are super wealthy, so this was her big chance to be the underdog. The school's administration held like a mini-trial about my "consistent microaggressions" against my roommate. They found that I'd been insensitive in my behaviour. And that I had flaunted Nazi imagery. Like I should have torn off my own skin rather than offend some rich, private school bitch from Manhattan. I was forced to move out, to an apartment off campus. The school newspaper made fun of my defence. No one believed that I had a tattoo based on Harry Potter. The paper called me Hermione Goebbels. Hermione for the character from Harry Potter, and

Goebbels for Hitler's chief propagandist. I was devastated. I stopped going to class and I started doing more drugs.'

Jess is crying now. The memory of those first few months at school is once again as raw and painful as it was when it happened.

'I'd always kept my drug use pretty PG. Weed, coke occasionally. I'd tried Oxy only a few times. But after the trial, I was so depressed and fucked up, I started doing a lot of Oxy. One day, my dealer was out, but he had fentanyl.' Jess wipes her nose on the sleeve of her parka. 'I ended up in the hospital. And that's when I met Alex. And you know the rest.'

Aaron stares off into the subdivision, his head bowed as if in prayer. Finally, he says, 'So, your friends and school accused you of being a neo-Nazi? Are you?'

'No.'

'No. Of course you aren't.' He smiles. 'Now tell me this, Jessica: why do you want to remain somewhere that made up lies about you, that's caused you so much pain?'

'I don't know.'

Aaron stands up and starts to walk again. Jess follows, snow crunching underfoot.

'You're special, Jessica,' Aaron says. 'I knew it the moment we met. Do you remember? I was walking to the stage at the GME, and this presence called out to me. I could feel vibrations speaking to me on a new, unique frequency.'

Jess smiles at the memory. 'You touched me on the shoulder. You thanked me for coming.'

'Do you think I do that for every new arrival?'

Jess shakes her head. 'No.'

'Ah, she finally concedes a point.'

Jess laughs.

'My little acolyte, you don't see how extraordinary you are, or that you're destined for greatness. But you will.'

'Thank you.'

'Don't thank me. Greatness comes at a cost. One that you must be willing to pay. Remember: there is no progress without pain.'

Jess nods. 'I think I understand.'

'And we can't leave it all to fate. When opportunity comes, we have to take it. The universe offers you a path forwards only so many times. Do you understand what I mean?'

'I think so.'

A cold wind howls.

'You'll keep your ears open? Do you promise?'

'I promise.'

Aaron smiles. 'That's all that I ask.'

# 51

Lou takes a deep breath. *Play it cool*, he thinks. *There's no point getting angry.*

But he's already angry. Very angry. Murderous, in fact. He wants to scream. He wants to punch Frank on his fat chin. Frank has a terrible temper, though. If Lou goes in ready for a fight, Frank will oblige. *Better to be methodical, impassionate.* And anyway, Lou isn't certain Frank lied.

But there's no other explanation.

The floor of the Manhattan office is nearly empty at this hour. Frank is at his desk. Dinosaur that he is, he's reading a hard copy of the *Post*.

'Morning, Lou,' Frank says without looking up from the paper.

Lou sits at the neighbouring desk and stares at his partner's jowls and receding hairline. The face that used to make Lou smile, now fills him with revulsion.

Last night, against his better judgement, Lou met Harper and Tom Park for a drink at a pub near campus. They'd called that afternoon, saying they had important information. It was testament to how little Lou had to go on, how desperate he was for new information, that he said yes. He didn't realise their 'important news' didn't involve the recent and unsolved murders he was investigating, but the case he closed and ended with a conviction. At first, Lou protested. 'You dragged me out here to talk about the Knox case?' But once they started, Lou wanted to hear it to the end.

'So, Frank,' Lou says, 'tell me if you've heard this.'

Frank doesn't bother to look up from the paper. 'Sure.'

'Six months before the Karma Killer murdered seven people in cold blood, he gave his home to Nelson Hamilton, son of Stuart M. Hamilton, banking magnate.'

Frank stiffens like a corpse. He looks up but can't quite bring himself to meet Lou's eyes. 'What are you talking about?'

'Don't tell me this is news to you, Frank. You looked into Knox's house, back when we were making the case. And you told me there was nothing there. So that means you're either dumb as rocks or you lied.'

'Honestly, Lou . . . I . . .'

Lou drops a copy of the deed Harper gave him onto Frank's desk. Two names are highlighted in bright yellow: William Thomas Knox and Hamilton's numbered company.

'Did Borelli know?'

Frank runs his fat fingers through his thinning hair. 'Yeah. He knew.'

'You know what the worst part of being lied to is? Having two civilians tell me the truth, like I'm a fucking idiot. On the bright side, I probably didn't perjure myself. Hard to perjure yourself if you've been lied to. But it's a shitty consolation on an overall shitty day. Don't you think?'

'Listen, Lou, I get that you're mad but—'

'What is it, Frank? What could possibly explain you lying to me?'

'I was under orders, OK?'

'Orders? From whom?'

Frank looks around to make sure no one is listening. 'I'm not supposed to tell you. It's nothing personal. You think I liked lying to you? But it's not related to the Knox case. It's . . .' He looks around one more time and lowers his voice. 'Abigail Hamilton has had some . . . issues. The director and Borelli didn't see any need to drag her into this.'

'What do you mean, *issues*?'

'She's an addict. Opiates. Heroin. She went missing a few years back.'

'Since when do we care about someone's drug problems? How does that change our investigation?'

'Her family . . . they're big political donors. They've written a lot of cheques to a lot of powerful people. Borelli didn't want to rock the boat. And you know the director – his political ambitions aren't exactly a big secret. I think Nelson, Abigail's brother – he called Borelli. Asked him for a favour.'

Lou is shaking his head. 'And what? Everyone decided to keep me out of it?'

'No offence, Lou, you're a great agent, but you're not exactly a team player. The director didn't want the Hamiltons involved. He thought it cleaner just to keep you out of it.'

Lou is about to lay into his partner, but stops. *What's the point?* He stands up and starts to walk away. Frank grabs his arm.

'I know you're mad, Lou, but this had nothing to do with Knox.'

'We didn't do our jobs.'

'We got the conviction,' Frank says. 'That's what we're supposed to do. *That's* our job. Who gives a shit if we cut corners to get a conviction?'

Lou stares at Frank's hand until he lets go of Lou's arm. Then he walks away.

'Let it go, Lou,' Frank calls after him. 'Don't piss off the wrong people!'

## 52

Harper is vaping, staring out the window, watching a group of students on the field below. They're being led through an early morning workout, which, to Harper, seems like one burpee after the next. Tom is in the other bed, sound asleep.

Harper barely slept – an hour or two tops. Since Foster was killed, the nights have been hard and are getting worse. She'd never admit it to Tom, but the stress of the job is getting to her.

When she'd agreed to work for Tom after Mitch's murder, he'd seemed inconsequential compared to Mitch. It made sense someone wanted to kill Mitch. He was unapologetic for the harm he'd caused. He was caustic, mean, a bully. Tom, on the other hand, was a charming PhD student. He wasn't even employed by Apollo Pharma. Harper – whether consciously or unconsciously – didn't think the task of protecting Tom would be the same as protecting Mitch. Not a cakewalk, but easier. Even when Tom was doxed the first time in New York, it seemed like something she could handle. But there's been a relentless focus on Tom, a building momentum. Harper can feel it.

Most nights, rather than sleep, she opts for her vape and staring out the window, hoping to spot whatever might be coming. It's only a taste, though, just a few puffs to turn the valve and release the pressure. It's a necessary compromise. The stress would be unbearable otherwise.

Harper's train of thought is interrupted by a buzzing sound. She gropes the floor, sifting through rumpled clothes, until her hand lands on the tablet. She picks it up and sees the security app was triggered. She thinks of the man in the balaclava outside Tom's home and her heart rate accelerates. She doesn't start to relax until she opens the app and sees Agent Diaz standing outside of Appleton Hall. He's typing a text on his phone. Harper receives the end product moments later.

It's Lou. I'm outside. Meet me at the front door.

Harper is surprised to see Lou. Last night, they'd met him at a bar, ordered beers, and laid out everything they'd learned about the Hamiltons and Knox's home. Lou didn't say (a) you're crazy or (b) I already knew all that. He just stood up and left. He looked angry – that was obvious. But it wasn't exactly clear why or at whom.

Tom turned to Harper and asked, 'Did he have no idea?'

Harper shrugged. 'Maybe not.'

Harper throws on jeans and meets Lou outside. It's raining lightly. Lou is waiting under the overhang of the building.

'The school doesn't mind you staying here?' Lou asks. 'Aren't the rooms filled with students?'

Harper leans against the half-open steel door. 'It's empty. They're tearing it down next spring, apparently.'

'Uh-huh.' Lou looks like he's about to ask more questions but decides against it.

'A bit early for a drop-in,' Harper says.

'You won't mind. Trust me.'

'Yeah?'

'You were right,' Lou says. 'About Nelson Hamilton.'

Harper wants to ask, 'Who's the amateur now?' but thinks better of it.

'I didn't know, but people I worked with did.'

That's the extent of Lou's explanation. Harper wonders if she'll ever know more.

'After we talked,' Lou says, 'I did some digging.'

Lou hands Harper a manila folder. Inside, there's a photo of a short, chubby man, with little dark eyes, wearing an orange prison jumpsuit.

'Who's this?' Harper asks.

'Abigail Hamilton's guru. He's had several aliases over the years. These days, he goes by Lama Aaron. His real name is Brent Coughlin. He's from North Carolina.'

Harper flips to another photo, a younger version of Aaron. He's wearing a pinstripe suit and tie. The collar on his button-down shirt is a touch too big.

'He was – or claimed to be – some math whiz,' Lou says. 'He dropped out of MIT in the Nineties to start a pyramid scheme where housewives sold stock options. He was charged with fraud and spent two years in federal custody. After that, he started peddling a new-age healing schtick. He was arrested again, at the start of this year. One of his followers is seventeen. Her parents accused him of statutory rape. But there was a lack of evidence – the girl refused to testify – so the charges were dropped and he was released.'

'So . . . he's . . . ?'

Lou shrugs. 'A con artist, a criminal, worse.'

'Are you sure? Nelson Hamilton didn't seem like the type to get beguiled by a con artist.'

'Being rich doesn't make you impervious to manipulation.'

Harper flips through the file. The last page is an aerial view of a property, with one large building to the east, and dozens of smaller buildings to the west. 'What's this?'

'Another property the Nelsons own. You have to penetrate a web of dummy corporations, but they bankrolled this and other real estate investments for the Movement, Coughlin's meditation group. That big building there was once a hockey arena. Abigail bought it and neighbouring land five years ago.

It's about an hour's drive outside of town. I figure this is the best place to start.'

'Start what?'

'Listen, you were right. With Knox there were loose ends. So why don't you dig some more and see if those loose ends are connected to Mitch's murder?'

'You didn't want to make this trip yourself?' Harper asks.

'I can't.'

'Why?'

'I've got something else I need to do. This conversation never happened. OK? I was never here. I'm going against protocol and my better judgement. But I trusted Charles, and Charles trusted you. So I'm going out on a limb here.'

'You sure you don't want to come with?'

'I can't. I've got someone I have to talk to.'

# 53

Harper is lying on the forest floor. Paper-thin leaves crunch under her weight. She raises the binoculars to her eyes and glasses the compound. She adjusts the dial counter clockwise and the image clarifies into dozens of buildings. They'd parked a mile up the road and approached through the woods, but all of their precaution seems pointless now.

'It's abandoned?' Tom asks.

Harper hands the binoculars to Tom. 'Looks like it.'

Tom glasses the compound. 'Strange.'

'Shall we take a look?'

They move slowly through the woods, just in case they're wrong. But once they're walking the grounds, it's so obviously devoid of human life, they move quickly, from building to building, most of which are unlocked. The first is an office – or what's left of one. Empty filing cabinets, barren desks and little else. The next two buildings are living quarters, obvious from the stripped bunk beds and empty chests of drawers. They find one building that's locked. They peek inside through a window. There are stairs into a basement or bunker.

'Think they're down there?' Harper asks. 'Waiting for the Apocalypse?'

Tom gives her a look. 'Nothing would surprise me right now.'

In another building, there are long tables, with random computer cords strewn about, and the odd monitor, but no hard drives. In the corner is a shelving unit on wheels that Harper recognises as once housing a server, but is empty now.

Outside they follow the dirt path past the buildings and into the forest, for a hundred yards or so, and then into a clearing. There's a wooden stage and benches where an audience would sit. Harper and Tom walk down the aisle. Harper steps onto the stage and stares out at the invisible audience. She squints, furrowing her brow. 'Did they put on plays or something?'

Tom finds a firepit to the side of the stage. They walk closer and find a cast-iron cauldron with a metal rod inside. Harper picks up the rod and examines the symbol fashioned on the end.

'Are these cattle brands?' Tom asks.

'I don't have a clue.'

Harper clears forest debris and makes a clear flat surface in the dirt. She dips the brand in a nearby puddle of water, presses it into the dirt, and pulls it away. What's left is a familiar image.

'What's that?' Tom asks.

'I don't know,' Harper says. 'But I've seen it before.'

# 54

The correctional facility is a lifeless building, devoid of hope, comprised of concrete, thick windowless walls, topped by spiralling barbed wire. Lou parks his Ford Taurus in the visitor parking lot and checks his phone. The hospital is supposed to update him immediately if there is any change to Charles's condition, good or bad.

No messages. Which means he's still alive, but still in a coma. Which means the state of excruciating paralysis continues.

Lou was reluctant to drive across the state. He didn't want to be on the other side of Connecticut if something happened to Charles. Especially if he took a turn for the worse.

Lou would never admit it, but it's been hard to focus on his job while worrying about Charles.

*Is this why I'm helping Harper Scott? I'm not thinking clearly?*

Possibly. The love of your life lying in a coma will make you do some strange shit. Plus, the revelation that his partner lied repeatedly during an investigation hasn't helped. It's made Lou second-guess everything that's happened.

And then there's Borelli. He used the Knox trial to get where he wanted to go. He didn't want to rock the boat by dragging the Hamiltons into the case. And he wanted the simplest case possible because he wanted to win. He stuck his head in the ground and prosecuted the narrative that gave him the path of least resistance. *What other corners did he cut? What evidence did he purposely keep from the judge and jury?*

At the security gates, Lou trades his gun in for a visitor's badge and a guard escorts him inside. The hallway is broken up by a series of security doors, a buzzer sounding before each one opens.

'Is the film crew interviewing you as well?' the guard asks as they walk down the hallway.

'Film crew?'

'The documentary. Netflix, I hear.'

'You're shitting me.'

'It's true. They've been in here a lot, filming the outside. We won't let them inside, but they call Knox and interview him on the phone.'

*The last thing Knox needs*, Harper thinks, *is more media attention.*

The guard takes Lou into the warden's office. He's eating a bacon and egg sandwich, grease glistening on his thick moustache. He doesn't stand up or offer his hand. He starts with a complaint. 'You didn't give me much notice, you know.'

'I'm only here to gather information.'

'Information about what?' The warden takes a massive bite of his sandwich and egg drips down his chin and onto his beer belly. He chews with his mouth open. 'Your email had little information to offer.'

'Does he have internet access?'

'Who? Knox? Absolutely not.'

'So you're certain there's no way he's online?'

'Not a chance.'

'I'm going to need access to your system so my colleague can double-check.'

'Is he here?'

'No. It can all be done remotely. And when I meet with Mr Knox, I want his room searched. Thoroughly.'

The warden shrugs. 'We'll search, if you really want. But I can tell you right now what we'll find. A big fat nada.'

## 55

A slab of three-inch plastic divides the visitor room in two. The concrete walls have been painted white.

Lou sits and places his pad of paper and pen on the concrete desk.

The guard asks, 'All good?'

Lou gives a thumbs up and the door on the other side of the partition opens. A guard briefly fills the space before stepping aside. Then the Karma Killer – hobbled with shackles – shuffles into the room. His beard is long, and unkempt. His eyes are as striking as ever, icicle blue, with a vacant expression, unable, or unwilling, to focus on the world before him. Knox sits. The guard tethers him to the concrete desk.

'Mr Knox, I'm Special Agent Diaz. Do you remember me?'

Knox stares over Lou's shoulder.

'How are they treating you here?'

Knox doesn't answer.

'If there is something you need, I'm sure I could arrange it.'

Knox keeps staring over Lou's shoulder.

'I'm here because I'd like to ask you about something.' After Knox's vacant expression doesn't change, Lou adds, 'Something that happened before you murdered Skip Buchanan.'

Knox finally focuses his eyes on Lou. 'I didn't murder anyone.'

'You confessed.'

'Untrue. I said Skip Buchanan deserved to die. You know that. You were there.'

*He's right*, Lou thinks. *At the time, I thought that was as good as a confession. But now?*

When Lou had first interviewed Knox, Knox had been on leave from the university for months. To make ends meet, he'd taken a job as a delivery driver for Hugonecs Inc., a company that delivered online orders across Connecticut. His phone was one of more than a hundred and sixty that had accessed the cellular network via a nearby cell tower on the night of the murders. Because Knox was a delivery driver, Lou had assumed he'd have good reason to be in the area. It was supposed to be a quick interview. A box they checked before moving on to the next name on the list.

Lou attended the Hugonecs warehouse with Deputy McClellan, from the sheriff's department, and Borelli. It was a Monday. They'd cleared the meeting with Knox's employer first and the shift manager let them use his office. They all sat, except for Deputy McClellan, who slowly paced from one corner of the office to the other. It was Lou who questioned Knox.

'Mr Knox, where were you the night of November 21st?'

'I don't recall.'

'Were you working?'

'I don't recall.'

'Do you know Skip Buchanan?'

'I know who he was. Yes.'

'Well, who was he?'

'He was a murderer.'

The interview had been routine up to this point. But when Knox made this statement – coolly, without emotion – Lou sat up with a start. Deputy McClellan stopped pacing. Borelli leaned forwards. And they were silent for a moment, letting Knox's statement sink in. Lou carefully pressed on, trying to draw him out.

'Who did Skip Buchanan murder?'

'The innocent.'

'How did he do that?'

'The *how* does not matter. It's a distraction. It is the *why* that's important.'

'All right. *Why* did he murder the innocent?'

'For profit. For status.'

'And is this why he was murdered?'

'His death had utility. He deserved to die.'

'Sure, William. I think I understand what you're trying to tell me. Did you kill Skip Buchanan?'

Knox suddenly stood up and ended the interview. Deputy McClellan began to reach for his firearm, presumably to place Knox under arrest. Lou signalled for him to stop. What Knox had told them was odd, chilling, and certainly suspicious. However, it was not sufficient grounds for arrest. That would come later.

Now Lou says, 'Maybe you didn't confess. But a jury of your peers convicted you on charges of murder, based on overwhelming evidence.'

Knox doesn't answer.

'Why did you give your house to Nelson Hamilton?'

Knox looks at Lou with a different expression than before, with a clarity he'd lacked. It doesn't last long, but Lou's certain he's seen it.

'Don't you want to ask me about Mitch Buchanan's murder? Maybe I know something about that?'

Lou fights the urge to curse. *Prisons are sieves*, he thinks. Cigarettes, drugs, information – it all flows through prison walls with little resistance. He was hoping to catch Knox off guard, but he clearly knows what happened to Mitch Buchanan.

'OK. What do you know?'

'I want an hour with an internet connection. Only then will I answer the questions you have.'

*This was a mistake.* Lou stands and starts to pack up.

'You didn't travel all this way to leave empty-handed,' Knox says.

'Well, I figure it's going to happen either way. Might as well get on the road sooner than later.'

He signals the guard and he starts to unlock the door.

'Don't you want to know who's next?'

Lou stops but doesn't turn around.

*He doesn't know anything*, he thinks. *Don't give him the satisfaction.*

'Have a good life, professor.'

# 56

'You're sure it's the same image?'

The road ahead is empty, black asphalt gradually tapering into oblivion. To their right, the forest is a green blur.

'Yes. Definitely the same image.'

'And it's on the wall of Appleton Hall?' Tom asks. 'In the room we're staying in?'

'Yes.'

'How is that possible?'

Harper doesn't answer. Her green eyes are on the rear-view mirror.

'What's wrong?'

'There's a grey sedan behind us,' Harper says. 'It's been following us for ten miles or so.'

Tom turns in his seat and watches the car. Harper gradually slows down. The sedan maintains the same distance.

'He's definitely following us,' she says.

'You have a gun, right?' Tom is suddenly very nervous. 'If you're driving, I should hold the gun.'

Harper snorts in disbelief. 'What are you going to do? Shoot the tyres out?'

'Come on, Harper. I've taken lessons. I can handle a gun. Where is it?'

Tom searches the car, starting with the glovebox.

'Relax,' Harper says, patting under her left armpit. 'I have it. But I think you're overestimating how useful a gun is. They aren't a magic wand. You don't wave them and a problem disappears.'

Tom nervously eyes the car through the rear window. 'What are we going to do? What if that's the same man who murdered my uncle?'

'Don't worry, I've got everything under control. Watch.'

Harper slams on the brakes and the SUV comes to a screeching halt. The grey sedan that had been following them does the same. The distance between the two vehicles goes from two hundred yards to twenty feet.

A moment of excruciating silence follows. Harper can feel her pulse pounding through her carotid artery.

They both watch the sedan. But its windows are tinted, so it's impossible to see inside.

Harper focuses on her breathing. Tom looks like he forgot to breathe altogether.

The sedan suddenly guns its engine and barrels past the SUV.

As it disappears out of sight, Tom sits in stunned silence before erupting in nervous laughter. 'That was incredible. Well done.'

With the threat removed, Harper feels the full force of the pressure that's built up. It's pressing outwards, on her ribs, on her lungs. It's excruciating and she has to release it ASAP. She has her vape, but when she looks at Tom, as their eyes meet, she settles on a more drastic measure. She flicks an invisible switch and her green eyes radiate invitation. She purses her lips ever so slightly. That's all it takes. Although he's hidden it as best he could, Tom has been a tinderbox since day one. And Harper's green eyes just lit the flame. He stops laughing, his breathing grows heavy. He leans forwards and presses his lips against hers. They kiss.

Harper undoes her seatbelt and throws herself onto Tom, straddling him. She bites his lip. They kiss and claw at each other's clothes.

Tom stops abruptly, tapping on something in the rear pocket of Harper's jeans. 'What's this?'

'It's nothing.'

Without asking, Tom pulls the object out of Harper's pocket and examines a square plastic package with a foil seal. 'Narcan,' he says, reading the label. 'Is this for allergies or something?'

'It's for opioid overdoses. It can save someone's life.'

'If someone's OD'ing. You mean if *I'm* OD'ing?'

Harper slides her hand past Tom's waistband and takes hold of him. 'I want to be prepared. For anything.'

Tom's eyes glaze over. He's too distracted to critically appraise Harper's contingency plan. 'Smart,' he mutters before flinging the Narcan into the back seat.

They resume, this time without any distractions.

# Day 422

Alex parks her BMW. She doesn't reach for the door. Neither does Jess.

'When's the funeral?'

'Thursday.'

'So what's tonight again?'

'I don't know,' Alex says. 'An I-feel-sorry-for-you pot luck. A please-don't-kill-yourself get-together.'

'It's so sad.'

Alex examines her nails. 'Aaron can't save everyone.'

'Yeah, but she was so young.'

Alex smiles at Jess, admiring her naivety. 'She won't be the last, Jess. With so many addicts in the Movement, we have to steel ourselves to tragedy. That's what Aaron says.'

'I know.'

Alex unclicks her seatbelt. 'Shall we?'

Meryl answers the door. She's wearing a white apron over a purple blouse. 'You're late.'

As they follow Meryl inside, Alex looks at Jess and rolls her eyes. A dozen congregants are spread out in the living room. Jess can hear more in the kitchen. Dana is sitting on the couch, clutching a Kleenex, her eyes red and raw. Brent is sitting on the La-Z-Boy, nursing a Diet Coke. Jess and Alex sit on the couch, next to Dana. There's a bowl of spinach dip on the coffee table.

'Where is he?' Alex asks.

'In his room,' Brent says. 'Resting. Aaron's with him.'

'How's he doing?'

Dana and Brent look at each other.

'He was yelling before,' Dana says. 'Then he started crying.'

'So, not great,' Brent says.

'At least' – Dana pauses to blow her nose – 'I've heard, with an overdose, it's not painful.'

The others nod.

'You overdosed before joining the Movement,' Dana says, staring at Jess. 'Is that right?'

'I did. Yeah.'

'Did you . . . did you see anything? Sometimes . . . I've heard . . . some people say they see a bright light.'

'I remember a door.' Jess shivers, recalling her overdose. 'It was closed. Someone was calling to me from the other side.'

'Do you think that was heaven?'

*No*, Jess thinks. *Whatever it was, it wasn't heaven.*

'Maybe.'

'That poor girl,' Dana says. 'Why did she have to use that *poison*?'

A small black cat materialises beside Jess on the couch. He stares at her, blankly.

'When did she start?' Jess asks.

'Her doctor prescribed Oxy,' Brent says, 'after she had knee surgery. A few years ago.'

'Aaron tried with her,' Dana says. 'He went above and beyond. The attention he showed her . . . I blame the doctors, prescribing pills they didn't understand and their patients didn't need.'

'They're not to blame,' Alex says. 'Not really.'

'No? Then who?'

'You know what Aaron says. In the modern world, blame can be measured in dollars and cents.'

'That's right.' Brent nods. He's staring intently at the spinach dip. 'The company who makes Oxy – everyone who works there – they're all corrupt. They're the real villains. In fact, there was something published today. Emails between people at one of the pharmaceutical companies. I only saw the headlines on Twitter, but apparently it's pretty damning.'

The doorbell rings and new arrivals filter into the room. Abigail and her brother – the redhead; Jess can never remember his name – are among them. They've brought a pie in a white cardboard box.

Aaron emerges, descending the stairs. The group goes quiet and looks at him.

'How's he doing?' Alex asks.

'He's a survivor,' Aaron says. 'But we all know how dear Tara was to Professor Knox. He's going to need our help in the weeks ahead. We need to come together and support him in his time of need.'

'What can we do?' Jess asks.

'I'm sure the universe will show us,' Aaron says. 'We only have to keep our eyes open.'

# 57

It's dusk when Harper and Tom arrive back at Appleton Hall. Once upstairs, they sit on the floor with their backs leaning against the bed and proceed to get high.

They barely spoke on the drive back. Tom stole the occasional look at Harper, but neither wanted to discuss what happened – probably because any hint of logic would lead, inevitably, to the conclusion that having sex at the side of the road wasn't a great idea.

Harper saw it as a mechanical necessity, the release valve that demanded immediate, drastic attention, rather than an act of passion. Tom, on the other hand, had a look Harper had seen before. Doe-eyed, a goofy grin. *It will fade*, she thought on the drive home. *Hopefully.*

Back in the room, they vape in silence, waiting for their respective highs to take hold.

'OK,' Tom finally says, 'where is it?'

Without a word, Harper drags one of the desk chairs to the door and pats the seat. Tom hops up and Harper points to the pattern etched into the top of the door frame. 'It's not an exact match,' Tom says, as he runs the tips of his finger across the wood. 'But it's close.'

They try plugging descriptions of the image into Google but it's hard to work backwards, from a description without any context. Out of ideas, they resume vaping.

'Any chance you got a look at who was driving the car?' Tom asks.

'No, the tinted windows made it impossible to see inside. I memorised the plate, though. Maybe Lou can run the number for us.'

'Who do you think it was?'

'No idea.'

'How did you know the car would just speed up and leave like that?'

Harper shrugs. 'If they wanted to do something, I figure they'd already have done it.'

Tom takes the vape from Harper. He suddenly tips his head to the side like a concerned parent. 'Harper, I know you've been smoking weed more than you let on. Before you say anything – don't worry. I know you're taking the job of protecting me seriously and you only smoke when it's safe to, early in the morning or late at night. And I know it's how you cope, that it's a form of self-medication. I just wanted you to know, I think you could benefit from seeing someone.'

Harper snorts sarcastically. 'Says the guy smoking weed?'

'I'm serious, Harper.'

'So when I get high, it's self-medicating. But when you do it – what? – you're just having a good time?'

'No, it's a crutch for me, too. Since Uncle Mitch was killed – it hasn't been easy. But something tells me it pales in comparison to whatever you've been through.'

'Don't try to fit me into some cliché you have of a veteran with PTSD.'

'Actually, the first thing that came to mind was a moral injury. I'm not an expert – it's not really my field; and it's relatively new in terms of a diagnosis – but from what I've read, a moral injury is when someone does or witnesses something that goes against their core moral beliefs, it can cause a sort of spiritual trauma. Veterans are being diagnosed with this more and more. But not just veterans.'

'So you sleep with me and now you feel comfortable diagnosing me? Jesus fucking Christ, Tom. You're a walking cliché. If you're bored, go watch *The Deer Hunter* or something and leave me the fuck alone.'

Tom puts his hand on Harper's shoulder. 'You're amazing, Harper. You are. How you handled that car today. Or how you got me through the crowd outside the theatre. I'm in awe of you, if I'm being honest. I know you're the right person to protect me. One hundred per cent certain. But no one's perfect. Everyone needs help at some point. Cognitive therapy, meditation – there are proven techniques for treating trauma.'

'Meditation? Like Knox?'

'Meditation is a powerful tool. Just because some con artist used it to manipulate people . . . there are scientifically proven benefits to meditation. You shouldn't discount it.'

Harper takes another long drag, holds the vapour in her lungs for three seconds, then exhales.

'I saw someone after my third combat tour, a psychiatrist. We tried meditation. And breathing techniques, to cope.' She shrugs, embarrassed that she's said too much. 'I stopped going. The guy was a prick. But the breathing techniques I use sometimes. When I feel . . .' – *like my heart is going to jump out of my fucking chest* – '. . . not myself.'

Rather than look disappointed, Tom looks excited. He tries to hold Harper's hands. 'Harper, that's incredible. I can work with you, if you want. To expand your coping techniques.'

Harper yanks her hands away from Tom's. 'I'm fine, Tom. Find another hobby.'

They glare at each other until the sound of the tablet vibrating ends the stalemate. Harper finds it buried under a heap of clothes. Once again it's the security app. Harper unlocks the screen.

Tom peers over her shoulder. 'Is that . . . ?'

'What's she doing here? At this hour?'

# 58

Harper opens the steel door. Rain is now falling in heavy sheets.

'Vice-Dean Perkins,' Harper says, 'are you here to see me?'

'Yes.' The vice-dean is standing under the cement awning, out of the rain. She's wearing a black trench coat. A manila folder is pinned between her left arm and ribcage.

'How did you know I was here?'

The vice-dean flashes her pained, toothless smile. 'It's my school, Ms Scott. I know just about everything that happens on campus.' Her eyes take in Harper's jeans and rumpled T-shirt. Disgust tightens her lips into a purse. 'How long *do* you intend on staying with us?'

Harper shrugs. 'As long as it takes. Is this what you came to talk with me about?'

Perkins shakes her head. 'No. Here.' She hands Harper the folder. 'I was doing some digging on Mr Knox after we spoke.'

'Oh yeah?' Inside the folder are two sheets of paper, dated from two years ago. Harper sees at the top of the page: *Revolutionary Russia – Class 202*. Underneath is a list of names. 'What's this?'

'It was the class taught by Mr Knox, before he quit. The semester his daughter passed away. I thought you might find the list of students interesting.'

Harper looks up, confused.

Perkins opens her umbrella and steps out into the rain. 'Read the names, Ms Scott.'

As Perkins walks away, Harper retreats inside. Under the buzzing fluorescent lights, she reads every name. She takes her time, afraid she'll miss whatever she's supposed to be looking for.

But her caution proves pointless. She recognises one name, couldn't have missed it if she'd tried. About halfway down the list of names of students who were enrolled in a course at Everly College on Revolutionary Russia, which was taught by William T. Knox, among the various 'Ps', is Harper's employer: Tom Park.

# 59

It's a shitty feeling knowing you've been played. Infuriating, embarrassing. *God, is it embarrassing!* It makes you re-examine every moment that came before, every exchange, every gesture.

*But just because Tom was a student in Knox's class, it doesn't mean . . .*

Harper isn't sure what it means. It raises questions, though. Big questions. Why didn't Tom tell Harper? Not even once? Why pretend not to know anything about your former professor? Has Tom been laughing at Harper this whole time?

Harper doesn't get past the stairwell. She sits on the steps, furious and confused, trying to decide what to do.

Outside, the wind has picked up. She can hear it whistling under the cement awning, a whipping howl.

When she finally heads back upstairs, she finds Tom sitting at one of the desks. He looks up from his laptop and flashes a victorious smile. 'You should see this. I found something on the Movement. It's an article about meditation groups. There's not a ton here, but I've found the reporter on Twitter. I sent him a DM. Maybe he'll meet with us.' Tom is staring at Harper and she can tell he sees something is off. 'What did the vice-dean want?'

Harper stands on the threshold of the room, frozen with indecision. Tom hasn't noticed the folder. He points at a bottle of bourbon. 'You want a drink?' It looks like the bottle he'd opened in Manhattan. It must have made the trip to Connecticut, though Harper never saw it packed. 'After today,' Tom says, 'I need something strong.' He pours himself a drink and takes a sip.

Harper starts to pace. Tom returns to the desk and resumes whatever he'd been doing on his laptop.

'Oh good,' he says, reading from the screen. 'The reporter has written me back already, and he's agreed to meet.'

Harper's mind is buzzing. *Is there actually a reporter?* she thinks. *Is he manipulating me?*

Tom looks up from the computer. 'Are you OK?'

Harper slams the folder onto the desk.

'What's this?'

Tom opens the folder and reads. Harper watches as sickening realisation forms on Tom's face. His head drops.

'What the fuck, Tom! What in the *living* fuck.'

Tom finally looks up. His eyes are red, as though he could cry at any moment.

'You knew him,' Harper says. 'You *knew* Knox.'

'I didn't know him.'

'You took his class!'

'Yeah, but it . . . I don't know what you think this means.'

'Why don't you tell me what this means?'

'I need another drink first.'

# 60

'This all happened when I was still taking my undergraduate degree here at Everly. I needed an elective. I don't know how I picked the Russian Revolution. A whim, I guess.' Tom is sitting on one of the twin beds, cross-legged. He's on his second glass of bourbon. 'When I enrolled in the class, it was before Knox was Knox. Before he . . . did what he did. But it was the semester his daughter went missing, and he took a leave of absence. There were rumours Knox's daughter was addicted to Oxy. I'd always been aware of Oxy's impact, good and bad. But it was mainly in *theory*, if that makes sense. I knew Oxy was helping people who experienced chronic pain – it really was. At the same time, though, some people were becoming addicted to Oxy. But I'd never actually known anyone who'd been addicted.'

Tom sips his bourbon and then takes a deep breath.

'My mom used to tell me things, about the business. She'd drink too much and tell me stuff she probably shouldn't have. I guess the guilt was getting to her. I don't know. For years, I ignored what she told me. Or not so much ignored it as stored it in one compartment of my brain, without analysing or thinking it through. I just parked it there and lived my life. The lies we tell ourselves, right? But then when Professor Knox's daughter went missing, and I knew my family's hands weren't clean, I started to feel this immense sense of guilt. I knew I had to do something. First, I dropped the class, because I didn't want anyone to make the connection between me and Knox. (You could drop or switch out of any class three weeks into the semester. I don't know where Perkins got that list, but most records won't say I was a student in Knox's class.) And then I started visiting my mom more in New York. She thought I was homesick. She didn't know what I was really up to.' Tom sips his bourbon. 'I started going through her documents at night, when she was asleep. She'd been on the board of Apollo Pharma for decades, and she had an office full of records. I started making copies, at a twenty-four-hour Kinko's down the street. I'm not sure what my plan was. I just wanted a record of the truth. It lessened my guilt.'

'It was you,' Harper says. 'The leak to the press.'

Tom nods. 'I sent two boxes of documents to reporters at the *LA Times* and *The Washington Post*. Anonymously. The story broke weeks after Knox's daughter died. You've read Borelli's book. Knox saw the story. He obsessed over it, over my family, over everything Skip and Mitch had done. Knox wanted Skip dead. So he killed him. It was all my fault.'

Tom drops his head. He's on the verge of crying. Harper moves closer and rubs his back.

'It's OK,' Harper says.

Tom makes eye contact with Harper, then tries to kiss her. She stands up and takes a step back. 'Are you kidding me?'

'I just thought . . .'

'You thought what?'

When Tom doesn't say anything, Harper grabs her jacket and keys and makes for the door. 'I need to clear my head.'

'Where are you going?' Tom asks.

Harper's only reply is the door to Room 212 slamming shut.

# Day 480

Alex is lying on Jess's bed, on her chest, swishing her feet back and forth. She's scrolling on her phone, flicking her index finger like there's an invisible bug on the screen.

Jess is reorganising the box in front of her, trying to cram a mandolin, mismatched mugs, and silverware into a box labelled 'Kitchen Items'.

'You won't need those,' Alex says, without looking up from her phone. 'You should just donate them.'

Jess bites her lip. 'Are you sure?'

'First of all, there's a kitchen that has everything. And second, bringing your own personal items is antithetical to the whole idea of the ashram. It's supposed to be a group project, a collective. I'm not even sure where you could store personal property there.'

'Really? What are you going to do about your car?'

'That's different. We'll still need to get around.'

Jess nods. 'That makes sense.' Using a black Sharpie, Jess crosses out 'Kitchen Items' and writes 'Donate', closes the box, folds the flaps inwards, and then seals the top with packing tape.

Alex resumes scrolling on her phone. Without looking up, almost as an aside, she says, 'Aaron's been very impressed with you, all that you've accomplished in so short a time.'

Jess smiles. 'That's good to hear.'

'In fact, we were debating whether you could be involved with something – something super important.'

'Oh yeah?'

Alex puts her phone aside and sits up. 'Actually, we've been talking about you for a while now, and I've been advocating for you. Aaron and I both think you could do more for the Movement, that you're capable of a bigger role. But' – she tips her head to the side – 'we need to know you're one hundred per cent committed before you can move forwards.'

Jess places her hand on her chest, like a squire waiting to be knighted. 'You know I'm committed. You've seen how hard I work.'

'Sure. But people change their minds.'

'I wouldn't. I mean – what can I do? I want to take the next step.'

Alex reveals a black USB stick.

'What's that?'

'The answer to your question. This is how you prove your loyalty.' Alex's eyes hold Jess's like they always do: in a loving chokehold. Her smile radiates calm. 'All you have to do – at this stage anyway – is upload a few files to your computer.' She sees Jess's unease and adds, 'It's only red tape, Jess. A speed bump on the road to a newer, better you.'

Jess looks around her small bedroom – if only to break the spell of Alex's gaze for a moment. But Alex's big blue eyes draw her back in.

'We need to trust you,' Alex says. 'I know you're in this for the right reasons. But everyone else – they need to see you buy in, that you're committed as the rest of us. What we upload on your computer – it's like insurance.' She checks her nails. Her voice is pure serenity. 'It's a trust exercise. I had to do it, too.'

'Yeah?'

'Oh, for sure.'

'What's on there?'

'Well, you're free to look if you want, but I wouldn't recommend it. Maybe change your password so Josh and Susan can't go snooping. Until you've moved out, I mean.'

'Seriously?'

Alex joins Jess on the floor, on her knees. She takes Jess by the hands and looks into her eyes. It feels to Jess like they're about to exchange wedding vows.

'Do you trust me?'

'Yes. Of course.'

'Do you trust Aaron?'

'Yes. Equally.'

'Then you've got nothing to worry about. If you didn't trust us, then – yeah, of course you shouldn't do this. But if you do – if you trust me as much as I trust you – nothing can go wrong. And believe me, it's worth it. You have only experienced one part of what the Movement has to offer. In order to move forwards, you need to destroy yourself. This will be the end of you, and the beginning of us. I know this is confusing, but I promise it will all make sense later. We all have so much faith in you.'

'I understand,' Jess says.

'And you're ready?'

'Yes.'

'Good,' Alex says. 'Step into the hallway. I only need a minute. Then, your new life begins.'

# 61

Harper sneaks back to Appleton Hall a little after three in the morning. Tom is asleep in his bed, splayed out in his underwear.

Harper had escaped to the nearest pub, nursed a pint of Budweiser, and pondered her next move. The way she saw it, she had two options. Option #1: Don't believe a word Tom said, cut her losses, and leave. Maybe go back to Ohio. Figure it out from there. Option #2: Believe Tom and finish the job. She figured staying on wasn't an option unless she trusts Tom. But could she truly trust him after he lied the way he had?

Then she thought of Foster, clinging to life in the hospital, and the idea of whoever did that to him walking away, without consequence – that was out of the question. So she settled on Option #3: Finish the job, but watch Tom like a hawk. With her mind made up, she paid her tab and drove back to Appleton Hall.

Harper strips down to her underwear and a tank top and slides into her bed. She's close to falling asleep when she hears the tablet vibrating. It's buried under clothes on the floor, so the sound is muffled. She finds it, unlocks the screen, and swipes back between the different locations. She can't find what triggered the app and is about to toss the tablet onto the floor when she sees something. Movement in the hallway of Appleton Hall, on the second floor, by the stairwell. The silhouette of a man.

A shiver travels down Harper's spine. It's not so much the hour or that Appleton Hall is supposed to be abandoned. What's terrifying is the phantom's predatory calmness, as he stalks from the stairwell towards Room 212.

Harper shakes Tom awake, keeping her hand on his mouth to stop him from making any noise. She points at the screen of the tablet and Tom's eyes go wide. Harper directs him to the corner of the room, under the desk.

Next, she places the tablet on the bed and then checks the chamber and clip of Jay's Sig 9.

Tom is watching her with wide, unblinking eyes.

Harper kneels in the corner of the room opposite Tom, the gun in her right hand, the tablet in her left. She toggles her gaze between the tablet and the door.

The phantom is halfway down the hallway. He's wearing a balaclava. Harper makes out what she thinks is the shape of a gun in his hand. For days she'd envisioned this moment, someone coming for Tom in the dead of night. She'd hoped their only weapon would be a needle filled with an opioid. A gun complicates matters.

The phantom stops outside Room 212.

Any second now it will start. The man in the hall will kick in the door and start shooting. That's how Harper would do it. The moment of surprise provides the seconds needed to fill the room with bullets. Or maybe he has a key, and his plan is to quietly enter the room and inject Tom with fentanyl.

Either way, it's about to start. Now is the time to act.

Toggling between the tablet and the door, Harper lines up where she thinks the man's head is, tilts the gun a few degrees up, and then fires two shots.

The sound is deafening. Tom buries his head under a cocoon of limbs.

Harper had been kneeling in the corner of the room opposite Tom. With the sound of the gunshots still echoing in the room, she calmly walks to Tom's side of the room, kneels, shielding Tom from what could come next, and watches the phantom on the tablet. He's fallen backwards, as the bullets sailed over his head. He sits up, gathers himself, raises his gun, and fires three shots in the general direction of where Harper had been seconds earlier.

*Mine were warning shots*, Harper thinks. *His weren't.*

Using the tablet to judge where the target is, Harper aims the Sig 9 at the door. She fires two shots. A cry of pain seeps in from the hall. On the tablet, she watches the phantom stand and run.

Harper flings open the door and races down the hall, barefoot and half-naked.

The man in black reaches the stairwell, stops, turns, and raises his arm. Harper dives to the ground just as two shots fly over her head.

Harper shoots blindly from the floor, as the phantom disappears into the stairwell.

'Idiot,' Harper mutters to herself.

She gets up and sprints, but stops at the door leading to the stairwell.

She listens.

She can't hear footsteps. So she waits. There's a wheezing sound. Panting, maybe. Harper sees drops of blood leading into the stairwell. *He's injured. But how badly?* Harper pictures the man in the balaclava on the landing, gun raised, waiting for Harper to emerge, a deadly game of chicken.

His patience runs out first. He shoots three bullets into the door and Harper drops to the floor. She listens but she can't hear anything. *He's not running*, Harper thinks. *Not yet.* If you're here to kill someone – sure it went off the rails, but that doesn't mean it can't be salvaged. Especially if one of the targets is dumb enough to chase you into a stairwell.

Harper quietly hurries back to Room 212. Tom is where she left him, huddled in the corner of the room. He watches Harper.

He can sense the danger hasn't passed, so he doesn't say a word. Harper slides on her jeans and stuffs the Sig 9 into the waistband. She drags the window open, pops the screen out, and then, feet first, squirms through the small window and lowers herself outside. She lets go and drops to the ground, absorbing as much of the force as he can with her long, thirty-four-year-old legs. She muffles a groan as her knees burn like hell. She stands and positions herself in front of the entrance to Appleton Hall, her Sig 9 aimed at the steel doors.

Harper waits.

*Breathe.*

Suddenly the door swings open. The man in the balaclava takes one step outside. He's huddled over, his gun aimed at the ground. His free hand is holding a wound in his left flank.

'Drop it!' Harper screams.

He starts to raise his gun.

Harper pulls the trigger.

# 62

Red and blue lights glide along the cement wall of Appleton Hall. A cacophony of law enforcement and first responders zig and zag their way through the crime scene. Dozens of vehicles are parked on the road and the field, black and white patrol cars, two ambulances, a fire truck.

Lou steps out of his Ford Taurus and watches Frank walk towards him. Lou received the call on his drive back from upstate. Another person was dead at Everly College. When they told Lou it happened at Appleton Hall, he'd assumed it was Harper or Tom Park, but was too afraid to ask. He just hung up and drove.

'Lou,' Frank says with a curt nod.

'Frank.'

They haven't spoken since Frank admitted he lied to Lou during the Knox investigation. Lou would have liked to given Frank the cold shoulder for a few more days at least, but it's hard to act petty when there's a dead body to deal with.

Frank leads Lou through a maze of first responders and then under the cement awning of Appleton Hall. Two state troopers are kneeling beside a body. Frank disperses them with a flick of his chin.

The corpse is wearing a balaclava. There's two bullet wounds, one in the head, between the eyes, the other in the sternum. Frank kneels and gently yanks the balaclava off the corpse.

Lou is happy to learn he doesn't recognise the victim.

'Who is he?'

Frank shrugs. 'The fuck if I know! But this has to be our guy. Has to be.'

'What happened?'

Frank rubs his large belly. 'Inside is a mess. We're trying to make sense of it, but at least ten shots were fired. We figure this guy' – he points at the corpse – 'came to kill Tom Park. He had a syringe in his pocket. We have to test it to know what's inside, but we can both guess what was in it, and he had keys to the building.'

'Oh yeah? How'd he get those?'

Frank shrugs. 'Green eyes and him exchanged gunfire. Somehow they ended up outside. And then ... well ... the only part we know for certain is how it ended. No mystery there.'

'Scott had a firearm?' Lou asks.

'Yup. You want to guess the make?'

'Sig Sauer?'

Frank nods.

'Did she admit it's Hollinger's?'

'Not yet. I didn't press her on that, seeing as how someone just tried to kill her. But we've confiscated the weapon and will run the serial number. We should know soon enough.'

'I want to talk to her.'

Frank leads Lou to the ambulance. The double doors in the back are open and Harper's sitting on the back bumper, her long legs nearly touching the pavement. She's in jeans and a tank top, her tangled black hair is tucked behind her ears. Tom Park is sitting beside her, his hands on her arm, offering what comfort he can.

'Hey, kids,' Lou says. 'Busy night?'

Harper is staring at the ground. Lou puts his hand to her chin and angles her head up, until their eyes meet. 'You OK?'

She nods.

'What happened?'

Harper shrugs, as if that answers Lou's question. Once released from the prop of Lou's hand, she goes back to staring at the ground. Lou asks again and Tom starts to explain, right up to Harper shooting the intruder. 'I was watching from the window,' Tom says. 'Harper didn't have a choice. She shot him in self-defence. Do you think he killed my uncle?'

Lou doesn't know the answer so he ignores the question. 'Tell me everything that happened since I gave you details on Coughlin, the Hamilton's guru.'

'I'm sorry, you what?' Frank asks.

'Ignore him,' Lou says to Tom. 'Tell me everything.'

Tom describes the abandoned compound, the grey sedan that tailed them on the highway, Harper slamming on the brakes, the sedan barrelling past. He shows Lou pictures he took of the metal rod with the strange symbol and explains that somehow there's a similar image carved into the wall of Appleton Hall.

Lou turns to his partner. 'What do you think, Frank? Should we go have a look?'

Frank looks wistfully in the direction of the fresh corpse. 'Don't we have our guy? I'm not interested in extra credit, here.'

Lou stares at Frank until Franks sighs and says, 'I hate this fucking case.'

Lou and Frank gently slip past the bullet-riddled door to Room 212. Inside there are two deputies from the sheriff's department taking pictures.

'Give us a minute,' Frank says and the deputies leave.

Lou starts to pace the room, absorbing every detail. Bullet holes in the door, slugs in the cement wall. There are two beds, both unmade. He squats and examines Harper's bra, which is lying on the floor. He lifts it up using a pen. It strikes Lou as intimate to leave something like this out, on the floor. Then he remembers the way Tom was holding Harper's arm outside, the familiarity between them.

*It makes sense*, Lou thinks. *Two attractive people, locked in a room. I'd be surprised if they weren't sleeping together.*

'Where'd they say it was?' Frank is on his knees, examining the baseboards.

'Not there,' Lou says. He moves closer and sees something etched into the upper part of the door frame. It's small, the size of a thumb. He drags a desk chair over to the door and hops onto the seat. He runs his index finger lightly over the impression in the wood.

'What is it?' Frank asks, his face scrunched up in a puzzled squint.

Lou takes out his phone and takes a picture. 'I don't know.'

'What does it mean?'

The flash from the camera on Lou's phone emits a white pulsing light.

'It means we're not done yet.'

## 63

Tom's house near campus is spotless. On their hasty exit six days ago, they'd left dirty plates in the sink, beds unmade – who knows what else? Skilled cleaners have since come and gone, unseen and – aside from the faint smell of eucalyptus – without a trace. With Appleton Hall a crime scene, the choice was to come back to Tom's home in Petersburg or find a hotel. They opted for what they knew. And with Mitch's killer likely dead, the risk of returning to a doxed home seemed low.

Harper drops her duffle bag by the door, heads straight to the liquor cabinet, and removes a bottle of bourbon. Breaking her rule not to drink in front of Tom, she pours herself a double and downs it in one gulp. An arrow of warmth slides from her throat to her belly and the valve turns a quarter inch. The excruciating pressure eases, slightly. She sits on a stool at the kitchen island and waits for her vape to heat up. All of this she does before Tom's finished taking off his shoes and coat. He comes into the kitchen and sits on the neighbouring stool. He puts his hand on Harper's arm.

She takes a drag from her vape. The valve turns another quarter inch.

'I think we should talk about what happened,' Tom says. 'If we don't address it, then . . .'

Harper sighs. 'Listen, Tom, I appreciate that you're trying to help. But I went to war, remember? That's not the first time . . . I'm fine.'

'But if there's some underlying trauma—'

'There's not.'

'You just killed someone. You don't feel anything?'

Harper shrugs. 'Maybe I'm in shock.'

'You just downed two and a half ounces of bourbon.'

'I was thirsty.'

Tom sits and stares at Harper, a doctor examining his patient. 'OK, if you're fine, you don't mind telling me about what happened at Dark Star, the reason you quit?'

'It's a boring story.'

'I doubt that.'

Harper shrugs.

'Humour me. We're not going to sleep right away – not after what just happened. A story would help us kill time.'

Harper tries to plot her quickest way to end the conversation. *Just tell him and move on.*

'Fine. Why don't you pour yourself a drink and get comfortable.'

# 64

'It was supposed to be an easy job. Medium risk, high reward. Mordecai said—'

'Sorry. Who's Mordecai?'

'My former boss. Before founding Dark Star he'd been high up in the Israel Defense Forces, a second lieutenant or something like that.'

'He sounds like a character.'

'He was a prick, but smart. Too smart for his own good. Anyway, where was I?'

'Medium risk, high reward.'

'Right. Mordecai said we'd get paid six figures, maybe seven for the data we were going to take.'

'You told me Dark Star was corporate espionage, but that sounds an awful lot like stealing.'

'Mordecai said Dark Star was a Swiss army knife. But essentially we did for companies whatever they paid us to do. A few times we were asked to obtain information from a competitor. Mordecai called it "competition research".' Harper sucks on her vape and shrugs. 'But yeah, you could call it stealing. But if one billion-dollar company wants to steal data from some other billion-dollar company – I never saw it as a big ethical dilemma. It was a game. That's what I told myself, anyway.'

'What sort of data?'

'It's complicated, and I'm not sure I totally understood it. Let's call it an algorithm. OK? The target was Stuart Munn. You may have heard of him. A "tech-bro" is the best description I can think of. He developed and sold some website in the Nineties. And ever since he's made a living investing in internet start-ups. He's very rich. Richer than you. He'd spent every summer since his second divorce on the Mediterranean, going from port to port in his massive yacht, sleeping with the sort of women who were impressed by massive yachts. We'd worked this angle before, the fragile ego of an aging, lonely man.'

'Let me guess. You were the bait?'

Harper shrugs. 'I look good in a summer dress.'

'I bet.'

'I wore spaghetti straps, red lipstick, and too much mascara, and sat myself down at the bar of the douchiest bar in Santorini. Weird lighting, electronic music no one with a soul would willingly listen too. I waited fifteen minutes and Munn tried to pick me up.'

'What was his opening line?'

'He asked if he could buy me a drink?'

Tom feigns throwing up. 'That sounds about right. I can't picture you putting up with a guy like that. Heck, I can't picture you saying anything other than "Fuck off" in response.'

'As much as I'd love to tell him to fuck off, that wasn't the plan. But I didn't coo either. That wouldn't work. Not with a guy like Munn. You have to make him work for it. So, rather than say, "Yes, please buy me a drink," I gave him the best look of disappointment I could muster and said no. He couldn't stand the rejection, of course. Not with his ego. Mild resistance from the pretty girl at the bar is like a puzzle he has to solve. He begged until I said yes. Then he spent forty minutes or so bragging about his life achievements. Near the end of our second drink, just before he invited me for a tour of his yacht, I slipped him Rohypnol.'

'A roofie?'

Harper nods.

'Jesus.'

'Then he led me down the quay to his yacht. He had a security team on board but they barely paid attention to the girl in spaghetti straps. Munn gave me a tour that ended with the main cabin on the upper deck, just as his legs started to tingle. I sat in front of his computer – some monstrosity with four monitors – and asked to go online quickly. I said my phone was dead and I just needed to check my flight. The roofie was already starting to take effect. He wasn't all there. He said, sure, no problem and typed in his password. Once he'd finished, he lay down on a leather couch and shut his eyes.'

'And just like that, you're past his firewalls?'

'Yup. It had all gone according to plan. While Munn was unconscious, I poked and prodded his hard drive. But just as I finished copying the files we needed, Munn woke up.'

'No shit.'

'He wasn't totally with it, but he was conscious. He asked what was happening. I pulled the USB stick from the computer, as subtly as I could, and dropped it in my purse. I went and sat beside him, playing it cool, but he knew something was off. He said, "What were you doing on my computer?" I said, "Checking my flight. Remember?" He wanted to know what was in my purse. I said no. He had some surge of adrenaline – maybe he'd started replaying the evening in his head and realised how monumentally stupid he'd been – and he lunged forwards. I grabbed his wrist and sent him head over heels, onto his back. As I was leaving the cabin, I could hear gunfire. I knew it was Mordecai. I was late and he wasn't going to take any chances. Then I heard Munn scream for help.'

'There was someone from Munn's security team on the upper deck. He tried to put his hands on me. I broke his nose. And then I jumped.'

'What do you mean? Into the water?'

'Yeah. I kicked off my heels, threw my legs over the railing, and dove.'

'Did they see you come up?'

Harper frowns. 'Someone did, I think. I swam fifty yards underwater and came up on the other side of a small ship on the neighbouring dock. It was my rendezvous point with Mordecai and Jennings, the other member of our team that night. It was dark and I couldn't see well and I figured it was Mordecai or maybe Jennings who fished me out of the water. But once I was on the dock and finally caught my breath, I looked up and saw it was one of Munn's men.'

'What did he say?' Tom asks.

'He only had time to smile.'

'Before what?'

'Before his head exploded.' Harper is staring at her bourbon. She takes a long sip.

'What do you mean?'

'Mordecai shot him. In the head.'

'He must have seen Munn's man at our rendezvous point and waited for a distraction.'

'Oh my God! That's . . . horrible.'

Harper nods. 'Mordecai stepped over the corpse and yanked my purse out of my hands and started rummaging inside. He was furious. He said, "Jumping into the water was stupid." At first, I didn't take my eyes off the dead man on the dock. His bullet had gone in the back of his head and out of his eye socket. So the one side of his face was fine. The other . . .' Harper absently sips from an empty glass. When she notices, she puts the glass back on the counter. 'Once the shock passed, I got to my feet and screamed at Mordecai. About how he didn't have to kill Munn's man. "Just cleaning up your mess," he said. Jennings was there.

He'd been hanging back but then he stepped forwards. "Let's keep it down," he whispered, "They're searching the docks as we speak."'

'Mordecai found the USB and held it up to the moonlight. He said, "It's wet and probably fucked. Ten million. Gone. Just like that. Because you took a swim rather than shoot your way out. Fucking pussy."

'I figured my days with Dark Star were probably over no matter what. I'd been spotted in the middle of a job, by someone with a lot of money and connections, a fuck-up that's impossible to unwind. And Dark Star operated on anonymity as much as anything. Mordecai would have had to cut ties. Maybe there was a five per cent chance he kept me on, in some diminished role, back in the lab, typing away. But when I punched Mordecai on the chin and he toppled into the water – that sealed it. I screamed, "I quit." But Mordecai was two feet underwater at the time. So, no wonder in his version I was fired.'

'Did the man from Munn's security detail have his gun drawn? Was what Mordecai did self-defence?'

'It wasn't self-defence.'

'Was this your first time seeing someone shot like that?'

'I've been to war. I served in Afghanistan, I saw some horrible things. But this was the first time I witnessed a cold-blooded murder. For money.'

'I see.'

'And I was part of it.'

Tom puts his hand on hers. 'Tonight was different, Harper. If you didn't do what you did, that man would have killed you. And after he killed you, he'd have headed back inside and killed me.'

Harper nods. 'Yeah. That's true. But all the same, I could have done without killing someone today.'

She stands and wobbles. Tom grabs her arm to steady her. Harper tries to push him away, but it's a dismal effort. Soon she's leaning on him for support.

'Come on,' Tom says, 'let's find you somewhere to lie down.'

He takes her to his bedroom. At the foot of the bed, he gives her a gentle push and Harper tips over and lands face first. Tom takes Harper's boots off and unfurls a blanket over top. She's asleep a moment later, buried under a shroud of linen.

# Day 488

It's late, after midnight. They're in the north cabin, on the eastern edge of the ashram, Jess's new home. Bunk beds are packed between the walls like anchovies in oil. An electric space heater hums in the corner. But the brutal February cold leaches its way inside. Jess can feel the sharp pang of winter in her lungs and the soles of her feet.

Alex hands Jess the blindfold. She sees Jess is uneasy, so she gives her a short pep-talk – the third today. 'You'll be all right, Jess. I promise. And remember: there's no progress without pain.'

Jess takes a deep breath. She nods.

'You're ready for this.'

'I know.'

Alex leaves, shutting the door behind her. Jess takes off her clothes, even her wool socks, ties the blindfold tightly around her head, and, as instructed, sits at the end of her bed. Her mind drifts back to three nights ago, when Alex uploaded the USB stick onto her laptop. That's when she told Jess about her maniple.

'Your what?' Jess asked.

Alex smiled. She loved the intrigue, the inscrutable term. 'It's a phrase we borrowed from the Roman army. It's a military unit.'

Jess was sceptical. 'Are we going to war?'

'Yes.'

'With whom?'

'Our enemies. People who deserve it.'

'Who are our enemies?'

Alex patted her leg. 'All in good time, Jess.'

'What do I have to do?'

'What do *we* have to do? We're doing this together. As a unit. It's important to remember that.'

'You said this is "your" maniple. How many other maniples are there?'

Alex shrugged. 'I'm not sure. Only Aaron knows.'

'Not even your mom?'

'No. And that's the thing – what I need you to understand before I leave here today. This is an absolute secret. You can't tell anyone else you've been invited to join my maniple.'

'OK.'

'I'm serious, Jess. I know you mean well, but sometimes you can be a bit naive. Don't trust anyone with this. Not even Aaron. He speaks to me about Maniple business, and I speak to you and the others in our unit. Understand? You need to follow my orders exactly or we consider it a betrayal. It's like the army. We need absolute devotion and respect for hierarchy.'

'I understand.'

'Because if you betray the maniple, Jess, we make one call to the police, they check your computer, and you'll spend a very long time in jail.'

'Jesus! Are you serious? What was on that USB?'

'It's best you don't know. Don't think about it. In fact, that's your first order as a member of my maniple: forget about what's on your computer. Don't look. Got it?'

Jess felt light-headed.

Alex repeated her question. 'Got it?'

Jess nodded. 'Yes.'

Now a bell rings. Jess hears the door open and a man's voice – gruff; one Jess can't quite place – tells her to stand. She suddenly feels the full weight of her nakedness. She wants to cover her breasts, her crotch. But she stops herself. Aaron's voice, his sage wisdom, reaches the cool, rational side of her brain. 'When opportunity comes, we have to take it.'

*I want this*, Jess thinks. *More than anything.*

She stands, proudly. Chin up, shoulders back. She feels strong and confident, because she has a purpose. The woman who would do this – she's already a far cry from the girl who had to snort Oxy to get through the day.

The bell continues to ring. Jess is led by the hand down a path of hard-packed earth. The air is freezing cold, the ground even colder. Her nipples harden. The soles of her feet burn. She's led down a small hill, and up onto a wooden platform. She waits. She can feel eyes on her, watching.

Hands take Jess by the shoulders and gently pull her down onto a wooden stump. Then fingers press on the inside of her knees and push her legs apart.

An eternity passes.

Jess's confidence waivers. She feels exposed, dirty. She wants to run.

A chant starts up, slow and methodical.

*How many people are here?*

She thinks about what brought her here, where she was only fourteen months ago. Her first month at Everly College – how it left her ostracised and alone. How she turned to drugs. Her anger, her loneliness, and how everything changed when she met Alex. How she found focus, a vocation, a purpose.

A bell brings the chanting to a close. Then a voice, deep and commanding, speaks. 'Moral purity,' the voice – Aaron's voice – says, 'starts today.'

Silence follows. It stretches out, like an elastic band, tension building the longer it goes.

And then white-hot steel is pressed into Jess's inner thigh. A wave of excruciating pain washes over her.

Her skin literally sizzles. She can hear it, with horrible clarity, before her scream overtakes it.

As her leg is cauterised, burned with a scar she will carry forever, beneath the wave of vivid pain, she feels . . .

Joy.

# PART THREE

# THE SWEET SPOT

# 65

'The Movement is so fucked up, I don't even know where to start.'

Simon Clegg claims to be thirty-two, but he doesn't look a day over eighteen. He's short, wide-eyed, and his chin as smooth as polished chrome. Clegg is the reporter who'd written about the Movement. Tom had reached out to Clegg and organised the meet-up hours before Harper shot and killed the man who broke into Appleton Hall. Harper figured the intruder was Mitch Buchanan's murderer, and so Tom's life wasn't in imminent danger. But Tom wanted to keep the meeting, to learn what he could about Knox's connection with the Movement, and how it fits with Mitch's murder. 'Maybe the threat has passed,' he told Harper this morning, 'but we don't know that for sure.'

At Clegg's suggestion, they've met on the patio of a coffee shop in Brooklyn. Clegg is sitting on the edge of his seat, incessantly tapping his foot, producing enough nervous energy to fuel a small car. *Hasn't this guy discovered weed?* Harper thinks. *He's a journalist living in Brooklyn for Christ's sake.*

'I shouldn't even be talking to you,' Clegg says, looking around, making sure no one is listening. 'They ruined my career with lawsuits, bankrolled by Abigail Hamilton. The site I was working for is on the verge of bankruptcy.' He shakes his head. 'The legal system in this country is nearly as fucked up as the Movement.'

Clegg lights a cigarette. Harper watches as his first, long drag sends a tiny ripple of serenity through his system and briefly flattens his nervous edge.

'It started about a year ago. I found them by coincidence,' he says. 'I was trying to come up with article ideas and a friend of mine went on a meditation retreat. No smartphones, no email, no social media. He *hated* it. I thought I could do the same and write about it. You know, a tongue-in-cheek commentary on our society's dependence on the internet and social media. How technology has changed the chemistry of our brains. Do you know what I mean? I used to be able to concentrate for more than thirty seconds. Now I'm lucky if I can sit for five without scrolling on my phone.' Clegg sips his coffee, fuelling his metronome of a foot. 'Anyway, I was Googling meditation groups, looking for the most extreme I could find. I thought that would, you know, give me the best material for an article. The link I found – it was just dumb luck. Are you familiar with Aaron? Or Lama Aaron or Father – whatever he calls himself now? First, I found an excerpt of his book, *The River*. You could download an excerpt for free. It was bat-shit crazy. So I started Googling Aaron and the Movement and figured out where they met every Saturday morning.'

'Did you go?'

'I tried to. But they stopped me at the door. I wasn't in the right attire. They said my green shirt would screw up the room's vibrations.'

'What did you do?' Tom asks.

'What could I do? I went home. But I came back the next week, dressed in the colours of a Buddhist monk. Maroon, mainly. They let me in, but only after I'd paid an initiation fee. Five hundred dollars. Can you believe that? I stayed for the whole ceremony and, believe me, it was as batty as the book excerpt. He was like a philosophy professor with verbal diarrhoea. And people lapped it up. I mean, right then and there I knew it was a cult.'

'Really?' Tom asks. 'Your article didn't say anything about it being a cult.'

'Well, no. Not my first article. That article was about meditation groups, like I said. And I wrote about a few different ones, including the Movement.'

'But if you thought it was a cult, why write something positive? You called Aaron a "paragon of serenity".'

'Listen,' Clegg says, 'I knew that I had to get on their good side if I was going to get any access. Once I had access, then I could write what I really thought.'

'So you ingratiated yourself to them?'

Clegg puts his arms up, showing his innocence. 'Hey, this is how it works. You write a few puff pieces to get better access. I wasn't doing anything any other reporter wouldn't do.'

'Did it work?'

'Yes and no,' Clegg says. 'The day I went, I milled around the group afterwards, asking questions, introducing myself. I met this woman, Meryl. She was Aaron's second-in-command, I think. Or third. (Power changed hands there like a war-torn country.) I told her I was writing a piece about meditation groups, that I thought the session I attended was incredible. I told her I'd love to meet with Aaron, ask him some questions.' Clegg laughs. 'She may have bought Aaron's bullshit, but she wasn't buying mine. Not at first. But I kept at it. I emailed her the story when it came out. She liked it and invited me to their compound. The meditation session I'd attended was in this big building, an old hockey arena or something. And the Movement had bought all this land behind it, where they built a small village. They called it the "ashram", but it reminded me of a summer camp.'

'Why did Meryl invite you back?' Harper asks.

Clegg shrugs. 'She wanted good publicity. And I think she thought she could manipulate me. But they were careful. Someone was with me at all times. I got to watch different meditation sessions, and these strange group meetings called a criticism circle where they insulted each other. At first, I thought it was right out of Mao's Cultural Revolution. But when I was doing my research, it turns out there was actually a cult in California called Synanon – have you heard of it? – it basically did the same thing. The more I researched cults . . . the overlap is nuts. They borrow from each other. Or maybe it happens by accident. Trial and error as they figure out ways to control people.' He takes a drag of his cigarette. 'I was surprised they let me watch. But I think they honestly thought I'd be impressed. I don't think they had any idea how nutty it all was. And they tried to show me they were living this beautiful way of life that wasn't dependent on technology, but that was a lie. One of their cabins was essentially a computer lab. Later, when I got my source, I figured out what that was about.'

'Your source?'

Clegg nods. 'Yeah. Like I said, I was watched the whole time I was in the compound. I handed out cards, so people could contact me if they wanted to. But during my third visit, I realised these people were in so deep, they were probably being watched as closely as I was. So I started handing out two cards at a time, so they could hold on to one if they wanted to, and make a show of throwing the other one out, if they were being watched.'

'And that worked?'

'It must have,' Clegg says. 'Because I got an email a week after my last visit.' He looks around nervously. 'Maybe we better take this discussion inside.'

'You wanted to meet here,' Harper says.

'I know, I know. I wanted a public place. I didn't know who I was meeting. Not really. But now . . . you seem OK. Like you are who you say you are. And a public space like this . . . You never know who's listening.'

## 66

Clegg walks them around the corner to his tiny Brooklyn apartment. Harper and Tom take a seat on a futon draped in rumpled clothes. A zipper digs into Harper's tailbone. Clegg brews more coffee and returns as the gentle gurgle of percolation fills the room.

'The email,' he says, finally resuming his story, 'came from some anonymous account. It said, "I can tell you everything you need to know about the Movement." And it gave me a time and a place to meet.' Clegg lights another cigarette. 'There's a small museum near Everly College. The email told me to wait in front of an exhibit about the Salem witch trials. Which I did. I sat there for an hour. Then a woman sat beside me. I recognised her right away. I'd seen her on my tours. She had been attached at the hip to a blonde woman in the ashram. But she was by herself at the museum.'

'What was her name?'

'I can't say. I promised I wouldn't reveal her name until she was free and clear of the Movement. And that's what I'm going to do – even if she's probably dead. It's been hard, though. My career has gone to shit protecting her. And with the material I have, I could get a job with the *Times* or the *Post*. They'd eat the story up with a spoon. The Movement's sued the website I wrote for, but it's a small, up-and-coming site – it's only been around for a few years – and it didn't have the resources to fight back. Not like the big outlets.'

'What happened when you met?' Tom asks.

'We only talked for a moment. She didn't feel comfortable talking out in the open, so we agreed I'd rent a hotel room, where we'd meet. We picked a time that coincided with her trips into town. It was about a week later.'

'And?'

'What she told me ... it was everything I'd suspected was going on: brainwashing, groupthink. She – let's call her "Jane Doe". Jane was in a bad place when the Movement came calling. She'd been bullied at school, started using drugs. When she met the blonde I mentioned, a pretty twenty-something high up in the Movement, she'd overdosed and was in the hospital. A lot of the Movement's followers – they call themselves congregants – most of them, like Jane Doe, were addicts, or related to addicts. Aaron promised to help his followers kick their addiction. And you know the state of the opioid epidemic in this country. It gave him an endless trove of potential marks.'

Tom blushes at the mention of the opioid epidemic.

'Tell us more about Jane Doe,' Harper says. 'And the blonde.'

'The blonde brought Jane to her first meditation session,' Clegg says. 'At the first one, Aaron acknowledged Jane. He put his hand on her shoulder, said he was glad she came. Keep in mind she'd overdosed not too long before. Her life was in the toilet. And then suddenly Aaron made her feel special. He had a gift for this, sensing what people needed and then using it to exploit them. She – my source – she watched him do it to others. And it wasn't just Aaron. The group itself made her feel amazing at first. One day you're lonely and friendless. The next you've got texts and emails and Facebook invites from dozens of people. It's only when you're fully integrated into the group and can't imagine living without them, it's only then that they invite you to the weird shit.'

'Like the criticism circle?' Harper asks.

Clegg ashes his cigarette. 'Exactly. And once you're doing that . . . It's like Aaron studied how to brainwash people. A system of rewards and punishments, fear and isolation, a closed system of logic. Have you ever heard of a thought-terminating cliché? It's a phrase designed to end a debate. We use them all the time, like saying "everything happens for a reason". But the Movement – like a lot of cults – used them to control its members. "There's no progress without pain" – that was a big one. Anytime someone felt uncomfortable with what they were asked to do, or had done to them, their friend would say, "There's no progress without pain", and they'd feel pressure to say it too. And so whatever they were feeling was justified, and it stopped further discussion on the topic. My source walked me through all of this. We met twice at the hotel, and she was working up to something big, I think. Something she had to tell me. But we were building trust. We were supposed to meet a third time but she never showed. I drove by the ashram, but . . .'

Clegg pauses for dramatic effect, but Harper knows the punchline: 'They were gone.'

Clegg nods. 'Yeah. How did you know?'

'We've been there,' Harper says. 'When did this happen?'

'Let me see,' Clegg starts counting his fingers. 'Less than a year ago. My source sent me the email after Christmas, sometime in January, I think, and the whole ashram was missing a few weeks after that.'

'Do you know where they went?'

'Lama Aaron was arrested. Apparently the mother of one of his young congregants accused him of statutory rape, and he spent a few months in jail, before the charges were dropped. But as for everyone else in the ashram – who knows? I spent months poking around, but I never found a lead.'

'And you think your source is dead? Because she didn't show?'

Clegg nods.

'You think they're capable of that?' Harper asks. 'Of murder?'

Clegg shrugs. 'Isn't everyone, in the right circumstances?'

'Have you gone to the police?' Tom asks.

'Yeah, of course. I went to the sheriff's department. And I left messages for the FBI. They said, "A source not calling a reporter is not a crime." The problem is I *know* a crime occurred. I just can't prove it.'

'Have you thought of writing a story about the Movement, but keep Jane out of it for now?' Tom asks.

Clegg snorts, sarcastically. 'Are you kidding? Like I said before, Abigail Hamilton is bankrolling the Movement's lawyers. They buried my old website in litigation. It was so bad they fired me. No paper or website will publish the story. Not without someone on the record.'

Harper takes out her phone and shows Clegg a picture of the symbol etched above the door to Room 212. 'Do you know what this is?'

'Sure. That's the endless knot.'

'The what?'

'It's a Buddhist symbol. The Movement co-opted it. My source . . .'

Clegg stops himself, unsure if he should say more.

Harper leans forwards. 'They branded her with the symbol, didn't they?'

'How did you know that?' Clegg asks the question but he doesn't give Harper time to answer. Now that the cat is out of the bag, he's happy to tell you everything he knows about the cat. 'She had it burned into her inner thigh. You should have seen the wound it made. It was months old when she showed me, and it was still so red and raw. They had this fucked-up ceremony.

She was blindfolded and then – boom! – they pressed a smouldering hot brand into her thigh.'

Harper and Tom exchange a look. They figured this was what the brand was used for, but it's strange to hear it said aloud.

'Did you know William Thomas Knox was with the Movement?' Tom asks. 'A congregant or whatever they call it?'

'The Karma Killer was with the Movement? How . . .' Clegg's voice trails off, his mind spinning with too many questions. 'Did the police know?'

'We believe the DA's office knew,' Tom says. 'And someone in the FBI. But we're not sure how much they knew about the Movement itself.'

'It'd be pretty messed up if someone from the Movement killed Skip Buchanan,' Clegg says.

'Why?'

'Well, maybe they're a cult, but all they do is preach about how to make the world a better place. It's like their main concern.'

'But you just said you think the Movement killed your source?'

'I know, I know. It doesn't make sense, does it? It's just that I could see them doing whatever was necessary to protect themselves. But to murder someone in cold blood – it doesn't fit with their philosophy.'

Clegg leans back in his seat and takes a drag of his cigarette. He shakes his head, lost in thought.

Harper leans forwards and touches Clegg's arm. 'I know you're only trying to protect your source but we need her name. It's important.'

Clegg shakes his head. 'I'm sorry. I am. I can give you a copy of the Movement's videos. I've got VHS material dating back to the Nineties. I ordered it on eBay and converted them all to digital. And Aaron's books. But other than that . . . I can't give up the name of a source. I can't.'

# 67

Outside of Clegg's apartment, the sky is the colour of asphalt. Harper and Tom walk half a block to the SUV.

Harper has been unarmed since the FBI confiscated Jay's gun. It's not ideal, but she's nearly certain the threat to Tom's life has passed, that whoever she shot and killed outside Appleton Hall was the same man who'd doxed and killed Mitch Buchanan, and who'd been terrorising Tom. Harper still feels naked without a firearm – especially out in the open like this, as they dash to the SUV – but the risk feels manageable and equal to the task.

'I can't believe he wouldn't give us the name of his source,' Tom says as they're climbing into the SUV. 'If we could find her . . .'

'I tried snooping around his desk when I went to the washroom.'

'And?'

'His desk was empty. He must have had everything locked away, including his laptop.'

'So we're at a dead end?'

'Not necessarily. I left him a present. As long as he opens it, we're OK.'

'What kind of present?'

'A USB.'

Tom squints. 'What are you talking about? A memory stick?'

'Yes, infected with malware. It's something we did at Dark Star to gain access to computers.' Tom stares at Harper blankly so she continues. 'OK, there are two ways to get into a computer.

Hardware or software. Both are based on the idea that people are trusting, curious and stupid. You know, those emails you get that try to get you to click on a link. The email claims your bank account has been hacked, and you need to click on the link ASAP to sort it out. Once you click on the link, the hacker has access to your computer. That's the software route. Hardware is based on the same principles – trust, curiosity, stupidity – but rather than an email, you use a memory stick and hope it gets connected to a computer. Say a USB is left on the premises of some company. Ted in accounting finds it. He's curious. He wants to know what's on it, so he plugs it into his computer to see. It didn't seem like a big deal, but it's monumentally stupid. Now the computer's breached, at the mercy of the hacker. Are you following?'

'I think so.'

'Well, I used that trick with the USB, but with an upgrade.'

'What's the upgrade?'

Harper smiles. 'I labelled the USB. I wrote "porn" – P-O-R-N – in big capital letters.'

'So he thinks there's porn on it?'

'Right. And there is. But there's also malware that gives me access to their computer.'

Tom laughs. 'Does that work?'

'You'd be surprised. Much better than leaving it unlabelled. With an unlabelled USB, I'd say we had a fifty per cent success rate. When poor Ted from accounting finds the USB, curiosity eats away at him. He really wants to know what's on it. He doesn't *need* to know. But he wants to. Sometimes though he remembers the training IT provided when he joined the company. Or he's cautious and he checks in with IT, and they tell him "for the love of God, don't plug that into your computer". But when I wrote "PORN" on the side of a USB, I had a one hundred per cent success rate. No one's calling IT to ask if they can look at porn.'

'Seriously?'

Harper shrugs. 'Add the promise of porn to Ted's natural sense of curiosity, and it's hard for him to resist.'

'Are men really that disgusting?'

'Predictable is the word I'd use.'

'But did you leave it on his desk? Isn't that suspicious?'

'Not his desk. On his bathroom floor. Near the toilet. So he thinks it fell out of my pocket when I used the washroom.'

'Smart,' Tom says. 'OK, say your plan works, how long will it take?'

Harper shrugs. 'Clegg has to find it and plug it into his computer. A couple of hours, maybe longer.'

'Wait. Does this mean you came prepared for this? You brought with you a USB armed with malware?'

'I had the hardware from my time at Dark Star, so it didn't take long to set up. I figured why not come prepared.'

'Still, seems like a long shot. Doesn't it? He has to find the USB and hook it up to his computer. Wouldn't he be extra paranoid about security with the Movement breathing down his neck? You saw him in there. He was *so* nervous.'

'Hundred dollars says we are in Clegg's computer before midnight.'

'You're on.'

Harper puts out her hand and Tom takes it. They shake, finalising the bet.

'So what now?' Tom asks.

'Once Clegg plugs the hardware into his computer, I can get inside from anywhere. I figure we head back to Everly and wait,' Harper says. 'Unless there's something you want to do in the City before we leave?'

'Now that you mention it.'

# 68

The medical examiner is eating a sandwich at her desk.

'Hi Gladys,' Lou says, as he wraps his knuckle on the open door. 'You have a name for me?'

Gladys shakes her head as she dabs her mouth with a cloth napkin. 'Not a name.'

'No? Agent Dreser said you had a name. Why'd I come down here if you don't have a name?'

Gladys drops her sandwich. 'Is your time *so* precious, Agent Diaz? You can't spare half an hour?'

Lou shrugs. 'Spare or waste?'

Gladys sighs. 'You're going to feel bad in about five minutes.' She stands. 'Come on. I have to show it to you because I can't describe it.'

Lou follows the medical examiner into the morgue, to a gurney with a naked cadaver, the body Lou last saw out front of Appleton Hall. There's an incision along the stomach and the man's insides are on full display. Lou's stomach turns. He looks at the ground until Gladys says, 'Here. Right here. Thought you'd want to see this.'

Lou looks up and sees Gladys pushing the cadaver's knee to the side, exposing the inner thigh. Lou's revulsion evaporates when he sees the marking. He moves closer. 'Is that . . . ?'

'It's a brand,' the medical examiner says. 'Burned into the skin. Like he's cattle. I didn't know how to describe the image. And I thought you'd better see it. So do you feel bad now, about being rude?'

'I'm glad you called, Gladys.'

'You know what it is?'

'No, but I've seen it before.' Lou leans closer, until his nose is two inches away from the brand. 'Can you tell how old it is?'

'I'd say it's at least six months old. Other than that, no.'

'So it could be years old?

'Sure.' Gladys is looking at her notes. 'I'm going to call it an "unknown pattern" in my report. Unless you've got something better to call it?'

'Unknown pattern works for me. For now, anyway.'

# 69

'There she is.'

Penelope Buchanan descends the steps of her psychiatrist's office, an unmarked brownstone on Seventy-Fifth Street.

Tom steps out of the SUV and waits in the middle of the sidewalk. Penelope sees him and stops walking. She's surprised, then angry. She considers crossing to the other side of the street. Penelope's butler Zorro is at her side.

'Hi, Pen,' Tom says.

Penelope glares at her cousin. 'You lied to me. Harper's not your girlfriend. She's your bodyguard.'

'I'm sorry, I really am. But I can explain,' Tom says, pointing at the SUV. 'Can we talk in private. Please.'

Penelope bites her lip, thinking. She finally nods, signals Zorro to wait on the street, and follows Tom into the back seat. She sees Harper behind the wheel and scoffs. Tom joins Penelope in the back seat and shuts the door. 'Who told you that Harper wasn't my girlfriend?'

'Wells,' Penelope says. 'He called me the day after you visited. He couldn't believe you hired someone from Uncle Mitch's security team, after what happened.' Penelope steals a quick, judgemental look at Harper.

Harper remembers Wells from the family meeting in New York. He was the loudest and rudest of the cousins, the 'man-child' as Tom called him.

'Ah, yes, Wells,' Tom says, 'the paragon of decision-making. For the record, Harper's saved my life twice this week.' Tom takes Penelope by the hands. 'And I'm sorry I lied, Pen. I am. But I needed your help. Harper's not only protecting me, she's been helping me figure out who killed Uncle Mitch. I needed you to talk to us, and I didn't think you would unless I lied. Did you hear what happened last night in Petersburg?'

'No.'

Tom describes in brief detail the break-in at Appleton Hall. He paints Harper as a hero but leaves out the part where she shot and killed the intruder. 'We're on to something, Pen. I don't know what, exactly, but it's something.'

Penelope's expression changes, from angry to overwhelmed. Her eyes glisten, portending tears. 'What do you want from me?'

'Last time we talked, you were holding something back. You seemed nervous or ... I don't know. I think there's something you didn't tell us about that night.'

A tear travels down Penelope's cheek.

'Please, Pen,' Tom says. 'I know you're scared, but we need your help.'

'I heard something,' Penelope says.

'You mean the night Skip was killed? What did you hear?'

'Chanting.'

'What?'

'I don't know.' Penelope drops her head in her hands. 'See! This is why Borelli asked me to keep it quiet.'

'It's OK. Take your time.'

'It was after I'd heard the gunshots, after I'd gone up to the loft of the barn. It was dark, and there were no windows, so I couldn't see anything. Grandpa Skip said he was going to take a look. He stepped out of the barn, and – I don't know – maybe thirty seconds later I heard another gunshot. Then I heard Skip's panting. He kept saying "No, no, no." Because of the marks in the snow, and the trail of blood, Borelli said Skip tried to crawl away from Knox. I guess that's what I heard. But then it was quiet. I don't know for how long. A minute, maybe two . . . And then I heard something. It sounded kind of like chanting . . . But I wasn't one hundred per cent sure, so Borelli said, "Don't put doubt in the mind of the jury. Do that and Knox will go free. And then he'll come for you." He said only tell the jury what makes sense, and that you're one hundred per cent sure of. So I didn't say anything about it at the trial. I didn't lie, really. The other lawyers just didn't know to ask.'

'It's fine, Pen,' Tom says. 'You did what was asked of you. I'd have done the same. But I'm not sure I'm following. What do you mean, chanting? What did it sound like?'

'I don't know. It sounded like chanting. Like "UMMMMMMMMMM".'

'If Knox was chanting when he killed Skip,' Tom asks, 'does that mean it was like a religious experience for him?'

'No,' Penelope says. 'I mean . . . maybe. I don't know. But that's not what was so strange. I think . . . it wasn't just Knox chanting.'

'What do you mean?'

Penelope shakes her head, annoyed she has to say it aloud. 'I mean Knox wasn't alone.'

# 70

Bacon sizzles on a flat-top grill.

'Coffee?'

Lou and Frank nod in unison before their waitress pours coffee into their mugs.

'Do you boys know what you want?'

'Eggs and sausage, pancakes on the side.'

'Egg white omelette.'

They return laminated menus to the waitress. Once she's out of earshot, Frank hands Lou a manila folder. Inside there's a printout of an employment file from Everly, tax forms, payroll.

'What's this? You got his name?'

'His name and more.'

'Brent Amendola? That's the name of the guy who shot up Appleton Hall?'

Frank nods.

'And he worked at Everly College? No shit.'

'A janitor. We found keys and an access card on him, which meant he could get inside practically any building at Everly. We'd assumed it was stolen, but when I checked with the caretaker department, I walked into their office, and there was his picture on the wall. He was on their baseball team. The head custodian raved about Amendola. Great worker, never been late. He'd worked at Everly for more than a year. And he was a student before that, nearly seven years ago.'

'That's strange, isn't it?' Lou asks. 'To have a degree from a school like Everly and end up a janitor?'

'Those fancy degrees aren't what they used to be.'

'Did you find any connection to Knox?'

'Nothing yet.'

'But you think this is our guy?' Lou asks. 'The man who attacked McMurtry and who killed Mitch Buchanan?'

'It has to be. He had a key and access card to Cielo House, which would explain why there was no sign of forced entry. He had a syringe for crying out loud. The lab hasn't confirmed yet, but my money is on fentanyl. Just like what was used on Mitch. I figure he broke into Cielo House Friday night and waited for Mitch to return.'

'Maybe.'

'Maybe? Come on, Lou. Think about it. This is our guy. Has to be.'

'But the cameras in Cielo House weren't shut off on Friday night until after Mitch was back in his room. So your theory doesn't fit. Maybe Amendola came after the cameras were shut off. But how'd he time it, how did he know the cameras would be off? And some guy with a liberal arts degree takes out two members of Buchanan's security detail all by himself? And what about the symbol?' Lou hands Frank the pictures he took at the medical examiner's office. 'Scott found the cattle brand in the Movement's abandoned compound, and that same image was branded into Amendola's thigh. And Knox was a member of the Movement. There's clearly a connection here.'

'Can we really trust what Scott found?' Frank asks. 'What does she know about conducting an investigation?'

'I know you don't want to talk about the Movement,' Lou says. 'You don't want the corners you cut during the Knox investigation to come back and bite us in the ass. But something is off here, Frank. I drove by the guru's home when you were at the school asking about Amendola.'

'And?'

'It was empty,' Lou says. 'Mail was overflowing from the mailbox. The lawn hadn't been cut. Just like the ashram or whatever the fuck they called it. Where did this guru and his followers go? Why did they leave town?'

'Aren't you overthinking this? We got our guy. He's on ice in the morgue.'

Lou's phone rings. He answers.

Their food arrives. Frank leans down and smells his pancakes.

Lou hangs up and places his phone on the linoleum table.

'Who was that?' Frank asks, as he's flooding his plate with syrup.

'Harper Scott.'

'Did you agree to meet her?'

'She says she has new information.'

Frank laughs. 'We should be charging her with lying to the FBI, not making her an honorary agent or something?'

Lou surgically cuts his omelette into one-inch pieces. 'Foster liked her. Called her a bulldozer.'

'Foster this. Foster that. You really trusted him, didn't you? How did you know him again? Did you serve together?'

'Yes.' Lou nearly leaves it at that, but this is the first time Frank has asked directly about his relationship with Foster since Foster was shot. And to simply describe the man he loves as 'someone he served with' while Foster's fighting for his life – it feels like a betrayal. So, without thinking it through, Lou adds, 'He's my boyfriend.'

'Boyfriend?'

Lou nods. He braces himself for Frank's reaction.

'So you're gay?'

'Yes.'

The expression on Frank's face is pure puzzlement, like he lost his keys and is trying to mentally retrace his steps to find them.

Then he nods and takes a bite of his pancakes. 'Looks like I owe Greg Downing fifty dollars.'

'Greg from the office? Why? What do you mean?'

'We had a bet.'

'About what? Whether I was gay?'

'He wanted to ask you out. I said don't bother. He's not gay, he just has great taste in suits.' Frank sips his coffee. 'Sorry. Maybe you wanted to date Greg Downing or something.'

Lou smiles. 'Don't worry. I'm out of his league.'

Frank winks. 'That's what I figured.'

# 71

On the drive from New York City to Everly College, they talk through Penelope's revelation, but Tom is reluctant to draw any conclusions. 'Just because she thinks Knox wasn't alone, that doesn't mean she's right.'

'I'm all for being sceptical,' Harper says, 'but at a certain point we have to decide what's true and what's not.'

'We're getting close, but we're not there yet.'

'Penelope says Knox wasn't alone. Knox was part of some group called the Movement. And Clegg confirmed the Movement is some fucked-up cult. You're not ready to draw a line from A to B?'

'Like I said, we're getting close, but jumping to conclusions is how you make mistakes. Maybe Clegg's source will give us what we need.'

Once they're inside Tom's bungalow, Harper sets up her laptop in the kitchen and checks her Trojan horse program.

'Anything?' Tom asks.

'No.'

She checks the time. 'Our bet was midnight, right? It's not looking good for you.'

'It's only seven. I'm not worried.'

Tom grabs two beers from the fridge. They drink in the kitchen, leaning against the counter.

'So is there really porn on the USB?' Tom asks.

Harper laughs. 'Yeah. It would be suspicious if there weren't.'

'Do you ever think about what the person's doing while you're hacking their computer?'

'It's best not to.'

They smile and sip their beers. They stare at each other. Harper says, 'I'm going to lie down, get some rest while I can.'

Tom looks disappointed. He nods. 'Sure. You can use my bed upstairs if you want.'

'Thanks.'

Harper walks to the stairs, stops, and looks over her shoulder, her green eyes alive with an intensity that wasn't there moments before. 'Are you coming?'

It takes Tom a moment to process the invitation. Then he hurries after Harper, following her upstairs.

They meet in Tom's bedroom, at the end of the bed. They kiss. Harper takes hold of Tom's shirt and helps him peel it off. They do the same with Harper's. Then they resume kissing until they hear an electronic *ping* downstairs.

'What was that?'

Harper smiles and checks her watch. 'That's the sound of me winning our bet.'

'You mean . . . ?'

'We're in.'

# 72

**Transcription:**
**Interview of** ▮▮▮▮▮▮▮▮▮▮▮▮▮▮ **– DAY 2**

SIMON CLEGG: All right, let's begin. I've started the recording. The time is 2:36 p.m. We are in my hotel room, at the Marriott in . . .

▮▮▮▮▮▮▮: Do we have to say where? You didn't last time.

CLEGG: Sure. We can leave that off the record, if you like. But remember, as I explained before, I'm taking every precaution to protect your identity. I'm the only person who will hear this recording. I will transcribe our interview myself, and I will redact all reference to your real name. The transcript, my notes and the recording will be kept on an encrypted hard drive, which will never leave my home. No one will know we've met. Not until you tell me it's OK to go public.

▮▮▮▮▮▮▮: If you say so.

CLEGG: You think they'll find out? Even with all of the precautions we're taking?

▮▮▮▮▮▮▮: He'll find out. Eventually. He's brilliant. You know that, right? He's literally a genius. He has an IQ of 160.

CLEGG: Who do you mean? Aaron?

▬▬▬▬▬: We call him Father now.

CLEGG: Like a priest? That's . . . interesting. When I visited the ashram, everyone was calling him Lama Aaron.

▬▬▬▬▬: Once his vibrations reached a certain frequency, Meryl started calling him Father. So we all started to do it.

CLEGG: I see. OK. I want to come back to that idea of vibrations later, I'm not sure we've covered that yet. But just to close the loop on whether this interview will be discovered, I'm sure Aaron – or Father, sorry – is a smart guy. But there is no way he'll know that we've met. Not until you say it's OK for me to publish my story. You understand that, right?

▬▬▬▬▬: It's getting late. Maybe we should just start.

CLEGG: All right. Sure. Last time we met, you told me about the initiation process into – what was the group called again? Let me just check my notes.

▬▬▬▬▬: The Maniple.

CLEGG: Right. The Maniple. M-A-N-I-P-L-E. Which was – or is – a secret group within the Movement. I was looking up the name since we last spoke. Is it a reference to the bit of cloth a priest uses? The liturgical garment?

▬▬▬▬▬: Yes, but it's also a division of a Roman legion. So there's a double meaning. Father is big on double meaning. We are holy and violent. Soldiers of God and Truth. The Hand of God. It was an honour to be invited to join. I told you that, right? Only a select few are ever invited to join.

CLEGG: Yes, you told me. That's very . . . uh, impressive. When you described the initiation, you said that they marked you, but you didn't explain how. Or where. Are you comfortable telling me now?

██████: I don't know.

CLEGG: If you're not, I understand. I just—

██████: You know what? Fuck it.

CLEGG: Why are you unbuttoning your pants?

██████: Here. Right here. This is it.

CLEGG: I – um – for the record, you've stood up, unbuttoned your pants, and pulled them down to your ankle. And you're now pointing at a scar on your inner thigh. Oh my . . . did they . . . did they brand you? Like cattle? Does it hurt?

██████: It's gotten a lot better, but fuck did it hurt at the time. I mean . . . I don't know how to describe it. I broke my ankle once and this was about a thousand times more painful. I had to clean and dress it constantly, changing the bandages twice a day. It took months to heal, and it hurt the whole time.

CLEGG: You must be angry they did this to you?

███████: What do you mean?

CLEGG: Well... they burned you. They mutilated you. And it sounds like you didn't have much warning. Or choice.

███████: To tell you the truth, I hadn't thought about it like that. Being branded wasn't something to be mad at, but something I had to endure. Because this *was* an honour. I was proud that I'd been invited to join this super-secret group. I'd earned it. And we were going to do something to fix this fucked-up world. There's no progress without pain.

CLEGG: How were you going to do that?

███████: Well, at first... we started small. I realise now that Father had a grand vision for us, an ultimate goal. But we had a lot to learn before we focused on our true purpose. I moved to the ashram not long after I joined my maniple. I was meditating a lot, reading Father's books, and I was praying a lot. At his core, Father was a Buddhist, but he incorporated all these different faiths into the Movement.

Anyway, one day, it must have been a month after I'd joined Alex's maniple, Aaron was preaching about the Uyghurs. They're a group of people in China. Muslims, I think. (It's starts with a "U" and a "Y", but it's pronounced *Wee-gurs*. You probably don't know how to pronounce it because no one literally gives a fuck about them.) I guess the Chinese government was trying to – well, I'm not even sure what they wanted to do. Kill them off, I guess. They were locking the Uyghurs up, sending them to re-education camps. Like Hitler did with the Jews, but this time no one cared. Father learned that there were clothing companies – like Swish, the sports brand – that were using cotton picked by

Uyghurs who'd been locked up by the Chinese government. They were profiting from forced labour. It was horrific. There were calls on social media to boycott Swish and the other companies. But Father said this wouldn't go anywhere. People will bitch and moan, and then they'll get on with their lives. Father said, 'If only there were people who could hold them to account. Superhuman beings who could ensure balance was restored to the universe.'

When Father was saying this, Alex reached out and clawed at my thigh. She had long nails, so it *killed*. Afterwards, in the parking lot, Alex whispered to me, 'Did you hear the message Aaron sent us?' I said, 'What are you talking about?' And she said, 'About Swish. Aaron gave our maniple a target.'

We went to work the next day. We had dozens of burner accounts – you know like fake accounts. On Twitter and Facebook and Reddit. We started posting about how the CEO of Swish deserved to die. We were trying to spark something. Outrage that would actually lead to change. We wanted to start a movement. It was trial and error. We saw that the most vile posts got the most engagement. People either loved it or hated it, which is the sweet spot for getting people engaged online. That's actually what we called it when our posts went viral, 'the Sweet Spot'. And eventually, rather than say he deserved to die, we started writing that we were going to kill him.

CLEGG: Your plan to make the world a better place was by making death threats?

████████: Yes.

CLEGG: How was that supposed to work?

████████: What do you mean?

CLEGG: Well, how would threatening someone – how would that improve the world?

███████: It's common sense, isn't it? It's – what's the word – deterrence. Don't tell me you don't believe in deterrence because – as Father said – it's like the foundation for criminal justice in the Western world. The death penalty? Hello? Let me put it this way. No one gave a shit about the Uyghurs. People kept buying clothing made by slave labour. So, the CEO of Swish wasn't deterred from using slave labour because there was no negative incentive. But if enough people wanted him dead, if he felt that his life was truly in danger – voilà! there's your deterrence. And then, obviously, retribution, or payback – that's the other reason to try to hurt the CEO. He deserves it. Father is a big proponent of karma. Horrible acts deserve commensurate punishment.

CLEGG: Isn't there a certain irony there? Committing an immoral act to punish another immoral act?

███████: Only if you forget who these people were. Father taught us that it doesn't matter what you're doing so much as who you're doing it to. The enlightened mind sees this. And you know what? It felt good to threaten this rich and powerful CEO. He was a piece of shit and he *did* deserve to die.

CLEGG: But that's not really karma, is it? I'm obviously no expert, but isn't karma the idea if you're horrible in this life, you'll come back as a beetle in the next? What you're describing is something different. You're describing revenge.

████████: Father says that at its very heart, the idea of karma is cause and effect. And so's retribution, what you'd call revenge. They're similar principles.

CLEGG: OK, I think I know what you're trying to say. And you continued to use burner accounts to make these threats online?

████████: Yes. We had to. Anonymity was key to protecting ourselves and continuing our work. Vigilantes need a persona. Bruce Wayne has Batman, we had burner accounts.

CLEGG: Was it hard to come up with names for every burner account? When I rented this hotel room, I used an alias. But I struggled to think of one.

████████: We had a system. You watched one of our criticism circles, right? You know, that Father says the day you join the Movement is auspicious. And so we count the number of days that each congregant is with the Movement. We just adopted the same naming system for any new burner account. The number of days we'd been with the Movement and the word karma. So if I created a burner account on my two-hundred and second day with the Movement, my name would be @Karma202.

CLEGG: From these burner accounts, you'd threaten people?

████████: And spread Father's teachings.

CLEGG: Alex was in your maniple. Who else?

████████: Next question.

CLEGG: Is it still a secret?

██████████: Maybe. I don't know ... I mean the reason I'm talking to you ... things got so fucked up, what we did ... but I swore an oath.

CLEGG: You told me Alex was the leader. You were comfortable telling me that much.

██████████: Did I say that? She said she was the leader of our maniple. But I don't know. The way it was set up, siloed into tiny groups, and all my thoughts had to be filtered through Alex, I couldn't be sure who our *actual* leader was. Alex implied she took instructions directly from Father, but I never saw that. To tell you the truth, I thought Alex's mom was the real leader of our maniple. It was just this sense I had.

CLEGG: Alex's mom was in the Movement as well?

██████████: Oh yeah. She was the longest-serving member. When I first met Alex she said her mom started taking her to the Movement when Alex was addicted to Oxy. But that was bullshit. I'm not sure why she lied. I saw pictures of her mom with Father from the Nineties.

CLEGG: Did Alex tell you what you wanted to hear so you'd join the Movement?

██████████: No. She wouldn't do that. Let's stop talking about Alex. OK?

CLEGG: Sure, ▮ Let's go back to what your maniple did. You said you would threaten people online. Is that mainly what you did?

▮: For a while, yeah. We were getting engagement online, but it wasn't breaking through to the real world. It wasn't sparking the revolutionary change Father wanted. Alex told our maniple that we needed to do more to inspire fear in those who aren't afraid, the wolves who should be the sheep. We started breaking into homes of different targets. We'd make a mess and usually leave a mark. The same one we branded each other with. We'd carve it into the wall, or the banister, of some family that deserved to have karmic repercussions. Alex called these Karmic Raids. They were exciting, for sure. But they were hardly ever mentioned online or in the press. In terms of sparking real change, the Karmic Raids weren't getting the job done.

CLEGG: You mentioned the Uyghurs and the CEO of Swish. Is that who your maniple focused on?

▮: Those first few months we targeted whoever Father referred to in his sermons. CEOs, a senator, a few Karens, the manager of an Applebee's. But then a story leaked to the press and we realised that there was one family we should have been targeting. One family who'd caused so much pain and suffering. And not just pain and suffering in an abstract sense, but specifically to our congregants. Father became obsessed with it, what came out in the press release. It became our sole focus. The injustice of it. And at the same time one of our congregants had just lost his daughter. He didn't take it very well.

He was gambling and drinking. Aaron said we needed to help him focus on something, on making the world a better place.

CLEGG: I'm not sure I understand what you mean. Can you walk me through it? What lead? Which family?

███████: Why are you looking at me like that? You're judging me. It was our targets who were bad. Not me. Not Alex. They deserve all the evil shit our maniple brought down on them.

CLEGG: I'm not judging you, Jess. I only want to hear your story.

███████: I should go. If I'm much longer, they'll suspect something.

CLEGG: Can we meet again?

███████: Yes. Next week. I'll come to this room again.

# 73

Tom is reading the transcription over Harper's shoulder. Once he's finished, he says, 'Well, there's one mystery solved.'

'I counted a few. Which do you mean?'

'The usernames of their burner accounts. The word "karma" and then some numbers. It's people in the Movement.'

'Borelli was wrong,' Harper says. 'He took these posts, assumed they were Knox, and then said they were Knox's manifesto. But it was more than one person, including Clegg's source. They were – what's the phrase she used? – "spreading Father's teaching".'

Tom is shaking his head, but out of disbelief, not because he disagrees with what Harper's said. 'And it's them. They're the ones who have been threatening and doxing my family online.'

'Only a fraction of the posts we see online had that sort of username.'

'That's true,' Tom says. 'I can't believe it, but they achieved what they were looking for. They set out to inspire the masses, to stoke a mob, by making murder threats a viral movement. And they did it! Fucking hell.'

Harper scrolls up. 'And did you see? On page eight. Clegg meant to redact his source's name throughout, but he slipped up. Here. Her name is "Jess".'

Tom brings his nose an inch from the monitor. 'Holy shit.'

'He probably redacted it in the final version,' Harper says. 'What we found is a fragment of the original Word document on his hard drive. He did his best to protect her, he's just shit with computers.'

'May I?' Tom asks, pointing at the laptop. Harper stands up and Tom takes her seat. 'I want her full name. She's our answer to this puzzle. I'll try Googling "Jess" and "the Movement".'

After thirty seconds, Harper asks, 'Anything?'

'No.'

'Try Jessica, Everly College, and Appleton Hall.'

'Why?' Tom asks as he's typing. 'Because of the endless knot that's carved into the door frame? That's a bit of a long shot, don't you ... Wow!'

'What?'

'It worked. I got a name, Jessica Andrews.'

Over the next half an hour, they read everything they can find on Jessica Andrews, articles about her time at Everly College, mainly in the school paper, but a few national outlets as well. The school paper called her anti-Semitic and, in at least two stories, a neo-Nazi. The national papers couched those descriptions as 'allegations', but essentially made the same claims. The story stemmed from an argument between Andrews and her roommate in Appleton Hall, which led to an investigation by an expensive New York law firm, and culminated in a hearing on campus.

Harper reads the articles, but doesn't understand how any of it was newsworthy. 'Why would national papers document an argument between two teenagers?' She thinks of all the shitty things she said at that age, and she's grateful reporters weren't there, recording it for posterity. 'Do you remember this happening?' she asks Tom. 'You'd have been here at the same time?'

Tom nods. 'Yes, vaguely. I didn't remember the name, but the Nazi roommate story was all anyone talked about for a few weeks. But then the story disappeared. We all moved onto some other controversy. I don't think I've thought about it since.'

Tom doesn't find any reference to Andrews joining the Movement, but there is one reference to her going missing twelve months ago – not nearly as widely reported as the fight with her roommate. In fact, not a single news organisation reported the story. Tom found the information on the sheriff's department website. According to the short press release, Andrews dropped out of school and went missing not long afterwards.

They call Special Agent Diaz. He's still in town, investigating the incident at Appleton Hall. They agree to meet at Tom's in an hour to discuss what they found.

After Harper hangs up, she heads for the door.

'Where are you going?' Tom asks.

'The vice-dean isn't the warmest personality, but she's been helpful so far. I'm going to see what she has on Andrews.'

'It's after eight, you think she's still in her office?'

'She doesn't strike me as the nine-to-five type. Dropping by her office is worth a shot.'

# 74

Three dozen students are holding a candlelight vigil for Mother Earth. All but one participant are dressed in black and gripping a candle. The woman playing the recently departed Mother Earth is dressed in white. She's lying on a mock funeral pyre.

Harper skirts past the demonstration and ducks inside the redbrick building. On the second floor, the vice-dean's secretary has gone for the day. But as Harper predicted, Olivia Perkins is in her office.

'Ms Scott,' she says, with a brief glance from her monitor. 'You're back.'

'I am.'

Harper takes a seat across from Perkins.

'I'm surprised you're not in jail,' the vice-dean says as she removes her reading glasses. 'Didn't you shoot someone?'

'It was self-defence.'

Perkins flashes her pained smile. 'I'm sure it was. And what did Mr Park have to say about his semester under the tutelage of Mr Knox?'

The revelation that Tom was Knox's student seems like a lifetime ago. Harper would have faked indifference if it were necessary. But her shrug is genuine. 'A coincidence.'

Perkins waits for more of an explanation but Harper declines to give it.

'Well,' Perkins says, 'is there something I can help you with?'

'I need information on a former student.'

'And who would that be?'

'Jessica Andrews.'

The vice-dean leans back in her chair. 'Jessica Andrews?'

'You know who I'm talking about?'

'It was more than three years ago, but a hard incident to forget.'

'What incident? The trial?'

Perkins laughs. 'It was hardly a trial. There was an investigation, followed by a hearing. It was nothing, really. A dispute between two students. But the national media picked it up. Who knows why. A slow news week, maybe. Or they needed more fuel for the culture wars.' She shrugs. 'Absent the media involvement, it was just another day on campus. We deal with disputes between students all the time.'

'But big enough to hire lawyers to investigate, and to hold a hearing.'

'We have processes that must be followed. Complaints of anti-Semitism must be investigated thoroughly. We have a responsibility to the students.'

Harper shakes her head. 'I don't know how you do it.'

'Do what?'

'Work here. Deal with all this bullshit. Everyone's mad at everyone all the time. I'd be sick of it if I were you.'

The vice-dean's eyes narrow to frosty slits. 'I appreciate the input, Ms Scott, but perhaps I'm missing something. How was Ms Andrews' case related to Mr Buchanan's murder?'

'We spoke to a reporter ...' Harper checks herself. She's already betrayed Clegg's trust by hacking his computer and learning the name of his source. Why go further if she doesn't need to? 'Listen, if you can't provide her file' – she stands – 'I'll try President Flowers. Do you know where his office is?'

'No, no – let's not bother Winston with this.' The vice-dean waves at her to sit down. 'As I've said before, I'm happy to help.'

She opens her desk drawer and then holds up a key. 'I'm not sure if I can provide her entire file – likely that's confidential. I'll have to check. I wasn't vice-dean at the time, you see. My predecessor handled the Andrews case. But perhaps there are public records from the hearing. Let me go have a look. It won't take long. You can wait here if you like.'

Perkins leaves. Harper texts Tom: Progress!

# 75

'Where's Harper?' Lou strides into Tom's home.

'She's gone to ask the vice-dean for help. She'll be back soon. I can catch you up.'

Lou follows Tom into the living room. A laptop is connected to a 45-inch television. The quality of the image on the screen isn't great, coarse pixels, with colours and lines that bleed into one another. Lou makes out a man on stage in a baggy suit, with a large collar, orange button-up shirt, and long hair. The background is pastel – very Nineties or early 2000s.

Tom presses play and then sits cross-legged on the floor, a few feet from the television. He picks up a pad of paper. His notes – pristinely printed out in blue ink – fill the page.

'What are you watching?' Lou asks as he sits on the coffee table.

'This is the Movement's earlier iteration, "Meditate to a Successful Life". We met with that reporter, Simon Clegg. He converted a bunch of VHS videos he'd ordered on eBay to digital and gave me a copy.'

'How are they?'

Tom adjusts his glasses. 'Mind-numbing. I can't believe people bought into this garbage.'

'I bet.' Lou sits on the arm of the sofa. 'And what did the reporter say?'

Tom explains everything they'd learned from Clegg about the Movement. Visiting their ashram, a source reaching out to him in secret, a name that he wouldn't give up. 'But we were able to figure out the source's name.'

'How?' Lou asks. But when he sees Tom's grimace, he puts up his hands. 'Actually, I don't want to know. Keep going.'

Tom explains everything they found on Jessica Andrews.

'She's been missing how long?'

'More than a year. Harper's gone to the school to see what she can dig up.'

'And this was Clegg's source? A neo-Nazi?'

'We don't know if it's true or not.'

Lou shrugs. 'Where there's smoke there's fire.'

'Can you imagine having all that written about you, when you're eighteen years old? It would be devastating. She'd be perfectly primed to join' – she points at the television – 'this.'

On the screen, the man in the baggy suit is standing beside a woman sitting in a director's chair with a blindfold on. The video is muted, but it looks to Lou as though the man is leading the woman through a meditation.

'Who's the guy in the suit?' Lou asks.

'Lama Aaron. Although he wasn't using the "Lama" moniker yet. Here, he's just Aaron.'

Lou moves closer to the screen. He didn't recognise the man in the suit as Coughlin, but now he does. 'This isn't what I expected. When I heard meditation group, I pictured . . . I don't know. Crossed legs and whale sounds.'

Tom nods. 'Yeah, I watched a more recent video and it was like that. Aaron was wearing a saffron-coloured leisure suit and a gold Rolex. But this is his earlier stuff, from the late Nineties. I think he's adapted to tastes over the years. This is more oriented towards success in business. But as tastes changed, he slowly started to move towards a new-age vibe.'

On screen, the woman in the chair finishes her meditation. Aaron removes her blindfold. She's beaming with pride, on the verge of crying. She stands up and hugs Aaron. To Lou, a born sceptic, the scene looks rehearsed, meant to give the impression the woman's life has suddenly improved – modern snake oil. The woman leaves the stage and a blonde woman takes her place. She shakes hands with Aaron.

'She looks familiar,' Tom says. He slides closer, bringing his nose a few inches from the screen. 'Holy shit.'

'What?' Lou asks.

'Holy fucking shit!' Tom takes off his glasses and keeps staring.

'What?'

Tom points at the woman on the screen. 'Do you know who that is?'

# 76

Harper paces the wall of photos to kill time. In one, the vice-dean is shaking hands with former Vice-President Al Gore. In another, she's sandwiched between Bruce Springsteen and Condoleezza Rice.

Students are chanting in the quad outside. The faint glow from the candles below gives the window a yellow hue.

The vice-dean returns, holding up a stack of papers. 'Success, Ms Scott.'

Harper points at the wall of pictures. 'These are impressive.'

Perkins drops the papers on her desk and joins Harper by the wall. 'Yes, we have quite a few celebrities come through our school. One of the perks of being vice-dean is that I can corner them for a picture.'

Harper points at a picture of the vice-dean beside a pretty young woman wearing a graduation robe and cap. She has blonde hair and blue eyes.

'Who's this?'

'My pride and joy,' Perkins says. 'My daughter, Alex. She graduated from Everly College a few years ago.' She turns to her desk and points at the stack of papers. 'As I was saying, Ms Scott, I've found the file on Jessica Andrews, but I don't think you can take any of this with you. Do you mind reviewing it here, in my office?'

Harper fights back a sigh and nods. *It's better than nothing.* She takes a seat and, holding the stack of papers in her lap, starts to flip through the material. Perkins busies herself behind Harper, by the door.

Harper's phone vibrates along her thigh. She drags it out of her pocket, props it between her shoulder and ear, and continues to scan the papers.

'Where are you?'

It's Tom. He sounds anxious.

'With the vice-dean,' Harper says, 'in her office. I'll be back soon.'

'Get out of there now. It's not safe.'

'What?'

'She's one of them, Harper. She's *in* the Movement. Get out of there *now*.'

Just then Harper feels a sensation along her neck, a sharp pinch.

Instinctively, she reaches for her gun, but it's with the FBI, not holstered under her arm. She stands and the papers in her lap scatter to the floor. She whips around and sees Perkins standing directly behind her. The vice-dean's lips are stretched into a malignant smile.

A pulse of euphoria travels through Harper's limbs. Then, just as quickly, extreme exhaustion overwhelms her, like she'd just finished driving twenty-four hours straight.

Harper drops the phone and reaches for her neck. Her hand closes on a smooth cylinder of plastic. She pulls at it, feels something slide out of her. The realisation that she's holding a syringe doesn't fully bloom because the opioid has already started flattening her consciousness.

Her legs wobble. She desperately wants to shut her eyes, to go to sleep.

'W-why?' she asks.

'I'm sorry for this, Ms Scott. We would never harm a citizen if it weren't absolutely necessary. But if you keep asking questions about Jessica Andrews, then soon enough you'll discover she was with the Movement. (Or maybe you already knew that?) And if you keep digging, no doubt you'll find out I'm with the Movement as well. And our work isn't done yet. Inspiring real change takes time and *immense* effort.'

Harper grips the back of the chair she'd been sitting on for balance.

'This is sad but necessary. And you're not entirely innocent, are you? You accepted blood money in exchange for protecting Mr Park. You knew the risks.'

Harper knows she has seconds until her eyes close, maybe for good. Once she does, she'll be at the vice-dean's mercy. She has an overwhelming desire to escape, that everything will be fine if she can just get out of this room.

'And you should thank me,' Perkins says. 'This is a humane way to go. It really is.'

Summoning all the strength she can, Harper lifts the chair over her head and tosses it through the window. The crowd below screams as the chair and shards of broken glass rain down on the quad. Harper staggers towards the hole in the window.

She doesn't make it.

She collapses.

Her eyes shut.

A tide of poisonous bliss drags her away.

# 77

Tom screams into the phone, 'Harper! Harper!'

Lou swerves the Impala around a plodding van and slams his palm on the horn.

Up ahead a traffic light turns amber. Lou accelerates. The force pushes them back against their seats.

'I've lost her,' Tom says.

'Call an ambulance.'

Lou hops a kerb and flies across a grassy field. A dozen kids playing Ultimate Frisbee flee in terror. He brings the car to a screeching halt on the quad, beside a smashed wooden chair and shards of broken glass. They sprint inside and up the stairs. Inside Perkins' office, there's no sign of the vice-dean. Harper is lying on her back and unconscious. She's clutching a syringe in her right hand.

Lou drops to his knees and puts his ear to Harper's chest. 'Shit.'

'Is she breathing?'

'I can't tell.' Lou traces his fingers along Harper's ribcage and then places the palms of his hands at the apex. But before he can start CPR, Tom grabs him by the elbow.

'Wait.'

Lou is about to tell Tom to get out of his way, but there's a certainty to Tom's voice that gives him pause. He watches Tom reach for the back pocket of Harper's jeans and remove a plastic container the size of his palm. He peels back a sheet of tinfoil and removes what looks like nasal spray.

'What are you . . .' Lou starts to ask, but his voice trails off.

Tom inserts the tip of the bottle into Harper's nose and pumps Narcan into her nasal cavity.

She doesn't move.

Lou is about to start CPR.

And then Harper gasps, sucking air into her lungs, like a newborn, taking her first breath of a new life.

# 78

Harper opens her bleary eyes.

*Beep beep beep.*

The world clarifies. Slowly.

She recognises the aesthetic of a hospital: industrial, hygienic, functional. Her mouth is dry, like she's been chewing plaster. It feels like a giant sat on her chest.

'Oh, thank God.'

Tom is sitting on the chair beside the hospital bed. Harper tries to prop herself up on an elbow, but a torrent of blood rushes to her head and she has to lie down. Tom stands and places his hand on her shoulder. 'Don't push yourself, Harper.'

'What happened?'

'What do you remember?'

'I don't know. Why don't you start at the beginning?'

Tom tells her. When he's finished, Harper asks, 'You saved my life?'

'Yup.'

'It's supposed to be the other way round.'

Tom smiles. 'The alternative was letting you overdose.'

'OK, that would have been worse.' Harper takes another stab at sitting up. 'What was in the needle?'

'The doctors say it must have been an opioid, because the Narcan worked. But I haven't heard anything more specific than that.'

'And you saw Perkins in the Movement's early videos? Which means she's been a member of this cult for years?'

'Yup.'

Memories of her conversation with Perkins come back to Harper. 'I asked about a photo on the wall. She said it was her daughter, Alex. It didn't register, but that's the name of Andrews' friend, according to Clegg's interview notes.'

Tom takes out his phone and Googles 'Alex Perkins'. He shows Harper a picture.

'That's her.' Harper laughs, derisively. 'Perkins told me her daughter's name maybe ten minutes before she tried to kill me. If I'd died, I'd have deserved it.'

'Don't be too hard on yourself, Harper. No one would have put that together. Not until . . . you know . . . Perkins attacked you with a needle.'

'Has Lou found Perkins?'

Tom shakes his head. 'The FBI went to her house, but she wasn't there. And her car was left in the Everly College parking lot. She must have had her escape planned out.'

'I fucked up,' Harper says. 'Going directly to Perkins like that.'

'Actually, you accelerated our investigation. We've learned more in the last few hours than we have in a week.'

'But I asked Perkins about Andrews.' Harper closes her eyes and thinks back to her conversation with the vice-dean. 'Shit, I think I mentioned a reporter as well. How long until Perkins puts two and two together? I put Andrews' life in danger.'

'Clegg thought she was dead already.'

'Is that supposed to make me feel better?'

Tom leans forwards and squeezes Harper's hand. 'Harper, listen. I've saved the best news for last. Foster's awake.'

It takes a moment for Tom's statement to register. Harper stares at him blankly. Then she's struggling to stand. 'I've got to talk to him.'

'Harper, stop. You're not ready to walk.'

'I have to see.' Harper's legs give way the moment she steps onto the floor. Tom helps her sit up.

'Harper, stop. He's alive. There's no rush.'

'Get a wheelchair, Tom. Get a wheelchair or you can watch me crawl to Foster's room.'

# 79

'You look like shit.'

Tom wheels Harper into Foster's hospital room. He looks anaemic and weak. Still, it's an improvement from Harper's last visit.

'I was shot three times,' Foster says. 'What's your excuse?'

Tom parks the wheelchair a foot from Foster's hospital bed.

'You go first,' Harper says.

Foster shakes his head. 'Uh-uh. You first. I need my bearings.'

Harper tells Foster everything that's happened since the Friday night, from the Hamiltons, to the abandoned ashram, to Perkins stabbing a needle into Harper's neck.

'So Perkins nearly killed both of us? Now I don't feel so bad.' Foster starts to laugh until a sharp pain makes him clutch his side.

'All right,' Harper says. 'Your turn. What happened that night?'

'I suppose it starts with the phones.'

'Whose phones?'

'Remember how I told you Mitch Buchanan had three phones?'

Harper's expression is blank. A lot had happened since Friday afternoon.

'I could swear I told you . . .' Foster shakes his head. 'It doesn't matter. I was light on the details because he – well – not to speak ill of the dead, but Mitch Buchanan was a philanderer. A real dog. He had one phone for work, another for I don't know what exactly, and a third for cheating on his wife. He had it registered with someone who works for him, some kid in the mailroom at Apollo Pharma. Mitch had it with him all the time.' Foster moves slightly and grimaces in pain. 'Anyway,' he says, 'that night – Friday – you may have noticed Mitch was flirting with the vice-dean.'

'It looked an awful lot like arguing to me.'

'If I didn't know him, I'd agree. But, trust me, for Mitch that was all foreplay. At the time, I thought Perkins wasn't into it, but now I think she was playing him from the start. That's what he wanted, a conquest, and she knew it.'

Harper recalls her own words to Tom: men are predictable.

Foster shakes his head again. Harper can sense the emotion welling up inside of her friend.

'After the shitshow at the theatre,' Foster continues, 'Mitch started texting her. I have no idea when or how he got her number, but he had it. He texted her from this third phone – his philandering phone – and invited her over for a drink. She was coy in her messages. She said, "If I'm caught on video, sneaking into the hated Mitch Buchanan's room in the middle of the night, I could never live it down. The students would run me off campus." Something like that. So Mitch asked me to turn the cameras off for a few hours. I told him to fuck off, no way I'm turning the cameras off. He threatened to fire me, threatened to sue. He said it's just some woman coming over, and what the hell is he paying me for if I can't keep him safe for two hours without a camera.' Foster shakes his head a third time. 'I said yes and it cost Jay his life.'

'They'd have found a different way,' Harper says.

'Maybe.' Foster nods. 'Still, it was a stupid fucking decision. Anyway, it was about half an hour after I turned off the cameras that Perkins knocked on the door. Just after midnight.

I tried to check her bag and pat her down, but Mitch told me to leave her alone. He mixed her a drink. They talked on the couch a while, rehashing what happened at the theatre. Mitch had that aura about him after something like that. You know? That happy-to-be-alive vibe. Perkins didn't. She was running in neutral, like nothing had happened. That should have set off my alarm bells. Whose fine after that? A psychopath. That's who. Anyway, eventually they go to the bedroom. Perkins took her purse. I could hear them laughing, like they're having fun. Then other noises.'

'You thought they were screwing?'

'Yeah, that's what it sounded like. But who knows? At some point, Jay and I heard a noise in the hallway. I think it was three, three-thirty. Jay left the room to have a look.' Foster squints as he tries to remember the sequence of events. 'I watched the door to the hall shut. Then I heard the door to the bedroom. I turned and there was Perkins, aiming a gun at my head.'

'It was coordinated,' Harper says. 'The noise to draw Jay out. Perkins waited until you were alone. Do you think she killed Mitch before or after she shot you?'

'I don't know. She could have given him the shot before, but that would have been risky. If he struggled, maybe I would have heard something. My bet is she convinced him to let her tie him up. Then she gagged him. Once she'd shot me, she goes back in and fills him full of Oxy or whatever they used.'

'And she shot you before whoever was in the hallway shot Jay?'

'I think so. I figure the plan was to draw one of us out into the hall. When Jay heard the shots in the room, he'd have turned back towards the room, and they probably shot him then. Maybe they were hiding in a room. I don't know.'

'Did she say anything?'

'Who? Perkins? No. She had a shit-eating grin, with her gun aimed at me, as she soaked up my helplessness. But she didn't say a word. Just stood there, smiled, and then shot me.'

'Then what?'

'The force sent me back and I landed on the floor. From there I had a clear view of the door before I lost consciousness. I heard two shots in the hallway, then two people came into the room. A man and a woman.'

'Did you recognise them?'

'No. I'd never seen them before.'

Harper pulls up a picture on his phone. 'Any of these guys look familiar?'

The first photo is Brent Amendola, lying dead on the ground outside Appleton Hall.

'That's one of them. A friend of yours.'

'He tried to kill me and Tom in Appleton Hall.' Harper swipes her phone and shows Foster another picture.

'Yeah,' Foster says, stiffening. 'That's one of them. Who is she?'

'Alex Perkins,' Harper says. 'The vice-dean's daughter.'

'No shit. That's some family.'

'Come on, Harper,' Tom says. 'We should give Charles time to rest.'

'I'm fine,' Foster says. 'I slept a whole week. Remember? Tell me more about the Movement. Does this mean Knox is innocent?'

Harper and Tom exchange a look. 'We don't know. We still think he was involved, but we don't think he was alone.' Harper tells him everything they learned from the reporter Clegg and Penelope Buchanan.

'They were chanting?' Foster shakes his head. 'Like this was some sort of religious experience for them? That's fucked up.'

'Did you see or hear anything like that?' Tom asks.

'No. I blacked out after the other two came into the room.'

'Do we know where she is?' Foster asks. 'Perkins, I mean. Her and the rest of her friends?'

Before Harper can answer, Lou Diaz materialises in the doorway. His eyes are red like he's on the verge of crying, but he's smiling.

'Come on, Harper.' Tom grips Harper's wheelchair and starts to back it up. 'Let's give these two some privacy.'

As they're backing out of the room, they watch as Lou sits on the edge of the hospital bed and takes Foster's hand.

'I'll be back, Charles,' Harper says. 'And we can come up with a plan.'

If Foster hears, it's anyone's guess.

# 80

Harper slides on her T-shirt just as Tom hovers, waiting to help.

'You don't think you're pushing it?' he asks. 'I'm sure you could stay another night.'

'No rest for the wicked.'

'Careful, Harper. That sounds like one of those thought-terminating clichés Clegg told us about.'

Before Harper can answer, there's a knock at the door.

'Hello, Ms Scott.' Professor Collins is standing in the doorway. Harper recalls how surprised he was to see Harper four days earlier, and figures Collins couldn't have been half as surprised as Harper is now. 'Apologies for the interruption. I was . . . Oh. Hello, Mr Park.' Collins had started to filter into the room but stops when he sees Tom. 'I'd heard what happened,' he says to Harper, 'and I wanted to . . .' He looks back at Tom, unsure of whether to continue.

Tom, sensing the man is too polite to ask to be left alone, says, 'I'm going to go check with the nurse.'

'As I was saying,' Collins says, once they're alone, 'I heard what happened and I wanted to see how you were and . . . apologise.'

'Apologise? Don't tell me you were in the cult as well. I can't handle another academic making an attempt on my life.'

'A cult? Was it a cult? I don't know all the facts . . . and a cult is so . . . such a strong . . . well, it doesn't matter what Olivia was mixed up in . . . And I obviously would never . . .' Collins takes a deep breath to gather himself. 'What I'm trying to say is that I feel responsible. When you spoke to me about Knox, I sent you off to Olivia, and you eventually ended up here. You thought I was trying to help, but my motivations were selfish. Petty, in fact. I thought you would annoy her. For years, Olivia and I have been engaged in a cold war of sorts. Little did I know who I was really dealing with.'

'You had no idea?'

'No. Not at all. But now, with hindsight . . .' He sighs dramatically and stares at the ceiling. 'Of course, I knew she saw Knox outside the university. They were friendly. And I saw how she tried to distance herself from Knox after he was arrested. How she denied a friendship with him, as much as logic would allow. But I thought it perfectly normal after our colleague was revealed to be a monster. Do you think she was with Knox the night he . . . ?'

Harper shrugs. 'I don't know.'

'Ah, that reminds me.' Collins reaches into the breast pocket of his tweed blazer and pulls out three Post-it notes. Elaborate cursive handwriting in blue ink fills the square yellow pages. 'Do you remember when you visited me and I tried to quote Orwell? Well, I tracked down the quote I'd butchered. It's from Orwell's essay, "Revenge Is Sour".' He looks down at the note and reads. 'Orwell said, "Revenge is an act which you want to commit when you are powerless and because you are powerless: as soon as the sense of impotence is removed, the desire evaporates also."'

'That's . . . umm . . . great. But why did you come here, professor? And why are you quoting Orwell? Are you worried about what I'll do to Perkins?'

Collins laughs. 'Oh, I'm not worried about Olivia. No, I . . . I don't know you well, Ms Scott. But for the reasons I explained, I feel responsible, like I exposed you to an avoidable disease. And if I had to pinpoint what I was worried about, I suppose it would be you. Or, more precisely, what an act of revenge against Olivia would do to you.' He hands Harper the Post-it note with the Orwell quote. 'I thought you should at least have this, unbutchered, in the hope it offers some wisdom.'

'So you'd let her run off scot-free?'

'Of course not. I don't pretend to say any of this is easy.' Collins takes a deep breath and stares at his hands, which are clasped across his belly.

Harper nods at the second and third Post-it notes, crushed in the professor's hands. 'What are the others for?'

Collins looks down at his hands. 'Ah, yes. Of course.' He laughs. 'I tracked down the quote you'd referred to. It was Seneca. You were right.' Collins reads his messy handwriting. '"It does not matter what you bear, but how you bear it."'

Harper narrows her gaze. 'I didn't butcher the quote. Maybe you just assumed I had it wrong.'

'Perhaps. If that's the case, then maybe I'll hold on to this one. It will be good for me to keep in mind in the weeks ahead.'

Collins folds the second Post-it note and slides it into his wallet.

'And the last one?' Harper asks.

'This one you'll want, I think.'

Collins hands Harper the Post-it, with the words 'Fiesta Inn'.

'What's this?' Harper asks.

'Olivia made several trips to Mexico over the last few years. But she'd never say where. At the time, I thought, "Oh, she just doesn't want word to get out about her favourite vacation spot." About a year ago now, I was in her office, and she'd left out an invoice on her desk. As I was leaving, I saw it was in Spanish. I read the name of the letterhead aloud and asked if that was her secret Mexican getaway. She was upset and immediately ripped the invoice off the desk and flung it into a drawer. She said it wasn't a hotel and ushered me out of her office. The way she acted – I was suspicious. I went back to my office and Googled the name. Sure enough, it was a hotel in Mexico, though it didn't look like a hidden gem. Poor reviews, little in the way of amenities, in some small town. I remember thinking, "What is she up to, going to this horrible spot?" I actually went to the trouble of calling the hotel and making a reservation. I was going to go . . . but then I lost interest.'

'You think this is where she is?'

'I don't know. But I believe it might be a place to start.' The professor stands to leave. 'I fear that, in my attempt to make amends, I'm doing what I came here to apologise for. Sending you off to Olivia while she's sharpening her knives.'

'I'm a big girl, professor. I can handle myself.'

'Of that, I have no doubt.'

Without another word, the professor turns and leaves, disappearing into the fluorescent-lit halls of the hospital.

# 81

Harper doesn't wait for Tom to return before heading to Foster's room. Special Agent Diaz is once again at Foster's bedside. This time he's more composed, and is sitting with his legs crossed and a manila folder across his lap.

'Have you been discharged?' Lou asks, nodding at Harper's jeans and leather jacket. 'Looks like you didn't get very far.'

'Shouldn't you be out tracking Perkins?'

'Play nice, Harper,' Foster says. 'Lou has news.'

Lou plays dumb. 'I don't know what you're talking about, Charles.'

Harper rolls her eyes. 'Oh, please. Not more of this I-can't-share-information bullshit. Your investigation would be nowhere without me.'

'Come on, Lou,' Foster says. 'You told me. What's the difference?'

Lou isn't convinced. He shrugs.

'Maybe I have news too,' Harper says. 'And I'm willing to trade.'

Lou is doubtful. He frowns. 'What could you have figured out from your hospital bed?'

'You'd be surprised.'

'Oh, for fuck's sake, Lou,' Foster says. 'Don't try to out-stubborn Harper Scott. You'd have more luck with a brick wall. Tell her already.'

'Fine,' Lou says with a sigh. 'The janitor you shot, Brent Amendola, a few years ago he was a student at Everly College. And – surprise, surprise – he was a member of the Movement.'

Lou hands Harper the manila folder. Inside are photographs. In the first, Amendola is at a barbeque, smiling, drinking a beer. In a second, he's meditating, with his legs crossed and eyes closed. In a third, Harper recognises Alex Perkins. They're holding hands and clearly an item.

Lou says, 'We got a warrant issued that gave us access to a private Facebook account for the Movement. There are pictures of Amendola, Knox, Perkins, Andrews, the Hamiltons. One big happy family.'

'So this has been their plan for months?' Harper asks. 'Amendola took the job so he could help murder Mitch Buchanan when he came to open the library?'

'That's the theory.'

'And why was there such a lag in time between Skip's murder and Mitch's?'

'Lama Aaron was arrested not long after Skip was murdered, and spent six months locked up before the charges were dropped. Maybe his followers couldn't function without him.'

'Tell her about the jet,' Foster says.

Lou gives Foster a look, a don't-rush-me squint, before turning back to Harper. 'Nelson Hamilton has a private plane,' Lou continues. 'It flew to Mexico City the night Perkins attacked you. We think the Movement relocated to somewhere in Mexico, possibly after Skip Buchanan was killed.'

'Interesting,' Harper says.

'Which would explain the empty ashram,' Foster says. 'And why Lou can't track down any key members of the Movement. And why Andrews stopped meeting with that reporter.'

'So, after Perkins stabbed me with an opioid,' Harper says, 'she hopped on a private jet to Mexico?'

'That's the theory,' Lou says. 'After murdering Mitch Buchanan, she stuck around Connecticut as long as she could. But when you started asking questions about Andrews, she probably figured her window to escape was closing.'

'I fucked up asking her about Andrews, didn't I? Now Perkins knows she was talking to the reporter Clegg, and she's in danger.'

'Maybe they already knew. Who knows,' Lou says. 'Anyway, it's your turn now. Tell me what you know.'

Harper explains what Professor Collins told her. 'If they're in Mexico,' she says, holding up the Post-it, 'I've got a good idea of where.'

'Great.' Lou puts out his hand, waiting for Harper to hand him the note.

'Will you bring me with you?'

'I know you're pissed off, Harper. I understand the desire to get your hands dirty. But that's not how this works. We're not flying to Mexico, guns drawn, and dragging Perkins and her guru back to the US. Diplomats will talk, there will be negotiations. The process will take months.'

'Maybe I'll go alone then.'

Lou smiles. 'No offence, Harper, but that sounds like the plot to a bad movie, a big fucking cliché. You've done enough. Give me the name of the hotel and let us take it from here.'

Harper stares at Lou.

'She's worried about the girl,' Foster says. 'Andrews. She thinks she's in danger.'

'Because of me,' Harper adds. 'I told Perkins about speaking to a reporter, and I asked for information about Andrews. There's no way Perkins didn't put two and two together. If she knows Andrews spoke to a reporter . . . God knows what she'll do to Andrews.'

Lou nods, sympathetically. 'I hear you, Harper. We'll do everything we can to save Andrews, I promise. But the name of the hotel Perkins visited – it will narrow our search from a country to a city.'

Harper stares at Lou for a good ten seconds, but then hands him the Post-it. He reads it before folding it in half and sliding it into his wallet.

There's a knock at the door. All three turn and see Tom on the threshold to the room. 'There you are,' he says to Harper. 'Ready to go?'

'Where to now?' Lou asks.

'I'm making Harper stay with me in New York for a few weeks to recover.'

'Is Appleton still a crime scene?' Harper asks. 'I'd love to grab what's left of my belongings before we head back to the city.'

Lou shrugs. 'It's the sheriff's crime scene. But I owe you one, Harper. I'll take you there myself. Make sure you get everything you need.'

'Can you drop her at my place near campus afterwards?' Tom asks.

Lou smiles. 'Sounds like a plan.'

# 82

When Harper finds herself once again outside the door to Room 212 on the second floor of Appleton Hall, she's mildly surprised to find the door riddled with bullet holes. So much has happened over the last forty-eight hours, she'd nearly forgotten exchanging gunfire with Amendola.

'Looks like a war zone,' Harper says.

Lou shrugs. 'It was.'

Harper steps inside. 'Yeah, maybe you're right.'

Lou reads a text on his phone and says, 'I need to drop by President Flowers' office. You OK to find what you need?'

Harper nods. 'Sure.'

'Great. I'll be back in half an hour. If you finish, you can meet me at the car.'

Lou leaves. Harper packs her personal belongings into her duffle bag. At first, she moves quickly, not wanting to linger. She's had enough of Appleton Hall and Everly College. But memories of the attack forty-eight hours ago – of her shooting and killing Amendola – start to come back, and she can feel the pressure building up inside of her, so she sits by the window and smokes her vape.

*Anyway, I'm off-duty*, she thinks. *Or retired.*

She can hear students on the field outside, cheering in unison. She stares at the door to the hall, at the endless knot etched into the frame of the door.

Something about the carving nags, though she can't exactly say why.

She calls Lou. He picks up. 'You done already?'

'Who carved the endless knot into the door frame?'

'Can't this wait? I'm still walking to see Flowers.'

'Humour me. Please.'

Lou sighs. 'We found the carving all over Appleton Hall. We didn't find any correlation between the one in your room and the attacks. My advice: don't overthink it.'

'At first, I thought it was Andrews,' Harper says. 'Tom and I Googled the name "Jessica" and Appleton Hall, and that led us to articles about Andrews. But I think that was just dumb luck. She didn't join the Movement until *after* she was kicked out of Appleton Hall and was living off campus. That's when she met Alex Perkins. So the timing doesn't line up.'

'Like I said, best not to overthink it.'

'Could it have been Amendola?'

'I don't know, Harper. At this point, we'll need to make arrests and interrogate people. Investigations like this take time. You have to be patient.'

Harper keeps staring at the symbol etched into the wood.

'The night Amendola broke into Appleton Hall, he set off the hallway camera Foster had set up. But not the one out front.'

'So what? There's a back entrance to the building. Foster didn't have a camera there.'

'What if . . .'

'Harper, for fuck's sake. You won. You kept Tom alive, exposed Knox's fucked-up cult. Somehow you survived a shootout and an opioid overdose. Relax. Take your victory lap, finish packing up your things, come outside, and wait for me at the car.'

'Sure,' Harper says. 'I'll be out soon.'

# Day 848

Jess is brushing her teeth in the communal washroom when Alex appears in the mirror, a spectre over Jess's left shoulder. She's dressed in black. 'It's time.' She doesn't say for what. 'We're meeting outside his cabin in ten.'

Jess spits white foam into the sink, rinses her mouth, then trudges along an icy path, through the ashram, to her cabin. The walk is treacherous. It snowed the night before, just before the temperature dropped a million degrees, freezing the snow and slush into a hard, slippery crust. She changes into black – black jeans, black sweater, black jacket, black wool hat. She's the last to arrive. The rest of Alex's maniple – Alex, her boyfriend Brent, and Professor Knox – are already on Father's porch.

Father ushers them inside his cabin and through a guided mediation, as he manifests their shared destiny, the higher path they've chosen to tread.

'Remember,' Father says, as they're readying to leave, 'there is no progress without pain.' The maniple repeats the maxim in unison.

Outside, Olivia, Alex's mother, is waiting for them. Meryl had displaced Olivia as Aaron's number two, but Olivia has worked her way back into Father's good graces, and now she and Meryl seem to share the number two role.

Olivia takes her daughter by the hands. 'Make me proud.'

'I will, Mother.'

They drive along the I95, heading south. Massive snowploughs are out salting the road, their hazard lights glistening off the black asphalt.

Jess has a vague sense of something in the distance, pulling her towards it, as though fate had the force of gravity. But somehow she's indifferent to it. She doesn't analyse it or fear it or think about it at all, other than to note it as a novel experience. The future is inescapable, as Father would say. Inevitable.

After forty-minutes or so, Brent exits the highway and heads west, along a county road, before pulling onto a gravel driveway. He parks and shuts off the engine. With the heat off, winter quickly starts to seep through the windows. Silver moonlight reflects off the windshield.

Alex hands Jess a knife and Jess's sense of time and space alters, like she's taken a psychedelic drug that both dulled and heightened her consciousness. She could hear a fly land on a flower petal, but can't form a coherent independent thought, like 'What do I need a knife for?'

Knox loads a revolver and hands it to Alex. Then he loads a second.

The chime of a text message echoes through the interior of the car. 'What the fuck, Knox,' Alex says. 'We weren't supposed to bring our phones!'

Knox curses under his breath, turns off his phone, and leaves it in the glove compartment.

They exit the car. Jess feels a sharp pang in her lungs, as she breathes in the pitiless December air. Knox points beyond a thicket of trees. 'It's this way.'

'Have you been here before?' Jess asks.

Knox doesn't answer her question. Brent turns on his flashlight, and they follow him into the forest. Alex lights a cigarette. They walk five hundred yards or so before Jess sees a light beyond the trees. Once they reach the clearing, a large home comes into view. It has peaked windows and a column of smoke twisting out of the chimney. They walk towards it, snow and ice crunching underfoot.

On the front porch, Alex tosses her cigarette and then tries the front door. It's unlocked. She turns back and smiles.

The foyer is dark and empty. Jess examines framed pictures on the wall. Two feature a grey-haired couple, smiling proudly outside the Temple of Heaven in Beijing, and arm-in-arm on the dock beside a sixty-foot sailboat, gleaming white in the Caribbean sun. In another photo, the same man – with his full head of silver hair and thick white moustache – is standing in the centre of the frame. To his immediate right is a man that could only be his brother. He has auburn rather than silver hair, but both men are short, with the same cheekbones, and the same self-satisfied smile. The brothers are surrounded by forty or so people, all wearing matching navy Patagonia vests, with a corporate logo stitched onto the breast. The logo is too small to make out, but the banner behind the group offers a clue. Written in large white letters: APOLLO PHARMA CORP.

Alex flicks her chin, ushering them onwards. As instructed, the maniple disperse, like furies, pursuing justice, dissolving into the shadows.

Jess and Alex walk towards the sound of laughter coming from the kitchen. There, they find two women in their sixties, sitting at the kitchen table, splitting a slice of chocolate cake. The one with grey hair is facing the hall. She sees Jess and Alex and stops talking mid-sentence. Her mouth opens wide but no words come out. The brunette turns and says, 'Oh my God.'

'If you scream,' Alex says, 'I'll shoot you in the head.'

The women are in shock. Colour drains from their faces. Alex ushers them into the living room and forces them to kneel. The brunette starts to cry.

Knox joins them. 'No one's upstairs.'

Alex points her gun at the grey-haired woman. 'Where's your husband?'

'He ... he's away.' Jess recognises the grey-haired woman from the photos in the foyer. 'On business.'

'He's here,' Alex says. 'Check out back.'

Knox rushes off.

A Latino couple walks into the foyer. Brent is behind them, his revolver aimed at their back. They're dressed in pyjamas and wide-eyed, like the terror of the moment has robbed them of the ability to blink.

Alex orders them to kneel beside the two women. Brent binds their wrists behind their backs, using strips of a thin, orange nylon rope.

'Just take what you want and leave,' the grey-haired woman says.

'Rob you?' Alex drops to her knees and looks the grey-haired woman in the eyes. 'Rob you? Like you robbed the American people? Should I make money off of your misery, like the way you made billions off the misery of others?'

The brunette whispered to her friend: 'Don't try reasoning with them, Cecilia. They're insane.'

'Insane?' Alex's expression cracks briefly, then she stands and collects herself. 'Far from it. We have clarity of mind. And that's why we know what must be done.'

Brent starts to gag the four captives, shoving sheets of fabric into their mouths, and seals their lips with duct tape. He starts with the two older women. As he's gagging the Latino woman, her husband jumps to his feet and races into the kitchen. Brent rushes after him, disappearing into the kitchen.

There's a heavy thud, as though someone tripped and fell to the ground. Then three gunshots echo through the walls. *Bang. Bang. Bang.*

The women scream but they're all gagged, so the sound is muted.

Brent returns from the kitchen. Blood is splattered across his face. 'We'd better hurry up.'

Alex brandishes her knife and steps towards the grey-haired woman. She stops and looks at Jess. 'If you're just going to stand there, find Will. Tell him to hurry up.'

Jess hasn't moved for some time. She'd been quietly watching events unfold as though it were a play, and she was in the audience. But when Alex speaks to her it breaks the trance. And once she has permission to leave, she flies from the living room, through the kitchen and out the sliding glass door. She barely thinks about where she's going, only on the act of moving away from where she was, on putting distance between her and the living room and what is about to happen there.

In the back yard, she follows an icy path down a hill. Her pace slows once she's out of the house. She carefully places one foot after the next, doing her best not to slip. Soon she hears strange sounds coming from the bottom of the hill. Someone is panting, like a wounded animal.

There's a barn at the foot of the hill. Light escapes the open door and penetrates the darkness. On either side of the path, the snow is perfectly smooth and frozen, like a porcelain soufflé. Except for a narrow path that has been recently tilled. Jess looks in the same direction the narrow path is headed and sees someone kneeling in the snow. She knows it's Knox by the shape of his torso, long and skinny. As she draws closer, she can see, on the other side of Knox, a man is lying in the snow. His shoulder is bleeding from a gunshot wound. It's the wounded man who's panting wildly and fighting to get away. But when he sees Jess, he abruptly stops struggling. He thinks he was in the fight of his life against a stranger with a gun. But now a young woman has arrived, luminous in the moonlight.

Jess recognises the man – not only from the photos in the front hallway, but also from months of online research. She recognises the thick mane of silver hair and matching moustache of Skip Buchanan, the CEO of Apollo Pharma.

The first domino, as Father has come to call him.

Jess steps forwards and kneels beside Skip. He watches her, puzzled, trying to discern her purpose. Knox opens his duffle bag and removes gauze and medical tape. He hands both to Jess and she starts to dress Skip's wound. He lets her, his eyes never blinking.

Knox unzips a black case the size of a Bible and removes a syringe and bottle of clear liquid. He stabs the tip of the needle into the bottle, draws back the plunger, and fills the syringe. As he holds it up to the moonlight, Skip finally snaps out of his trance. 'What do you want? What is this?'

Knox stares at Skip. 'Tara Knox.'

'What?'

'Tara Knox.'

'I don't know who that is.'

Knox had been calm up until this point. But Skip's indifference and failure to know the name of his daughter – it's too much. Hate boils over. 'Karma,' Will says. 'That's what *this* is.'

Skip understands enough to know he's in danger. He starts to struggle again. Knox hands the needle to Jess, straddles Skip's ribcage, and holds Skip's arms down at his side. Skip whips his head from side to side. 'No, no, no.'

'Do it,' Knox screams.

Jess hesitates.

'Do it!'

Suddenly Alex and Brent are there. Alex straddles Skip's right bicep, with her ass aimed at Skip's head, and locks her hands on Skip's right wrist. Brent wriggles the sleeve of Skip's shirt sleeve up, revealing a forearm, and then helps hold his legs in place.

'Come on, Jess,' Alex says. 'Find a vein if you can.'

Jess stares at the syringe in her hands.

'Do it,' Knox says. 'Now.'

'Jess,' Alex says. 'Look at me.'

Jess meets Alex's eyes. 'Come on, Jessica. You can do this. Remember: there's no progress without pain.'

Jess nods and mutters the same words back to herself. 'There's no progress without pain.'

She slowly slides the needle into Skip's forearm.

Using her thumb, she presses the plunger down.

Skip's resistance recedes. His breathing slows.

Alex, Knox and Brent stand and watch.

And then the opioid that has taken the lives of so many people adds another name to the list.

# 83

Harper finishes her call with Lou, drops her phone on the bed, takes one last drag from her vape, and then slides off her sneakers. She moves slowly, carefully, her sock feet barely making a sound on the parquet floor. She once again laments that her firearm is still with the FBI, and so she finds the extendible baton buried under a pile of clothes, extends it with a flick of her wrist, grips it tightly in her hand, by her hip, and then exits Room 212.

The hallway is empty, the stairwell too. She stands on the landing and listens. *Up or down?*

She ascends. On the third floor, the door to the hallway is boarded up. Harper probes, tugging at the plywood, but it's nailed in place. She finds the same obstacle on the fourth and fifth floors. *Down it is.*

She descends, gliding past the fourth floor, past the third, past the second. On the ground floor, there's a door to the basement. It's made of heavy steel. The beige paint is faded and chipped. Harper pushes on the silver bar that's perpendicular with the floor and a metallic click echoes as the door unlatches. She grimaces at the sound, steps through the door, and gently closes it behind her. A weak, pulsing light clarifies filthy cement stairs.

Halfway down, she sees an endless knot on the wall. It's small, maybe the size of a quarter, drawn in permanent black marker.

Her heart rate quickens. A voice in her head screams to call Lou – *Don't do this alone!* – but the stubborn, dominant side of her brain takes over and propels her forwards.

There's another steel door at the bottom of the stairs, another silver bar she has to push. Harper is more delicate this time, the metallic click barely audible. She pushes the door open just wide enough to see a hallway, lit by a dangling, uncovered bulb. The endless knot is everywhere, covering nearly every inch of the cinderblock walls. The dimensions vary, from the size of a thumb to that of a car tyre. Half are black, the other half a range of vibrant colours, pink, purple, indigo blue.

Harper quietly closes the door behind her and slips into the hallway. She passes a closed door on her right. A second door is further down the hallway. This one is a few inches ajar. Harper stops and waits. She listens for thirty seconds and then pushes the door open. She grips the baton tightly. Her knuckles go white.

Once the door is halfway open, Harper looks inside. The room is empty, except for metal piping along the far wall, and a woman. She's sitting on the floor, facing the door. Her mouth is covered with silver duct tape and her arms are tied behind her back, with plastic ties that are looped through the metal piping. She looks unconscious or close to it: her chin is a few inches from her chest, and her head is lolling to the side. She has black hair and tattoos along her arms.

Harper darts to the woman, kneels, and peels the duct tape off her mouth. The woman's tongue pokes out, from between her lips. Harper grabs her by the temples and forces her head up.

Harper asks, 'Are you Jessica Andrews?' even though she knows the answer.

Andrews' eyes struggle to open. 'Father,' she mumbles.

Harper finds a piece of glass on the ground, what looks like a broken beer bottle, green and sharp, and carefully cuts the plastic ties from Andrews' wrists. Once she's freed, Harper slaps her ferociously. 'I'm going to get you out of here, but you need to *wake up*.'

Andrews is conscious enough to nod, but her eyes are still unable to open fully. Harper slings Andrews' arm around her shoulders and together they walk to the door.

Andrews starts to babble. 'I didn't. I didn't. I swear.'

*They must have drugged her*, Harper thinks. *And God knows what else.*

Harper clamps her hand on Andrews' mouth. 'You have to be quiet. Everything will be OK, but I need you to be quiet. Or they'll hear.'

Harper releases her grip on Andrews' mouth and starts to drag her down the hallway, towards the stairs. Her eyes lock onto the door between her and the stairs. *We have to get past that door.*

Andrews starts to babble again.

They're five feet from the closed door, twenty from the stairs.

'No!' Andrews yells, her voice suddenly alive. 'Forgive me, Father! Forgive me!'

Harper stops moving. She listens. There's nothing at first.

Then the door opens. Two men step into the hallway. When they see Harper and Andrews, their expressions are shocked, then angry. The one in the lead rushes forwards. Harper drops Andrews. Then, as she's back-pedalling, she swings the baton. The hallway is narrow, so she has to start the baton up high and swing down. The ballpoint end connects with the crown of the man's head. His body instantly goes limp and he falls to the ground.

The other man stares at his fallen friend. He's in shock but Harper doesn't have time to use this to her advantage. Maybe she could have sprinted past while they were distracted, but now more people are streaming into the hallway. Another man, then another woman, a blonde that Harper guesses is Alex Perkins, the vice-dean's daughter, and then Perkins herself.

Before Harper can plan her next move, they rush forwards, as a unit. She tries to swing the baton but it's useless. She's overwhelmed and tackled to the dirty cement floor.

Someone hits her, in the face and stomach. Someone else wrenches the baton out of her hand. Then they drag her by the feet into the room they'd come out of. She uselessly claws at the cement floor.

Inside the room there are cots along one wall, a makeshift computer lab and a television set in the corner. It's playing an interview of Wells Buchanan, of all people. A short, chubby man with long brown hair, and a rugged beard is sitting a few feet from the television on a cheap plastic chair. Somehow his entire attention is focused on the television, not the melee on the other side of the room.

'Hold her down,' Perkins says, as she's pulling on latex gloves. 'Don't let her move.'

Someone sits on Harper's legs. Others pin her arms to the ground. She thinks of Mitch Buchanan, the position he was in when he overdosed on fentanyl. She struggles, using every ounce of her energy to break free, but it's useless.

'I don't know how you lived after what I gave you before.' Perkins is filling a syringe, sucking clear liquid from a glass vial. 'But this time there will be no rising from the dead.'

Harper screams, 'Wait!'

She's out of breath from struggling. Raising her voice takes extreme effort.

'Relax, Ms Scott,' Perkins says. 'This will all be over quickly.'

'Wait!' Harper's mind races, trying to think of a way out. 'You can't kill me. I'm not a Buchanan.'

Perkins keeps moving towards Harper, but her brethren look thrown. Doubt creeps in. A woman with short hair and glasses says, 'Stop, Olivia.'

'Don't interfere, Meryl.'

'We must consult Father.'

The room turns and stares at the chubby, bearded man watching the news. He doesn't deign to look at his subjects. He merely waves his hand, as if to say, 'Go ahead.'

The sliver of hope Harper was grasping evaporates. Perkins walks towards Harper holding the syringe. When she's close, she kneels beside Harper. Her smile is victorious.

And then her head explodes, leaving a hole the size of a fist above her left eye. Harper only hears the gunshot afterwards. The echo in the small room is deafening. Over the top of the gore that is Perkins' head, she sees Lou standing in the frame of the door, behind the smoking barrel of his Glock.

'No one move,' Lou says. He flicks his chin at the man sitting on Harper's legs. 'Get the fuck off of her.'

Once the weight is removed from her legs, Harper scrambles to Lou's side.

'There's another gun at my ankle,' Lou says.

Harper kneels, finds a .22 in a hidden ankle holster. She scrambles to her feet and aims the gun at the eleven remaining members of the Movement.

'Everyone lie down on your chest,' Lou says, 'hands behind your head.'

The congregants stare at each other, then at Lama Aaron, unsure of what to do.

Lama Aaron sighs loudly, with an exhausted air. He stands up and, for a moment, it's unclear what he'll do. Lou aims his gun at the guru, ready to shoot. But Lama Aaron drops to his knees, and then lies down, with his chest on the cement floor.

Lama Aaron's followers stare at their leader in disbelief.

'How long until the cavalry is here?' Harper asks.

'A few minutes,' Lou says. 'Until then, shoot anyone that moves.'

# Epilogue

On the banks of the Ohio River, on the top of a hill, with an unobstructed view to the south, to Kentucky, there's a small cemetery. Here, at around one in the afternoon, Harper Scott walks the tombstones, toting a six-pack of Budweiser. The sound of glass bottles gently colliding is as soft as windchimes. The air has a bite to it today: fall is finally here.

Derrick's tombstone is beside their grandfather's, two granite slabs surrounded by wild, unkept grass. Harper opens three beers. The first two she leans against each tombstone, the third she keeps. She sits down, leaning her back against the trunk of an oak tree.

When Harper had planned this visit, she'd imagined a conversation, one-way but heartfelt. There were things she wanted to say, things she wanted to get off her chest. And that's what people do in the movies, isn't it? Talk to a gravestone and eventually you reach some sort of cathartic moment. But now that she's here – alone and obviously staring at a slab of granite, not her brother – speaking out loud seems silly. So Harper settles on drinking her beer in silence.

After twenty minutes, she hears a twig snap. She looks up and sees Tom, who was supposed to give her an hour alone. He waves, sheepishly.

It's been four weeks since Harper found a dozen members of the Movement hiding in the basement of Appleton Hall. Olivia Perkins was pronounced dead on the scene, Jessica Andrews was taken to the hospital for evaluation, and the remaining ten, including Lama Aaron, were arrested.

For years the Movement had proved to be a remarkably secretive and close-knit group, but once arrested and subject to questioning, they quickly turned on each other. Members willingly divulged the crimes of their fellow congregants in the hopes of lessening scrutiny of their own. Agents Diaz and Dreser – happy to correct their past failure – slowly and methodically learned who was there the night Skip Buchanan was murdered. William Knox, Alex Perkins, Brent Amendola, and – according to Alex Perkins – Jessica Andrews. In fact, Perkins claimed that it was Andrews who delivered the fatal dose of Oxy to Skip Buchanan.

Harper had developed a soft spot for Andrews and doubted her involvement in Skip's murder. (After all, who could trust what Alex Perkins said?) But Lou thought the story had the ring of truth to it. 'Maybe she didn't kill Skip, but my money says she was there. A guilty conscience would explain why and when Andrews started talking to the reporter Clegg.' Once Andrews was discharged from the hospital, she was arrested and charged.

The willingness of the Movement's members to implicate each other had only one limit: Lama Aaron. Each congregant was taken through Lama Aaron's criminal history and multiple arrests, the allegations of grooming and sexual abuse, and how he amassed a small fortune via his followers. But they were unmoved. Lama Aaron, they said, was being persecuted because he is so enlightened, because he is a prophet, because a revolution is coming. His intentions are pure. He knows and sees all.

'Tell me he's not getting off,' Harper said to Lou when she'd heard the latest update.

'Don't worry,' Lou said. 'Even without their testimony, we've got enough to put him away for a long time. And once they get some distance from their cult, once the brainwashing starts to fade and the prospect of a long prison sentence becomes more real, someone will crack.'

Following the arrests, information about Olivia Perkins started to leak to the press – her involvement in the Movement, her connection to the Karma Killer. And when it became clear that *at least* two professors and three students from Everly College had been involved in a Manson family-like cult, hiding in an abandoned building on campus, the school hired a law firm to conduct an investigation. An interim report concluded that there were no additional cult members in Everly's faculty or student body, but noted that the school's president, Winston Flowers, had fostered a 'toxic environment and culture', and Flowers – seeing the writing on the wall – stepped down.

After Knox's involvement with the Movement became public, a former member of Borelli's team from the Knox trial gave an interview with *60 Minutes*. She explained how Borelli strong-armed witnesses, including Penelope Buchanan, into avoiding any detail that didn't fit with their theory that Knox alone committed the murders. She didn't directly blame Borelli for Mitch Buchanan's murder, but the implication was obvious to anyone paying attention.

Soon there were rumours, reported breathlessly in the national outlets, that Borelli would be charged with prosecutorial misconduct and fired by the network for failing to uphold journalistic standards. But the network dragged its feet and – probably due to the high ratings Borelli was now garnering – ultimately did nothing more than issue a statement expressing disappointment.

Once Foster was discharged from the hospital, he and Lou flew to Rio de Janeiro and disappeared. Harper figured they'd surface when the storm had passed.

As for the Buchanans, some tried to spin the Movement's murderous plot into sympathy for the family. Cindy Buchanan gave no less than seven interviews, perfecting the solemn pause when asked about how *she* felt when she'd learned the extent to which her life was in danger. She'd look directly into the camera and exclaim, 'I'm just happy to be alive ... and to focus on my clothing line.' Apparently Wells Buchanan was in discussion with Spotify to produce a podcast about his experience.

The family's media push seemed to work, at least in part. There was less debate in the mainstream press on the pros and cons of the #KarmaKillings. The revelation that the murder of the Buchanan brothers wasn't a movement of concerned citizens fed up with billionaires escaping punishment, but much more a fucked-up cult doing what a megalomaniac asked them to do – it took the wind out of the sails of those claiming there was an upside to harassment and murder.

But there was no *mea culpa* in the news or the online discourse, no exploration of the role social or old media played. In the relentless fight for attention – for likes or retweets, for social cachet, for the nirvana of going viral – Knox was useful. And then he wasn't. So the world moved on.

Tom chose a different path than the rest of his family. Initially, he tried to disappear in the churn of New York City. (Returning to Everly College was out of the question. The anonymity he once enjoyed there was eviscerated after what happened.) But even in New York he couldn't escape the connection to his family or the media's newest obsession, the Movement. When Harper said she was leaving to spend time at home, Tom tagged along. He's a fish out of water in the mid-West, but somehow, in a town that was ripped apart by Oxy and the opioid epidemic, no one seems to have a clue who the Buchanans are.

'Sorry,' Tom says as he walks across the graveyard towards Harper. 'I'm early.'

Harper stands and dusts off her jeans. 'Don't worry about it.'

'I didn't want you to miss your appointment.'

'Seriously. Don't worry about it.'

'How was it?'

'Staged,' Harper says. 'But nice.'

They drive to a strip mall on the outskirts of town. Tom walks Harper to the door and kisses her on the cheek. 'Good luck.'

Inside, the secretary behind the desk motions for Harper to sit in the waiting room. A few minutes later, a balding man in a camouflage jacket and a short woman in a flowery blouse enter through the office door. The man warmly thanks the woman several times before limping off. The woman smiles at Harper. 'Good morning, Ms Scott.'

'Good morning, Doctor Taylor.'

Doctor Taylor leads Harper into her office. They sit and talk. Pleasantries at first, then she asks how Harper slept.

'Did you dream of the man with the green eyes?'

Harper shakes her head. 'No.'

'How long has it been?'

'Seven nights now.'

'That's good. Very good.'

This is Harper's third week seeing Doctor Taylor, a clinical psychologist. She came highly recommended by an old colleague of Tom's. Harper likes Doctor Taylor. She hasn't rushed to judgement or pried into Harper's past. They're taking it slow.

'Are you ready to begin?'

'Yes.'

Doctor Taylor dims the lights and takes a seat near Harper.

'Close your eyes.'

Harper closes her eyes.

Doctor Taylor has been teaching Harper 'helpful coping mechanisms', including meditation. Harper sees the irony in learning to meditate after nearly dying at the hands of a meditation group. But Tom said meditation was scientifically proven to be effective. 'Maybe that's how Lama Aaron was able to gain the trust of his followers,' he said. 'They were recovering addicts who experienced the bona fide benefits of meditation.' And to Tom's point, one of Doctor Taylor's stated goals, through therapy and meditation, is to lessen Harper's dependence on weed. Harper hasn't seen any progress there – not yet anyway. But again, they're taking it slow.

The moment Harper closes her eyes, her mind starts to travel at light speed. She thinks of Tom, their walk through the cemetery this morning, his smile when they parted; then she thinks of his family, their wealth, where they got it, which makes her think of Derrick.

'Feel yourself sitting, and know that you're sitting.'

Harper focuses all of her attention on her ass and the small of her back making contact with the chair. She waits for that sense of stillness, that sense of calm.

'Focus on your breathing, as it enters your nostrils and expands your chest and belly.'

Harper Scott takes a long, deep breath.

# Acknowledgements

This book would not have been possible without my agent, Sam Copeland, and my editor, Ben Willis. I'm indebted to both for their advice, insight, and encouragement.

Thank you to the teams at Rogers Coleridge and White and Bonnier, particularly Georgia Marshall.

Thank you to Elyse Strathy for her keen editorial eye.

A very heartfelt thank you to my wife, Anna, for her steadfast love and support, sense of humour, and for reading and commenting on early drafts. I'd be lost without her.

Thank you to my children, Hazel, James and Margaret. Without you, I'd have finished this book years earlier, but life wouldn't have been nearly as fun or meaningful.

Thank you to Kristin Inglese who designed the graphics in the book.

I read widely on the opioid epidemic but found two books particularly helpful: *Empire of Pain* by Patrick Radden Keefe and *Dreamland* by Sam Quinones.